M...
WEARS BLACK GLOVES

"What do you think you are doing?" she gasped. "Get out of my bed, sir. Have you lost all sense of propriety?"

"I'm sure I must have," he answered soberly, pulling off his black long-tailed coat. He propped one of the pillows on the headboard and leaned back against it. "You tend to have that effect on a fellow, Frances." And he reached out and pulled her to him. . . .

MISS ROMNEY
FLIES TOO HIGH

Graymarsh pulled Sarah into his arms. His face was pale. His voice shook. "I thought I'd lost you forever." And, unable to adequately express the horror and bleakness of that prospect, he abandoned the attempt and held her closer, then met her upturned lips with his.

No sooner was that contact made than Sarah soared again. She was light-headed—she was spinning—she was flying—it was glorious, beyond belief. . . .

By Marian Devon
Published by Fawcett Books:

MISS ARMSTEAD WEARS BLACK GLOVES
MISS ROMNEY FLIES TOO HIGH
M'LADY RIDES FOR A FALL
SCANDAL BROTH
SIR SHAM
A QUESTION OF CLASS
ESCAPADE
FORTUNES OF THE HEART
MISS OSBORNE MISBEHAVES
LADY HARRIET TAKES CHARGE
MISTLETOE AND FOLLY
A SEASON FOR SCANDAL
A HEART ON HIS SLEEVE
AN UNCIVIL SERVANT
DEFIANT MISTRESS
THE WIDOW OF BATH
THE ROGUE'S LADY
DECK THE HALLS
MISS KENDAL SETS HER CAP

Books published by The Ballantine Publishing Group are available at quantity discounts on bulk purchases for premium, educational, fund-raising, and special sales use. For details, please call 1–800–733–3000.

MISS ARMSTEAD WEARS BLACK GLOVES

MISS ROMNEY FLIES TOO HIGH

Marian Devon

FAWCETT BOOKS · NEW YORK

Sale of this book without a front cover may be unauthorized. If this book is coverless, it may have been reported to the publisher as "unsold or destroyed" and neither the author nor the publisher may have received payment for it.

A Fawcett Crest Book
Published by Ballantine Books
Miss Armstead Wears Black Gloves copyright © 1985 by Marian Pope Rettke
Miss Romney Flies Too High copyright © 1986 by Marian Pope Rettke

All rights reserved under International and Pan-American Copyright Conventions. Published in the United States by Ballantine Books, a division of Random House, Inc., New York, and simultaneously in Canada by Random House of Canada Limited, Toronto. *Miss Armstead Wears Black Gloves* was originally published by Ballantine Books in 1985. *Miss Romney Flies Too High* was originally published by Ballantine Books in 1986.

http://www.randomhouse.com

Library of Congress Catalog Card Number: 96-90889

ISBN 0-449-22612-3

Manufactured in the United States of America

First Edition: March 1997

10 9 8 7 6 5 4 3 2 1

Contents

Miss Armstead
Wears Black Gloves

Chapter One

MISS FRANCES ARMSTEAD WAS NOT AT ALL DECEIVED BY Mr. Albert Yarwood's studied indifference. Even had she not heard him burst through the downstairs door, come racing up the stairs, and then slow down to a decorous walk just before entering the morning room, where she was hard at work contriving to net a purse, his countenance would have eventually given him away. Bertie Yarwood's somewhat round, slightly babyish, almost handsome face was not accustomed to being wiped clean of expression. Animated good humor punctuated by sudden storms of awesome, though brief, duration was more in its usual line. So now the prominent blue eyes could not quite dampen their sparkle, nor could the corners of the pursed mouth quite control a tendency to twitch.

Mr. Yarwood carelessly pulled up a caned-seat armchair by the window next to Miss Armstead. He stretched out a pair of muscular legs encased in skintight breeches and crossed the ankles of his boots casually. He studiously brushed the dust from his riding coat sleeve, much to the detriment of the Aubusson carpet. "Hullo, Frankie." He yawned lazily as he gazed out the window, seemingly absorbed by the showy attempts of a male peacock to bedazzle a female of the species. "Fine day, ain't it, Frankie? Warmish for October." Miss Armstead risked another peek then, up through thick, dark lowered lashes. There was no doubt about it. Bertie Yarwood was simply awash with news.

3

Frankie had developed more than a sixth sense where Bertie was concerned. Their estates bordered each other, her uncle and his father were the best of friends, their ages were only six months apart—with him the elder, as he never tired of pointing out—and they'd been constant, bickering companions since they were both in leading strings. So now as she covertly studied him, Frankie had no doubt that whatever it was that Bertie was momentarily holding back was bound to be something that she would not like at all. The thought caused her to botch the work in hand. "Oh, bother!" she muttered under her breath as she strove to undo the damage she'd just done.

At the exclamation Mr. Yarwood withdrew his attention from the peacocks to study her. What he saw was a young lady of average height, delicate bone structure, and what he was prone to describe as Frenchified coloring—dark hair and eyes which contrasted quite dramatically with very fair skin indeed. If pressed, Mr. Yarwood might have gone so far as to admit that much to his surprise, Miss Armstead had turned out to be quite pretty. No Nonpareil by any means, but all things considered, Frankie really didn't look half bad. But as a general rule Mr. Yarwood failed to think of Miss Armstead in those terms. And certainly at the moment he was diverted by her frowning concentration as she tried unsuccessfully to undo a snarl.

"What the devil do you call that thing?" He gestured toward the netted mass. "No, don't tell me. Let me guess. A rabbit snare?"

Frankie shot him a look that tried but failed to wither. "It's a purse," she informed him, then instantly was sorry.

"A purse!" he whooped. "What do you plan to carry in it, cabbages?" Miss Armstead looked down darkly at her handiwork. It did seem to have developed a life of its own and had far outstripped the dainty proportions of the illustration she'd been following. "Maybe you'd better give it to Old Ned for a game bag," her closest friend continued. "I know you ain't really up to snuff when it comes to clothes, Frankie, but I shouldn't think even you would be caught dead carrying a thing like that."

"Well, since I don't go out anyhow, I can't say that it really matters," she spit back, then suddenly wished she could recall

4

her words. For from the sudden gleam of triumph in Mr. Yarwood's eyes, Miss Armstead's instincts told her that she had somehow unwittingly fallen into a trap.

With the studied nonchalance of a bad actor recognizing a spoken cue, Mr. Yarwood picked up her words and seemed to savor them. "You don't go out, you say? Oh, well, now, all that's a thing of the past you know—your not going out and about, I mean. By George, the matter slipped my mind there for a bit, but I had meant to tell you right away. There's no need for you to wear black gloves any longer, Frankie."

Miss Armstead tried to match her nonchalance to his, with equally poor results. "What a peculiar thing to say. I'm not wearing black gloves, as you well know."

"I'm speaking only figuratively, of course." Bertie looked rather proud of the expression. "What I mean to say is, you can give up your fakey mourning. Greville Wainwright's very much alive."

"Good God!" The reaction exceeded Mr. Yarwood's fondest expectations. Miss Armstead's mouth flew open. She dropped the netted purse from nerveless fingers and turned chalky white. "Lord Greville alive? B-but he can't be," she finally gasped.

"Tell him that." Bertie broke into a wide grin, deciding that the time had come to lay his emotional cards out on the table. It had the wrong effect. Frankie's horror turned to incensed suspicion.

"Bertie Yarwood, is this your idea of a joke? If you're roasting me, I swear it, I'll—"

"No, no, 'pon my honor." He hastily snatched away the straw she clutched for. "Would I fun about a thing like that? Oh, Lord Greville's alive all right. And"—he paused dramatically while Frankie turned all the paler—"what's more, he's back here at Alton Hall."

Bertie stooped down to pick up the aborted purse and began to toss it back and forth between his hands while he studied his companion's face with a relish he no longer attempted to disguise. "Well, the fat's really in the fire now, I'd say. Hoist by your own petard, ain't you, Frankie? Now, didn't I tell you it was a rackety idea right from the start?"

"You did not!" Frankie spoke between clenched teeth. Indignation overran her horror as she observed Bertie's enjoyment of her discomfort. "And what's more, you quite failed to come up with a better idea. And since you did agree to go along with my scheme—which I should not have to remind you, Albert Yarwood, was as much to your advantage as to mine—it ill becomes you to sit there crowing over me like a—like a—fox in the hen house."

"Never saw a crowing fox in my life," her friend retorted, "though I've ridden down a many of the bushy little beggars."

"Oh, do be quiet about pointless foxes, Bertie, and try to tell me the whole business straight for once. Are you quite sure he's back? Couldn't it have been someone else? I mean, he did go down with the *Arrow* and drown in the Mediterranean. So it just doesn't stand to reason he could be back here. Oh, my God," she moaned, "if you can't count on a thing like that, what can you count on?"

"I say, Frankie," Mr. Yarwood suddenly interrupted her heart-burnings. "Could you ask Parkinson to fetch tea and a bit of seedcake or something? I'm fair famished. I mean, I rode right over here the moment I heard and—"

"Bertie!" Miss Armstead's voice had a dangerous edge to it. "If you don't tell me everything you know immediately, I swear I'll strangle you this instant with this netting."

"Be the only useful thing you've done with it yet," he jibed; then, fearing his hostess's imminent apoplexy, if not her threat, he added hastily, "I got the news from Charles just this morning." Charles was the Yarwood footman. "He's walking out with the Wainwrights' parlor maid, you know, and was over there last night. Well, they'd had a letter from London just that day—Lord Greville was back and would be home tomorrow—that's today, actually. Seems he'd just learned himself that he'd been listed dead. Seems he wasn't drowned at all. In point of fact, he's been to Trafalgar and fought with Nelson—been decorated—promoted—the whole business." Mr. Yarwood suddenly succumbed to the ridiculousness of the situation and barely managed to gasp out between his whoops, "I will say this for you, Frankie, when it comes to picking fiancés right out

6

of the blue, you certainly don't stint. Lord, you might just about as soon have picked on Nelson—or Wellington—or, oh, my God, I don't suppose even Prinny himself would be above your touch!" He held his sides and doubled up with laughter to the peril of the delicate chair he sat in, while he barely managed to gasp out, "Just think, Frankie, this so-called fiancé of yours, that you managed to make up out of the whole cloth for yourself, is not only not drowned and eaten by the fishes; he's alive and well and a full-blown hero. And just what do you plan to do now, Miss Armstead?"

Miss Armstead didn't know. When on the spur of the moment she'd invented a fiancé, it had seemed at the time a stroke of genius. Considering that she'd had to improvise there on the spot, pinned down by Uncle Matthew's disapproving eye, Frankie thought she'd done rather well in coming up with an instant reason why a marriage should not be arranged between Albert Yarwood and herself. When she'd explained that fond as she was of Bertie (what a whisker!), her heart belonged to another, Uncle Matthew had looked absolutely thunderous. His beefy face, florid at the best of times, had flushed a port wine color while he'd swelled with indignation to the peril of his already straining waistcoat buttons. "We'll have no more of that nonsense, Miss," he had bellowed at her. "I can't help it if he is the eldest son of my closest friend. Evelyn Yarwood is nothing but a gazetted fortune hunter!"

"Well, when it comes to that," Frankie was stung into saying despite all her resolutions, "why on earth would Bertie marry me except for my fortune? And isn't it a bit odd to give me to the second son and not the eldest? Evelyn, at least, stands to inherit Ashwood Park."

"That's as may be," her uncle replied darkly. "George Yarwood may think twice before he lets Evelyn send his estates down the River Tick. The thing is, I had always intended you for Evelyn and I let his father know it. But that was before the boy turned out to be a gamester. He's practically ruined George already, and he'd run through your fortune in a minute, Miss. So we'll hear no more of that. No, Bertie may have his faults, but he's no gamester. Besides, he'll be content to settle down here in Hampshire instead of racketing around London all the time like Evelyn. Why, Bertie would rather ride to the hounds any day than stand in White's bow window ogling ladies through a quizzing glass like some damned Macaroni."

"Nobody says 'Macaroni' in 1806." Choosing not to comment on just what she thought of Bertie's stay-at-home proclivities, Frankie corrected her old-fashioned relative instead. "You could say like some damned beau, or some damned Corinthian, or some damned out-and-outer, if you like."

"Well, I don't like. I mean to say I don't like hearing you using such language, Frances. It ain't becoming to a female. Now, where were we?"

"I was just about to explain that you'll have to tell Mr. Yarwood very tactfully that I can't marry Bertie, for my heart has been given elsewhere."

"Damn it, girl!" Mr. Armstead exploded again. "As long as I'm your guardian, I'll never consent to your marrying Evelyn. Now get that maggoty notion out of your head once and for all."

"It is out of my head, Uncle," she answered patiently, if untruthfully. "What I've been trying to say, if you'd only listen, is that I can't marry Bertie because I've an understanding with Greville Wainwright."

"I b-beg your pardon?" Uncle Matthew had stared at her as though one of them had taken leave of their senses and he wasn't quite sure which was the afflicted one.

"You heard me, Uncle Matthew. Greville and I have an understanding."

"Don't try and flummox me, Miss. It ain't the kind of joke that I enjoy."

"I'm not funning, Uncle Matthew. Greville Wainwright and I are betrothed. Secretly, of course."

"Betrothed! That's the biggest pack of nonsense I ever heard. Damme, Frankie, you don't even know the fellow. How could you know him? He's one of those navy coves, always out to sea."

"Well, he wasn't at sea six months ago," she shot back at him. "He was at Aunt Maria's house party, which is where we met and fell in love." Frankie was warming up to her work now, spurred on by an actress's instincts that she was just about to hook her audience.

"Lord Greville was at Maria's? You never mentioned it." Matthew Armstead's attitude was that of the almost-converted sinner, who really wishes to believe.

"That's because he felt we should keep our tendre for one another secret. He was concerned about the great difference in our ages, for one thing."

"It ain't as great as all that," Mr. Armstead interrupted. "He's Evelyn's age exactly, as I recall."

"Oh." Frankie was momentarily set back upon her heels. She'd no notion at all of Lord Greville's age, or indeed of much else about him, since she'd only exchanged the briefest civilities with him upon introduction. He'd certainly seemed older, due to his distant air of consequence perhaps. "Well, mostly he was concerned that since we'd had so little time together and he'd be away so long, that I might have a change of a heart," she tried again. "Which is ridiculous, of course. But then too, he felt I should reach my majority before he spoke to you."

"He said that, did he? Well, now, by George, if that ain't just like Lord Greville. The man's a gentleman through and through. Which makes a change from some of the rackety types you've attracted in the past, I don't mind saying. My God, Frankie! You're actually going to marry Lord Greville Wainwright!" The enormity of the miracle was beginning to sink in. "If it don't beat all. And ain't you the sly puss, though. Who'd have ever thought you'd come up with a prime catch like that? Why, just wait till I tell George Yarwood!"

"Oh, no, you can't!" Frankie had yelped.

"Have to, you know, How else can I explain that you'll not be marrying Bertie? Lord, even George will be the first to understand that I couldn't possibly turn down Lord Wainwright's grandson for friendship's sake. Why, it's like one of those far-fetched fairy stories, Frankie, you knocking Lord Greville right off his feet. You'll be the *on dit* of the county."

Frances Armstead had never seen her uncle so elated. And for the first time she began to have serious second thoughts concerning her selection. For when she'd hit on the idea of a counterfeit fiancé, Lord Greville had possessed the only qualification of any importance in her eyes: he was thousands of miles away. That, coupled with the fact that their meeting had taken place in her aunt's country house when no one of her acquaintance was around to give the lie to her fabricated romance, made him the logical choice among a very few candidates for the spurious office. She'd failed completely to recognize the fact that in the eyes of the world the heir to the Wainwright estates and title might have a few other points of eligibility in his favor. She looked uneasily at her uncle Matthew as a case in point, for while she'd fully expected him to approve the match, she'd certainly not expected him to be in such transports over it.

Of course, if she'd taken time to think about it, she would have realized that the Wainwrights were definitely above the Armstead touch. But in point of fact the enormity of what she'd done simply had not occurred to her. Now Uncle Matthew was babbling on about ten thousand pounds a year, the richest estate in Hampshire, and a title that went back several generations. Well, it was all purely academic in any case. But it was certainly going to make things more difficult when she did reach her majority and elope with Evelyn Yarwood. That particular marriage would be a blow to her uncle Matthew, of whom she was truly fond, no matter what. But now she could see that she'd greatly compounded the difficulty. For her to jilt a future baron for a rake (only in Uncle Matthew's eyes, of course) might well finish her guardian off. But she'd simply have to face that crisis when it came, the resilient Miss Armstead decided. Right then the immediate problem was to prevent her uncle from spreading abroad the good news of her betrothal.

"Please, Uncle Matthew, if you must tell Mr. Yarwood about my understanding, be sure and get his solemn oath that he'll tell no one else. And don't you say a word either. Greville was most insistent that we keep our betrothal secret for a while. You see, he has yet to tell Lord Wainwright of it."

"Thinks it will come as a blow to the old gentleman, does he?" Since he himself had just pronounced the Wainwrights above their touch, it did seem unreasonable of Uncle Matthew to sound a bit offended now, Miss Armstead thought. "Well, now, your fortune ain't to be despised, m'dear, even if it does come from commerce, and French trade at that. And certainly no one moves in more tony circles than your aunt Maria. She may be a foreigner and rackety as they make 'em, but there's no denying the fact she's married into two of England's finest families. Come to think on it, I expect that meeting you there among the Fashionable Set is what gave Lord Greville the notion to offer for you," Mr. Armstead mused, his good humor beginning to be restored. "Well, now, I don't think Lord Wainwright will be too displeased. It no doubt ain't the match he'd have chosen for his grandson and heir, but it ain't like the lad's bringing home an opera dancer."

"Just the same, Uncle Matthew," Frankie had said firmly, "Greville wants to break the news to his grandfather himself. And since he did not have the opportunity before he went to sea—his leave was cut short, you may recall—" she improvised, "it's only proper that he be the one to speak to Lord Wainwright upon his return. Why the old gentleman would have every right to be set against the match if he were to hear of it through rumor-mongering."

Frankie had thereupon extracted a solemn promise from her uncle to keep the matter secret. But being of a perceptive nature, she could not fail to note in the weeks that followed how her neighbors' attitudes toward her began to change. If she was not exactly toadeaten, she almost certainly was constantly deferred to. Even the servants, who heretofore had tended to treat her as a favorite though somewhat troublesome child, now stopped themselves with apparent difficulty just barely short of forelock-pulling.

To make matters worse, Bertie learned of his reprieve from Mr. Yarwood, and Frankie had felt compelled to take him into her confidence. He of course pretended to have known all along that "the whole thing was a hum. Didn't think it likely that Lord Greville would have formed a tendre for you. He couldn't have been at sea that long! Of course," he added in the spirit of fair play, "I didn't believe that my brother Evelyn could have formed one for you either, so I guess I was led down the garden path there for a bit. But then I thought it over and decided you must be playing deep."

After that it had seemed necessary to explain the situation to Evelyn and scotch any rumors that might reach him. Therefore, Frankie had written a letter which Bertie obligingly carried to London for her. He fetched back the answer, in Evelyn's hasty scrawl, congratulating her on her ingenuity, but wondering why she had to pick out a stiff-rumped cove like Greville Wainwright to become engaged to. "Still, come to think of it," he'd ended facetiously, "I can't think of anyone whose fiancée I'd liefer run off to Gretna Green with. Yours, Evelyn."

So what with one thing and another it had come as a considerable relief when the news reached Hampshire that the "HMS *Arrow*, sloop of war, escorting, along with the bomb vessel HMS *Acheron*, a valuable convoy of merchant ships, was attacked by two large French frigates and, after a four hour battle, sank, all hands reported lost." Frankie was not, of course, so totally lost to proper feeling that she did not find it tragic that a young man with so much to live for had been cut off in his prime, or that she failed to grieve for the poor old gentleman in the Hall who not only had lost his only son in an accident years before but was also now bereaved of his grandson and heir as well. But still Miss Armstead would have had to be sapskulled not to recognize that she had been extracted from a situation with all the potential for a major scandal.

There was, however, an unlooked-for complication in this new development. Frankie was forced into a bogus period of mourning that she found more distasteful in its hypocrisy than in its confinement. For, though social by nature, she found being barred from assemblies and rout parties a small price to pay for having Uncle Matthew tactfully abstain from renegotiating the abandoned match with Bertie. Even a "secret" fiancée, it seemed, was allowed a year to wear the willow for a naval hero gone to his final, watery resting place. So Miss Armstead had been more grateful than not for the state of limbo Lord Greville's death had placed her in. That was, of course, before Bertie Yarwood had interrupted her purse-netting to drop his bombshell and blow her complacency to smithereens.

And now it was that young man's obvious enjoyment of the situation that goaded Miss Armstead into rallying her troops to meet life's latest onslaught. "Well, of course I'm very glad to hear that Lord Greville is not drowned after all," she said. And if her face failed to carry a conviction to match this declaration, for once Bertie decided not to point up the discrepancy.

"That goes without saying," he answered piously. "But there's no need to try and wrap the whole thing in clean linen, Frankie, 'cause it won't do. Fact is, Greville Wainwright's resurrection has left you in the devil of a coil."

"I don't see why," the resilient Miss Armstead replied stoutly. "He won't be here long, I'm sure. Sailors never are. Why, he had to leave that house party days before anyone else did in order to get back his ship." Her voice increased a notch or two in optimism. "I'll bet you a monkey right now, Bertie, that he's just popping down to Hampshire to reassure his grandfather and let the old gentleman see his heir in the flesh after the shock of thinking he was dead. Then the admiralty's bound to whisk him off again, and things can go back to being the way they were."

Mr. Yarwood was prevented from commenting on this rosy version of the future by the butler's entrance with a heavily laden tray. "I took the liberty of having cook prepare refreshments for Master Bertie," he murmured as he set the tray on a loo table that occupied the center of the room. Parkinson, who had been a contemporary and confidant of Frankie's father, was fond of both the young people, though prone to think of them largely in nursery terms.

"I say, Parkinson, this is famous." Bertie all but licked his lips. "I told Frankie to give the bell a pull, but you know what females are, always thinking of their own shapes while a fellow starves."

Frances Armstead barely restrained her impatience while Parkinson fussed around pouring tea and making sure that "Master Bertie" was amply supplied with the gingerbread nuts which, so he informed that young gentleman, "cook put into the oven the very moment she got the word that you were here, sir, knowing how partial to them you are."

"Master Bertie," Frankie mimicked, "is partial to anything that can be shoved into his mouth and swallowed." This observation earned her a duet of injured looks.

"Well," she said disgustedly after Parkinson had finally withdrawn, "is that all you're going to do, stuff yourself?"

"Lord, Frankie, what else should I do? Quit looking so Friday-faced and taste the nun's cake."

Miss Armstead complied reluctantly. But as she sipped her tea she took the conversation back where it had broken off. "You do agree, don't you, Bertie?" Anxiety had crept back into her voice again.

"With what?" he asked through seedcake.

"That Greville Wainwright will probably just pop in and out of Alton Hall and then be off to sea again."

"Well, as to that, Frankie, I really couldn't say. But I do know one thing Charles told me. The Hall's on its ear right now. The old gentleman hasn't entertained since Methuselah was just an infant, so Charles said. But now his lordship's planning to give a ball. Right away, in fact. Plans to ask the entire county to it."

"Oh, no!" Miss Armstead looked aghast. But then she conceded philosophically, "Well, it's to be expected, I suppose, that he'd want to celebrate his grandson's return to life."

There was a long, pregnant pause while Mr. Yarwood deliberately picked up the scattered crumbs from the front of his waistcoat with a dampened index finger and popped them in his mouth. A sly grin twitched the corners of his lips as he surveyed Frankie with the kind of scientific interest that a small boy accords a beetle rolled helplessly over on its back. Frances Armstead, too well acquainted with all his moods, returned his gaze warily.

And then Mr. Yarwood played the trump card he'd been concealing up his sleeve ever since his entrance. "I don't think it's exactly a 'coming-to-life party' for his grandson that the old gentleman has in mind. Actually, if you want my opinion, it's more likely a 'welcome-to-the-county' for the beautiful lady friend Lord Greville's brought down from London with him."

Chapter Two

THE FOLLOWING DAY WAS FILLED WITH WAITING. Matthew Armstead, who had also heard the news of his niece's fiancé's miraculous return, kept looking out the window, waiting for the hero-lover to appear upon his doorstep. Miss Armstead, however, kept waiting for the arrival of their card of invitation to the Wainwright ball.

Needless to say, it was the card that got there first. And after Frankie had snatched the crested invitation off the silver tray in the hall where Parkinson had placed it, she could not decide whether what she felt was horror or relief.

Relief won the day, but only barely. Since news of the ball was bound to reach her uncle's ears, their omission from the list might be a bit awkward to explain. Not that contriving a suitable excuse for not attending would be much easier.

In point of fact, Uncle Matthew showed little sympathy for her preliminary symptoms on the morning of the ball. When Frankie failed to appear at breakfast, sending word that she was suffering from a putrid fever, he arrived unexpectedly in her bedroom, where she was dealing with the heavily laden breakfast tray that her maid had thoughtfully provided. "Nerves," he diagnosed while Frankie endeavored to conceal the tray underneath the covers and look invalidish. "Best thing in the world for you to do is to get dressed and go for a walk. Fresh air and exercise. That's the cure for any ailment."

Wishing it were possible to turn pale on command, Frankie

settled for making her voice as faint as possible. "I don't think I can stir out of bed today. I'm so sorry about the ball. You'll have to go without me."

"Nonsense. Of course you're going to Lord Wainwright's ball. Why, even if you weren't going to be one of the family"—and at this point Frankie was unaware that she'd just succeeded in turning pale—"it still wouldn't do not to show up when invited. Why, I'd sooner turn down an invitation to Carlton House. At least I don't have to live in the same neighborhood with the Prince of Wales. Tell you what I'll do, though. I'll have cook mix up a dose of bark mixture for you. That should set you right in no time." Here Frankie's pallor took on a slightly greenish cast.

Matthew Armstead then leaned over and patted his niece on the shoulder with a great deal more tenderness than he was wont to show. Frankie was a sight to elicit any elderly gentleman's compassion, her dark eyes enormous with apprehension, her nightcap slightly askew with a tangle of dark curls escaping to give an even more distrait appearance to her countenance. "There, there, m'dear. It's natural enough that you've got the wind up a bit over the prospect of seeing Lord Greville after all these months. Afraid he might have had a change of heart, then, are you? Nonsense!" he said heartily as she nodded. "Who's he going to have changed it for, some mermaid he spotted as his ship went down?" He laughed heartily at his little joke. "Now just get all such maggoty notions out of your head, child. I'll admit it. I thought it queer at first that he didn't show up here soon as he got home. But it wouldn't have been at all the thing to do, leaving Lord Wainwright alone after all the old gentleman's been through. Besides, I wager he's been kept busy with the preparations for their party. Well, now, I expect we can look for an announcement there, eh?" And he pinched his niece's cheek playfully.

"Oh, no," Frankie gasped, appalled by the very notion of such an expectation on her uncle's part. "Nothing like that will happen." At least she prayed there'd be no announcement of a betrothal, as she thought apprehensively of that "Diamond of the First Water," in Bertie's words, whom Lord Greville had brought home with him. "Why, he hasn't even spoken to you yet, Uncle." She tried to dampen Mr. Armstead's enthusiasm. "Besides, this ball isn't really in Greville's honor at all. You see, he's brought a visitor from London with him. His cousin, in point of fact," she fabricated. "The party's planned for her."

"Ah, is that so?" Mr. Armstead was beaming, much to her surprise. "Well, ain't you the sly one, Frankie. Imagine you knowing a thing like that. So you have seen Lord Greville! I was the least bit suspicious when you went riding yesterday and wondered just what you were up to and—well—I confess that I suspected an assignation. No, no." He waved the subject away as she opened her mouth to deny the meeting. "I'm not one to pry or scold. Even if you are still underage and in my protection, it ain't as if you're not betrothed. Besides, if Lord Greville ain't a gentleman to be trusted, well, I don't know who is. His cousin's here, you say?" He frowned thoughtfully. "Didn't know he had any. His father was an only child, you know. Thought his mother was one, too, but she couldn't have been, now could she? Of course, she came from Dorset." For some reason that Frances failed to understand this seemed to explain the matter to her uncle's satisfaction. He left her then with strict instructions to drink the bark mixture, which he intended to have sent up immediately, go for a brisk walk, take a nap in the afternoon, and be prepared to leave at eight.

Since there seemed no way short of death—a bit drastic even for the circumstances—to avoid the Wainwright ball, Frankie did the next best thing and contrived to make them as late for it as possible. This maneuver had decided drawbacks, since it involved spilling tea on her favorite ball gown and having to change into one less becoming that had made more appearances in county society than she liked to think of. And it also involved driving Bess, her dresser, almost to the point of tears when she, uncharacteristically and repeatedly, found fault with the way her hair was dressed and insisted upon having it done a half-dozen ways. When she finally pronounced it "passable," the frustrated maid eyed the mass of ringlets and the chignon with exasperation and forgot herself enough to mutter under her breath, "It's exactly the way it was the first time."

But Bess's state was mild compared to the temper Uncle Matthew was in when Frankie finally joined him in the lower hall, where he'd been pacing and shouting up at her for close to an hour and reporting the implacable movements of the clock hands.

He continued to scold for the entire length of the carriage drive to Alton Hall, lecturing her on the folly of making a poor impression on her betrothed's grandfather by being tardy for this important function.

"Well, if he'd wanted us on time, he could have invited us to dinner, could he not?"

Her uncle Matthew looked quite shocked. "It was an honor for us to be asked to Alton Hall at all," he said reprovingly. "You could hardly expect us to be invited to dinner first. That honor is reserved for Lord Wainwright's most intimate acquaintances. Of course, though, in the future—well, that will be quite a different matter, will it not?" And Mr. Armstead's humor was suddenly restored by the prospect of the dizzy rise in status he'd experience once his niece had married the future baron of Alton Hall.

Seeing a sudden smile replace the petulance that had marked her uncle's countenance since the beginning of the carriage ride, Frankie had no difficulty guessing the direction of his thoughts. His restored good humor perversely plunged her into a deeper gloom. Her spirits sank another notch as their carriage swept between the imposing pillars that flanked the Alton gate and raced as rapidly as was seemly up the final half a mile that brought them to the turnaround before the hall. And at the sight of that imposing edifice Miss Armstead's spirits sank to the level of her evening slippers.

But if the massiveness of Alton, built as it was with rectangular solidity flanked by four square towers, intimidated Frankie as she climbed the two tiers of steps that led to the main entrance, the hall they entered undid her nerve completely. It was enormous, in the old style, two stories high, with a marble floor expansive enough to encamp an army, which might indeed have felt right at home beneath the plaster replicas of ancient weaponry that adorned the walls. Pedestals topped with marble statuary—a mixture of ancestral busts with Greek and Roman heroes, Frankie surmised—did little to give the place a cozy feel. Even the two cherubs who blew their trumpets over the marble archway that separated the great hall from the saloon looked sinister, in spite of dimpled cheeks and baby plumpness. Perhaps it was the Wainwright coat of arms they flanked that robbed them of the usual endearing cherubic qualities. Frankie barely managed to suppress a groan as she surrendered her cloak to one of several footmen and made her way with Uncle Matthew toward the saloon where the orchestra was hard at work providing the music for a minuet in progress. She gazed up for another look at the demonic cherubs as they passed beneath them and could have sworn that their hollow marble eyes winked knowingly. "Here comes the impostor," their trumpets seemed to blare.

Lord Wainwright greeted them at the saloon entrance, courteously brushing aside Mr. Armstead's elaborate apology for their tardiness that centered around a horse unfortunately casting its shoe just as they reached their own carriage gate, and presented them to a rather Friday-faced elderly spinster whom he identified as Miss Austen, companion to their guest of honor, Lady Venetia Sellars, who was unfortunately already on the dance floor. Frankie studied his lordship covertly through lowered lashes as he made the introductions and wondered if she'd find him half so forbidding if it were not for her ill-advised charade.

Certainly he was distinguished-looking. Except for a slight bulge where his waistcoat met the top of satin knee breeches, he was quite trim of figure. His ramrod-straight carriage and his well-shaped calves beneath his white silk hose belied his rapidly approaching octagenarian status. His hair was long in the fashion of the last century and tied behind his neck with a neat black ribbon. But it no longer required the powdering that had once made it à la mode, for nature had turned it to a snowy white. There was nothing out of date, however, about his long-tailed waisted coat, Miss Armstead noted. Indeed, the quality of its cut made her uncle Matthew, who was similarly attired, appear ill-dressed by contrast.

Once these formalities had been taken care of and they'd moved farther into the room, Frankie seized the opportunity to look around her. The saloon, even larger than the great hall, was packed with guests. That the baron had been able to produce so great a crush on such short notice was certainly a tribute to his consequence, as well as a testament to the joy the county felt at the return of the Hero of Trafalgar from his watery grave.

A good portion of the guests were now engaged in performing the minuet, a dance as antiquated as the host's hairstyle, but equally dignified and distinguished, Frankie concluded while she watched. She stood by Uncle Matthew's side trying to look as if attending such a gathering were an every-night event for her, while in fact she longed to ooh and aah over the beauty of her surroundings. Above the dancers, a myriad of candles sparkled through the crystal pendants of faceted glass belonging to an enormous chandelier suspended from the center of the ceiling, and bathed the multicolored gowns of the female guests and the severe black and whites of their partners with a fairy dust of light. The saloon walls were banked with flowers and greenery. A parade of gilt chairs framed the dance floor to accommodate those guests either too fatigued, too old, or too partnerless to participate. Miss Armstead was leading her uncle Matthew toward two of these when their progress was impeded by the sudden materialization of Mr. Albert Yarwood.

"Are you just now getting here?" he demanded. "Lord, I've been watching for you for ages."

"You mean you were asked to dinner?" Frankie was diverted into asking. Her uncle Matthew seemed equally intent upon hearing Bertie's answer and looked rather more pleased than not when the young man answered, "Good lord, no. Wouldn't expect to be. But I did get here promptly at ten, you know, and I've been looking for you ever since. What kept you, anyhow?"

At that point Mr. Armstead forestalled any explanation his niece might have made by turning her over to Mr. Yarwood's keeping in order to seek out his own cronies, who, his lordship had informed him, were gathered mostly in the drawing room, where tables had been set up for cards. This left the young people free to seek out the chairs Frankie had targeted and have a private whispered conversation.

"To tell you the truth," Bertie began, "I'd given up on you. Thought you'd funked it. And lord, Frankie, I can't say that I'd have blamed you." He looked around, wide-eyed at the magnificence. "I must say it again"—he choked with laughter suddenly—"when you decide to dream up a fiancé, you don't do the thing by halves. My God, Frankie, what ever put such a maggoty notion into your head?"

"I don't know," she answered miserably. "Well, yes, I do, actually. You see, all I knew of Lord Greville was that he was miles away. I'd no idea he was such a Nabob."

"Well, you should have known it," he answered practically. " 'His lordship' and all that."

"Having a title doesn't necessarily mean you're rich as Croesus," she retorted. "Besides, I never expected things to come to this sort of pass. Where is he, anyhow?"

"There." Bertie gestured toward the minuet.

"Where?" Frankie finally had to ask after perusing the ranks of dancers in vain for several seconds.

"Right in front of us," Mr. Yarwood hissed as the dancers shifted positions in slow three-quarter time.

"I still can't find him," his companion whispered back. Mr. Yarwood's shoulders began to shake with choked-off laughter. "He's close enough to bite you, stupid. Lord, Frankie, you mean you can't even recognize your famous fiancé? I knew the engagement was all a hum, but I thought you'd at least seen the fellow. Been at a house party with him, you said. Listen, I ain't one to preach as a rule, but if you keep on telling whiskers at this rate, there's no telling—"

"It wasn't a whisker. We were both at the house party, and I did meet him. But I don't see anybody that—my God, is that he?" She clutched Mr. Yarwood by the sleeve to the detriment of his valet's attempt to achieve wrinkle-free perfection to help offset the stigma of provincial tailoring. "It can't be!"

"Don't see why it can't. In point of fact it is. Here, Frankie, want my quizzing glass for a better look?"

"But I'm sure he didn't look like that," she croaked, waving away the proffered glass, which Bertie had hung around his neck with a black ribbon according to the dictates of *Le Beau Monde* for fashionable Full Dress. "Why, he looks more like a gypsy than a lord." Frankie stared with a stunned look at the man opposite them, who was bowing to a lovely lady who wore a clinging muslin dress.

He was tall as his grandfather with the same clear gray eyes. There were even the same fine lines crinkling at their corners. But there all resemblance stopped. He looked less benign than ruffian. His dark hair was cropped short above his collar, with more regard to function than to fashion. His evening clothes were impeccable but conservative; his shirt points were not so high as to cause discomfort nor did his stock appear modishly designed to choke him. He wore no fob or quizzing glass. Indeed he appeared free of ornamentation of any kind. But it was his complexion that drew Frankie's disapproval. Among the pale faces of the local gentry his stood out darkly, sunburned, and swarthy. "He looks—mahogany," Miss Armstead breathed.

"Well, what would you expect after months at sea in the Mediterranean?" her companion answered. "But quit ogling him for a minute, would you, and look at the beauty with him. How's that for a rival, Frankie?" Bertie sniggered.

The minuet now concluded, the dancers were deserting the dance floor. The ladies plied their fans vigorously from the exertion, either flirting with their present partners or casting their eyes about for new ones. The female with Lord Greville belonged to the former category. Her hand remained attached to her escort's sleeve. Her lovely blue eyes sparkled up at him as she tossed her golden curls and laughed in appreciation of whatever witticism his lordship had just uttered.

"Did you ever see such an angelic face?" Mr. Yarwood sighed in Miss Armstead's ear. "Or such an absolutely divine figure?"

"Humph!" Frankie came perilously close to snorting. "I don't think I've ever seen so much of anybody's figure."

In truth, the provincial Miss Armstead was a trifle shocked.

She had heard, of course, of the English imitators of the scandalous French ladies known as Les Merveilleuses. These elegant, useless ladies of fashion had adopted the Greek style of clothing and carried it to the extreme. But Lord Greville's partner was the first example of this fashion that Frankie had ever seen. Lady Venetia was wearing a chemise dress of transparent muslin over pale pink silk body tights. This was risqué enough, but Miss Armstead suspected that the lady had actually dampened her gown in order to assure that it clung to her graceful curves revealingly. A simple pink ribbon was twined in among the golden curls, matching the ones crossed over and over up the leg, again in the classical Greek manner, to hold her tiny flat sandals securely in place. Her neckline was quite scandalously low, revealing lovely milk-white breasts. But here the Marvel had thrown Greek simplicity to the winds by donning an elaborate diamond necklace that rivaled the crystal chandelier for sparkle. Lord Greville did not strike Frankie as the type of man to wear his heart upon his sleeve in public, so his face revealed little of what he was feeling. But there was no denying the fact that the lady with him held his complete interest as they moved off the floor or that in marked contrast to his lordship's reserved attention, Frankie's companion and childhood friend might well have been the target for a whole quiverful of Cupid's arrows.

"I say, Frankie," he breathed, "you've really gone and done it now. Nobody's going to believe for one minute that Greville Wainwright's lost his head over you when he's got a prime 'un like that beauty dangling after him." Bertie had been ogling Lady Venetia's progress across the saloon, but he now turned his quizzing glass back on his companion. For several seconds he seemed to weigh Frankie in the balance and find her wanting. "You should pay more attention to your clothes, Frankie. Ain't I seen that dress before?" His disapproval of her pale yellow, tambored, nontransparent muslin gown was obvious.

The fact that she herself had been regretting the spider gauze she'd ruined did not lessen her resentment of the criticism. "Yes, you have. Twice, in fact, though what that has to say to anything I can't—oh, no!" She broke off in horror, her eyes

23

riveted upon a scene over her companion's shoulder. He swung around to see what was happening. "Oh, no!" he echoed as his chin dropped.

The object of all his attention was Mr. Matthew Armstead, who had reentered the saloon in time to waylay the guests of honor as they left the dance floor. He was now engaged in pumping Lord Greville's hand and slapping him upon the back with a familiarity that caused his niece to cringe. The Trafalgar hero's face was devoid of all expression. They saw him appear to reply civilly but briefly to the effusive greeting.

"Look at him," Miss Armstead groaned. "I made him promise me particularly that he'd not approach Lord Greville."

"Well, never mind," Bertie answered comfortingly. "His lordship's no doubt accustomed to being toadeaten. Ain't likely he'll refine too much on it—my God!" This time it was he who clutched at Frankie. "Your uncle's actually dragging the fellow away. Frankie, they're headed right for us!"

Miss Armstead had already spied the danger. Her defense was to leap to her feet and give her stunned friend's arm a jerk. "Quick," she hissed. "Come dance with me." And she endeavored to lead her transfixed companion to the floor, where sets for a country dance were being formed. Her strategy failed however. "Just a minute, Frances!" her uncle called out in a voice accustomed to setting to rights a pack of baying hounds off on the wrong scent. "There's someone here who'd like to see you."

Heads turned their way curiously, and Frankie felt her face flame red as she turned, with Bertie cowering behind her, to face her nemesis.

"Well, now, Lord Greville, I don't believe you've met me niece. Frankie, here's Lord Greville Wainwright."

Chapter
Three

IF MR. ARMSTEAD'S STILTED VOICE WASN'T ENOUGH TO make it clear that the fakey introduction was being made for the benefit of the people pricking up their ears around them, the broad wink and nudge to the ribs he gave his lordship underscored the point. "There's nothing at all odd about you two having a dance together, now, is there?" he added under his breath in a conspiratorial tone. "Nobody can refine the slightest bit on that. Doubt that your grandfather will even notice." And he gave Frankie a push in his lordship's direction.

Even in the midst of her shame and humiliation, even while she prayed to be stricken dead upon the spot, somehow Frances Armstead was able to spare a thought for the efficacy of good breeding. Greville Wainwright's face remained expressionless. Nor did his cool gray eyes betray the annoyance he must have felt. And if the tone in which he then inquired, "May I have the honor?" seemed a trifle dry, no one, especially Frankie, could possibly have faulted him for that.

Since her body refused to obey her command to swoon, and since Lord Greville was extending a gloved hand, she saw no alternative course of action that would not make the hideous scene more ghastly still. She laid a trembling hand on his and allowed him to lead her out upon the floor.

After they'd taken their places in the set and had stood in awkward silence for a while, he asked, "Do you live in the neighborhood, Miss Armstead?" The question, though polite, was not accompanied by the inquirer's attention, Frankie observed. Indeed her partner's eyes were busily scanning the ballroom. They finally came to rest upon Lady Venetia, now taking her position in another set, partnered by a middle-aged exquisite whom Frankie did not know. "She's beautiful, isn't she?" she blurted, then felt herself coloring again as Lord Greville at this point gave her his full, though slightly annoyed, attention.

However grudgingly it was given, Frankie decided to take advantage of the fact that she'd captured her partner's interest and of the loud music for the boulanger that the orchestra had just struck up, which should cover their conversation for a bit. "I do hope you'll overlook Uncle Matthew's 'peculiarities,' " she plunged in, placing considerable stress upon the final word. "Those of us close to him hardly even notice his—er—eccentricities—any longer. Indeed, he's perfectly harmless, you understand. And perfectly normal most of the time." Frankie warmed up to her explanation, seeing that she had her partner's full attention. "Indeed, our physician, Dr. Carstairs—do you know him?" Lord Greville nodded and she continued. "Dr. Carstairs says that Uncle's condition is quite similar to the malady suffered by King George. Only"—she felt compelled to add in a fit of conscience—"of course Uncle Matthew has never been so bad as to need the constraint of a straitjacket like our beloved king."

"I'm very sorry to hear of your uncle's problem," her host murmured, and unbent in his expression enough to seem quite human for a moment. It was evident also that a mystery had just been cleared up for him.

It was soon their turn to dance, and Frankie suddenly began to enjoy herself. For one thing, despite the great amount of time he must have spent at sea, his lordship was an accomplished dancer—though not quite as skilled nor half as good-looking as Evelyn, she thought loyally. But the fact remained that Miss Armstead had been in exile from all social functions for several months now while she supposedly mourned the demise of her present partner. So it seemed only poetic justice that he should be making up for some of the inconvenience he had caused her by now quite adding to her enjoyment of the dance.

Indeed, the set was far too soon concluded. His lordship thanked her for the pleasure and nodded politely to Bertie as they rejoined that young gentleman, who had remained rooted to the spot where they had left him. Then the two friends stood silently until their host was out of earshot, and Bertie hissed, "Quick, before I bust. What did he say to you? I tell you my heart was in my mouth the entire time, Frankie. Oh, my God, your uncle! He couldn't have made a bigger cake out of himself if he'd practiced for a year. Whatever did Lord Greville say?"

"Lord Greville is too much the gentleman to refine overly upon the oddities of lesser mortals," Miss Armstead loftily informed her friend. "Actually, I found him very pleasant company." As Bertie gave her a look that was pregnant with disbelief, she gave his hand a tug. "Oh, forget Lord Greville and come on. They're forming another country dance. Do let's join in. I've had my fill of schemes and of naval heroes who won't stay drowned. Now that I'm here and the worst is over I intend to enjoy myself. Do come on, Bertie, or we'll be too late."

Unfortunately Miss Armstead's assessment of the evening was proven wrong. The worst, she soon discovered, was far from over. Although the company was liberally spiced with members of the ton come down from London, the majority of it was made up of the Armsteads' friends and acquaintances from the immediate vicinity. And among these folk Frankie had always been a favorite, with her ready smile and ingenuous manner. The story of her betrothal to the Wainwright heir had become a widely known secret in the neighborhood, regarded somewhat in the light of a Cinderella fairy tale. Frankie had earned a great deal of sympathy when the news of the sinking of the *Arrow* had drifted back to Hampshire. And the rejoicing over the hero's marvelous survival had been as much for her sake as for his. And it had added a definite spice to an evening, memorable in any case for providing the opportunity of a lifetime to enter Lord Wainwright's stately home, that the star-crossed secret lovers were about to be united under their very noses.

At first, Lord Greville's apparent coolness to his betrothed was written off as a marvelous bit of playacting on his part for the sake of the old gentleman. But as the evening wore on and he seemed oblivious to Frankie's presence while he dangled after the beautiful and somewhat scandalous lady from London, more and more dark looks were sent the hero's way and Frankie became more and more the object of sympathetic murmurs and hand-squeezes. At first she managed to ignore all the innuendoes having to do with perfidy and fickleness. But when she took the floor with Bertie's father, a rotund version of his second son, who announced that for two pins he'd put a flea in a certain nobleman's ear, she became alarmed. Especially so since they were in the same set with Lord Greville who had just committed the solecism of standing up for two times in succession with the dampened Lady Venetia, thereby creating an atmosphere of tension and hostility in their group that, besotted though he no doubt was with the lady twinkling up at him, was beginning to prick his awareness, Frankie feared.

"Promise me you won't say a word," she whispered to Mr. Yarwood, sounding so alarmed that he finally grudgingly agreed to keep his opinions to himself even if it killed him, which it might soon do if his lordship continued to look calf-eyed at a certain hussy who, if Frankie wanted his opinion, was, in spite of all her airs and title, no better dressed than your average light-skirt.

After the crisis of that set had passed, Frankie was able to relax a bit and enjoy the ball again. She certainly was at no loss for partners. The lesser Hampshire gentry seemed determined to make it clear that if a certain member of the ton could not appreciate the true loyalty and worth of a local girl, well, then there were plenty of others that were able to. In the middle of a cotillion Frankie observed her uncle Matthew accosting Lord Greville as the young man sought to pass him. She saw the look of annoyance on his lordship's face, but since she knew that she'd scotched all possibility of Lord Greville placing the slightest significance upon any words her uncle uttered, she returned her divided attention to the comments that her partner had been making. But at the end of that dance when Bertie practically snatched her out from under the nose of another gentleman waiting to partner her, she knew from his horrified expression that the fat must be well and truly in the fire.

"Frankie, I think he knows," he hissed into her ear as he hurried her to the opposite end of the ballroom from the spot where the unfortunate Lord Greville was hemmed into a corner by an enormous lady in purple satin who was obviously haranguing him.

"Who knows what?" Miss Armstead whispered back, more in an effort to delay the ax's drop than from any ignorance. But Bertie was in no mood for fatuous questions.

"You know damned well who and what," he said as he pulled her down on a chair beside him some distance from any possible eavesdroppers. "My father and Lady Landon had their heads together there for at least half an hour, yammering away like bosom beaux. And no sooner did Lord Greville hove in sight on his way to the punch bowl than she jumped up and set sail after him. Now look at them."

Frankie did. The three purple ostrich feathers that crowned Lady Landon's coiffure were waving emphatically with every word she uttered.

"What's so remarkable about Lady Landon talking to her host?" she asked with more bravado than she felt. "You know how encroaching she can be. She'd never pass up an opportunity to toadeat."

"Don't you believe it." Bertie squelched her hopes. "She and my father were talking about you. I know because I heard 'em. And from the look on her face when she made for Lord Greville, well, if you think she merely wants to do the polite, you're caper-witted. But I tell you what I'll do, Frankie," Bertie said in a flash of inspiration. "I'll get us some punch."

"Punch! I do not want punch! Do you always have to be thinking of refreshments? You would think that at a time like this—"

"Don't be such a gudgeon," he interrupted witheringly. "I'm going for punch so I can go by them and hear what the old behemoth is saying. And if she ain't ringing a peal over him for dangling after Lady Venetia and behaving so shabbily toward you, well, then, I'm a Frenchman!"

But as it turned out, Frankie didn't need to wait for Bertie's confirmation to realize that she was indeed the subject of the Lady Landon-Lord Greville discussion. No sooner had her friend set off on his spy mission than she saw Lord Greville turn toward the dance floor and sweep it with his eyes while her ladyship's lips continued to vibrate in the vicinity of his ear. Frankie grew more and more uneasy when Lord Greville's gaze hardly paused at all on Lady Venetia, who was dancing in his vicinity. She had a moment's hope that she was not, after all, the object of his quest when the gray gaze skimmed over her and kept on going. But even before she was able to exhale the breath she'd held, he backtracked and targeted her with all the impact of a broadside. At that precise moment Lord Greville was distracted, though, by a punch-bearer who bumped into him and paused to apologize profusely. Frankie took advantage of Bertie's diversionary tactic to retreat behind an enormous potted plant some distance from the chair where she'd been sitting.

Two dowagers gossiping nearby gave her a rather curious look as she disappeared behind the foliage; so as she cracked a window she remarked for their benefit, "I do need air." The ladies nodded sympathetically and went back to their conversation. Frankie fortified her position by rearranging the baskets of flowers around her into a cozy bower. She then sat down on the window ledge, prepared to stay there until Lord Greville was engaged once more upon the dance floor and she could slip out of the saloon and through the hall and have a footman send for her coach to fetch her home. In the meantime she occupied herself by peeping furtively through the foliage. When she saw Bertie pass by only a few feet from her with two cups of punch and a searching eye that failed to spot her, Frankie relaxed, feeling then quite secure in her hideaway.

Secure, but bored. She turned and looked out through the window at the bright moonlight that bathed the gardens. Lord Wainwright, like all thoughtful hosts, had timed his party with the full moon so that his guests could travel at night with little risk to horse and carriage. While she perused the ghostly formal garden down below her, Frankie noticed a ladder propped beneath the window, telltale evidence of the haste of preparation for the party that had caused a harried servant to leave it carelessly behind. An idea formed in Frankie's head as she looked at it.

Still, departing through the window from the most tonish party she'd ever attended did seem rather rackety. Perhaps the coast was by now clear and she could exit in the more normal way. She rose from the windowsill and risked another peep through the greenery—and almost gasped aloud. Lord Greville was so near that she could have reached out and touched him. Fortunately his back was toward her, and he was engaged in conversation. Not with Lady Landon still. It was Dr. Carstairs who had him in tow this time. But though the supporting cast had changed, the topic of conversation still appeared the same. Frankie's ears burned as she heard her name in among the doctor's flow of talk.

"As a matter of fact I was just looking for her," his lordship replied, coolly and distinctly. Which was all the prodding Frankie needed. She turned and eased the window up, thankful for the husbandry at Alton Hall that saw to it that this could be done so silently. She had just squeezed her way through the opening, mentally cursing the inconvenience of her long, rather narrow skirt, and had just discovered the top rung of the wooden ladder with a groping satin toe when to her horror one of the gossiping dowagers called out, "Do you mind very much closing the window, m'dear? It's creating an unpleasant draft."

Frankie dawdled no longer. She hastily planted the exploring foot. Disregarding both her loss of dignity and a flounce she ripped in her haste, Frankie began backing down the ladder at a prodigious pace. She was only halfway down, however, when a male voice spoke pleasantly above her. "Oh, there you are. I'd wondered where you'd got to."

Frankie jumped the last few rungs. She snatched the ladder away from the side of the house, sending it crashing into the herbaceous borders. And then she ran. Even as she mentally gauged the odds of her finding her carriage and making a clean getaway before Lord Greville could leave the building in the more orthodox manner, some instinct caused her to look back across her shoulder. The shock sent her careening into an oak. For Lord Greville, in gleaming pumps, silk hose, satin knee smalls, frilled shirt, and long-tailed coat was now dangling from the second-story window ledge by his fingers. And even as Frankie watched, he dropped.

Miss Armstead hitched up her skirt then and ran harder, to more purpose. But although she gave the exercise her very best, she still felt the same futility in the endeavor that a Greek classical hero must have felt when trying to sidestep one of the more unpleasant prognostications of the Delphic Oracle.

Indeed she hadn't even made it to the corner of the building when Lord Greville grabbed her. "I want to talk to you," he said, still in the same dangerous, pleasant tone with which he'd hailed her on the ladder.

"Well, you certainly have an odd way of going about it," she managed to say with some asperity. "You might have broken your neck back there."

"Hardly."

"Well, I suppose sailors do develop good heads for heights, what with climbing the rigging and all, though when it comes to that, if naval officers go climbing into crows' nests, I never heard of it."

"Young woman, would you stop babbling for a moment, before I shake you. I want to talk to you." Lord Greville thereupon seized Miss Armstead somewhat roughly by the arm and steered her firmly down a path into the formal garden until he found a bench well concealed from the windows of the house. "Sit!" he commanded. She might have been his Labrador, Frankie thought.

"It's damp," she countered.

In reply he drew forth a snowy linen handkerchief and applied it to the dew. "Why a female who just risked life and limb, to say nothing of reputation, by leaving a ball through the window and down a ladder should be concerned over a little dampness is more than I can fathom," he said nastily.

"Well, you do have a point, I suppose," she answered

sweetly. "Besides, I almost forgot. Dampening my gown will put me in the pink of fashion, will it not? Just like the London ladies you admire so."

The moonlight revealed every nuance of his expression as Lord Greville towered above her with folded arms, scowling down fiercely while she arranged her skirts carefully to conceal the ripped and dragging flounce. His gray eyes darkened at Frankie's damp-gown hit.

"Don't push me," he growled at her. "I'm well and truly tempted to keel-haul you as it is. Now, I think Miss Armstead, that you owe me an explanation. So let's have it."

"Well, I felt faint, you see, and needed air. And then I saw the ladder and thought I might just as well go down it and find my coachman, since I wasn't up to doing the polite, you know—"

"Stop it!" he exploded, and she cringed. "You know damned well I'm not talking about your odd way of leaving parties. What I want to hear is an explanation for half—no, make that three-quarters—of the county treating me like some kind of leper in my own house."

"Now, how would I know a thing like that?"

For a moment he was almost persuaded. "You are Miss Frances Armstead, are you not?" Frankie was just opening her mouth to deny the charge when he caused it to shut again. "Of course you are. You're the girl from the boulanger. The one with the demented uncle," he added grimly. "And you're the one the county's up in arms over. The one they want to nail my hide to the hall for betraying. You are, in fact, according to all the hints and innuendoes and, finally, the flat-out statements, my fiancée."

"Oh, dear God," Miss Armstead groaned.

"Amen," his lordship snarled. "Now, would you mind explaining just how it is that after fourteen months at sea I come home to find myself betrothed to a caper-witted female I've never even seen before?"

"You have seen me before." Frankie was becoming more than a little piqued. "We were both guests at the Paxton house party."

"Oh, were we, indeed? Well, I'm sorry, Miss Armstead, but I don't remember you."

"Of course you don't. As I recall you were pursuing some yellow-haired female to the exclusion of the rest of the company. It was the *on dit* of the week. She was not unlike Lady Venetia, come to think of it. I must say, you do run true to type. But when it comes to that, I didn't recognize you at first either. I thought you were some Romany," she finished rather nastily.

"I'm getting a bit wearied by your conversational tangents, Miss Armstead." His lordship sounded dangerous. "I would appreciate some straight answers to my questions. We have now established the fact that I have met you. At the Paxtons'. But as you've just tastelessly pointed out, I was indeed enjoying a flirt with another lady. And I'd be quite astonished if I exchanged a dozen words with you. And I certainly did not get so inebriated as to propose marriage to you. So just how, Miss Armstead, did this slanderous story get started?"

Frankie groaned again. "Well, I suppose I'll have to tell you."

"Yes, I rather think you will."

"It all had nothing whatever to do with you, you know." As his eyebrows shot up sardonically she continued with more spirit, "Well, you needn't look so Friday-faced. It's true. If you think I'd any desire to be engaged to marry you, well, you're much mistaken in the matter. You would never have come into the picture at all if I had not suddenly needed to provide myself with a fiancé, which was not all that simple at a moment's notice. And then suddenly I recalled meeting you at my aunt Maria's and it seemed a reasonable way out of the coil that I was in to say we were betrothed. But you may believe this, my lord"—Frankie was propelled by a basic need to puncture his self-esteem—"the only reason I had for picking on you was the convenient fact that you were in the Mediterranean and likely, so I thought, to stay there. And the whole thing was supposed to have been kept secret anyhow," she added bitterly, "because of your grandfather, you see, who was not likely to be pleased by the alliance."

"Do you know," his lordship interposed smoothly, "that that is the first statement you've uttered that finally makes some sense?"

"There's no need to be insulting," she snapped back. "Until I came here tonight I saw nothing so very odd in the notion that we might be betrothed. I certainly had no idea you were so plump in the pocket as you seem to be. And it's not as if you would have been the first jumped-up baron to be quite happy to lower your sights and snap up a fortune."

"I'm after your money, am I?" He looked enlightened. "At least I'm glad I had one sane motive for such a lunatic proposal. But forget that for a minute and get back to the main channel. Now, if I've followed this Banbury Tale so far, the plot is that you needed, for some obscure reason, to provide yourself with a mythical fiancé and picked on me because I was not there to defend myself. Am I right so far?"

"More or less. Though when you put it that way—oh, very well, then. As I said, I hadn't thought to inconvenience you at all, for I expected to be married myself before you ever came back to Hampshire." His brows went up another notch. "And then the word came that you had drowned—which really seemed to take care of everything."

"How convenient," he said darkly.

"Well, it was rather. Of course, I was sorry for your death on principle," she added hastily, "but as you yourself pointed out, it wasn't as if we ever actually knew each other."

"True," he answered quite matter-of-factly. But his eyes seemed to glitter in the moonlight.

"And for my purposes it worked out even better, if you'll forgive my saying so," she added diffidently. "And I must say it does seem rather—irresponsible," she continued, "of the admiralty to put such stories about until they're sure. They seem to have no proper notion of the havoc that they're wreaking."

"Well, it's an understandable oversight," he said. "I myself hadn't the slightest notion either of the repercussions of my demise."

"There's no need to be sarcastic. Granted, no one could have foreseen the complications it caused me, but it didn't take much imagination to foresee the pain the news of your drowning would inflict upon your grandfather—and upon any number of golden-curled ladies, I collect. It still strikes me as a shatter-brained sort of thing to do. And while we're on the subject, just how did you manage to survive the *Arrow*'s sinking?" He smiled sardonically at the tinge of regret with which her tone was colored. "Or were you even on it?"

"Oh, yes, I was on her right enough. As to how I survived, it was by the simple method of swimming over to the *Acheron* and being taken on board her."

"Well, really! That certainly goes to prove the point I was making about irresponsibility. You certainly would think, would you not, that someone might have at least considered that possibility."

"Well, yes, you would think so. I must admit that the same thought has occurred to me. But you have to expect a certain amount of confusion in wartime. And since we sailed on to join Lord Nelson, and since I transferred to another ship, well, I'm afraid officialdom rather lost track of me there for a moment. But, as I was saying, I'm sure they'd no idea, no more than I had, of the problem they were creating for *you*, Miss Armstead."

"When it comes to that, and please forgive my indelicacy, it was more a solution than it was a problem. For with you alive there was no telling when you might suddenly pop up unannounced and I'd be found out. But once you were in your watery grave I had twelve months' grace."

"Do please overlook my denseness," the other remarked. "It's a condition that seems to have become chronic after meeting you. Believe it or not, I'm generally considered quite astute. Now I'm afraid I fail to understand why my death gave you any such reprieve."

"Why, I went into black gloves for you, of course."

"You did? Well, thank you."

"Not literally, you understand. But Uncle Matthew knew that it would be indelicate to talk of another marriage until I'd been through a suitable mourning period for you. And since by then he and Mr. Yarwood between them had told the entire county about our secret tendre for one another, they all respected my grief and sent no more cards of invitation. Do you realize," she said accusingly, "that this is the very first party I've attended since you drowned?"

"Am I supposed to find your devotion touching?"

"Well, yes, you might just a bit. I mean, you might stop thinking of yourself just long enough to think of all I've been through to keep Uncle Matthew from posting the banns and forcing me to marry Bertie."

"Bertie?"

"Albert Yarwood. It was his father, I expect, who mentioned that you're supposed to be engaged to me."

"Among others, yes."

"Well, he has been even more eager than Uncle Matthew for Bertie and me to marry. And I must say that choosing you for a fiancé was a better inspiration than I'd any notion of when I came up with the idea. For Mr. Yarwood's sensibilities were not wounded in the slightest when Uncle explained that you and I had developed a tendre for each other. There was no winking at the fact that, even in Mr. Yarwood's eyes, you were a far more brilliant match than Bertie."

"Thank you."

"I do wish you'd break yourself of the odious habit of heavy sarcasm. I am not one of your deck hands, Lord Greville."

"Pity. Until this moment I've always been opposed to the cat-o'-nine-tails. But do continue."

"As I was trying to explain, Mr. Yarwood, who is Uncle Matthew's oldest and dearest friend, was not at all offended by my turning down Bertie to marry you. But when he finds out it was all a hum, well, I'm afraid I shall have put a period to a lifelong friendship."

"Pity you did not consider that possibility a bit sooner."

"You are determined to be as unpleasant about all this as possible are you not?"

"I suppose you could look at it that way."

"Well, I don't see why it would hurt you to be a little cooperative."

"Cooperative!" He stared at her incredulously. "Surely, Miss Armstead, even you can't have sufficient gall to suggest that I participate in this damnable charade of yours. If you think for one moment that I plan to pretend to be betrothed to you, you're queerer in the attic than you tried to dupe me into believing your uncle is. Though come to think on it, your uncle probably is insane. If a few minutes with you can have this effect, I don't like to contemplate what years of your company would do," he finished bitterly.

With considerable effort Frankie choked on the setdown she longed to hurl back in his teeth. For tact at this point seemed the more prudent course, since she was contemplating casting herself upon his mercy.

"No, of course I don't expect you to pretend to be betrothed to me. All I'm asking you to do is simply not shout from the house tops that we are not betrothed. Surely it would not require so great a sacrifice on your part just to say nothing at all while you're home on leave. I'm certain of this much—no one is going to drop any hints to your grandfather about me. Or to that dampened Nonpareil you're with. So you see you should really suffer no great inconvenience during the few remaining days that you have left. And you can rest comfortably when you're back at sea knowing that when you hit port again, I shall have reached my majority and be wed to the man I love. So I really can't see that it would hurt you to do me one small favor. All I'm asking is that you not speak out. I've only six more months to go, you see, until I can do precisely as I please. So can't you just spend your leave in the normal manner—except that, well, perhaps you could see the way clear to calling on me once or twice for Uncle Matthew's sake—no, no, of course that's a perfectly shatter-brained notion. Forget my mentioning it," she added quickly as he looked thunderous. "The only thing I really require of you is your silence until you go back to sea. That's not such an unreasonable thing to ask, now, is it?"

"Unreasonable? I don't even know the meaning of that word after trying to converse with you, Miss Armstead. So let's set it aside for just a moment. I feel I should point out that even if I fell in with your little scheme—which I've certainly no notion of conceding—there is one small hitch to your plan that you seem to have overlooked."

"Oh? And what is that?"

"I'm not going back to sea, Miss Armstead."

38

Frankie stared at him in the moonlight, hoping for some softening of his frowning countenance to show that he was teasing. "But you have to go back to sea," she protested. "You're a naval officer, after all."

"Was an officer," he calmly corrected her. "After the drubbing the Frenchies took at Trafalgar, I no longer feel a duty to the navy. My grandfather isn't young. He needs me. Taking care of my responsibilities at home now seems a more pressing demand than military service. So I've resigned my commission and propose to settle down in Hampshire and run the estate. And," he added with weighty deliberation, "I also intend to marry. But not with you, Miss Armstead. Most definitely not with you."

Chapter Four

IT SEEMED TO MISS FRANCES ARMSTEAD THAT HER LIFE had boiled down to a series of awkward moments. Certainly the garden scene with Lord Greville Wainwright had been difficult. But compared to the carriage ride home with her uncle Matthew, during which she'd confessed everything, that encounter had paled into insignificance. "You mean Lord Greville knew nothing of the betrothal?" Mr. Armstead had managed to blurt out after several seconds of shocked silence during which Frankie had feared apoplexy.

"Yes," she'd admitted. "He was quite as surprised as you, sir. But I must say," she improvised, for even the coach's shadows could not obsure the alarming hue that still suffused her uncle's complexion and she wished to pacify him, "his lordship took it rather well. At least"—her voice faltered under the stricken gaze—"I think he calmed down quite a bit after I had made it quite clear that I was only trying to get out of marrying Bertie and had no designs upon him at all."

Her uncle's response to this observation was a heartrending groan, followed by the observation that she'd brought down disgrace upon his head, followed in its turn by the oft-repeated statement that he'd never be able to hold up the aforementioned head again. "A hissing and a laughingstock," he intoned Biblically, "that's what you've made of my old age, a hissing and a laughingstock."

The rest of the carriage ride had been completed wordlessly. The only sounds were the horses' hooves, the back axle's squeak, Matthew Armstead's groans, and his niece's snivelings.

And now, once again, a mere three days later, Frankie braced herself for another scene. She stood on the doorstep of her aunt's townhouse in Grosvenor Square, staring at its highly polished knocker as if the brass jaws of the lion staring back were capable of opening wide and snapping off her fingers if she touched it. Her uncle's coachman was busily transferring her boxes from the carriage. The luggage pile around her feet had grown to formidable proportions. It would be immediately obvious that she was there to stay. And how she was going to explain this sudden materialization, like some poor waif left in a basket at the convent portals, was more than she'd yet been able to decide.

Indeed she'd rehearsed and discarded speeches to her aunt all the way from Hampshire. Absorption in this task had made her immune to the heady excitement she'd experienced in the past upon entering London and being caught up in the brick and cobblestones and smoke and shipping, in the street cries of ballad sellers, knife grinders, gingerbreadmen, chimney sweeps, cats' meatmen; in the rush of wheels and feet and hooves, in all the hustle and bustle and commotion that made up the greatest city in the world—ask any Englishman. She'd even quite failed to be impressed by the grandeur of Grosvenor Square. Nor did she pause a moment to reflect that her aunt Maria must be plump in the pocket indeed to be living in such a house in such a neighborhood. She was, in fact, still rehearsing and discarding apologetic phrases even as she reached out for the knocker and gave the lion a resounding blow upon its snoot. The resulting sound could well have been the crack of doom.

For several seconds the portly butler stared at the clutter of trunks and bandboxes. Then he wrenched himself away to peruse the young lady in the dowdy brown pelisse standing in their midst. Only his eyebrows revealed his shock. They involuntarily rose to unseemly heights while his other features remained suitably impassive. "I'm Miss Armstead," Frankie told him. And when that bit of information seemed inadequate, "Lady Paxton's niece." As the butler's gaze once more was pulled away by the magnet of the luggage, she said quite unnecessarily, "I've come to stay awhile."

The majordomo rallied then and ushered her inside, dispatching some lackies to collect her boxes while at the same time steering Frankie through a door off the antechamber that led into a music room. The only possible reason she could think of being shown into a room of such huge proportions and overpowering elegance was that the butler was reluctant to admit her farther into the house upon just her say-so. He deposited her upon a gilt chair next to an even more lustrous golden harp quite near the exit, as if expecting her to while away the time that he was gone by plucking at its strings.

But even had she been so inclined, not to mention skillful, there would have been no time. For her aunt appeared almost immediately and stood poised in the doorway as Frankie rose guiltily to her feet. "Well, Frances, it really is you. When Dearborn said a young lady had arrived with enough baggage for Napoleon's army, I wondered if he'd been nipping at the port. So what sort of coil have you got yourself in, m'dear? I can only suppose that you've finally run away from your tiresome uncle Matthew."

Frankie found it impossible to tell whether her aunt Maria was annoyed, amused, or merely indifferent to having an uninvited guest descend upon her just when she was doubtlessly hoping to lie down for a few moments' recuperation from the rigors of the day in preparation for the evening's social demands upon her energies. Not for the first time the niece envied the older woman's poise and wondered just what it would take to cause her ladyship to lose even a little of her aplomb. The dark eyes, very like her own if she had but known it, were appraising her now quite shrewdly, leaving Frankie to conclude that her whole history was likely written on her face. Her aunt Maria suddenly confirmed that impression for her. "Don't look so stricken, m'dear. I really am quite glad to see you." She walked over then and kissed the girl coolly on the cheek. "Well, now, do take off that quite dreadful bonnet and pelisse"—the elegant Frenchwoman did not attempt to repress her shudder—"while I ring for tea. Come sit down with me and explain the circumstances of this unexpected, though of course delightful, visit," she continued as she led Frankie away from harp side to a grained rosewood settee situated near the warmth of a glowing fireplace. "Has Matthew suddenly married? Does a wicked stepaunt want you out of the house? No, of course not." She stopped her niece's denial with a tinkly laugh. "What an absurd notion. Matthew would never upset a comfortable routine by taking on a wife, even if he could find a creature silly enough to marry him. Oh, I am sorry, little one." She forestalled Frankie's protest. "That was tactless of me. He is, after all, your guardian."

"I am very fond of Uncle Matthew." Frankie felt obliged to say this, although she was aware she sounded rather priggish as she did so.

"Are you?" Her ladyship's eyebrows outdid her butler's for altitude. "How odd. Still, I suppose it does you credit. But enough of Matthew Armstead. I think we've dodged the issue long enough. To put it bluntly, m'dear, why are you here? Not that you are not welcome," she repeated, "but your arrival does smack a bit of mystery, you must admit. To suddenly appear unheralded, out of the blue, looking quite distrait and wearing a pelisse and bonnet that, had your dear mother lived, would surely have killed her anyway—well, it does seem to require some explanation. Forgive me if I'm wrong, Frankie, but somehow I cannot think that this is merely a social call. You are obviously running away from something. And if we rule out your uncle Matthew—we did rule him out, did we not?—well, then," she continued in response to Frankie's nod, "that only leaves one thing, a blighted love affair. You must be in flight from some young man."

"Oh, no," Frankie protested. "At least not exactly. Well, not in the way you mean, that is."

Dearborn appeared with the tea board then in time to cover some of her confusion. "Oh, do take those garments away with you." Lady Paxton gestured toward the chair where Frankie had placed her offending bonnet and pelisse as the butler deposited the tea things on the sofa table in front of them. "Burn them if the maids refuse to wear them, which no doubt they will. No need to look offended, Frances. I'd send the traveling dress you are wearing along with them, but modesty forbids it." She poured out two steaming cups of tea as Dearborn left the room. "Now, then, let's have your story. And don't hold back anything. Believe me, nothing you can possibly have done will shock me half as much as your abysmal taste in clothes. Can you possibly be half-French? Well, never mind. I'm only funning. And this obviously is not the time for levity. Now, tell me." She leaned back against the armrest, sipping tea from a Dresden china cup and giving her niece the same detached attention she might have afforded a performance at Drury Lane.

But instead of complying with the request, Frankie jumped up and crossed the room to retrieve her reticule. "At least this was saved from your bonfire," she remarked as she fished among the purse's contents and pulled out a folded paper from the depths. She carried it to her aunt, who set down her cup to take the epistle gingerly by one corner. "I think you'd best read Uncle Matthew's letter before I say anything. It seems only fair for you to hear him first."

The only sound in the room for quite some time was the ticking of a bracket clock upon the wall. Frankie kept her eyes anxiously upon her aunt's face as the Frenchwoman frowned at the letter, held it at arm's length, then began to rotate it.

"Could you please inform me, Frances," she finally commented in exasperation, "just why your uncle felt obliged to cross his letter when you were hand-delivering it? Is there a shortage of writing paper at Fairfield House?"

"No, of course not. I suppose it was merely habit. He couldn't have been thinking clearly. He was quite agitated, you see."

"Evidently." Her ladyship squinted once more at the epistle. "I really can't make head nor tail of this. But obviously there's some kind of coil concerning the opposite sex—there inevitably is, is there not? And the Wainwright name keeps recurring." She looked up at Frankie in astonishment. "Amazing. I knew Lord Wainwright years ago. He was a bosom beau of Ramsbury—my first husband. Quite handsome, of course, even then. And I understand he cut quite a swath among the ladies in his youth. But that was well before my time. Heavens, he must be older than Methuselah by now."

"He's eighty, I believe," Frankie volunteered, "though you'd never guess it. He's a most distinguished-looking man. Still has his hair. Teeth too, I imagine."

The Woman of the World looked taken aback. "Hair and teeth, you say?" she commented rather dryly. "Well, that, plus a fortune to put Midas to shame, is certainly recommendation enough. And since I married not one but two older gentlemen myself, I'm certainly not the one to question your motives. Though come to think on it, I only leaped one generation, not two. But that's beside the point. Frankly, I think I'm most surprised that Matthew would have any objections to the match. I'd have expected him to jump for joy. It shows more proper feeling than I've credited."

"For heaven's sake, Aunt Maria," Frankie protested, "will you stop jumping to these ridiculous conclusions? I've formed no tendre for Lord Wainwright. Indeed I've scarcely met him. And I'm sure he doesn't recollect me at all. It's his grandson Uncle refers to—and no"—she quickly forestalled the obvious question,—"there is no romantic attachment between us either. Quite the contrary in fact," she concluded bitterly. "Oh, do finish the letter, Aunt Maria, in all fairness to Uncle Matthew, who really is a very good man and deserves more understanding than you're giving him."

Tears welled up into Frankie's eyes. Her aunt looked at her thoughtfully. "Very well, m'dear. No need to upset yourself." She turned her attention back to the letter. "Hmmmm," Lady Paxton frowned, "there's a Yarwood mentioned. It would appear I'm not to allow him to darken the door while you're in residence." She rotated the letter once again. "No, that can't be right. He says he'll be coming up from Hampshire in a few days and could bring along anything you may have forgot. My God, what could that possibly be? Your pianoforte, perhaps?"

Frankie ignored the jibe. "Uncle Matthew knows that Bertie's father is sending him to London on a business matter."

"And Bertie is a Yarwood?" Lady Paxton shifted the letter so that the fading rays of the sun could strike it through the window. "I could have sworn that I did see some stricture about 'not darkening the door.' "

"There are two Yarwoods. It's Bertie's older brother he refers to." Frankie hoped that put a period to the discussion.

"Oh, I see." Lady Paxton's expression, though, failed to match the declaration. "Well, now. We've established that there are two Wainwrights, and now it would appear there are two Yarwoods as well. Tell me, Frankie, do all your beaux come two by two? There does seem to be a Noah's Ark theme to your uncle's letter." Maria Paxton frowned at the paper once again, then sighed impatiently and put it down. "Really, Frankie, it's the outside of enough to expect me to go through the indignity of having the servants fetch my spectacles merely to decipher your uncle Matthew's ravings when you are sitting there with a tongue in your head and could simply tell me what this is about. Now—not to beat about the bush— let's settle one thing immediately. Frances, are you *enceinte*?"

Frankie stared at her aunt. Then the blood rushed to her face. "Indeed no, ma'am," she said indignantly.

"No need to get on your high ropes. It does happen. Of course, if you were breeding, London would be the last place to send you. But then I wouldn't pretend to imagine what course your uncle would choose to take. And since he seemed so determined to wash his hands of you—and the word 'scandal' did keep cropping up—I jumped to the wrong conclusion. And did I not also see a reference to convents?"

Frankie giggled in spite of everything. "Uncle Matthew does regret that we are not Catholic so he could send me to a nunnery. At least till the scandal dies down. If it ever does."

"Ah. Now we're getting to it. Just what sort of scandal have you embroiled yourself in, my niece?"

It was not easy for Frankie to tell the story of her bogus engagement and watch the various reactions to her words play upon Lady Maria's face. Her aunt frowned occasionally. Her expressive eyebrows rose more than once. She even laughed aloud as Frankie described how her uncle Matthew had collared Lord Greville at the ball and forced him to dance with her. But never once did her ladyship interrupt.

When the halting recital was at last completed she gave her niece an enigmatic look and said, "Well, m'dear, you certainly have gotten yourself into a coil, though I do think your uncle is making far too much of it. Of course," she added shrewdly, "I'm sure you haven't told me all, but that's no matter. I probably would not wish to know it anyhow."

That observation caused Miss Armstead to flush guiltily, for she had indeed routed her narrative around any mention of Evelyn Yarwood. Somehow she felt she'd find little sympathy for that attachment from her world-wise aunt. "All for love and the world well lost" was not Maria Lefroy Ramsbury Paxton's way.

"Well, I can see that you'll be the *on dit* of Hampshire for some time to come," that lady said. "But then, somebody has to be. Had I been consulted, I should have counseled staying there and outfacing the gossipmongers. But never mind. You're here. Now what, besides giving sanctuary, does your uncle expect me to do about you? Surely even he hasn't chosen Grosvenor Square to serve '*in loco* convent'?"

"No, ma'am." Frankie blushed. "I rather think he hopes you'll launch me into society and get me married before the news about me reaches London. But that really isn't necessary."

"Before the news reaches London?" Her aunt smiled cynically. "If I know the world, the news has preceded you."

"Oh, no," Frankie groaned.

"Oh, yes. But don't look so tragic. By the time the story's spread it shall be distorted beyond recognition. And who knows"—she struck a pose—"you and Lord Greville could wind up as a sort of Romeo and Juliet—star-crossed lovers with the evil Lord Wainwright tearing you asunder merely because of your social inferiority."

"But that's ridiculous!"

"Of course. But not half as ridiculous as the truth, you must admit. And since it serves our purpose, I might just as well give the gossip a nudge in that direction."

"You wouldn't!" Miss Armstead was horrified. "Why, that would be telling a falsehood. And nobody knows better than I what that can lead to. I have taken a solemn vow never to depart from the truth again!"

"No need to look so Friday-faced. I won't have to resort to lies. Just a few knowing looks and a sigh now and then will no doubt turn the trick."

"But that's the same thing." Frankie stuck stubbornly to her point.

"Perhaps. But the end justifies the means if it keeps you from ridicule. You may behave as scandalously as you wish in society, Frances, as long as you do not turn yourself into a laughingstock. Pray remember that."

"I'm not half as afraid of being laughed at as murdered," Frankie mumbled under her breath.

"By Lord Greville perhaps?" Her aunt's eyes gleamed with amusement. "He didn't take kindly to your betrothal, then? Well, let's not concern ourselves with him. No matter what wild stories may circulate, they'll only make him more interesting. Lord Greville Wainwright is a gentleman. A peer of the realm, in fact. He is above scandal, while you are not."

The lovely Frenchwoman regarded her niece in silence for a while. When she did speak it was to give a summary of her thoughts. "You, Frances Armstead, are a young woman of dubious social background, considerable fortune, some claim, I think, to beauty, and abysmal taste in clothes. All those things I can deal with. In fact, my dear"—she was looking at her niece with the same gleam in her eye that a gifted potter might accord a lump of clay—"I think I shall enjoy the challenge of turning you into a social success. And if in the process we have to take a few liberties with Lord Greville's character, well, I'm sure he'll be none the worse for it. Indeed he may live to thank us for it. Who knows"—Lady Paxton's eyes gleamed with suppressed laughter—"I may outdo Pygmalion, who after all, had only Galatea. But in transforming you I may also manage to turn a most unromantic-sounding man into a heartbroken, tragic hero. For it's the way of the world, little one, to love a thwarted lover. Your Lord Greville may live to thank you yet. So cheer up, child, and welcome to the Metropolis."

Frankie managed then to come up with a wan smile. Better yet, she refrained from shuddering as the sudden recollection of a furious, aristocratic face and piercing steel gray eyes came back to overset her. She also managed to refrain from telling her aunt Maria that she was indeed very much mistaken if she thought that Lord Greville Wainwright would ever thank her, Miss Frances Armstead, for anything.

Chapter Five

FRANKIE WAS ACCUSTOMED TO COUNTRY HOURS. EVEN the fact that she'd tossed and turned all night did not keep her from rising on her Hampshire schedule. Her appearance in the dining room shortly before eight caused considerable consternation among the servants, who then scurried around to provide a breakfast for her. This was served by Dearborn along with the offhand information that "Madame always rings for chocolate in her room upon awakening and never before ten." Declaring her resolve to adopt a similar custom in the future, Frankie polished off her tea and sweetbreads, then went to the library in search of pen and paper.

It took several abortive attempts at composition before it occurred to Frankie that no explanation for being in London was necessary and that it was enough simply to inform Evelyn that she was in residence with her aunt in Grosvenor Square. The whys and wherefores could wait till he came to call. She thereupon perused her third and final draft, found it satisfactory if somewhat ink-splashed, sighed, and liberally sprinkled it with sand, dusted it off, folded it carefully, then went in search of a footman to carry it to the Manchester Street address. If the footman was a bit taken aback by this early-morning mission, the liberal vail that Frankie slipped him more than made up for it.

He was not, however, the only servant who set out from Paxton House that morning with a message. Before leaving for the theater the evening before, her ladyship had scrawled a note to London's most fashionable modiste. That lady and two assistants arrived promptly at ten-thirty, whereupon Frankie was summoned to join them in Lady Paxton's bedchamber.

She found her aunt propped up in bed upon silken cushions, sipping chocolate with a decided look of martyrdom upon her face. However, her Frenchwoman's love of fashion soon dispelled her jaundiced outlook as the dressmaker responded enthusiastically to the challenge of completely outfitting "Madame's niece."

"Such a pretty child," the modiste enthused in Gallic tones that quite paled Lady Paxton's slight French accent. "When I have finished, she will do you credit. You will see. She has the famous Lefroy look. It only needs some bringing out. Which I, of course, shall do."

"Yes, I do believe the raw material is there." Lady Paxton looked at her niece objectively as she sipped her chocolate.

"Thank heavens the Armstead traits aren't too apparent. The jaw is a bit too square perhaps. The mouth a trifle large. But she has her mother's hair and the same flawless complexion. Annette, you know, was the beauty of the family."

"Why, she couldn't have been!" Frankie blurted, looking at her aunt. For even without the benefit of her dresser's arts, even in her present dishabille, and even with a touch of headache, Lady Paxton, there was no denying, was indeed a lovely woman. Her heart-shaped face, near-perfect features, and large dark eyes were quite dazzling. So were the small even teeth she showed now in a pleased smile brought on by her niece's ingenuous remark.

"Thank you, m'dear," she said, "but it is true, you know. Fortunately your mother was older and never cast me in the shade. Nor had I any other reason to feel jealous of her—though I must confess that later on I felt a twinge or two when our uncle left his entire fortune to her. But long before I was eligible for the Marriage Mart, Annette had thrown herself away to wed your father and rusticate in Hampshire. She could have had any man in England, you know," the dead woman's sister sighed. "There was one earl in particular—well, enough of that, except to say that my poor émigré father took to his bed over it all. And he made me promise faithfully that I'd never be foolish enough to marry for love instead of profit. And I must say"—she dimpled—"I never disappointed him."

Frankie repressed any comment she might have liked to make. And indeed a rebuttal would have been mere guesswork on her part. For since both her parents had died during her infancy, she had no actual way of knowing whether her mother had "thrown herself away" or not.

At any rate she was soon distracted from that subject by the variety of patterns the dressmaker was spreading out upon the bed for their perusal and by the lovely fabrics her associates were displaying.

The next few hours flew quickly by in a discussion of Frankie's sartorial needs. "Surely I can never wear so many clothes," she finally protested. The exclamation won her twin looks of disapproval. "I do believe, Frances,"—her aunt frowned—"that Mademoiselle and I are better judges of the requirements of a London Season than you can be."

"Without a doubt," Frankie rejoined with spirit. "But I'm the better judge of Uncle Matthew. He'll never cough up the blunt for all of this."

"Do spare us your cant phrases, please. You are not riding down foxes in Hampshire or whatever it is you do there. Young ladies of the ton do not 'cough up blunt.' And if your uncle Matthew is too clutch-fisted"—she ignored her niece's smothered giggle at her own cant phrase—"to support your introduction into society, well, he'll simply have to accept you back, for I will not stand sponsor to a dowd."

Frankie had grown a bit weary of hearing herself so described. "It's a bit hard to be judged on the basis of one bonnet and one pelisse," she muttered. "No one has complained of my taste before." No one but Bertie, anyhow.

"Who was qualified, your uncle Matthew?" Her aunt snorted inelegantly. "And as for basing my judgment on a pelisse alone, my dresser assures me that even the maids are reluctant to accept any of your castoffs," she concluded witheringly. "Now, just be thankful that Mademoiselle Louise here is the last word in what is à la mode, and more importantly, in what is right for you."

"Ah, that is so." The plump little Frenchwoman sounded gratified as she plied her tape to Frankie's measurements. "But even I must defer to your aunt's superior taste. You are most fortunate, Miss Armstead, to have such an arbiter of fashion for your mentor."

"I know I am," Frankie replied with suitable humility. "Besides," she added as a sop to her country conscience, "if Uncle does think the cost excessive, he can always charge it to my estate."

This ethical point settled to her satisfaction, she began to enter into the spirit of things once more, even daring to argue the point when both daughters of France assured her that a profusion of knotted ribbon would *not* improve the simple ball gown of rose pink gauze they had both decided on. It was at this point that Dearborn entered the room with something akin to trepidation and announced, "There is a gentleman here to—"

"Dearborn!" his mistress interrupted with a frown. "Did I not say that I was positively not at home to anyone?"

"Yes, madame, you did indeed. But you see the young gentleman wishes to speak to Miss Armstead. And if I may say so, he is most insistent."

"To see my niece?" Her ladyship's eyebrows rose. "Now, who on earth could possibly—" Not waiting for a suddenly rosy-cheeked Frankie to reply, Maria Paxton turned her full attention back on her majordomo. "Does the gentleman have a name?" she inquired pointedly.

"He says he is a Mr. Yarwood." For some obscure reason, Dearborn chose to doubt it.

"Yarwood?" Her ladyship frowned. "Is he not the one that we're forbidden to receive. Do you think yourself capable of throwing him out, Dearborn?"

"No, madame," Dearborn answered with quiet dignity. "But I am certain that Charles or James—perhaps I should say that Charles *and* James could manage the thing if you desire it."

"Oh, no, Aunt, you wouldn't!" Frankie was horrified.

"No, I don't suppose I would," her aunt sighed. "Although your uncle probably does know best in this case, it goes decidedly against the grain with me to have him dictate whom I should or should not receive in my own house. Show the gentleman into the music room, Dearborn. And since he's an old friend of yours, Frances, I suppose he can survive the sight of you in that hideous muslin. Whyever do you wear that peculiar shade of orange? But do at least, child, contrive to subdue your hair a bit."

Frankie obediently stood in front of the cheval glass trying to curb her impatience while her aunt's maid brushed her hair. She thought wistfully of all the lovely clothes on order, wishing she might wear the yellow sprigged muslin this very minute and bedazzle Evelyn. Still, she thought philosophically, Evelyn had managed to fall in love with her just as she was, so surely he could endure the sight of her once more in her less than modish clothes.

For the first time, though, Frankie's newly awakened sensibilities made her stop to realize that the man she loved was, in Bertie's words, a Pink of the Ton, a Tulip of Fashion. Even the great Beau Brummel, according to Evelyn's younger brother, cut no better sartorial figure than did young Mr. Yarwood. She flinched a bit to think that Evelyn no doubt had viewed her taste with the same inward shudder that her aunt and the French modiste had accorded it. Well, no matter. At least it proved he loved her for herself. Besides, it would make her transformation all the more delightful a reward for his patient tolerance.

"Never mind, Maud," she told the dresser, who was contriving to give her hair the Grecian look with small success. "I'll have to do." With that, she dodged out from under the brush and raced from the room and down the steps with a speed that brought a sudden look of pain to Dearborn's face. The butler had positioned himself by the entrance to the music room, the dumping ground, so Frankie was beginning to suspect, for awkward guests. But no Friday-faced servant or overpowering grandeur was going to spoil the joy of this reunion. Frankie swept past Dearborn with the glad cry, "Evelyn!" then came to a disappointed halt. "Oh, my goodness, it's only you."

"Well, you don't have to sound so overjoyed." The second Mr. Yarwood rose from the spindle-legged gilded chair as if he, too, had been performing on the harp. "I've just passed up the chance to visit the Tower menagerie to stop by here. So don't come at me with that 'Oh, my goodness, it's only you' business. It ain't polite, for one thing."

"I'm sorry, Bertie." Frankie pulled up the companion chair to his as he sat back down. They faced each other through the harp strings. "It's just that you weren't due in London for another week, I thought, and I was expecting Evelyn."

"I know. That's why I'm here. I had thought when I got to his place last night and found he'd gone to Kent that I'd spend the morning seeing the sights, but then your letter came—"

"Evelyn's in Kent?" Frankie interrupted, sick with disappointment. "What on earth is he doing in Kent?"

"How should I know? I've never been there. I ain't the slightest idea what a chap does in Kent. But knowing Evelyn, he's sure to come up with something. For if there ever was—"

"Bertie!"

"Well, you asked the question and I'm trying my best to answer. All I know is what the servants told me, that Evelyn was invited to spend a fortnight in the country with Lord Marney. Which means, of course, that Evelyn's pockets are to let again, for he hates the country. Look at all the pains he's gone to get out of it. So I expect he's gone down there to sponge off Marney till his next quarter's allowance is due, if you want the truth of it."

"A fortnight?" Frankie was aghast at the bomb her friend had dropped. "He'll be away for a whole fortnight?"

"Not now, he won't. He went ten days ago, so that leaves"— he frowned with concentration—"four days to go. Not that I expect 'fortnight' to be taken at face value. A few days more or less would make no difference. So he could turn up anytime, I expect. Though on the other hand it could be another week."

"A week!" Frankie's groan made it sound an eternity.

"Still the best bet from my way of thinking is next Tuesday." Bertie continued to pursue the problem thoughtfully. "That's when he'll get his blunt and he ain't likely to stay a day longer than he has to. So Tuesday it is, then!" He beamed at Frankie, proud of having solved the riddle so handily.

"Tuesday." Miss Armstead's natural ebullience was returning. "By Tuesday, some of my new gowns will be ready, so that works out quite well. But Bertie"—she broke off in the middle of a vision of herself sweeping down the stairway clad in jonquil muslin while a bedazzled Evelyn gazed up at her— "you haven't said what brings you up to London a full week ahead of time."

"You, of course."

"Me? Whatever for?"

"I should say my father, actually. Didn't bring me, of course, but practically pushed me out of the house soon as he learned that Mr. Armstead had sent you packing. Wouldn't even let me wait till tomorrow after I'd told him that I planned to go fishing with Joe Talbert. Dammit, Frankie, I just now realized that I've missed a day's fishing and now the menagerie on your account. That really is the outside of enough. You could at least ring for tea, you know."

"But you still haven't explained anything." Frankie chose to ignore his refreshment needs. "Why on earth did your father think you should come to London a whole week before you planned to just because I have? Does he think people know that you were in collusion with me?"

"I was no such thing! At least if 'collusion' means I was a party to your sapskulled scheme to become engaged to Lord Greville, nobody's going to think that. For anybody who knows you realizes that you're perfectly capable of landing yourself in any kind of scrape imaginable without my help."

"So why did your father make you come to London?" Miss Armstead's patience was wearing thin.

"To dangle after you, of course."

"To what?" Her mouth flew open.

"You heard me. As soon as my father found out—and it was too devilish soon, believe me—that your engagement was all a hum and that your uncle had decided to place you on the London Marriage Mart he said that I must come to the Metropolis too and make sure that no gazetted fortune hunter snapped you up. No other fortune hunter, that is." He grinned suddenly. "You know, he really is determined that we get married," he added soberly. "What with our estates marching together and all. Not to mention the fact that Evelyn has us deep into Dun Territory. Oh, yes, and speaking of Evelyn—that's another reason I had to come to London early. I'm supposed to warn Evelyn off."

"Warn him off? I don't understand."

"It's simple enough. My father knows you prefer Evelyn over me. So he's supposed to back off and give me a clear running. My father knows, of course, that your uncle will never approve of you marrying a here-and-thereian like Evelyn. Of course, what he doesn't know is that you're ramshackled enough to elope without your uncle's blessing. Though it beats me why he wouldn't suspect something of the kind after you showed your true colors by making the county think you were betrothed to Greville Wainwright, of all unlikely things."

"*I* didn't make the county think anything!" Frankie's voice rose in protest. "The only person I ever meant to mislead was my uncle—which may have been shabby but necessary. And I must say it's unfair of you, of all people, to imply that I wanted it noised about that I was engaged to that odious—"

"Are you sure, m'dear, that you wish to apprise the servants of your views?" Lady Paxton's low-pitched voice, sounding slightly amused but still reproving, interrupted her niece's tirade. Though never requiring the five hours Beau Brummell deemed requisite for his appearance in society, she had dressed with unaccustomed speed, spurred on, perhaps, more by curiosity than by any desire to observe the proprieties and play chaperone. Now she stood coolly in the doorway surveying the flustered pair. "Frances, my dear," she prodded after the two had sprung rather guiltily to their feet and stood gaping at her, "should you not present your friend to me?"

"Oh, yes. Of course. I forgot you had not met. Aunt Maria, may I present Mr. Albert Yarwood. Bertie, my aunt, Lady Maria Paxton."

"Ah, Mr. *Albert* Yarwood." Her ladyship laid stress upon the given name as she advanced gracefully into the room and extended her hand to Bertie. The young man turned beet red and kissed it awkwardly. "Your servant, ma'am," he choked.

Lady Paxton gazed thoughtfully at the harp. "Dearborn always hopes my guests will play. Let's be more comfortable." She led them across the room, indicating that Bertie should join her on the sofa while Frankie sat in one of the carved and gilt armchairs that made up the grouping. "Now then," the hostess said, "we can enjoy a cose. I'm most eager to know my niece's acquaintances, Mr. Yarwood, and I understand that you are her oldest and dearest friend." She bestowed a dazzling smile upon the young man that caused him to squirm and blush once more, while Frankie shot him a look of undisguised disgust. It was obvious that her 'oldest, dearest' friend was putty in the hands of her practiced aunt. Though why Lady Paxton

56

should make 'that gudgeon Bertie' one of her flirts was more than her niece could understand.

"Shall I ring for tea, my dear, or have you already done so?"

"No, she ain't," Bertie said pointedly.

"Tsk, how remiss. Frankie, you must not forget that gentlemen, especially the athletic, outdoor type like Mr. Yarwood here, require more sustenance than we of the weaker sex."

"I could not possibly forget that Bertie, at any rate, needs constant feeding," Frankie replied rising and giving the bell rope a jerk.

While they drank their tea Frankie fluctuated between admiration of and annoyance at the subtle way her aunt went about getting the same information from Bertie that she'd prised out like a tooth extraction. True, he did try to wrap his visit in clean linen. He didn't actually say that he'd come up from Hampshire to dangle after her or that his brother was in the country on a repairing lease, but Frankie had no doubt that her aunt was quite adept at reading between the lines. Only Bertie was oblivious to how much of their affairs he was giving away. She could have kicked him.

But when he looked across the rim of his teacup and caught her glare, he completely misinterpreted it. "Oh, I say, I must be going." He quickly placed his nearly full cup on the sofa table and leaped then to his feet. "Overstayed myself," he explained in helpful response to Lady Paxton's look of surprise. "Twenty minutes, the limit for a morning call. Ain't that right, Frankie? Never could keep all that sort of thing straight, ma'am," he confessed.

"Oh, Bertie, don't be such a widgeon," Frankie snapped.

"She's right, you know," Lady Paxton interposed much more graciously. "We stand on no ceremony with you."

"Just the same, a cove should always do the polite." And with this dictum firmly in mind Bertie took formal leave of them. His graceful exit was somewhat spoiled, however, by his stopping at the door and snapping his fingers in vexation. "Bother! I almost forgot. Frankie." He turned to face her. "Meant to tell you who else is coming up to London."

"Yes?" she prodded as he waited expectantly.

"Lord Greville, that's who's coming." And though Bertie did not actually add the word. "Beware," his tone of voice managed to convey it all the same.

But if he expected the news to have a shattering effect upon his listener, he was doomed to disappointment. "Indeed?" Frankie managed to sound totally uncaring. "What does that have to say to anything, Bertie? I'm sure Lord Greville may come and go as he pleases. After all, hundreds of people come to London every day, so why shouldn't he? It's an enormous city, after all. We're most unlikely to meet in it."

Lady Paxton, who had been taking considerable interest in the exchange, now broke in to ask, "Is it Lord Greville *Wainwright* that you're unlikely to meet in London?" When her niece nodded in the affirmative, for some unfathomable reason her ladyship began to laugh.

Chapter Six

THE FIVE DAYS OF BERTIE'S ESTIMATED INTERVAL BEFORE Evelyn's return dragged by with an unbearable fatigue. Accustomed as Frankie was to frequent tramps through wood and meadow, fond as she was of horseback riding, there was just so much reading, tambouring, and sketching from the front window she could bear to do. She even endeavored for a while to learn the art of harp playing, but soon gave up the struggle when her aunt informed her that the servants were all threatening to quit.

"Well, how much longer am I to remain under house arrest?" she had asked rebelliously.

"I've explained, Frances," her aunt replied with a patience that had become sorely tried, "that I wish to present you properly to society. Afterward you may accompany me as often as you please." She was on her way to make a round of morning calls.

"I don't wish to accompany you. I only wish to get out of this house awhile. Could I not walk in the park if I put a sack over my head? I could cut out eye holes and—".

"All right." Her aunt laughed. "You've made your point." She looked at her niece critically. "Your new hairstyle is most becoming. And Mademoiselle did send some of your things this morning. I'm sure there must be a walking dress among them. Very well, then," she relented. "Maud is running an errand for me. I shall tell her to take you along. I shall also tell her to give you a careful inspection before you leave and make sure you do not wear the wrong bonnet entirely. In case you meet some acquaintance of mine I shall not have my reputation as an 'arbiter of fashion' ruined." She mimicked the French modiste's voice as Frankie giggled and hugged her. "Oh, thank you. This is famous. I should love to go shopping above all things."

Lady Paxton made her departure in a stylish barouche after telling Maud to procure a hackney carriage for Miss Frances and herself. Miss Frances, however, thought it a much better plan to walk, in order "to be able to peer into all the shop windows" as they went along. She therefore completely overrode Maud's protests of an ailing back, pronouncing with conviction that the exercise would do it good. And when the dresser gazed dolefully at the sky and predicted rain, Frankie convinced her of her own countrywoman's expertise, declaring it could not possibly rain for hours, if at all.

The purpose for the outing—the purchase of six pairs of French gloves for her ladyship—was soon discharged and the exhausted maid was ready to turn toward home. She was not heartless enough, however, to resist Frankie's plea to go "just a little farther" and visit a fashionable linen draper in Leicester

Square. Then there were other shops to be explored and their profusion of exciting things admired: silk stockings, tippets of fur and feathers, plumes of all kinds, ribbons, lace, and fancy trimmings in the latest mode. When poor Maud finally pronounced herself unable to go another step, Frankie took pity upon her and managed to flag down a hackney just as the first raindrops began to fall.

The citified dresser proved a much better prognosticator than the young lady of rural background. By the time the carriage arrived in Grosvenor Square, not only was the rain pouring but a blustery wind was propelling it in all directions. Indeed when Maud, her arms filled with purchases, had barely set her sensible shoes upon the cobblestones, a rain-filled gust snatched her carelessly tied bonnet from her head and blew it down the thoroughfare. "I'll get it. Run for the house!" Frankie added her share of the bundles to Maud's pile and dashed after the traveling headgear, oblivious to the rain's destruction of the modishly curled plumage above her own chapeau.

"Got you!" she squealed in triumph as the elusive bonnet came to rest against a wrought-iron fence. But as she stooped to snatch it up another gust sent it swirling into the street, and she followed in hot pursuit. She ignored the curses of a coachman as he managed against all odds to keep from crushing both the bonnet and its pursuer. She then had it almost in her grasp again when suddenly it was blown back once more in the direction it had come from to wind up at the foot of the steps that led to the oaken doorway of the house next to their own.

This time she pounced in time. Frankie had raised the bonnet with an air of triumph undiminished by its sodden, mud-stained condition, when the door above her suddenly burst open and a tall figure clad in a caped greatcoat and curly beaver came sprinting out of it. He leaped before he looked and sent her sprawling. "What the devil—Oh, I say, I am sorry," a familiar voice laced with unfamiliar contrition said as the tall gentleman helped her up from her prone position. But no sooner had Frankie regained her footing than the concern on Lord Greville Wainwright's face quickly changed to horror. "Oh, my God, it's you."

60

Frankie had no idea, of course, what her own face revealed. But she certainly knew insult added to injury when she heard it. "Do you always come out of the door like a cannon shot?" she inquired frigidly. "I might have been killed, you know."

Lord Greville seemed less distressed by that possibility than she could have hoped for. "I was trying to reach my carriage without getting soaked." For the first time Frankie noted that the curricle which had so skillfully dodged her and the hat was waiting for his lordship while the liveried driver observed their contretemps with interest. "I did not expect to find someone crouched upon my steps," Wainwright continued. "Just what the devil are you up to, anyhow? No, spare me the story for just a moment. I suppose I'll have to let you in before I drown. Crosby!" he whooped suddenly toward the coachman. "Put the curricle away for now." And before Frankie could realize his intent, much less voice a protest, his lordship more dragged than escorted her back up the steps and through the doorway. They stood in the antechamber, dripping puddles upon the black and white marble floor, while an astonished footman leaped forward to relieve them of their wraps. "Take off that wet pelisse, Miss Armstead," his lordship commanded. "You may deserve a putrid fever, but I'll not have your invalidism laid at my door. Bring some tea to the front parlor, John. Our interview won't take long, Miss Armstead, but never let it be said I allowed you to take a chill during it."

Frankie was so astonished by this strange turn of events that she automatically began to remove her pelisse upon command. The footman had already relieved her of Maud's bonnet; then when a stream of water from her soaked and flattened plume began to trickle down her nose, she added her own headgear to the servant's burden. "You don't mean to tell me that you actually live here!" she gasped up at his lordship.

"I certainly don't mean to tell you what you already know." He had taken her arm and propelled her into a small saloon hung with dark green damask. In spite of the fire just beginning to crackle in the fireplace, the room had the musty smell and frozen-in-time appearance of a place where the Holland covers had only moments before been whisked away.

The footman arrived almost on their heels with a silver tray, which he then deposited upon a sofa table near the struggling flames. As Frankie obeyed his lordship's imperious gesture and sat down, her first thought, "This is the most curious dream I've ever had," was quickly supplanted by "What on earth will Maud think has become of me?" In order to facilitate her quick departure she prompted, "Was there something you wished to say to me, Lord Greville?" as she poured and handed him his tea.

He choked on the hot beverage. "That *I* wished to say? I assume, Miss Armstead, that you have succeeded in tracking me down and were lurking on my doorstep to some purpose."

"Tracking you down!" she exclaimed. "I did no such thing, I assure you. If you think for one moment—"

"Miss Armstead," his lordship cut through her protest with a tone of voice usually associated with barking orders from the bridge, "I'm in no mood to listen to your dissimulations. I want it made plain right now that I take exception to—deeply resent, in fact—what I can only consider your harassment. It should have been enough to smear my reputation down in Hampshire. But to pursue me to London as well—dammit, that's more than my patience is set to bear. I've had enough of your little plots and schemes, Miss Armstead."

"Pursue you to London!" Miss Armstead rattled her cup back into its saucer lest she succumb to temptation and throw its contents in his face. "Pursue you to London!" Her voice rose another octave. "I did no such thing! I should not have to point out, if you were not such a conceited clodpole, that I was in London first. I might just as well say that you were pursuing me."

"Of course. That's just what you will do." There was murder in his lordship's eyes as he contemplated her across the tea board. "But let me warn you, Miss Armstead, if you begin to put word about London that I am secretly betrothed to you, that I'm in pursuit of you, or for that matter that I even know you, I shall expose you for the encroaching schemer that you are."

"L-Lord Greville." Frankie's rage was threatening her coherence. "You may call me a schemer if it pleases you, and I cannot deny it. But my schemes concerned only my uncle and myself. Do not dare to call me 'encroaching.' For the last time, let us hope, let me try to get it through your head—which must have become thickened past redemption from its soaking in saltwater—that you were never more than a figment of my imagination, a ploy, if you will. I could have chosen any other man just as well and pretended to be betrothed to him—and how I wish I had!" She rose to her feet then and glared down at him. "Lord Greville, pray watch my lips move and try, finally, to comprehend what I am saying: I do not wish, nor have I ever wished, to have anything whatsoever to do with you."

He stood too then and regained the height advantage. "I hear what you say, Miss Armstead, and am more than eager to believe you. Only forgive me"—he sneered—"but there is one little point you've failed to clear up adequately. If you want nothing to do with me, pray explain what you were doing on my doorstep."

"Trying to catch Maud's bonnet, naturally."

This was not the first time Lord Greville Wainwright had looked at Miss Frances Armstead as though convinced she had just escaped from Bedlam. She found, however, that the experience had grown no more tolerable through custom. "When we alighted from our carriage," she clarified haughtily, "the wind blew the maid's bonnet away. And since she's quite old, fifty if a day, and none too well and tired besides, I told her to get in out of the rain while I set out to catch it. It was just bad luck," she finished bitterly, "that the wind carried the bonnet to what turned out to be your front door just as you decided to do your famous flying leap."

His jaw dropped. "The Paxton House. Next door. You're staying at Paxton House? Oh, my God, I'd forgot. You did say you are Lady Paxton's niece."

"*I* not only said it; Lady Paxton did so as well when she presented me to you at her house party. An event you seem determined not to recall."

"I should have done so; I admit it. Warning cannons should have fired at the precise moment of that presentation. Or you really ought to wear a bell around your neck."

"Don't you think you are overworking your annoyance, Lord Greville?" Frankie was trying the effects of quiet dignity. "I can see where it may have come as a shock to find someone pretending to be engaged to you, but to go on and on about it seems excessive. After all, the embarrassment is all mine. You've been caused no inconvenience by it."

"No inconvenience?" he echoed with heavy sarcasm. "Perhaps some men might not find it 'inconvenient' to be treated like a leper by his neighbors. But I dare you to produce one who would not be inconvenienced by having the lady whose interest he hoped to engage refer to him as a heartless, callous libertine. It seems I now have the reputation of winning hearts for the sport of the pursuit and then breaking them," he wound up bitterly.

"Lady Venetia said that? I don't believe you! No one would have been so shabby as to tell her about me. Certainly not while she was a guest of yours. People we know are not so heartless."

"Perhaps not. But the same sort of scruples did not stop your Hampshire gossipmongers from confiding in her companion. I gather that their carriage ride back to London was most memorable. The first half of the journey was taken up by Miss Austen's recital of the tale of my secret betrothal, and the second became a trail of tears shed over the heartless way I'd treated you."

"Fiddlesticks!" Frankie snorted. "If you believe that taradiddle, you really have been at sea too long. If Lady Venetia Sellars was actually shedding tears—which I rather doubt, since she did not strike me as the type to suffer reddened eyelids gladly—it would certainly have not been on my account."

"What you think of Lady Venetia's sensibilities is quite beside the point, Miss Armstead," his lordship replied haughtily. "The point is that, thanks to you, she wrote saying her conscience would never permit her to receive the attentions of a man betrothed to another."

"Well, that does surprise me. I would have thought that was the sort of situation she'd have relished, making a conquest of someone supposedly out of reach, I mean. I understood that the

London beauties enjoyed such flirts as much as we country folk like riding to the hounds, and that even married men were fair game for their kind of sport. Well, I can see I've misjudged Lady Venetia, and I beg pardon for it. But," Frankie went on with growing candor, "if she is sincere in wishing to have no more to do with you, you may be fortunate at that. Uncle Matthew said that none of your neighbors liked her; they found her too high in the instep by half. And they particularly did not like her dampened dress and the fact that she made it so obvious that she was above her company. So if you do plan to live in Hampshire, as you say, you might find it rather uncomfortable to have a wife who is universally disliked. Not that she'd likely agree to rusticate," she mused. "She has too much town bronze by half to waste it in the country."

"Have you quite finished with your assessment of the lady's character?" His lordship was glaring daggers.

"Not quite. While we are letting our hair down, you might as well know that your servants did not like her either. That's always a true giveaway, you know. No one's quite as good as servants in judging a person's essential worth. So perhaps you are more fortunate than you know to have escaped further entanglement. Beauty doesn't last forever," she concluded primly. "Character is what counts most in the long run."

"Thank you for that little homily. Although it mystifies me how anyone so unprincipled can preach so eloquently." Frankie involuntarily backed up a step, scorched by the blaze in Greville's eyes. "And do forgive me if I fail to feel quite as fortunate to be victimized as you'd have me feel. The only bright spot in any of this business is that I cannot believe that Lady Venetia—in spite of what my servants say about her—is wanting for good sense. So when I tell her I've been the innocent victim of your Machiavellian plot to hoodwink your guardian, I've no reason to think she'll not believe me. But if she should be in doubt"—his gray eyes hardened—"believe me, Miss Armstead, I'm not above collaring you, dragging you into her presence, and choking a confession out of you."

Frankie was appalled. She stared up into his face in stricken disbelief. Tears gathered in her eyes. "You do not really intend to tell Lady Venetia Sellars that I fabricated a betrothal to you?"

"Have you left me any choice?" If his lordship noticed the threat of tears, there was no corresponding softening in his expression.

"I should hate her knowing above all things. She's bound to misunderstand, just as you have. Not to mention that she'll spread the story all over town. Uncle Matthew sent me here because I'm being talked of in every drawing room in Hampshire. Now it appears I'm to be the *on dit* of London as well."

"You should have thought of that possibility earlier."

"Now who's preaching? Well, I must say this. A real gentleman would not expose me to ridicule."

"You think not? Well, it just so happens that I feel absolved from playing the gentleman in your particular case, Miss Armstead."

A throat cleared in the doorway. "Oh, I say, Wainwright, isn't that cutting it a bit rough?" a masculine voice drawled lazily.

The two antagonists wheeled to face two spectators whose entrance had unfortunately been timed to coincide with his lordship's final statement. The butler was doing his best to look impassive while the handsome young gentleman beside him eyed Lord Greville through a quizzing glass with an expression that somehow contrived to look both bored and censorious.

The newcomer was dressed in a long-tailed coat of green superfine worn over a white waistcoat edged with the same green shade. His stockinette pantaloons were fawn, as were the soft leather gloves he wore. His shirt points were high, his cravat gracefully tied in the Oriental mode. In fact it was a prime example of the complete Corinthian who stood drinking in the scene.

"Mr. Yarwood to see you, sir." The butler at last recalled his duty, then tactfully withdrew.

"Evelyn!" Frankie gasped. Even in the midst of her astonished embarrassment she could not help but feel a surge of pride at the newcomer's appearance. Indeed, Evelyn was quite the most handsome man Frankie had yet to see, with his hair so blond as to be almost silver and his eyes of a clear sky blue. The resemblance to Bertie was actually quite pronounced. Indeed, no one could fail to mistake the two for brothers. But it was as if nature, having achieved perfection once, had then settled for a not too skillfully executed counterfeit.

Frankie stole a look at Lord Greville to see what effect Evelyn's magnificence might be having upon his self-esteem. She longed to announce to his arrogant lordship that this Paragon who so cast him in the shade was the man who loved her, her actual, genuine fiancé. And if that knowledge didn't puncture His Nib's insufferable superiority, well, then, she didn't know what would.

But at the moment the arrogance seemed in no danger of abating. In fact his lordship was glaring at the Tulip of Fashion with an expression that could not possibly have been mistaken for cordiality. "What the devil brings you here, Yarwood?" he asked.

"I'm on a rescue mission." Evelyn Yarwood's voice retained its drawl, but his eyes did narrow a bit at his host's imperious tone. "Out after damsels in distress, in fact. Never knew you were in the petticoat line, Wainwright. But this won't do, you know. Miss Armstead may be a green 'un and not up to snuff in the ways of the world, but she is a lady. And not without friends, you know." There was a definite note of threat in the final statement.

"Oh, for God's sake!" Lord Greville ran his fingers through his thick hair in a way to make the other young man, whose own locks were artfully arranged in a Brutus style, wince for a fleeting moment. "Are you threatening to call me out, Evelyn? Even you couldn't be such a gudgeon as to think I'm trying to seduce Miss Armstead!"

"What else is a man to think?" The eyebrows rose. "I arrive next door to find Lady Paxton's maid having a fit of vapors. One minute it seems, Miss Armstead was chasing the dresser's bonnet, the next she was being dragged in here by what the woman concluded was a White Slaver at the very least."

Lord Greville's muttered comment, perhaps intended to be inaudible, was not.

"You are not on shipboard, sir." Miss Armstead reproved him in a manner reminiscent of an early governess.

"No, more's the pity" was the acidic answer. He turned his attention back to Yarwood, who was looking pointedly at the tea things, clearly the evidence of a cozy tête-à-tête. "I have no intention of trying to explain all of this. I'll leave this entirely to Miss Armstead, whose inventiveness will doubtless rise to the occasion. Just let me tell you this." His voice was bitter. "If you thought to save Miss Armstead from seduction, your visit's a waste of time. That idea is worse than absurd; it's ludicrous. But on the other hand, your arrival may have been well timed at that. For ever since I've had the misfortune to meet this young lady, the urge to throttle her has been growing on me. And who knows when the temptation may become overpowering? Webster!" The butler, as his master had surmised, had been lurking within earshot. "Will you fetch Miss Armstead's wrap? Now, if you both will excuse me, I've some urgent business to attend to. Webster will show you out. Miss Armstead. Mr. Yarwood." Lord Greville Wainwright gave each of his visitors the briefest of nods and then went striding from the room.

Chapter
Seven

"I'D NO IDEA THAT YOU AND LORD GREVILLE KNEW each other," Frankie remarked over another tea, this one set up for her and Evelyn in her aunt's yellow saloon. After today, it occurred to her, she might well discover she'd formed an intense dislike of the popular beverage.

Evelyn, however, seemed to have no such qualms. His long, well-shaped legs were crossed at the ankles and stretched toward the fireplace while he sipped the steaming brew contentedly. "It was an acquaintance neither of us was able to avoid," he drawled. "Since we were neighbors and contemporaries, we were thrown together as children. I don't know who had the maggoty notion we should play together. His grandfather, I suppose. Greville was an only child, thoroughly spoiled, naturally, and impressed with his consequence even then. It was 'his lordship' this and 'his lordship' that from all the servants, of course." His lip curled at the memory. "At any rate, I was fetched to the manor occasionally to play with 'his lordship.' But to put it mildly, we didn't take to each other. In fact"—he laughed suddenly—"we finally had a terrible dust-up when 'his lordship' wound up with a blackened eye and a bloodied nose. Needless to say I was never asked back again. But then as luck would have it we both went to the same school. But we did contrive to see as little as possible of each other there. He was into games—cricket, rowing, the entire gambit, I suppose." He sneered. "Whereas the chaps I chummed with had more interesting pursuits to follow." It was on the tip of Frankie's tongue to inquire of their nature, but there was something about the wicked chuckle that escaped from him then that persuaded her to drop the subject. He changed it anyhow. "But enough of past history. Bertie told me that your cat was let out of the bag with a vengeance and that Uncle Matthew has sent you up here till the scandal blows over back home. But what I can't understand is why Greville Wainwright followed you."

Frankie giggled. "Lord, he'd have fits for certain if he heard you say that. He didn't follow me. He'd no idea I was in London. He came to mend some fences of his own. It seems that the lady he's been pursuing got wind of our so-called betrothal and rang a peal over him. So he's here to smooth things over with Lady Venetia Sellars."

"Venetia!" For the first time Evelyn Yarwood seemed jolted

out of his studied world-weariness. "Bertie told me that Wainwright had some beauty in tow, but I never dreamed it was Lady Venetia. For a man assumed to have drowned, he didn't waste much time," he concluded bitterly.

"You know Lady Venetia?" Frankie was not sure why she felt uneasy as she asked the question.

"Slightly."

"She's very beautiful, isn't she?"

"Yes, I suppose most would say so. Though I doubt many would go into the raptures my little brother used to describe her. By the way, Frankie, did I say that the worst upshot of your escapade is having Bertie foisted upon me? And Lord knows what it will take to get him home again."

"But Bertie hates the city."

"Not anymore," Evelyn chuckled with amused tolerance. "Little Bertie has suddenly discovered there's more to life than hounds and foxes." He thereupon launched into an amusing anecdote, amusing to him at any rate, having to do with Bertie's open-mouthed reaction to the sight of the crown prince tooling the ribbons in the park with his mistress at his side. Since Frankie did not enjoy poking fun at Bertie as much as his brother seemed to, she welcomed the interruption caused just then by the entrance of her aunt.

Miss Armstead was beginning to grow accustomed to the male reaction to Lady Paxton. Certainly Bertie's pop-eyed bedazzlement had seemed in character. But she did experience a twinge of jealousy as the blue eyes of his sophisticated older brother gleamed appreciatively. She caught herself wondering cattishly if Evelyn would be quite so smitten if he knew that the lovely lady was almost ten years his senior.

"Don't tell me. You need not say a word, cherie." Lady Paxton, suddenly becoming very French indeed, held up a graceful hand to forestall Frankie's introduction. She took in Evelyn's sartorial splendor and smiled appreciatively. "It is the *other* Mr. Yarwood. The city, not the rural one, of course. Still"—she waved away the obvious differences—"the family resemblance is quite pronounced."

Evelyn cocked one eyebrow quizzically. "I'm not sure

whether I've just been insulted or complimented, Frankie," he remarked, "but in any case do present me to this beauty."

"Oh, complimented, but of course." Again Lady Paxton breezed on past an attempted introduction. "I found your little brother to be quite charming, monsieur."

"In that case you are kind-hearted as well as beautiful." He kissed the older woman's hand with elegant grace as Frankie finally edged in, "Aunt Maria, as you have surmised, this is Mr. Evelyn Yarwood."

Frankie was rather surprised to find that it was Evelyn and not her socially adept aunt who controlled the conversation. He seemed to be at considerable pains to impress her ladyship. For instance, it took him no time at all to discover that he and Lady Paxton had several acquaintances in common and to divert her with all the latest *on dits* about them while Frankie smiled politely and felt excluded.

The only common denominator that Miss Armstead observed in the behavior of the two brothers was their strict observance of the proper length of time for calls, at least after Lady Paxton became one of the company. Frankie could only imagine that their mutual nurse had dinned this piece of propriety into them both. But whereas Bertie's exit had been awkward, if not to say precisely gauche, Evelyn extracted himself with his usual aplomb. "I have promised to take my little brother to Watier's"—he rose regretfully to his feet—"though I'm not sure that the club will survive it." He smiled ruefully.

"I did not know you were a member of Watier's," Frankie exclaimed. She was torn between an annoyance that surprised her at Evelyn's constant belittlement of Bertie and admiration that Evelyn with his rather ordinary antecedents belonged to this famous club for gentlemen. But then she recalled that Watier's, next to boasting Brummell for a president, was most famous for its all-night gambling. She thereupon bypassed both annoyance and admiration to look uneasily at the young man she loved. He, busily engaged in kissing her aunt's hand once more, was oblivious to the look.

"We must talk," she said sotto voce as she walked with him to the door.

"Certainly," he answered. "I'll call again soon. Perhaps we can snatch a private moment. But there's no hurry, is there, now that you're actually here for the Season." His beautiful eyes smiled down at her and her heart melted in response. "Isn't this famous, Frankie? The two of us in London at last? And may I say that you look splendid? Even after the blowing your new hairstyle took, I can see that it is very fetching. And as for your walking dress, it's by far the most becoming thing I've seen you wear." Frankie dimpled prettily, basking in his praise until he spoiled it all by adding, "Your aunt Maria has performed miracles, in fact." The Pink of the Ton placed his curly brimmed beaver at a jaunty angle and picked up his silver-topped walking cane. Frankie would have been pressed to provide a suitable reason for the fact she longed to kick him as he said good-bye.

After an hour spent in her room composing a letter to her uncle that said very little, Frankie was not surprised to get a summons from her aunt. It was too much to hope that Maud had not given a full account of her morning's adventures.

Lady Paxton rose from her library desk with obvious relief. "I'm more than a little tempted to hire a secretary, Frankie," she sighed as she moved gracefully to a wing chair near the fireplace and motioned her niece to join her there. Frankie did so without comment. She had long known that, much to her uncle's horror, Lady Paxton insisted upon conducting her own affairs and was in fact a shrewd businesswoman. "Would you care for tea, Frankie?" her ladyship inquired.

"No, thank you." Frankie barely repressed a shudder.

"It's time we had a comfortable cose, I think." Maria broke into a chuckle at her niece's expression. "Don't look so horrified. I'm not about to ring a peal over you. I do, however, feel I would be remiss if I failed to point out that young single ladies do not call, unchaperoned, upon bachelors in their houses. Now, what married ladies do—ah, that's another matter entirely. But even those affairs must be handled with discretion. Really, Frances, you must learn to be circumspect, my dear. A scandal will ruin your chances of a successful mar-

72

riage. It must not appear that you are pursuing Lord Greville Wainwright."

"Pursuing him!" Frankie's voice rose in indignation. "I cannot begin to say how weary I've grown of that accusation! Indeed, I cannot think of anything that would please me more than never having to see his odious face again."

"That may prove difficult," her aunt remarked dryly, "given the fact that he has taken up residence next door. Which, by the way, came as a surprise. Indeed, I've often wondered why Wainwright has kept his townhouse, since he never uses it. Although as a young man, he cut quite a figure in society, I believe. But now that young Greville has given up the seafaring life, I suppose the place will come alive again. I must say I'm glad of it."

"Well, I certainly am not. And I propose to send one of the servants out to scout for me each time I leave the house, so that I'll not be obliged to encounter his high and mighty lordship."

"No," her aunt replied thoughtfully, gazing into the flames that played over the coals. "I think that avoiding him would be a tactical mistake. I think that a better way would be to launch our own offensive."

"Whatever are you thinking of?"

"I merely believe, am certain of, in fact, that the best way to nip in the bud any rumors of a liaison between you and Lord Greville is to throw you into each other's company." She held up a hand to stop her niece's protest. "Allow me to explain, my dear, before launching into one of your famous high flights. I am intending to give a small party for your come-out. Only two hundred or so guests. Now, I collect it would be very odd indeed if we were not to include Lord Greville, who not only lives next door but is also a Hampshire neighbor of yours, and most importantly, whose grandfather is an old and valued friend of mine. But, of course, we shall also invite Lady Venetia Sellars."

"Oh, must we!" Frankie wrinkled up her nose.

"Indeed, we must. I would be obliged to anyway, even if Lord Greville had not developed a tendre for her. Her mother is considered a bosom beau of mine, you see, which is to say, we cannot abide each other." She chuckled wickedly. "But you must see that having Lord Greville dangling after Venetia at your come-out while you are too busy with your own social success to be aware of them will certainly spike the guns of any gossipmonger who has picked up that ridiculous story about his jilting you. Whereas if you avoid Lord Greville like the plague, it can only add to the story's credibility."

"I suppose you are right," Frankie admitted reluctantly.

"I know that I am."

"There is one slight drawback to your scheme, however."

"And that is?"

"It seems to depend a great deal upon my being a social success. There's certainly no guarantee or much likelihood of that."

"You will take. I'm sure of it. You underestimate yourself, my dear. You are very like your mother in one respect, I believe, that is to say you've no notion at all that you really are quite fetching. Especially when dressed properly for your age and type. And with me to guide you, your taste will shortly be impeccable." There was no conceit in her ladyship's tone. She was simply stating fact. "Besides," she continued, "I always believe in making doubly sure that all goes well. We will leave nothing up to chance. The Yarwood brothers will be on our guest list and if between them they do not insure your success, well, then, I'm a green 'un. Your friend Evelyn may be a rogue; indeed, undoubtedly he is one. But he's a fashionable rogue, and, I understand, aped by the younger men. Now, I do realize that your uncle has expressly commanded me to keep him away from you, and with good reason I have no doubt." She gave her niece a shrewd look from her intelligent black eyes and nodded a confirmation as Frankie colored. "But I see no reason to avoid Mr. Yarwood's company entirely when he can be of service to us. So, yes, he will be on our guest list. Along with Lady Jersey and Lady Cowper. Two Almack patronesses should be sufficient. We mustn't be too obviously encroaching." Lady Paxton had risen and was walking back toward her desk again, the guest list for her party beginning to take shape within her mind.

"Do you need me any longer, Aunt Maria?" Frankie asked.

"No, no, run along, dear. Later you can help me address the cards, but right now I need to plan. And, Frankie"—she looked up from her desk as her niece opened the library door—"when we do address the cards, you can lighten the tedium by telling me what you and Sir Greville did during the interval—some thirty minutes, I believe Maud said it was— you spent next door. And what Evelyn Yarwood had to say to his lordship when he came to fetch you home. And if that doesn't occupy all the time until the task is finished, you might also explain why it is that your uncle has forbidden you to have anything to do with the elder son of his best friend." She gave a throaty laugh at the look of consternation on her niece's face, then gazed at her thoughtfully for a moment longer. "You know, I think I've been quite wrong about you, my dear. I think I am mistaken to believe that you are so much like your dear departed mother. Indeed, I'm beginning to think that perhaps you and I are more closely related than your upstanding uncle Matthew—or you yourself, so I suspect— would care to contemplate."

Chapter Eight

On the day of Lady Maria Paxton's ball, given for her niece, the latter could not fail to admire the former's whirlwind efficiency. Frankie did wonder, however, if her aunt's energies were not somehow wasted upon such a frivolous endeavor. Would she not, perhaps, have been better employed in moving troops and supplies against that juggernaut Napoleon? Such an undertaking would call for only a slight increase in organizational skill.

Dawn had barely arrived before Pandemonium joined it. The street in front of their house became a snarl of tradesmen's carts burdened with supplies and dodged by errand boys, heavily encumbered. An awning was stretched noisily from the portico to the street to protect the ladies' ball gowns from Mother Nature's threatened dampener. A red carpet was then laid underneath it to insure that dainty slippers would reach the ballroom floor unsoiled.

Inside the house sweating servants were shifting furniture from room to room, some of it being hauled all the way up to the attics, to make space for the crush of guests. Huge baskets of flowers were being crammed in every nook and corner. Silver was being polished till it gleamed. Tables were set. Chairs were arranged for the convenience of the guests, the orchestra, and for the windband engaged to entertain during the supper that would follow dancing. Disputes between the house staff and the caterers were constantly arising and were just as quickly dealt with. Lady Paxton supervised it all, down to the most minute detail, seeming always to know exactly what was to be done and how to accomplish it with the least wear and tear upon everyone's ruffled nerves.

It was late afternoon before Maud could persuade her mistress to lie down and rest in preparation for the evening's revelries. "Oh, I'd no idea it was four already," her ladyship exclaimed. "Well, no matter. Barring calamity, we should be able to greet our dinner guests at eight as if the household hadn't a care in the world, let alone been running its legs off all day. Come, Frankie," she said to her niece, who had followed her to the kitchen and was now sampling a petit four, "you must lie down too." She forestalled any protests by adding, "No arguments, miss. If things go well, this may be your last chance to be in your bed till dawn. Besides, we'll have no one saying you look hagridden at your own come-out."

If indeed her ladyship had harbored any secret fears on that score, they were quickly dispelled when she walked into Miss

Armstead's bedchamber shortly before eight while Maud was putting the final touches on her toilette. "Oh, you do look lovely!" Lady Paxton exclaimed, causing Frankie's cheeks to glow with pleasure.

Even the critical Maud seemed more than satisfied with her results, having backed off to survey her handiwork while Frankie rotated slowly for her inspection. The debutante wore white spider gauze that sparkled with delicate silvery embroidering. Her dark hair was brushed into a chignon, the side curls pomaded until they glowed. A silver ribbon was threaded through her locks and served as the coiffure's only adornment.

"Yes, it's right, Maud. Perfect, in fact," Lady Paxton congratulated the dresser. "Will you object if I add just one touch, however?" She smiled wickedly as the maid began to bristle. "No, I do not mean to spoil her simplicity. Who would have thought that our harum-scarum Frankie could look almost ethereal? But I did wish to make you a present, my dear." She turned then toward her niece. "Something to remember this occasion by. If you will stop pirouetting and preening for just a moment, I'll put this on you."

"Ooooh," Frankie gasped as she gazed into the cheval glass while her aunt fastened a string of small, perfectly matched pearls around her slender neck. "Oh, Aunt Maria, they're lovely!" Only Lady Paxton's rapid backstep saved her from being clasped in an ecstatic embrace.

"Restrain yourself, my love," she laughed. "Do you wish to undo all of Maud's artistry? And if anyone rumples my gown tonight, let it be some gentleman who quite loses his head over me, not my overly exuberant niece."

"I can believe that any number of gentlemen are quite likely to lose their heads over you," Frankie replied seriously. She had been so absorbed in her own transformation that she had not, till that moment, taken in her aunt's elegance. "Well, I've just been put in my place" was the cheerful verdict as she gazed at Lady Paxton's sophisticated ensemble of lace over claret-colored satin. Diamond pendants dangled from Maria's ears; a diamond necklace bridged the cleavage of her breasts, daringly displayed by a shockingly low-cut bodice. "I'm glad I really stopped to drink you in before I went downstairs," Frankie commented philosophically. "Or else I might have gone on thinking I should become the belle of my own ball. At least I'll not be overset now by the sight of Lady Venetia Sellars. Even that golden-haired beauty cannot possibly measure up to you."

"Don't be ridiculous," Lady Paxton retorted, looking rather pleased at the compliment, nonetheless.

Dinner, where the conversation of the twenty distinguished guests sparkled even more brightly than the silver and the crystal in the candlelight, passed quickly. At its conclusion, Frankie joined her aunt at the ballroom door to greet their guests.

From the beginning the crush that filed by them insured that the evening was bound to be considered a success. No one, unless ill or out of town, had dreamed of refusing an invitation from Lady Maria Paxton.

While firmly entrenched among the ton, her ladyship still somehow managed to maintain an aura of mystery. No one could actually point to anything shocking in her history; even so, it was taken more or less for granted that she had had a succession of distinguished lovers at her beck and call. After all, she had married two men much her senior. And didn't gentlemen swarm around her like bees to the spring blossoms? And besides all that, she was a Frenchwoman, was she not? It was the potential for scandal that seemed to underlie the lovely widow's decorum that helped make her the figure of interest she had become.

After Frankie had been presented to wave after wave of guests, announced in Dearborn's stentorian tones, she was sure that her smile had become set like plaster. She was glad for its permanence, however, when Lady Venetia arrived upon her father's arm looking at least as lovely as Frankie had foreseen. But that lady's cool appraisal did a great deal to bolster Frankie's confidence. Instead of looking through and past her as she had done at Lord Wainwright's ball, her expression somehow conveyed that she now recognized a rival worthy of her steel.

Also, the separate arrival of the Yarwood brothers quite convinced Frankie that she was well on her way to becoming a success. Evelyn's eyes opened wide with appreciation and his lips lingered upon her hand a moment too long for strict propriety. It was Bertie, though, who capped her evening. He gasped in astonishment, then blurted, "My word, Frankie, you're beautiful. Who would have dreamed it?"

Lord Greville Wainwright was among the late arrivals. Frankie, who had not forgotten him for a moment, had begun to hope he would not come. Then she turned from a conversation with a gentleman who had known her father to find his lordship giving polite but brief replies to her aunt's inquiries concerning his grandfather's health. "He's taken more trouble than usual with his appearance" was Frankie's first impression. For Lord Greville was impeccably turned out in white satin knee breeches, white stockings, frilled shirt, and long-tailed coat. Even his hair was carefully arranged. Frankie almost giggled as she wondered just how long it would stay that way before he ran his fingers through it. It also had grown to a more becoming length. All in all, she concluded as she covertly watched him, he should have very little trouble in reclaiming the affections of Lady Venetia Sellars—if indeed he had ever lost them. Frankie thought she smelled artifice in the lady's tactics and wondered if her letter had not been a scheme to bring his lordship up to scratch.

By this time Frankie had grown accustomed to favorable reactions to her appearance and was rather piqued when Lord Greville displayed none. Not that he did not take a few seconds' time to look her over. But he did so rather in the same manner used to assess the position of an enemy vessel before one blew it from the water.

"Don't look so thunderous," her aunt whispered as Frankie stood glaring at Greville's back while he strolled into the ballroom to join a group of gentlemen in conversation. "He didn't respond to my charms either, and I turned them on full force. Perhaps he's dead." Frankie giggled then at her aunt's wry smile. The presence of Lord Greville Wainwright would cast no damper upon her come-out ball.

And Frankie did soon forget him in the crush of gentlemen

79

to claim her hand. Even she realized that their numbers and insistence went well beyond the demands of merely doing the polite. And though she rightly accorded her aunt's popularity with some of the credit for her success, there was enough left over for herself. She had "taken." There was no doubt. And if there had been, it was dispelled when Evelyn claimed her for the cotillion.

"Well, Frankie, how does it feel to be all the crack?" He smiled down at her.

"Am I, indeed, or are you funning?"

"Oh, be assured," he answered solemnly. "I had to step outside and run a dozen gentlemen through with my rapier before I could get a dance." She giggled infectiously. This was the evening's climax. Standing with her gloved hand in Evelyn's, she was sure that she was the envy of every female in the room.

If there was one small dark cloud on the horizon of her happiness, it was the attention that Evelyn accorded Lady Venetia Sellars. The two danced together in the same set with Frankie and a spotted viscount and seemed to be on quite easy terms together. It made Frankie wonder if, in fact, their acquaintance was as slight as Evelyn had intimated.

Later on she discovered that she was not the only one to harbor that suspicion. When to her amazement Lord Greville Wainwright outflanked three other gentlemen waiting to dance with her it was all she could do to keep her face composed as he led her into the set. "Have you gone mad?" she hissed under her breath as they took their places.

His eyebrows rose. "As usual, Miss Armstead," he replied in equally low tones, "I fail to take your meaning. Is there something peculiar in my behavior that I'm not aware of?"

"Well, of course. You're standing up with me. Which, when you consider that we both wish to nip in the bud any whispering about us, seems downright lunatic."

"You think so? I think it would appear more odd if I did not make some push to dance with the evening's honoree."

"Oh, merely doing your duty, are you?" she retorted. "Well, I assure you it's not necessary."

"I know." He grinned suddenly, looking quite human, much

to his partner's surprise. "I've noticed your success. I doubt it will prove necessary for you to go diving out one of these windows again tonight."

"That's a caddish thing—" The movements of the dance unfortunately cut short Frankie's scathing comment upon what she considered to be his complete lack of tact.

When they came together once again he seemed to have forgotten both Frankie and their previous conversation in his preoccupation with another set across the ballroom. Frankie followed his narrowed gaze and saw Lady Venetia standing up with Evelyn for the second time. The rush of jealousy she felt demanded an immediate target.

"I see your sense of duty does not require you to pay attention to your present partner, my lord. As I recall, the other time you honored me with a dance you spent the entire time ogling Lady Venetia Sellars."

"Your memory is better than mine, then," he answered, still keeping his eyes riveted on the handsome couple. "And I was not 'ogling,' I assure you. But I will admit to being surprised that she and Yarwood are so well acquainted. Though I suppose I should not be," he added. "The peripatetic Mr. Yarwood, he does get about, does he not?" He transferred his gaze back down to her. "I'm not mistaken, I collect, in assuming that he is your mysterious fiancé, the one I was a red herring for?"

"I really do not think that is any of your concern, your lordship," she answered with a hauteur that put his to shame.

"Nothing you do should be my concern, I grant you. Still, this doesn't seem to have prevented you from embroiling me in your affairs. But pray, don't answer my question if you'd rather not. It really is unnecessary. It doesn't take much effort on my part to deduce the obvious. Mr. Yarwood is your neighbor, it's common knowledge his pockets are to let, and you yourself apprised me of the enormity of your fortune, ergo—"

It was fortunate for the future baron that the dance separated them once again. When they were finally reunited, Frankie, while still livid, was beyond the point of murder. She substituted a whispered tongue-lashing in its stead.

"That was an infamous—cowardly—dastardly—despicable—" She choked as her list of adjectives ran out. "How dare you blacken Evelyn's reputation. You'd never do it to his face!"

He looked genuinely surprised. "Blacken his reputation? I'd no notion that I'd done so. Oh, by calling him a fortune hunter, you mean? Well, that should come as no surprise to Evelyn or anybody else. It's a well-known fact, hardly a calumny."

"And I suppose you think that Lady Venetia isn't?" Frankie hurled back nastily.

"Quite the contrary. I'm sure she is. That's why I'm surprised that she's wasting so much time with Yarwood. But then one can hardly blame her. He is every woman's ideal, I suppose. The proverbial Greek god come to life."

"Yes, he most assuredly is," Frankie replied with vicious sweetness. "So it's little wonder you have always disliked him. Jealousy ill becomes you, m'lord."

"Jealousy? The part about my disliking him is certainly true. But I deny being jealous of him. I'll leave the exercise of that emotion up to you, Miss Armstead. I'm sure he'll give you ample cause."

Fortunately the set came to an end just then. As Lord Greville led her from the floor Frankie remarked almost pleasantly, "I am quite determined that you shall not have spoiled my evening."

He looked startled for an instant. "Was there ever a danger of that? One dance wasted in an evening that must be considered a social triumph for you? I doubt that I have such power."

"Well, you obviously asked me in order to be as unpleasant as possible," she retorted as she parted from him. "But it will not wash, you see. I happen to know why it is that you belittle Evelyn. You still hold a grudge for that thrashing he once gave you." She tossed her head in triumph at her Parthian shot. The effect, however, was slightly marred by his lordship's reaction. For when she glanced back once more, she found to her chagrin that instead of being chastened as he should have been, Lord Greville Wainwright was, in fact, convulsed with laughter.

"Well, it's about time." Frankie found herself tugged into

another set that was being formed: "I must say, Frankie, that when you stop to consider how back home I was practically the only cove lining up to dance with you, it seems the outside of enough that you've ignored me for the entire evening here."

"I have not ignored you, unless you consider that I should have gone looking for you in this crush." Miss Armstead was still smarting from her encounter with his lordship. She glared at her old friend. "What is your problem, Bertie? Are you afraid of a scold from your father for not pursuing the heiress hard enough?"

"Well, what's got you into such a pucker?" Bertie was more curious than offended. "Greville Wainright, I suppose. I thought no good would come of it when I saw you two stand up together. What's he done, threaten to tell everyone you pretended to be betrothed to him?"

"No, but I expect he will soon enough, though," she said nastily. "It's just that he implied—no, he said it straight out—that Eve—that no one would marry me except for my fortune."

"If it's Evelyn that you mean, go on and say so." Bertie obviously was not about to take offense on his brother's behalf. "And if you're wondering whether he'd marry you if you hadn't a feather to fly with, well, the idea's absurd. What a gudgeon he'd be to do a thing like that with the estate all to pieces the way it is. But you ain't the only heiress around, you know, Frankie. And Evelyn has always had great success in the petticoat line. He is devilish handsome, you know." There was just a trace of envy in the younger brother's voice. "So I collect you ain't the only female he could talk into running off with him. But he did pick you."

Frankie did not doubt for a minute that Bertie's speech was intended to bolster her drooping spirits. But for some reason it fell short of expectations. They danced in silence for a bit, both deep in thought. It was Albert who broke it first. "You do realize, Frankie, that after tonight you could bring to heel about any cove in London, if you'd a mind to. Everybody's talking about how you've taken. Two or three fellows I spoke with are making perfect cakes of themselves, raving on about your beauty and about your sparkling conversation—all sorts of fustian. Still, though, I guess it ain't so strange when you stop to think of it. I was rocked back on my heels a bit myself when I saw you tonight. And I've known you ever since you were a grubby little girl. No telling what effect you might have on some cove you haven't been leading into mischief only to get him blamed for it all these years. So you don't have to let Wainwright bother you—or Evelyn either, when it comes to that. And if you're really concerned whether someone would snatch you up if you didn't have a farthing to your name, well, that's a pretty rum notion, if you ask me, but well, you just might be able to pull the thing off at that. Look at your aunt. She managed. Not just once, but twice. Of course, she married Methuselah both times, but you can't have everything. Point is, if she could find somebody, you could too. For you do look devilishly like her, don't you know."

What was probably the longest speech in Albert Yarwood's history came to an end as the music stopped. Frankie was claimed immediately by a new partner. And at some point during the ensuing country dance she realized that her good humor had been quite restored, though she was at a loss to know the reason why.

Chapter Nine

B ERTIE'S OBSERVATION PROVED TO BE RIGHT ON TARGET. Frankie had indeed taken. The days that followed her come-out brought with them a flood of invitations. Cards to routs, assemblies, balls, galas, fetes. Invitations to the theater, the opera. Requests for her company for tea parties, Venetian breakfasts, carriage rides. The silver tray could scarcely contain them all. And Dearborn was forced to post himself near the doorway and remain there in order to cope with the crush when Lady Paxton and her popular niece were receiving callers.

It was upon such an occasion that the butler appeared in the doorway of the withdrawing room, the yellow saloon having been abandoned as not large enough to contain the company, and announced with even more than his customary dignity, "Lord Wainwright."

Frankie, engaged in animated conversation with no less than four young sprigs of fashion, looked up in surprise, thinking that Dearborn for once had confused his terminology. She should have known better, though, for it was indeed the baron himself standing there gazing around the room at the twenty or so people present and looking slightly ill at ease.

As her aunt hurried forward to greet this unexpected guest, Frankie was struck once more by what a distinguished-looking old gentleman he was. She wondered fleetingly if his grandson would weather the years as well, but then found it unlikely that nature had endowed him half so well as it had his patrician ancestor.

Lady Paxton introduced Lord Wainwright to the company, but when he chose to come sit down by Frankie, the young men with her gracefully took their leave.

His lordship sighed as he watched their departure, regretting, perhaps, his own lost youth. He then turned to his young companion with a rueful smile. "You must forgive me, my dear, for driving off your beaux."

"Oh, I'd much liefer talk to you, my lord. I'm dying to know the news from home."

They spent the next several minutes quite amicably while his lordship diverted her with the various *on dits* from their rural society. She was surprised, considering his reclusive habits, how well informed he was. He must have read her mind, for he smiled and said, "The servants. They're the secret of my staying up to date. As you know, nothing we do ever escapes them."

If Frankie was made a little uncomfortable by that statement, the feeling passed immediately, for his lordship went on to speak of the unexpected pleasure he was experiencing from his first visit to the Metropolis in a dozen or more years. "I've discovered it's a mistake to write yourself off as old, m'dear, before the times arrives when you've actually no choice in the decision." He smiled engagingly and moved on then to enjoy a brief tête-à-tête with her aunt before he left them.

Later when Frankie had a moment alone with Lady Paxton in her bedchamber she commented on his lordship's charm. "A pity his grandson didn't inherit a bit of it," she sniffed. "I was astonished to see Lord Wainwright here. At first I wondered if he'd called because we're Hampshire neighbors. But then I realized that was absurd. His acquaintance with Uncle Matthew is only slight. I remembered then that he and your husband were bosom beaux."

Lady Paxton glanced up from the embroidery that was occupying her. She was reclining on a Grecian couch, while Frankie had chosen to plop down on the floor in front of the fireplace, oblivious to the pained look her aunt had given her. "Actually," her ladyship said casually, "your first instincts were right, you know. It is on your account that Lord Wainwright came to London."

Frankie sat bolt upright and stared at her. "Whatever do you mean?"

"I simply mean that his lordship got wind that his grandson had jilted a local girl and was much distressed by it. He has a highly cultivated sense of noblesse oblige, you know. He thought it his duty to come to London and confront his grandson with what he'd heard."

Frankie groaned. "Well, I'm surprised that he'd even call here, let alone treat me with such civility after finding out the truth."

"That's the strange aspect of the matter." Lady Paxton paused to clip a silk and rethread her needle. "It seems that his grandson was not exactly forthcoming on the subject. He was prone to dismiss it, in fact. The only comment his grandfather could pry out of him was that the gossipmongers have to chew on someone and it might as well be he. Which, needless to say, hardly satisfied the old gentleman's sense of honor."

"Well, I am surprised." Frankie's eyes had widened. "I wonder why Lord Greville didn't go ahead and tell him the awful truth and clear himself."

"Perhaps chivalry isn't dead in the Wainwright line after all," her aunt replied.

"I doubt that," Frankie mused. "If I know Lord Greville, and I think I'm beginning to, he probably resented the fact that his grandfather would suspect him of such rackety behavior and so got up on his high ropes and refused to discuss the matter."

Her aunt gazed at her thoughtfully. "That is one explanation, of course," she acknowledged.

"Well"—Frankie spoke with martyred resignation, looking a trifle ill, though—"I'll just have to go to Lord Wainwright and confess. It would be entirely too shabby of me to cause the old gentleman to lose respect for his heir."

"Oh, I don't think I should act hastily," Lady Paxton replied. "If Greville Wainwright was moved to protect your reputation—and it is not beyond belief, you know—it would be churlish of you to spoil his gesture. Besides, I think I was able to set his grandfather's mind at rest."

"You were?" Frankie looked at her aunt suspiciously. "You didn't tell the old gentleman a whisker, did you?"

"No, I merely said that I myself found it inconceivable that such a rumor could ever have been circulated, and pointed out that you most assuredly were not suffering from a broken heart. Quite the contrary, in fact. I told him that you have been enjoying your London Season tremendously. He seemed most relieved and remarked upon the fact that you do seem to be greatly admired. He also regretted not being fifty years younger himself."

"He actually said that?" Frankie looked quite pleased.

"Yes, he did. And I do think you might start feeling a bit less guilty about embroiling the Wainwright household in your affairs. For at least some good has come of it. You've succeeded in bringing Lord Wainwright out of retirement. Now I think the old gentleman is ready to kick up his heels a bit. At least he has invited us to share his opera box. I hope you do not mind, Frankie, for I've accepted for us."

"He did? You have? No, of course I don't mind. And Uncle Matthew will be ecstatic. Why, if Prinny himself were to ask me to the opera, Uncle Matthew wouldn't feel more honored. Perhaps," she observed wistfully, "this will take a bit of the sting out of what I did."

"Oh, undoubtedly." Her aunt's tone was dry.

"But you don't think—he didn't imply—that his grandson will be in the party, did he?"

"No, he did not say. But you can rest easy on that score, I think. I consider it most unlikely that Lord Greville will be joining us."

"Good," Miss Armstead declared with rather more conviction than she actually was feeling.

But in any case Lady Paxton's prognostication proved correct. For when on the appointed evening Lord Wainwright's old-fashioned crested carriage traveled the few yards from his doorway to theirs, he was the only occupant.

Frankie and her aunt had both dressed with particular care, Frankie in Urling's net over white satin and Lady Paxton in a black crepe frock over a black sarsenet slip. His lordship was lavish with his praise, congratulating himself for the good fortune of squiring two such lovely ladies to King's Theater.

It was Frankie's first visit to the opera house, a fact she made no effort to conceal. Indeed, when they first settled themselves in their chairs in Lord Wainwright's box she was so busy drinking in the grandeur of the decorated ceiling, the ornate chandelier, the tiers of boxes draped in crimson and trimmed with white and gold, and exclaiming over the size of the stage, gallery, and pit that she had little attention to spare for the audience. When she did find the time to peruse the other patrons, her eyes were mainly turned toward the pit and the tops of all those heads—turbaned, feathered, bejeweled, dark, fair, and bald—milling about like pieces of glass in a kaleidoscope as people greeted one another, gossiped, moved on to other groups, then finally found their seats.

Lord Wainwright, however, with the aid of his quizzing

glass, was looking at the boxes. "Me grandson's supposed to be here," he informed the ladies, "in Admiral Charing's party. He was to have had dinner with him and some other of his naval friends and then come hear the opera. Oh, I say, there he—no, I'm mistaken. I see Lady Venetia Sellars and Miss Austen and thought I spied Greville in the party, but it's not. Silly mistake, actually. That young man's hair is almost as white as mine."

Lady Paxton had her opera glasses trained in the same direction, but Frankie did not need to see her suddenly raised eyebrows to know whom she saw. Frankie followed the arrow of her aunt's gaze, though, to the box that had first captured Lord Wainwright's attention. There were eight people in the party: Lady Venetia and her chaperone, a distinguished-looking middle-aged couple who were the parents, possibly, of a rather ordinary-looking young lady who perhaps was only made to seem so by the beauty sitting next to her. Three young men rounded out the group, all vying for Lady Venetia's notice. But it was Evelyn Yarwood who hovered nearest and seemed to be captivating her at the moment with his conversation.

Evelyn must have felt all their eyes upon him, for he turned their way just then. But if he did appear startled for just a moment, he quickly recovered and bowed in their direction. Fortunately for Frankie's composure the curtain parted and she was free to direct all of her attention toward the stage. And it was greatly to the artists' credit that she was soon able to lose herself in their performance.

She did not risk another peek across the way until the intermission, and even then she was careful to conceal herself behind her rapidly moving fan. Evelyn had now left the field to Lady Venetia's other swains and was engaged in earnest conversation with his host and hostess. Frankie could not help but wonder, unworthily perhaps, if this change happened because he knew himself to be under scrutiny.

Her thoughts were interrupted by a visitor to their box. "Good evening, Grandfather." Lord Greville Wainwright was stiffly formal. "I was quite surprised to see you here. I don't believe you mentioned going to the opera."

"Oh, did I not?" His lordship rose to his feet innocently. "Probably didn't wish to make you jealous that an old dog like me could squire two beauties. Lady Paxton, Miss Armstead, I believe you already know me grandson."

Lord Greville bowed as the ladies acknowledged the acquaintance. Frankie's greeting was at least as reserved as his had been. In contrast, Lady Paxton turned on all of her considerable charm. "Do join us, Lord Greville." Her ladyship indicated a chair next to her own.

"Better still, let's walk about a bit," Lord Wainwright suggested. "It's a cruel thing to have to admit after just boasting about my prowess as a beau, but I begin to stiffen up when I sit too long."

Lady Paxton took his lordship's arm, which left his grandson little choice but to escort Frankie through the box curtains and out into the corridor. The older pair turned in the direction of Lady Venetia's box. "Oh, let's go this way." Frankie gestured in the opposite direction, then felt a need to provide a reason for her choice. "I long to see that statue closer." She gestured toward a distant alcove.

Unaccountably Lord Greville chuckled. But as his grandfather and her aunt were waylaid by some old acquaintances, he seemed glad enough to fall in with Frankie's plan. "By all means, let's go see the sculpture. Up close, of course."

"Oh, my heavens!" Miss Armstead blushed beet red as they reached their destination and paused before the nude Apollo. She glared up at Lord Greville, who was shaking with silent laughter at her embarrassment. "You know perfectly well that I didn't—" She choked in indignation.

He was studying the statue intently, his head to one side, his eyes narrowed, every inch the art connoisseur. "Yes, I see it now," he said thoughtfully. "By George, he is the very image of Evelyn Yarwood. From the neck up, at least. As for the rest, I could not say, of course."

"Lord Greville, if you think that I—"she began furiously, then laughed in spite of herself. "Oh, do come along. People are beginning to wonder at us. You really are completely odious. You knew all along that I'd put my foot into my mouth again, didn't you?"

"I knew that you were trying to steer us away from a possible meeting with Lady Venetia and your Evelyn and picked a rather unfortunate excuse to do so."

"Oh." She hated being so transparent. But since she'd been found out, she dared to ask, "Do you mind it a great deal?"

"That they're together?" He shrugged. "Let's say it doesn't particularly surprise me. Unlike my grandfather, I've never considered myself a beau. I also know it doesn't matter." His face was expressionless, his voice indifferent. "She may enjoy a flirt with Yarwood, but when it comes to choosing a husband—there'll be no contest. He won't be in the running."

Frankie stopped dead still to stare up at him as a group of splendidly dressed opera-goers dodged their way around them. "And you don't care?"

"Why should I?" was his calm reply.

"Why should you?" she echoed. "Don't tell me it pleases you to be married for your money and your position."

He shrugged once again while she took fleeting notice of the broad shoulders under the well-cut coat. His face, though not quite as sunburned as when she had seen him at the Wainwright ball, still seemed hard beyond its years. He answered cynically. "Do you know anyone in our set who marries for any other reason? Come, Miss Armstead, you yourself have surely heard Almack's referred to as the Marriage Mart, where all you young ladies go to await the highest bidder."

"That may be true in some instances, but certainly not in all."

"I beg your pardon, Miss Armstead. I forgot. You are a romantic. Just when is it that you are flying to the border? 'All for love and the world well lost,' no doubt."

"You need not keep harping on the same theme, Lord Greville. I'm not a slowtop, you know. I got your message the first time. You've already made it quite plain that Evelyn—or anyone else for that matter—would only wed me for my fortune." She had turned her head away, for to her mortification tears had begun to sting her eyes.

"Damnation." His lordship swore under his breath as he

took her arm and forced her to face him. "Look, please discount anything I've just said. You're right, I'm sure. People fall in love constantly—at Almack's—here—Grosvenor Square—Soho—And I can't imagine anyone more equipped with Cupid's arrows than you. You'll break any number of hearts before you're done, Miss Armstead. There now, that's better." His usually unreadable countenance had been shaken into real concern by her threat of tears. It now relaxed as she stared up at him suspiciously.

"That's doing it up a bit too brown, your lordship. On the whole I think I like you better when you're lashing out at me. It seems more honest."

"There's no pleasing you, then, is there?" He grinned crookedly and ran his fingers through his hair. "Well, I've just admitted I'm no beau."

"You certainly aren't." She giggled. "Not even Bertie Yarwood would make such a mess of the hairstyle your valet must have labored over. Wasn't that à la Titus before you wrecked it?"

"Oh, lord," he groaned. "I think so. At any rate the wretched man made me take a solemn oath I wouldn't touch it."

The patrons had begun to drift back toward their boxes. Frankie and Lord Greville followed suit. Her hand tightened upon his sleeve as they saw Lady Venetia and Evelyn talking with Lord Wainwright and Lady Paxton at the entrance to their box. "Smile, Miss Armstead," Greville directed under his breath. "You really must learn to dissemble. Why not let your fiancé be the one to feel jealous for a change?"

Indeed, Frankie noted then, Evelyn was looking at them through narrowed eyes while Lady Venetia actually appeared flustered.

"Ah, there you are, Greville, Miss Armstead," his lordship said, hailing their arrival. "That makes our reunion complete. We've been making plans behind your back. Lady Paxton had remarked that Miss Armstead sorely misses the opportunity to go riding, so we've arranged to meet in the park at nine to work in a gallop before the place fills up. How about it, children?

Lady Venetia and Mr. Evelyn here are game. What do you say, Greville?"

"Well, sir, I'm afraid—" From his tone of voice one might have suspected that Greville Wainwright was preparing some excuse, but the pressure of the gloved hand that still rested on his arm came perilously close to being classified a pinch. "That is to say, I should like it above all things," he concluded dryly.

"Well, then it's settled," his grandfather exclaimed.

A moment of rather awkward silence followed. Frankie plunged in to cover it. "What a lovely necklace, Lady Venetia. The design is most unusual." It would have been a breach of manners to add that the diamond and pearl creation, with a lovely cameo for its focal point, was clearly worth a fortune.

"Thank you," Lady Venetia replied politely. "It is a copy of one belonging to the Empress Josephine that my father had made for me. I am very fond of it on that account." While Frankie wondered just which was being honored, Lord Sellars or Napoleon's wife, the lady self-consciously adjusted the jewelry under discussion. "Oh, dear," she exclaimed as the choker began to slide off her lovely neck. "It's come unfastened."

"Here, allow me." Although Greville had made a slight move in Venetia's direction, it was Evelyn who was Johnny-on-the-spot to secure the wayward necklace. "Oh, I say," he exclaimed as he examined it more closely, "the clasp has broken, actually."

While they commiserated with the lady upon the temporary loss of her adornment, they also felt a need to add how fortunate indeed it was that she had not lost it, for instance, from underneath her cloak on her way into the theater. Evelyn gallantly placed the necklace in his pocket, volunteering to take it to the jeweler's for her as soon as the shop opened in the morning.

Further conversation was cut short by a rich soprano emoting upon the stage. The others made their polite farewells and went to rejoin their party, and Lord Wainwright and his guests settled themselves down again in his box to listen.

But this time the performance failed to charm. Indeed Frankie's head was so awhirl with so many conflicting impressions and emotions that she quite forgot to listen to it from then on.

Chapter Ten

"WELL, YOU ARE HARDLY A RAY OF SUNSHINE, I MUST say," Lady Paxton observed when her niece, dressed becomingly in a riding habit of slate-colored cloth, joined her in the hall. Her ladyship, similarly though somewhat more rakishly attired in bright blue velvet with a fetching small round hat of cork, had been waiting impatiently for some little time.

"This really was a maggoty notion," her scowling niece replied. "Tell me, was it your idea or Lord Wainwright's to form this peculiar party?"

"Mine, actually," her aunt replied, dimpling mischievously. "I knew, you see, how you've been longing for a ride."

"Well, if that's so, you knew more than I did," Frankie retorted as they emerged from their house to find the gentlemen from next door waiting, with the grooms from Tilbury of Mount Street holding their hired horses. The breath of men and beasts fogged in the morning cold. Lord Wainwright beamed at the ladies with genuine pleasure, whereas his grandson, Frankie observed, looked about as thrilled with the expedition as she was feeling.

Much to Frankie's surprise, Lady Venetia was waiting with her groom beside her at the appointed meeting place near the entrance to Hyde Park. I'd have bet a monkey that she'd keep us dangling for at least half an hour, she thought. But when the beauty moved her horse beside Lord Greville's and flashed a possessive smile up at him, Frankie concluded that being

punctual was merely the first step in a campaign to reingrati-
ate herself with him.

It was, in point of fact, Evelyn who kept them waiting, and
it occurred to Frankie to wonder if he'd had difficulty raising
the not inconsiderable blunt needed to hire a horse. But just as
they'd concluded he'd overslept and were preparing to move
on without him, he came galloping up, dapper as ever in a dark
green riding coat and boots that gleamed with blacking. But as
he reined in his horse Frankie noticed with unaccustomed criticism that the beautiful blue eyes were a trifle bloodshot beneath rather puffy lids and the handsome face showed signs of
dissipation. She thought of inquiring privately just how he'd
spent his time after the opera, then realized that she did not really want to know.

The party set off then at a rather decorous pace down a riding path that led deep into the park, a place of beauty even with
the trees stripped bare of foliage and the ground underneath the
horses' hooves crunching with the cold. Lady Paxton and Lord
Wainwright led the way. They were obviously enjoying each
other's company, hitting it off famously in fact, which was
more than could be said for Frankie and Evelyn, who came
after them, riding side by side in a rather constrained silence.
As for the couple bringing up the rear, Frankie's straining ears
heard no conversation from that quarter either. But perhaps
they purposely kept their voices low. She was quite determined
not to turn around and look.

"A penny for your thoughts." Evelyn broke the silence.

"I was wondering if you were up all night" was the blunt
reply.

"And suppose I was?" He raised an eyebrow.

"Well, it would account for the fact you kept us waiting and
that you look as if you must have shot the cat quite thoroughly."

"What's got into you, Frankie?" Evelyn studied her intently.
"It ain't like you to drag a fellow over the coals."

She looked appalled. "Was that what I was doing?"

"Close to it anyhow. And it does seem out of character. One
of the things I've most admired about you, you know, is that
you've always been one to live and let live, Frankie."

"I'd make an ideal wife, in fact."

"I've always thought so," he answered evenly. "Nobody wants to be leg-shackled to a shrew who'd always be going on at him over the least little thing."

"Like being late," she said with true repentance. "Oh, I am sorry, Evelyn. I truly am quite out of sorts this morning. Aunt Maria has already remarked on it. But I should not be taking my ill humor out on you."

"Well, now, that's better." He smiled his engaging smile and she responded. "You were right, though, about me shooting the cat," he continued. "Lord, I've the devil's own head this morning. But it's all your fault, you know."

"My fault?" Her dark eyes widened.

"Exactly. Have you any idea how it makes a cove feel to have his intended bride becoming one of the most sought-after women in London and not be able to come near her?"

As his horse almost crowded hers off the path she giggled. "You aren't doing too badly now, I'd say."

"Don't joke, Frankie. I'm deadly serious. It's hell having you here in London and not being able to claim you for my own. Why do you think I drink myself almost senseless at night?" Frankie glanced at him uneasily. It was hard to interpret the expression in his eyes. "You've grown into a very desirable woman, you know," he said huskily, "and I long to make love to you. Yet I shouldn't even be seeing you."

"Of course you can see me." She was uncomfortable under the intensity of his gaze. "We are seeing each other now, are we not?"

"This is hardly what I mean by 'seeing you,' and you damn well know it," he replied. "But even this is probably ill advised. If your uncle gets wind of the fact that we've been thrown together again, he'll yank you back to Hampshire so fast your head will swim."

"Possibly." Frankie thought it over. "But I doubt that he'd get into a pucker over Lord Wainwright's including another neighbor in his party. Besides, poor Uncle Matthew must feel well rid of me," she said sadly. "He was really shattered when he found I was not engaged to Lord Greville after all, and mortified by all the gossip. Oh, dear," she moaned, "I can't think how I was so hen-witted as to make up such a story. Which reminds me. I've been meaning to ask you, since you seem to be on remarkably good terms with Lady Venetia"—Evelyn shot her a searching look, but apparently read no censure in her face as she continued—"I'm wondering—" She paused again to look behind them and check on the other riders. Lord Greville and Lady Venetia had fallen far behind. The gentleman appeared fascinated by the lady's conversation. Reassured that they were well out of earshot, Frankie continued, "I'm wondering if Lady Venetia ever confided in you about her relationship to Lord Greville. Are they betrothed?"

"Not officially," he answered. "Well, that is to say, not at all. She does admit that he's been most attentive. And her father, of course, is throwing her at Greville's head. I think she has some reservations, though. Who could blame her?" he added with a trace of bitterness.

"Well, I trust her reservations aren't on account of that stupid betrothal that I invented." If Frankie was hoping to put some of her guilt to rest, this conversation was having the opposite effect. "Did she tell you that she accused him of being the kind of man who trifles with a girl's affections?"

He laughed mockingly. "Yes, and I told her she gave him too much credit. I can't see Wainwright somehow as a breaker of hearts." He gave Frankie a searching look. "But perhaps I mistake the matter?"

"Oh, how should I know?" She brushed the implication aside. "What I'm trying to find out, Evelyn, before the others overtake us, is whether you know how much Lord Greville told her about the Banbury Tale I invented. I'm puzzled by her attitude, you see. I had expected her to snub me completely and at the same time to spread the story all over London. And to my knowledge she has not done either. I mean to say, she treats me as she did from the first: that is, she holds me slightly beneath her notice but not quite beneath contempt. And if she's told the world I pretended to be engaged to Lord Greville, well, I have yet to hear of it. That might not be surprising, but neither has

97

Aunt Maria, and that would be. So how do you suppose his lordship explained away the rumors about him that she heard?"

"He didn't. Not to her satisfaction, at any rate. All he would say is that he'd no idea how such a preposterous story got started, but he could only suppose it was because the two of you happened to be at the same house party together. He gave her a lecture, it seems," Evelyn went on dryly, "on country gossip, trying to imply that making up scandal out of whole cloth was a country occupation."

Frankie's eyes widened. "Lord Greville said that? That was gallant of him. I would never have given him so much credit."

"Nor would I have." Evelyn's opinion, though, did not seem to undergo drastic change. He half turned in his saddle to observe the couple behind them, still deep in conversation. "But don't award him his halo quite yet. Unless I miss my guess he's filling her in on the details right now."

The tree-lined path that they'd been following now crossed a carriage road, and Lord Wainwright and Lady Paxton had reined in their horses and were waiting for the others to overtake them. Frankie and Evelyn urged their mounts ahead. Lady Venetia and Lord Greville also soon caught up.

"Well, now"—Lord Wainwright beamed at them—"wasn't this a good idea?" The old gentleman was obviously enjoying the exercise. His grandson, however, was studying him intently and did not appear entirely pleased by what he saw.

There was some discussion then about the route to follow, which ended in a decision to keep to the carriage road until they came to an open space where they'd be at liberty to give their mounts free rein. Since there was very little traffic at such an unfashionable hour, the group was able to ride together and hold general conversation for a bit. Lord Wainwright was entertaining them with an anecdote about the old king, "Farmer George," when his story was interrupted by the sound of carriage wheels. The six riders obligingly guided their horses to the edge of the roadway to give the vehicle ample room to pass. Instead the driver of the smart curricle reined to a stop beside them. "May I speak to you a moment, Mr. Yarwood?" its lone passenger called out.

Since she was mostly blocked from view by Evelyn and his mount, Frankie felt free to gawk. And indeed the young lady seated in the blue silk-lined vehicle was no doubt accustomed to such scrutiny, though perhaps not from a member of her own sex.

For the intruder managed to cast even the lovely Venetia Sellars in the shade. Her eyes were a trifle larger and of a deeper blue. Her cheeks were rosier, though it did occur to Frankie to wonder if they had some help in this department. And her hair was of a slightly more golden tint. In fact, the stranger was definitely the type Lord Greville Wainwright favored. Frankie looked in his direction to see if he had yet succumbed. But he seemed impervious to the beauty's charm and was, in fact, studying Evelyn's face with something close to amusement on his own.

The lady's smile was apologetic and took in the whole group. But her low and vibrant voice, with only the slightest trace of an accent to betray her antecedents, addressed Evelyn once again. "What a fortuitous circumstance, Mr. Yarwood, to find you out so early in the park. May I presume to request a few words with you?" She smiled once more at his companions. "I promise I shall not detain him long."

"Then why do we not ride on ahead?" Lady Paxton suggested, her face giving no clue whatsoever to her thoughts. "You know our direction, Mr. Yarwood."

Evelyn was looking thunderous, Frankie saw, feeling rather sorry for the lovely lady and wondering what she might have done to incur his wrath. Indeed, everyone was behaving most awkwardly, she noticed as she prodded her horse gently with her boot heel. The two Wainwrights were as expressionless as cardsharps, while Lady Paxton's eyes were twinkling with amusement. Lady Venetia's color had heightened considerably, as if in competition, and her lips were tightly compressed.

"Who is she?" Frankie inquired of Lord Greville as soon as they were out of earshot. He was riding between the two young women in the wake of the senior members of the party. "It was odd of Evelyn not to introduce us."

"It was rather, now you mention it." Lord Greville seemed

99

to be enjoying a private joke, but Lady Venetia shot Frankie a set-down look across his chestnut. And suddenly the light dawned. "Oh, my goodness!" Miss Armstead blurted. "Don't tell me that she's a Fashionable Impure!"

"I'm sure that no one intends to tell you that." Lady Venetia spoke icily.

"Tsk, tsk," his lordship chided in low, reproving tones, "Don't you know that no lady speaks of such things, Miss Armstead?" Frankie looked at him suspiciously, somehow divining that he might soon fall right off his horse in helpless laughter.

"Oh, do they not? Well, then, I stand reproved. Though I fail to see why it's so much worse for me to say aloud that she's Evelyn's light-skirt than for you both to know it and pretend not to."

His lordship did choke then. Her ladyship shot Miss Armstead a look that almost blasted her from the saddle, then spurred ahead to join Lady Maria and Lord Wainwright.

"Well, I've said the wrong thing again," Frankie muttered to herself.

"Is that supposed to be a newsworthy observation? Should I perhaps contact the *Gazette*?"

Frankie chose to ignore his jabs. Instead she said, "Well, since I've already sunk myself below reproach, you might just as well go ahead and tell me who she is."

"What makes you think I'd know?" He tried to look affronted.

"Oh, you know all right. Gentlemen, so I've been told, always seem to know that sort of thing. Which doesn't say a lot for your sex, Lord Greville." She cut short any rebuttal he might have made by adding, "Besides, I saw that knowing look that passed between you and your grandfather. Now, that does shock me, I'll admit. That such an upright gentleman as Lord Wainwright—and an ancient one at that— should instantly recognize Evelyn's demirep friend—well, it's most disillusioning."

Lord Greville whooped then, causing the others to turn and look at them curiously. "In justice to my grandfather, Miss Armstead," he said when he'd recovered, "let me suggest that it was the type he recognized, and not the person."

"Well, frankly I don't see how." She frowned thoughtfully. "True, she is very beautiful, which must needs be a prerequisite, I should think." She looked up at his lordship questioningly.

"No doubt it helps," he answered solemnly.

"Then she must get on splendidly, for I've never seen a lovelier female in my life. I thought she quite cast your Lady Venetia in the shade, don't you agree?"

"No, I do not," he answered firmly.

"Well, there's no accounting for taste, then, is there?" She smiled at him mischievously. "You still have not told me who she is. And don't deny you know her, for I'll not believe it."

"But you forget that I've spent most of my adult life at sea, Miss Armstead."

"Not all, though," she answered shrewdly. "However if you're determined not to say, I can't force you."

"True. And since I am several years your senior, perhaps you won't take it amiss when I point out that this conversation has been most improper, as Lady Venetia's example indicated."

Frankie gave him a scornful look. "Well, I certainly didn't expect you to be as prim and proper as she is. Nor did I think to have to stand on points with you after what we've been through together."

"What we've been through?" He looked at her in astonishment. "You've lost me again, Miss Armstead. I can't think what that could be except"—he choked—"a certain upstairs window."

"I simply meant," she answered haughtily, "that since from the first our acquaintance has not been built upon the artificial rules of polite society, I felt that I could speak my mind freely to you without fear of censure. I see that I was wrong and that you're every bit as starchy as Lady Venetia. You two are obviously made for each other. I wish you joy of it." She urged her mount forward to join the others and he followed, a length behind.

The gallop required for Evelyn Yarwood to overtake their party could have been the reason he was looking flustered as he rode up. For there was no doubt that his usual urbanity was missing. Frankie knew him well enough, however, to realize that he was mortified by his encounter with the Fashionable Impure. Nor did she believe that his embarrassment was on her account. She was quick to see that he was assessing the reactions of Lady Venetia and Lord Wainwright in that order.

He rallied quickly, however, with a rueful smile. "I do beg pardon for the delay."

Lord Wainwright graciously accepted Evelyn's apology. Then he and Lady Paxton took the lead once more. As the others followed, Evelyn confided in a lowered voice, "My first inclination was to ignore it when that—uh—personage accosted me." He was the image of injured rectitude as he continued. "But now I am very glad, in one sense at least, that I did not deliver the snub that I'd intended. For the creature actually wished to do me a good turn. Or to be more accurate, to do my brother a good turn."

"Bertie?" Frankie blurted in disbelief.

"Do keep your voice down," Evelyn cautioned, glancing at the two chaperones, who were once more absorbed in their own conversation. "If Lord Wainwright should get wind of Bertie's—er, peccadilloes—he might in all conscience feel obliged to report the matter to our father. I do beg your pardon, Greville."

"Not at all," his lordship murmured, his face as usual revealing nothing of his thoughts.

"But I don't understand." Frankie obligingly lowered her voice to a whisper level. "What does Bertie have to say to the fact that a ladybird fairly snatched you from our midst?"

For just a fleeting moment Lord Greville's face lost a bit of its impassivity, while Evelyn appeared inclined to throttle his bride-to-be. "Bertie has everything to do with it," he snapped, "as I'm trying to explain, if you'll stop interrupting." Frankie looked chastened and he continued. "The lady—er, young woman, I should say—said she recognized me by my close resemblance to my brother."

"You and Bertie look alike? Well, strange I never noticed it and I've known you both forever. You are much better—still, come to think on it, Aunt Maria did say much the same thing when she first—"

"Miss Armstead." Lord Greville's voice was calm and low,

but there was still about it a quality of one accustomed to command. "Do be quiet a moment and allow Evelyn to continue."

"Oh, I am sorry. Do go on."

"Thank you," Mr. Yarwood remarked dryly. "As I was saying, the young person recognized me—by whatever method—and having become, er, 'friendly' with my brother, and no doubt sizing him up for the flat he is," he added disparagingly, "she thought it in his best interests to warn me that the young idiot is flying too high by far. Or to be more precise, that Bertie's been playing deep at the gambling tables and has got himself into hock to Carter the moneylender himself."

"Bertie!" In spite of all her resolutions, Frankie was shocked once more out of her silence. "Oh, how could he?" Her cry was truly anguished.

"Just what I've been wondering myself," Bertie's brother muttered.

"I should have thought that he of all people would have had more sense than to be taken in by cards. After all he's had to say about how sapskulled you—" The look of pure venom that Evelyn shot at Frankie brought her up short. "How sapskulled you always said such conduct is," she finished lamely.

"It is certainly most regrettable, but not at all unusual, I understand, for a young man upon his first visit to the Metropolis to lose his head a bit." The world-wise Lady Venetia tried to set some of Evelyn's obvious anxiety to rest. "I'm sure your brother will come about, Mr. Yarwood. And be all the better for the lesson he has learned."

Evelyn flashed his beautiful smile. It was filled with gratitude. "Perhaps you are right, Lady Venetia. Certainly for Bertie's sake—and for the family's—I pray so."

The two of them rode ahead, for the path narrowed, while Lady Venetia filled Evelyn in on a series of examples from her acquaintance with young men who had had one bad experience at the gaming tables only to become completely reformed characters.

Miss Armstead's view of the situation was not quite so charitable. "Just wait till I get my hands on Bertie Yarwood," she muttered between clenched teeth.

Lord Greville, who unlike her seemed to have had his original bad humor blown away by the morning ride and now appeared to be enjoying himself almost as much as his grandfather, chuckled suddenly. "Oh, come now, Miss Armstead, you surely don't think that young Bertie has had any dealing with that Exquisite we saw back there. I think you give him too much credit. Or too little, if you prefer."

"Are you implying that Evelyn is lying?" Frankie appeared very haughty then indeed. "Jealousy does not become you, Lord Greville." She looked pointedly at the two blond heads, as close together as their horses would permit, in earnest conversation. "I know you are determined to think as little of Evelyn as possible."

"Now, there you are wrong. Think little of Yarwood? Quite the contrary, in fact. I find my admiration for him growing by leaps and bounds. Also I've decided that you and he seem perfectly suited to each other. I had not thought such a thing possible, but I now must concede that he may well be your equal in inventiveness. Or, forgive me, possibly your superior."

Miss Armstead used a term to describe his lordship that she'd heard the groom employ when he'd thought himself well out of earshot. Lord Greville remained unruffled. "Yes, now I think on it," he continued, "you and Yarwood are even better suited than Lady Venetia and I. While she and I have only, 'starchiness,' I believe you said, as our chief bond, just think of the tedious hours you and he can while away telling each other your fabrications. Just a minute there, Miss Armstead." He forestalled a furious departure by reaching over and taking a firm hold on her horse's bridle. "Before you ride off in high dudgeon, satisfy my curiosity on one small point."

"Yes?" Miss Armstead inquired icily.

"Explain if you can," Lord Greville inquired softly, "just why you were so much more shaken by young Bertie's alleged flurry at the tables and his intimacy with a Cyprian than you were when your betrothed seemed to be the culprit."

104

Chapter
Eleven

THE FACT THAT SHE'D BEEN UNABLE TO SUPPLY A READY
answer to Greville Wainwright's impertinent question and
had flounced off—or as nearly as one can flounce on horseback—and had snubbed him for the remainder of the ride did
not cool Miss Armstead's ire at Bertie Yarwood. Indeed, when
that unsuspecting young gentleman paid a morning call next
day, it was his misfortune to step into a hornet's nest.

"Good lord, Frankie, I don't even know the Gilded Lily."
Mr. Yarwood had tried to exit with the last of the callers in
Grosvenor Square, but Frankie had dragged him back to sit beside her on the sofa. "At least I suppose it must be her you're
talking about. That is, if the woman in the park actually was a
Nonpareil, for I've known you to call some pretty odd-looking
females 'beauties.' Elizabeth Pembroke, for example. Why,
she's actually horse-faced!"

"Bertie! Forget Elizabeth Pembroke. This woman was a
Nonpareil. Ask Greville Wainwright if you don't believe me.
No, don't," she quickly qualified.

"All right, then, if she was a Nonpareil and if she was a
Cyprian, and for the sake of argument we'll say she was"—he
forestalled another outburst—"then given the yellow hair and
the blue silk carriage, it must have been Lily O'Malley. They
call her the Gilded Lily. Because of her hair I suppose too, but
mostly because she's the highest-paid light-skirt in the business. That's her own carriage she was driving. She owns a

house in York Place. And they say her jewels would make Queen Charlotte green with envy." Bertie was warming up to the subject. "And as for her—er—'clients,' well"—he lowered his voice—"she's been visited by Royalty—bigwigs in the government—top-ranking officers—only the genuine Nabobs can walk up her stairs, believe me. So how you can accuse me of—really, Frankie, you're shatter-brained even to think it."

She was finally convinced that Bertie was quite incapable of lying so convincingly. "Well, then, if you aren't a—particular friend of hers, whatever made her say such a thing?"

"That's easy enough," he answered promptly. "Of course she didn't."

"You mean Evelyn just made the whole thing up?"

"Stands to reason, don't it? But think just a minute, Frankie, before you go flying off up into the boughs. What was he to do? You can't go admitting to a gaggle of females, not to mention the two top Nabobs from your home neighborhood, that you're on easy terms with the most famous light-skirt in London, can you?"

"You can as readily do that as to say that your brother is on easy terms with her." Frankie's tone was censorious.

"Well, I grant you I don't like it above half either, but Evelyn had to say something, and I expect it was all he could think of on the spur of the moment," he said charitably. "I expect he was afraid Lord Wainwright would report him to Father. You know how that generation is. Sticklers to duty."

"Well, as far as that goes, he may well tell Mr. Yarwood that you're the Gilded Lily's pet and that you've just gambled away the family fortune. Oh, my heavens. I just assumed that part's not true either. It isn't, is it?"

"Good lord, no. The family fortune's already been disposed of. And as for Lord Wainwright telling Papa that I've been sowing my wild oats, well, it don't signify. He won't believe it."

Frankie looked impressed. "Why, Bertie, I'd no idea your father thought so highly of you."

"He don't," the second son answered promptly. "Thinks I'm a numbskull. Heard him say so any number of times. He happens to know, though, that I ain't one for gaming. Or the petti-coat line either, when it comes to that."

"Well, I'm glad." Frankie's face reflected strong disapproval. "For I can't help but believe that either one is reprehensible—no matter how accepted it is among gentlemen of the ton.

"But there's one thing I don't pretend to understand, Bertie. If as you say the Lily chooses her—friends—from only the very rich, how does it happen that Evelyn?—"

"I've wondered that myself. And all I can think of is that even a Venus Mendicant, when all's said and done, is still a female. And you of all people should know there's no one to beat Evelyn when it comes to getting on the good side of one of those." If after that statement Frankie was mentally agreeing with the absent Mr. Yarwood's assessment of his younger son's brainpower, Bertie was too filled by pride in his brother's social success to take note of it. "I guess the Gilded Lily just simply likes Evelyn. It ain't to be wondered at too much, when you stop to think on it. Most of her customers are oldish coves. Bald, I expect, with paunches. And there's no denying that Evelyn's devilishly good-looking. Makes a nice change, I shouldn't wonder." He suddenly stopped his musing and frowned reprovingly. "But really, Frankie, this conversation won't do, you know. We really shouldn't be having it. Can't think what got into me. Except I was caught off-guard by the idea that the Lily was talking about my affairs—which is ridiculous; she wouldn't have been. But we've been through all that. What I'm saying is that if I hadn't been set back on my heels, I'd never have dreamed of talking about light-skirts and such with you. For it ain't the thing. Not having a mother has kept you from being up to snuff in a lot of areas, Frankie." He was trying nobly to make allowances. "But take my word for it. A lady does not discuss Cyprians. At least not with a gentle-man," he qualified. "Lord knows what a pack of cackling fe-males get up to on their own."

"You can spare me your lectures, Bertie," Miss Armstead informed him. "I've already had that one, done up brown."

"Lady Paxton tried to set you right, then, did she?"

"No. Lord Greville Wainwright."

"What a whisker! Really, Frankie"—Bertie sighed—"you do need to learn to put a curb on that tongue of yours. Anybody who didn't know you as well as I do might not realize you're funning."

Mr. Yarwood almost succeeded in taking his leave then. But he had not quite made it out the front door, which Dearborn was holding open for him, when Frankie came running down the steps after him. "Oh, Bertie, hold up just a minute, will you?"

The young man turned toward her with a pained "what now?" look upon his face. "Really, Frankie, I've told you twice now that I'm due at the Scarboroughs'."

"This won't take a minute. Have you been to the Tower yet?"

"No. I tried to go once, remember? There's nobody like you, Frankie, for messing up a fellow's plans."

"Good. Then will you take me? I don't mean just to the Menagerie, but to Astley's Royal Circus and the Egyptian Hall—you know, all those places one longs to see but never can because the people who live here are bored to distraction at the very idea."

"My God, Frankie, what do you take me for, a tour guide?"

"No. I wouldn't trust you to find anything. Or know what it was even if you saw it. But I can't go alone. Please, Bertie."

Whether it was the pleading look in the large dark eyes or the memory of his pressing engagement that moved Bertie to acquiesce remained a mystery. "Oh, all right," he said rather ungraciously, and the thing was done.

"Next Friday, then," Frankie called from the doorway as he, like Greville Wainwright, leaped the marble steps. The only reply was a wave of the hand. Whether it was meant for her or the hackney cab coming around the corner, Frankie had no way of knowing.

During the next several days the only glimpses Frankie caught of Greville Wainwright were on those rare occasions when their entrances or exits to and from their separate houses coincided. But even then Lord Greville was, or seemed, unaware of her presence.

108

His grandfather, on the other hand, was very much in evidence. Not only did he squire Lady Paxton to several social events; he was often to be found with her in the yellow saloon drinking tea. Frankie returned from a shopping trip on one such occasion to find them, plus Evelyn Yarwood, with their heads together. Lord Wainwright was in the midst of an anecdote that the other two seemed to be enjoying. The threesome, Frankie was told when she drew up a cross-framed stool and accepted a cup of tea, had just decided to celebrate the first rainless day in four by driving in the park. When they urged her to accompany them during the fashionable hour of five Frankie made the excuse of wishing to finish Maria Edgeworth's latest novel.

After a bit, while his lordship went next door to order his carriage sent around and Lady Paxton excused herself to don her wrap, Frankie commented to Evelyn on the oddness of the expedition. "Won't you be bored to distraction in such company? I think Lord Wainwright is quite the nicest man I have ever met, but he hardly seems your style. Nor does my aunt Maria, though I doubt that anyone could possibly be bored with her."

"No indeed." Evelyn, for once, allowed himself to sound enthusiastic. "In fact, she's amazing. She somehow manages to make the younger beauties seem quite gauche. Present company excepted, of course." He smiled his engaging smile. "You are quite like your aunt, you know."

"Thank you," she answered politely, at the same time wondering how it was that Evelyn always seemed to know just which sort of compliment would please a person most.

If Evelyn noted a bit of reserve in her attitude, he gave no sign. "As for Lord Wainwright," he continued, "I do enjoy his company. He's a delightful old gentleman. Quite unlike his heir, who seems totally absorbed with his own self-consequence. Besides," he added with a mischievous grin, "being in Lord Wainwright's company won't do me any harm with my bucolic father, and being in Lady Paxton's good graces should make things easier with your uncle. So I do have ulterior motives, you see. I would not want you to think I'm a reformed character."

Frankie laughed then in spite of herself, and some of the tension that had grown up between them since the encounter with the Gilded Lily eased a bit. "You're wrong on one count, though," she added seriously. "Being in Aunt Maria's good graces won't help you at all where Uncle Matthew is concerned. He doesn't really approve of her, you see, and would not have sent me here had I not already sunk myself below reproach."

Mr. Yarwood, with a few well-chosen epithets, let it be known just what he thought of Mr. Matthew Armstead. "A priggish old antidote" was the most complimentary.

"I do wish you would not talk so about Uncle Matthew," Frankie protested. "He has always been kindness itself to me and I'm very fond of him. And I do wish above all things"— here her lip trembled slightly—"that I had not given cause to make him feel ridiculous. Uncle Matthew's dignity is v-very important to him."

"Not thinking of crying off, are you, Frankie?" The tone of voice was light, but the blue eyes narrowed.

"N-no, of course not. But it's just that—"

Whatever reservations Frankie was feeling had to remain unexpressed, for they were joined at that moment by Lady Paxton, who was looking even more ravishing than usual, so her niece thought, in a merino pelisse of a deep rose color adorned with white fur tippets.

After saying good-bye to the handsome pair and bidding them enjoy the carriage ride, Frankie retired to her bed chamber, sank down upon the couch there, and picked up Miss Edgeworth's novel. But although the book had been highly recommended to her, somehow the celebrated author failed to charm Miss Armstead. In fact she caught herself staring, unseeing, at the printed words for minutes at a time.

And during the following days Frankie was hard pressed to discover why it was that she had suddenly become disenchanted with the Metropolis. Certainly there had been no lessening of her popularity. Cards of invitation continued to be delivered to Grosvenor Square. She and Lady Paxton had, in fact, a great deal of difficulty choosing among so many.

But even a card to attend Almack's failed to bring a sparkle to her eyes.

"Really, Frankie," her aunt chided during the ride to the Assembly Rooms on King Street the following Wednesday evening, "I don't think you realize how privileged you are to be attending Almack's." They were enjoying the comfortable cushions of Lord Wainwright's well-sprung carriage.

"It's true, m'dear," his lordship chuckled. "It's easier to be asked to take tea with the queen than to get on the list at Almack's."

Frankie did smile back, if a bit wanly. She knew, though, that while his lordship perhaps exaggerated the case, there was truth in what he said. Almack's was where the crème de la crème of society met to dance, to gossip, to sip lemonade and cold tea, consume bread and butter and stale cake, but most of all to see and to be seen. Not for nothing was it called the Marriage Mart. And ladies of the ton schemed and connived for invitations into this Seventh Heaven of the Fashionable World. It was, however, presided over by a group of patronesses more formidable than Cerberus, who guarded Hades, since their function was in the main to keep the undesirables from entering. And many a young lady and young gentleman were cast into utter despair when they found themselves barred from that exclusive world.

"I do know that I'm fortunate, Aunt Maria." Frankie tried to put enthusiasm into her voice. "And I owe it all to you. I'm most grateful, truly I am."

Her aunt looked mollified. "I don't think it's true that you owe it all to me, m'dear. You deserve some credit. Ladies Jersey and Cowper seemed quite taken with you at your come-out party. But if you should thank anyone, it is Lord Wainwright here. I have not told you that he spoke of you to Princess Esterhazy."

"Oh, did you indeed!" Frankie turned impulsively to give the old gentleman a hug. "How excessively kind of you."

"Frankie!" her aunt scolded. "You really should learn to control yourself. What must his lordship be thinking?"

Nothing adverse evidently, from the pleased look on the

aristocratic face. "Harrumph, leave the chit alone, m'dear," he said. "Didn't you just give her a set-down for not being pleased over her invitation? That's the trouble with you ladies; charming as you are, you've no notion of consistency."

Frankie's demonstration had been due, however, far more to the fact that his lordship had been moved to trouble himself on her behalf than from any great desire to visit Almack's. Still, when they entered the sanctum sanctorum she was soon caught up in its atmosphere, attributable far more to its reputation for exclusiveness than to the remarkableness of its decor. And it was impossible not to feel at least a twinge of excitement, Frankie found, as his lordship pointed out leading figures of the ton to her. When these notables included no less a personage than the Duke of Clarence, his majesty's third son, she began to appreciate her opportunity and memorized his features to describe to Uncle Matthew.

But of more personal interest was the sight of Lord Greville Wainwright dancing, as they entered, with Lady Venetia Sellars. Frankie and Lord Wainwright spied them at the same moment, evidently, for his lordship breathed a sigh that sounded like relief. "Ahh, there's Greville. Glad to see him out and about again. Don't know what's got into the lad of late. He's been moping around the house, blue-deviled as can be."

Before Frankie could think of an appropriate comment, her hand was claimed by an admirer. Her two chaperones took themselves off to join some mutual acquaintance they spied.

The evening flew swiftly by. If Frankie was not permanently extracted from her fit of the mopes, she at least was given a brief reprieve. She was greatly in demand, and it was almost ten o'clock, when the festivities at Almack's would come to a close, before she finally was at liberty to sink down upon a chair and fan herself.

"I don't believe it," a dry voice remarked. Frankie looked up to see Lord Greville standing above her with folded arms, studying her intently. "The indefatigable Miss Armstead has finally collapsed. I've been trying to get near enough to solicit a dance all evening, but to be quite honest, I, too, would rather sit. Do you mind?" He nodded at the vacant chair next to her own.

"Oh, no. Please do." Frankie was a bit surprised to hear the warmth that suffused her voice and realized that she had just bestowed a smile upon his lordship that caused him to look momentarily startled. To cover her subsequent embarrassment she remarked as he sat down, "I collect that you are here with Lady Venetia and her parents. She looks remarkably like her mother. Do you not think so?"

He laughed at that. "Well, Miss Armstead, I was put off guard there for a moment by your cordiality, so you got me with your first rapier thrust. No, I do not think Lady Venetia looks like her mother, who must weigh at least eleven stone."

"I meant in her features and her coloring," Frankie said heatedly. "I was not referring to her weight."

"Oh, were you not?" His eyebrows rose.

"No, I wasn't. Though when it comes to that, Lady Venetia will probably look just that way in thirty years."

"Whereas you, Miss Armstead, will doubtlessly remain sylphlike forever. Like your uncle Matthew, for example?"

"Touché," she answered, then added, "I am sorry. I was very glad to see you, and I don't know why we always have to be at daggers drawn."

"Given our history, I don't find that half as puzzling as why you were glad to see me." He was looking at her rather oddly.

"I don't know either," she answered candidly. "I expect it's because you're from Hampshire. I own to being a trifle homesick right now."

He smiled crookedly. "You must be, indeed, to sentimentalize our first meeting. Hampshire or not, that memory has to be painful for both of us."

"That's certainly true," Frankie glared, "but I am getting a bit wearied of reminding you that it was *not* our first meeting."

"Oh, yes, the house party," he replied meekly. "I do beg pardon. But tell me this, Miss Armstead. How can you possibly be homesick for Hampshire here of all places? Don't you realize how many young ladies of quality—not even to mention their encroaching mamas—would kill to be in your position?"

"Talking to you, you mean?" She looked astonished.

"No, peagoose. Spending an evening at Almack's. But let me applaud you on your good sense. This place makes even me homesick for Hampshire. Or the Caucasus, come to that."

"You actually do not enjoy Almack's?"

"I find it a damned bore," he answered emphatically.

"Then why did you come? Oh, yes, of course. Lady Venetia likes it, I suppose. We've come full circle."

"Yes, I suppose she does. Most beautiful young ladies do. I expect it's perdition itself for the ones that never take," he observed with remarkable insight as they glanced at a group of rather plain young ladies sitting together with determined smiles fixed upon their faces. "But actually it was her father who was so set upon my accompanying them here tonight. He made such a point of it in fact that I couldn't possibly cry off without appearing boorish."

"Well, that's odd, for when I saw Lord Sellars he was dozing in a corner. Why do you suppose he wished to come here?"

"I expect it was because this was the one place he could be sure of my being in his daughter's company without having your Evelyn Yarwood for a rival."

"I don't know what you mean," she replied, bristling.

"Of course you do. You surely must be aware that he's constantly in her pocket. By the way, forgive me—this is tactless, I realize—but is Yarwood aware that he's betrothed to you? I know the question is indelicate"—he grinned—"but having been in the same spurious position myself and having observed his pursuit of Venetia, it has occurred to me that he might be totally in the dark as to your relationship."

"That is an odious thing to say!" Frankie's temper flared. "He most certainly is aware of our betrothal. Which does not mean that he has to dance attendance upon me. In fact, as you well know, he has been expressly forbidden by my guardian and his father to do so."

"Well, then, I must commend his compliance. I never suspected Yarwood of possessing such a sense of duty."

"I'm beginning to understand," Miss Armstead said frostily, "how Lady Venetia might prefer someone with Evelyn's amiable qualities. Don't you think then that you should take a cue from your future papa and go seek her out while you have a clear field? Since, as you have pointed out, Evelyn—yes, and Bertie too, of course—is not blue-blooded enough for admission here—as indeed I am not either; but then your grandfather vouched for me, and I'm sure no one ever doubts a Wainwright's worthiness—" She was in full spate now, but suddenly Lord Greville looked diverted.

"My grandfather vouched for you?"

"Yes, but I'm sure you can lock him in one of Alton Hall's towers when you get him home. That's the usual thing with Bedlamites, is it not?"

"Miss Armstead." His lordship's patience was becoming sorely tried. "Will you please come down off your high ropes and attend to me? You're in a better position to observe than I, but it strikes me that my grandfather has been spending an inordinate amount of time in the company of your aunt. Is this not so?"

"I don't know about 'inordinate.' " She rolled the word dangerously off her tongue. "But yes, they are quite often together. Is there anything wrong with that?"

"I don't know," the other answered slowly. "I certainly hope not. But given the change that's come over my grandfather in the last few weeks, plus your aunt's well-known penchant for marrying elderly gentlemen of means—there could be." Frankie stared at him in astonishment. But there was no mistaking the fact that he was serious. And concerned. "I'm genuinely fond of the old fellow." He spoke as much to himself as for her ears, it seemed. "And I'd hate to see him make a fool of himself after all these years."

Frankie was coming dangerously close to apoplexy. Indeed it was most fortunate that the last dance came to an end at just that moment and the guests began to mill about. That and the fact that Lord Greville rose abruptly to his feet saved him from possibly being the only gentleman ever to be struck sharply with an ivory fan there in the sacred halls of Almack's.

Chapter
Twelve

FRANKIE HAD BEEN LOOKING FORWARD TO SIGHT-SEEING as a welcome break in a round of social obligations that were rapidly becoming tedious. It would be a relief to explore London and not feel required to be on her best behavior. Bertie, however, she soon discovered, did not share her anticipation.

They had set out at an early hour with Frankie clutching the guide book she'd purchased, determined to see as much as possible. Mr. Yarwood bore up well enough during Westminster Abbey, flagged a bit at the British Museum, grew glassy-eyed at the Elgin Marbles, and absolutely refused to enter the portals of St. Paul's. "I thought you wished to sight-see," Frankie finally snapped in exasperation. "What is your trouble, anyhow?"

"Well, my feet for one thing." He looked grimly down at his golden-tasseled Hessians that gleamed, à la Beau Brummell, by means of a blacking dampened with champagne. "These damn boots are too tight. Don't tell Evelyn, though. He did tell me to go to Hoby for them, but this other cove was cheaper."

"Oh, for heaven's sake, Bertie, anyone should have more sense than to break in new boots on a sight-seeing tour."

"Well, frankly, it ain't just the boots. Truth is, I've had my fill of dead things."

He did, however, agree reluctantly to visit the Tower of London and seemed to forget the pinching boots in examining the various instruments of torture and visiting the Menagerie. But then he declared firmly that he'd had enough.

"You'd had enough before we even started," Frankie said to him accusingly. "Really, Bertie, I don't know why you ever agreed to come. The only things in London you've shown the slightest interest in are clocks. I've never known you to be so conscious of the time. You've been on pins and needles for the past two hours. All right, then, never mind, I'll let you off the hook. Though you did promise to spend the whole day, remember?"

"I know I did," her escort grumbled. "But I didn't know what a dead bore those museums and churches would turn out to be. And I certainly didn't know how hard they'd be on a cove's feet."

"Well"—Frankie frowned down at her map while the hackney coachman held the horses patiently near the entrance to the Tower—"now that we're this close I'd certainly like to go and take a look at the new docks." Bertie opened his mouth to expostulate, but she forestalled his protest with a withering "That certainly won't hurt your feet. All you have to do is sit in the coach."

"Oh, all right, then, but this'd better be it, Frankie," he mumbled ungraciously, and gave the coachman orders to drive on.

Long before they reached the docks they smelled them. With a martyred gesture Bertie extracted a snowy handkerchief from up his sleeve and clapped it to his nose as they drew near the water. Frankie, however, was too fascinated with the ships that thronged the harbor to be overly concerned with unpleasant odors. There were brigs and pleasure boats, men-of-war and merchant ships, barges piled high with cargo. Foreign flags seemed to outnumber the Union Jack, and the garbs and tongues of the various nationalities noisily conducting business gave the place an international coloring that was strange and most exotic to landlubber eyes.

Bertie, however, seemed more occupied with the chaos on dry land, where stevedores and travelers, carts and carriages, horses, dogs, cats, and rats milled about in a mass of apparent confusion. Frankie was astonished to hear her friend suddenly exclaim, "I say, look who's here!" How anyone could pick out an acquaintance amidst such bedlam, was more than she could know. "It's Lord Greville. Oh, I say, what luck!"

Frankie looked at him in amazement. Sure enough, as she herself had just confirmed, Lord Greville, seated alone in a high perch phaeton that afforded a marvelous view, no doubt, of the twenty acres devoted to England's sea-going commerce, was gazing pensively at the water. But why the sight of him should seem fortuitous to Bertie was more than she could comprehend, for Bertie, overawed by his lordship, was usually inclined to dodge him. She did not have to wonder about it long, however. After commanding their jarvey, "Hold up right here," her escort jumped from the hackney and reached a hand up to Frankie. "Come on quick, before he decides to leave."

"I have no wish to intrude myself upon Lord Greville Wainwright," she informed him. The memory of her last encounter with that gentleman still rankled.

"Well, I have," Bertie retorted, "and since we've been doing what you've wanted to do all day, it's high time I had a turn."

Frankie could not deny the justice of the statement. She climbed reluctantly from the carriage and allowed him to pull her through the crowd until they stood gazing up at the driver of the phaeton.

Lord Greville's mind seemed a million miles away. He not only was unaware of their presence, but also he seemed equally oblivious to all the noise and bustle. His eyes gazed seaward, but Frankie wondered if they actually were focused on anything. Indeed his aspect was quite trancelike.

Bertie cleared his throat. "Oh, I say, Lord Greville," he remarked diffidently, seeming of a sudden to doubt the propriety of accosting a mere acquaintance.

The other gazed down at them blankly and then seemed to wrench himself back into the present. "Miss Armstead—and Yarwood, isn't it? What the devil are you two doing here?"

As always Frankie found herself bristling at his tone, but Bertie seemed to find the question perfectly reasonable. "We're out sight-seeing," he answered with a notable lack of

118

enthusiasm. "And the thing is, you see, Frankie here would insist on seeing every old tomb in Westminster Abbey and every broken-up statue that Lord Elgin brought back from Greece, not to mention walking my feet right out from under me. But the whole thing is, you see, I did promise her the whole day, but that was before I knew there was to be this mill at Five Court. Bulldog Burke is fighting the Ferocious Frederick, you see. Oh, my God"—Bertie's eager face fell suddenly—"but of course you'd know that."

"How on earth would he know a stupid thing like that?" Miss Armstead interrupted witheringly.

"Don't be such a ninny-hammer," he replied in kind. "Any knowing 'un would. But Lord Greville in particular would be up to snuff. He strips with Gentleman Jackson himself." Bertie's voice was filled with awe.

In contrast, Miss Armstead sounded a trifle shocked. "He does what?" she asked as his lordship broke into a grin.

"Strips with Jackson," her escort replied impatiently. "And more than one cove has told me that Jackson said there ain't a gentleman around half so handy with his fives."

"Oh." The light was slowly beginning to dawn. "You mean he boxes." She wrinkled her small nose and sniffed.

"He doesn't just box." Bertie was becoming incensed in direct proportion to Greville's increased amusement. "I've been trying to tell you, Frankie; he's the top of the trees."

"How nice," Miss Armstead murmured flatly, while Bertie said apologetically to his lordship, "Shouldn't have bothered you now. For of course you'll be going."

"No, as a matter of fact, I'm not planning to attend the fight."

"Oh, I say, that is famous!" The sun of Bertie's countenance was abeam once more. "Then I was wondering—would you—since you do live next door and all—would you mind taking Frankie home? If I take her, you see, I'll miss the thing. Most of it anyhow."

"Bertie!" Miss Armstead protested.

"Oh, I should think you would miss all of it," was Lord Greville's opinion. "I don't think myself that Frederick can last more than six rounds with Burke."

"You think not?" Bertie began to swell with pride. "Thought the same myself. Fact is, I put a fiver on the Bulldog."

"Bertie, you never gamble. Or so you told me." Miss Armstead sounded dangerous. She was completely out of charity with her escort.

"It ain't a gamble. It's a sure thing. You just heard his lordship."

"He's right, you know," Greville offered. "But to answer your question, Yarwood, I'll be happy to escort Miss Armstead home." He was climbing down from the phaeton to hand her up.

Frankie turned toward Bertie and tried to convey with a series of contorted facial expressions that she desired him to change his mind. It didn't work. If Bertie rightly interpreted her pantomime, he chose to ignore it. "Oh, I say, thanks ever so much, Lord Greville," he said with heartfelt gratitude. "And don't worry, Frankie. I'll be back in plenty of time to take you to Astley's Royal Circus. I promise." He could not possibly have failed to hear the anguished "Bertie!" she hissed at him as he turned and fled, but he did not let it deter him or even break his stride.

Lord Greville heard, though, and chuckled. "Come on, Miss Armstead. You might as well give in gracefully. Not even you, in that fetching bonnet, can possibly hope to compete with Bulldog Burke and Ferocious Frederick. Face it, little one; no female could."

There was nothing for it then but to grit her teeth and put a gloved hand in his and be helped up onto the seat of his magnificent equipage.

"Oh, what a view," she breathed when she reached that elevation. The sunlight sparkling on the water, the forest of masts nearby, the white sails moving as a backdrop in the distance, seemed the most splendid thing she had seen all day. It was easy to understand how Lord Greville had succumbed completely to its spell.

"Yes, it is rather splendid," he answered her. "Are you in a great hurry or would you mind sitting here for a while?"

"I should like it above all things," she answered. "In point of fact this will be the only spot on my entire tour that I was not rushed through."

He laughed and they sat in silence for a while till Frankie broke it. "It was the other way around, wasn't it?"

"I beg your pardon?"

"The fight you had with Evelyn when you were boys. You blackened his eye. Not vice versa."

"Well, yes. But as I recall, the episode didn't reflect much credit on either of us."

"There was no reason to lie about it." Her voice was expressionless. "I can't imagine why he did."

Lord Greville shrugged. "Who knows? Perhaps he honestly forgot. Or perhaps he merely wished to impress you. That's rather understandable."

"The thing is," she continued after the slightest of pauses, "I doubt he even had a reason. Evelyn is rather unreliable, actually."

He gave her a sideways glance. "Well, perhaps that's not such a bad thing. Reliability is often judged as dullness."

"I don't agree. It's a quality I've admired greatly in my uncle Matthew. No, that isn't true," she amended in a rush of insight. "It's a quality I always simply took for granted. *Now* I admire it."

"I see," he commented gravely. "Well, have you given any thought to the other Yarwood? The one they want you to marry? Forgive me, as you know I am prejudiced, but he strikes me as being quite superior to his brother."

"Bertie?" It was obvious from her tone that the suggestion held little merit in her eyes. "No, Bertie and I would never deal together. Besides"—she was hard-pressed to keep from sounding the least bit affronted—"Bertie has not the slightest desire to marry me."

His lordship, to her disgust, laughed aloud at that. "I expect he doesn't consider himself up to the weight."

"What's that supposed to mean?" she replied, bristling.

"Simply that he could not go two rounds with you, Miss Armstead."

"I'm well aware of your opinion of me. There is no need to keep rubbing it in."

"I doubt you know anything of the kind," he answered evenly.

"Well, it doesn't signify. What I do want your opinion of is why you think it would be such a disaster if your grandfather married my aunt. Not that I think for a moment there's a possibility. I just resent the fact that you seem to think she is not good enough."

"I never said that. I simply think the whole idea is ludicrous. For a man of his age to marry, I mean."

"Well, I don't agree. Why not wed if he wants a cheerful companion who enjoys his company?—and I can see he might."

Lord Greville did not fail to recognize the insult and to counterpunch. "While she in her turn gets a sizable fortune in return for her cheerfulness?"

"Well, what's unusual about that? As you yourself have said, that's the way marriages are made in our society. And I can't see that a match between them would be as coldblooded as the one you're plotting with Lady Venetia. At least they're genuinely fond of each other. And if you feel anything for Lady Venetia Sellars, I'll be surprised to hear it."

"Oh, I feel something all right," he said dryly.

"We were speaking of fondness, not of lust."

"You do believe in plain dealing, don't you, Miss Armstead? Very well, then, what better motives for marriage can you imagine? Lust on my side. Money on hers. We should get on famously."

"But do you love her?" She looked at him curiously.

"I think this conversation's already gone too far, Miss Armstead."

"Lust's a fit subject, but love is not? You have some strange ideas, Lord Greville." She did, however, drop the subject. They both gazed at the moving ships for several minutes until the irrepressible Miss Armstead suddenly giggled.

"What now?" His lordship frowned down at her.

"I was just thinking what a huge joke it would be if Aunt

122

Maria and Lord Wainwright did get married and produced an uncle for you. No wonder your nose is out of joint. Is it possible, do you think? I mean, he's awfully old, of course, but can a man of his age. . . ?" Her voice trailed off delicately.

"That, I suppose, would depend on the man," he answered. "In my grandfather's case I couldn't say. But I will say one thing, Miss Armstead. I have had some of the damnedest conversations with you that I've ever had with any female. You've no notion at all of propriety, have you?"

"No, I don't suppose I have." She sighed. "At least Uncle Matthew has remarked the same thing on several occasions. And even Bertie has taken me to task. But I still would like to see it happen—you being cut out by your grandfather's infant, I mean." Her shoulders shook with the joke of it.

He looked down his aristocratic nose till some of her mirth subsided. Then he said with low intensity, "So would I, Miss Armstead. Believe me, so would I."

Frankie had thought of several responses, a scornful snort seeming the most apt, when something in his demeanor persuaded her to opt for silence. They both reverted to looking out over the harbor, and once again Frankie succumbed to the novelty of it all. She strained her ears to catch a shouted conversation between two ships flying the American flag and marveled how the Yankees could have so perverted their common mother tongue.

But as the sun disappeared behind the gathering clouds and she grew chilled from sitting still so long, she stole a glance at her companion to see if perhaps he too had drunk his fill of the nautical sights and sounds. But if the harbor's fascination was beginning to pall, he gave no indication. With difficulty Frankie repressed a sigh. And began to wonder if she had not, perhaps, been a little hard on Bertie.

Chapter Thirteen

I<small>N FACT,</small> L<small>ORD</small> G<small>REVILLE</small> W<small>AINWRIGHT</small> <small>SEEMED TO HAVE</small> forgotten all about Miss Armstead. He had picked up a brass telescope from the seat between them, extended it full length, and was now peering toward the harbor entrance with great intensity. "Ahh, there she is," he muttered to himself.

"There who is?" Frankie refused to be ignored.

"The *Constant*" was his brief reply.

Frankie squinted her eyes in the direction his telescope was pointing and saw across the collection of anchored crafts that a newcomer was arriving in the distance. She watched the small white speck grow rapidly, carried by the wind and tide, until soon without benefit of telescope she could distinguish three masts rigged with billowing sails. "What a beautiful boat," she exclaimed as the graceful craft drew nearer.

"Ship," Lord Greville growled. "My God, girl, don't you know anything?"

As she glared up at him, Frankie bit back a sharp retort. She was shocked by the misery and longing revealed on the usually guarded face as he watched the ship's approach. A fleeting thought crossed Frankie's mind: If he should ever look at a woman in just that fashion, she would be lost indeed.

"What boat—ship—is it, do you know?" For some reason she felt a need to break the spell. She was finding his tension quite unbearable.

"She's the *Constant*. I just told you."

"So what is the *Constant*, a warship?" Even Frankie found the query chuckleheaded now that she could see the firing decks.

"No, a whaler" was the disgusted reply, but she was glad to see some of his misery replaced by irritation. "She's a frigate," he went on to say.

"Oh," said the farmer's niece, not at all enlightened. Then after a moment's pause she got up her nerve to ask, "You sailed on her?" All in all it was an educated guess.

"Yes." The monosyllable closed that subject.

They sat in silence a few minutes longer till the ship drew near enough to distinguish the sailors swarming purposefully over the rigging and the decks, with here and there a blue-coated officer among them barking orders.

Lord Greville clucked suddenly at his matched team of greys and flicked them lightly with the reins. Their departure was so unexpected that Frankie had to clutch the sides of the red leather seat to keep from toppling off it. "Don't you want to stay and see it dock?" she exclaimed as her jockey-style bonnet blew back off her curls, saved only by its ribbon fasteners from sailing off toward the dock to join the frigate.

"No." Again, even the irrepressible Frankie felt that the subject was firmly closed.

They rode in silence, both deep in thought. Indeed their reveries lasted till they reached the Strand, a record for Miss Armstead. But then she blurted, "You really meant what you said, then, didn't you? About your grandfather and my aunt Maria."

"Oh, God, Frankie," he groaned, neither of them apparently noticing he'd used her name. "I wish I'd never brought up that subject. Forget it, will you."

"No, I can't. For now I realize you really were only concerned that the old gentleman was going to seem ridiculous. A thing you refine far too much on, by the by. But," she continued hastily as he looked murderous, "you'd actually be relieved, wouldn't you, if there were somebody else to carry on in your place?" With all the self-congratulation in her voice that Aristotle must have felt after uncovering some great truth, she went on to declare, "For what you really want is to spend your life at sea!"

He didn't deign to answer but flicked his team while drivers of the more workaday vehicles in his path cursed roundly as the phaeton threaded through the traffic at breakneck speed. Frankie was, however, also in full spate. She clapped one hand upon her bonnet and with the other grabbed his sleeve of superfine while she shouted in his ear. "That certainly explains a lot about you. I'm really glad that Bertie foisted me on you."

"Well, that makes one of us."

"It certainly explains your foul disposition." They were tooling through Charing Cross at an alarming clip. Frankie was too intent upon her mental voyage to notice he was not heading directly for Grosvenor Square. "It is a bit much," she continued, "to expect a person to be the soul of amiability when he's as deeply unhappy as you are. Although," she reflected, "it's hard to imagine you the soul of amiability under any circumstance."

He continued to drive in tight-lipped silence till they reached the relative solitude of St. James's Park and while Frankie craned her neck for a glimpse of Buckingham House he guided his team off the carriage road onto a verge that was thickly carpeted with fallen leaves. Then he turned and glared. "Now, just what is this latest bee in your bonnet, Miss Armstead? God help me, I'm a fool to ask, but what the devil makes you think that I'm unhappy?"

"Well, it should have been perfectly obvious from the start." Frankie seemed still engaged in pursuing her thoughts out loud. "I should have guessed it from the way you were so out-of-all-proportion angry because I'd pretended we were betrothed." She waved his opening mouth to silence. "No, let me continue. You thought I was trying to trap you. And resented that fact so deeply that you refused to accept my perfectly logical explanation. You wanted to believe I'd laid a trap, you see." She pounced on the notion triumphantly. "For you had every right to be angry about that—whereas you could not lash out against the real trap you were caught in, the trap of duty and filial responsibility." She finished her diagnosis triumphantly.

"Miss Armstead, you are without a doubt the most—" His

lordship, at a loss for words, came up with *fanciful*, and quickly discarded it. "No, by damn, 'demented' female I've ever seen."

"I am not. At least not in this instance. For I really have uncovered why you're such a care-for-nothing. And why you despise us all—up to and including the beauteous Venetia. She's part of the trap, too—don't deny it—because you want no part of the life she represents. No use getting on your high ropes and calling me all sorts of unflattering names, because I know I'm right. For I saw your face back there when your boat—ship—your frigate came sailing in. You looked—bereft. You are, first and last, a sailor."

"I don't deny," he replied stiffly, "that if I could choose the life to lead, I'd have stayed in the navy. But I do deny being angry over it. Believe me, Miss Armstead. It's not that bit of disappointment that so often makes me long to throttle you."

"Then why don't you do it? Not throttle me, of course," she said quickly as a wicked gleam came into his eye. "Go back to sea, I mean."

"You've just said why." He frowned at her slow-wittedness. "My grandfather is old and there's the estate to be looked after."

"You can hire a bailiff."

"We have a bailiff."

"Well, then, you see."

"I see nothing," he retorted. "There has always been a Wainwright on the land. No bailiff, no matter how conscientious, can take the the place of the lord of the manor. You've no idea of my grandfather's responsibilities."

"I certainly do have. I've spent more time in Hampshire than you have, remember? And I know that his tenants run to him for everything from legal disputes to christenings. But it doesn't have to be that way. A good bailiff could—"

"Marry? Produce offspring? Carry on the Wainwright name?" he asked sarcastically.

"Well, you could do those things and still have a naval career, could you not? Aren't most of those men back there married?" She waved dramatically in the general direction of the London dock. "Why, look at the great Nelson. He not only had a wife; he managed to keep a mistress as well. Oh, I am sorry," she said with true contrition, "I should not have spoken so frivolously about a man who must have been your particular idol. My point simply was that a naval career and marriage aren't contradictory."

"They aren't compatible either." He spoke with the conviction of a man who had given the matter considerable thought. "It's no kind of life for a woman, being married to a man who spends months, years, at a stretch at sea."

"Oh, I don't know," Miss Armstead replied solemnly but with a twinkle in her eyes. "The lady married to you might come to welcome it."

"Vixen!" His glare turned into a grin, however. "I must say, you have a decided way of taking the starch out of a fellow."

"But setting aside the fact I couldn't resist delivering a leveler," she went on, "I am perfectly serious, you know. I really can't see that your desire for martyrdom is doing you or anyone else any good."

"Martyrdom! You go too far, Miss Armstead. I really don't care for that term." His eyes narrowed.

"What else would you call it? Throwing your life away, making everybody miserable in the process."

"Just whom am I making miserable?" The sudden chill was enough to cause her to rebutton the top button of the cherry pelisse she wore.

"You certainly don't intend to deny that your grandfather is worried sick over the fact you're so blue-deviled."

"I do deny it."

"Well, you should not. It simply proves my point. You're too absorbed with your own dissatisfaction to notice what's going on around you. Why else do you think he followed you to London?"

"To find out why I broke the heart of one of our ramshackled neighbors."

"Well, aside from that, he really is concerned for you. He remarked to Aunt Maria just the other day how much you've changed since your—er—drowning incident. You know"— she broke off her previous train of thought—"I really owe you

128

an apology for that. I thought it was cowardice that caused you to give up your commission after your ship was shot out from under you. Not that I blamed you in the least." She shuddered. "I would have done the same myself."

"Would you indeed."

"No need to be so nasty. I had come to realize I mistook the matter even before I saw your ship come in back there. But as I was saying, you are only making miserable the very ones you're sacrificing yourself for. Besides your grandfather, there's Lady Venetia to consider."

"I know I'm a fool to ask, but in what possible way has your fertile little mind decided that I'm making her miserable? I've seen no signs of it."

"Well, you can't say that your pursuit has been exactly ardent, now, can you?"

"I can't—or won't—say anything about my pursuit of Lady Venetia, except to state that it is certainly no concern of yours."

"Maybe not. But it is one of the *on dits* of the various drawing rooms. Everyone is remarking on the fact that you've cooled off drastically. They say that when Admiral Webster introduced you to her you actually appeared besotted. And when you invited her to Alton Hall everyone expected to read a notice in the *Gazette* immediately. Then when no engagement was announced—you know how it is—people began to speculate. And"—she wrinkled up her nose distastefully—"a lot of people blame Evelyn. They say he has come between you. But I don't believe that for a single minute."

"Oh, do you not? Well, now, I can hardly wait to hear your theory."

"You have already heard it." She spoke reprovingly. "Pray pay attention. After the first few days of behaving like a moon calf—"

"Like a what?" He sounded dangerous.

"Like a moon calf. Remember I had a chance to observe you with another yellow-haired female at my aunt's house—even if you do choose not to recall that I was there. So I know that after months at sea you are inclined to make a cake of yourself over

129

a pretty face, and I can imagine that was how it was at first with Lady Venetia. But after things settled down a bit I'm sure you began to see her, too, as a part of the trap you were caught in."

"Have you quite finished reading my character?" His lordship was excessively polite. "If so, perhaps we should be on our way. I didn't wish to arrive home before you'd finished spouting all your nonsense. It would have been a shame to cut one of your famous high flights short. But it is possible that your aunt may wonder what has become of you. So before she begins to think that you've been kidnapped and has cause to celebrate, I had better take you home."

Miss Armstead looked at him thoughtfully. "You're angry with me, aren't you?"

"Did you think I'd be pleased?" His eyes glinted.

"Well, yes, I rather did. It always helps to understand our actions, don't you think? For it's only through such understanding that one can change."

"The only thing I understand is that if you don't break yourself of the habit of meddling in other people's affairs—the complexity of which you cannot begin to understand, in spite of your insufferable conceit—someone is going to throttle you."

"Well, really," Frankie stormed back at him. "Of all the ungrateful, arrogant, care-for-nothings God ever made—"

She got no further. She was grabbed by the shoulders and given a shake that caused her teeth to rattle. "Do be quiet, Miss Armstead." Then she was enfolded in two strong arms and trapped hard against a three-caped greatcoat. Her jockey bonnet was swept off her head to dangle helplessly by its satin ribbons. Her mouth was covered with his lordship's, who began to kiss her with an angry fervor. She was too stunned at first to experience anything except surprise. She had been kissed before, of course. When Evelyn had asked her to elope with him, he had sealed their betrothal by a cool, chaste kiss lightly upon her lips. It had in no way prepared her for this experience. As his lips burned into hers, his lordship's anger was rapidly becoming lost in another, far stronger emotion. Frankie parted her own lips and found herself suddenly swept away upon a tide of new sensation that she'd never before imagined, let alone experienced. Somewhere a voice—Uncle Matthew's perhaps?—was telling her that she was behaving outrageously. And somehow, unbidden, the image of the Gilded Lily smiled knowingly down at her.

It was Greville Wainwright who at last put a period to their unexpected, inexcusable intimacy. As he reluctantly removed his lips from hers Frankie remained immobile, pressed up against him, clasping the back of his middle cape like a drowning victim clinging to a spar. She stared up at him, lips still parted, studying his shuttered face. Only his eyes perhaps held a clue, but she couldn't interpret it.

"Don't tell me you're at a loss for words," he finally said huskily with a twisted smile.

"Why did you do that?" she whispered.

"God knows. Possibly because I'm a man and you're a woman and it wouldn't have been the thing to give you a leveler the way I longed to. Kissing you just seemed to be the only recourse."

Still clinging tightly to his coat, Frankie thought that over. Did he really imagine he hadn't handed her a leveler? Though it had been her good fortune to thus far, at least, escape that experience, it was hard to imagine that a right to the jaw would be nearly as devastating as what she'd just been through.

Lord Greville, very gently, pushed her upright on the seat and positioned her bonnet properly. "I'd better take you home." He sprang the horses.

As they came tooling into Grosvenor Square at his customary breakneck speed, his lordship said abruptly, "Damn it all, Frankie, I know I've behaved like a perfect cad and have been trying to come up with a fitting apology, but I can't seem to find the right words for it." He pulled the phaeton to a halt before her door and gazed down at her ruefully. She met his gaze unblinkingly.

"I expect that one reason you are finding it so difficult to frame a proper apology is that you are well aware that I cooperated quite fully with your caddish behavior." Her color was heightened, but her voice was cool. "So that would seem to nullify the need, would it not, Lord Greville?"

Without waiting for his reply or his assistance she made the long jump to the ground. As she ran up the front steps and through the portals of her house she was dimly aware that Lord Greville Wainwright had not moved, even though his team, so near the stables, jingled their harness impatiently.

With so many warring emotions at work within her, Frankie did not feel up to confronting the servants, let alone her aunt, at just that moment. Since the latter was certain to be in her room dressing for dinner and would no doubt call to her as she went past and inquire about her day, Frankie decided to delay going to her room. Instead she sought the sanctuary of the morning room until she could face the household a bit more calmly.

If she did not exactly tiptoe down the hallway, she did move quietly enough not to call attention to herself. And the well-oiled doorknob turned silently, giving no clue to her presence either as she stood frozen on the threshold, staring with dismay at the tableau in front of her.

Maria Paxton, her garments in disarray, reclined full-length upon the Grecian couch. Evelyn Yarwood, his coat of blue superfine upon the floor, sprawled on top of her. He was kissing her passionately while his busily employed hands put Frankie to the blush. Her quick involuntary intake of breath gave a warning of her presence. Lady Paxton, wrenching her mouth free, spied her niece across her lover's shoulder and whispered, "Oh, dear God" as Evelyn rolled off her.

As he scrambled to his feet in red-faced confusion, Frankie found herself thinking inanely that it was the first time she had seen him so out of countenance and the first time she'd seen him in disarray. She had just a moment to reflect that tousled hair and a shirt opened at the throat and half-tugged from his trousers were more becoming to him than all his polished dandyism. Then she snapped back to the realities of this terrible intrusion, gasped "I beg your pardon," felt herself flush, and fled.

She sought the sanctuary of her room, closed the door behind her, flung herself facedown upon her bed, and tried fiercely not to think.

When, seconds or minutes or eons later, she heard the door

132

open softly, Frankie began to breathe slowly and rhythmically. She thought of adding a slight snore but was deterred by the possibility of not being able to make a convincing job of it.

"I know you aren't asleep, Frankie," her aunt said gently as she sat down beside her on the bed. "I think that we should talk."

Frankie rolled over and propped herself up against the pillows. She tried to smile at her aunt, and if the results were a little shaky, the effort seemed to bring some slight relief to the other's troubled countenance. "I'm sorry, Aunt Maria," Frankie said, "much as I'd enjoy it, I really haven't time now for a cose. Bertie's due soon, you see. You may remember that we're to go to Astley's."

"I remember. You have plenty of time, though. And well, frankly, I don't think this should wait. I'm afraid Evelyn and I have just shocked you dreadfully."

"Oh, indeed no." Frankie laughed a rather unconvincing airy laugh. "Why, indeed, should I have been? I know that these things happen."

"Come now, Frances. This world-weary pose really doesn't suit you at all, my dear. You have every right to be furious. With Evelyn, of course, but with me most especially. What we did was inexcusable. But the thing is, my dear"—Maria Paxton looked at her niece with real concern—"I don't want you to attach more importance to the, uh, episode than it deserves. Which is next to none," she finished lightly.

"Oh, I do know that much." There was more conviction in the niece's voice than the aunt perhaps had hoped for. "I realize I'm not really up to snuff, Aunt Maria," Frankie continued with a trace of bitterness, "but I'm learning fast. And I do know this much. A gentleman needs little provocation to make passionate love. And any female, I expect, will do him. I expect just proximity is often enough to set one off when the impulse strikes. So really, Aunt Maria there is nothing for you to explain to me. It's all best forgotten. Believe me. I attach very little importance to the sort of thing I just witnessed. So let's say no more about it, shall we?"

"Thank you, I think, for your understanding," Lady Paxton remarked rather dryly. She sat studying her niece's face for a while longer, then rose reluctantly to her feet. "As you so wisely say, it's all best forgotten. And Bertie will be here soon." She walked across to the door, opened it, then turned hesitantly toward her niece. "Frankie, speaking of Bertie, have you ever thought that perhaps—"

"Oh, Aunt Maria," Frankie wailed, giving way at last to the despair she felt, "if you too are about to tell me that you think Bertie is more suited to me than Evelyn, please do not. Right now I think it would be the outside of enough."

"The thought had crossed my mind," the other admitted. "But I shall bite my tongue instead. Good night, m'dear."

The door closed softly behind her.

Chapter Fourteen

IT WAS OBVIOUS THAT BERTIE'S DAY HAD GONE MUCH better than hers. Frankie was grateful to be able to sit back in the rather smelly hired carriage that was taking them to Lambeth and let his enthusiasm swirl around her. So absorbed was he in reliving every feint and jab and punishing blow of the mill he'd witnessed that he hardly seemed to notice the apathy of his audience. Frankie, though, was caught up in contemplating physical encounters of quite another kind than the bare-fisted barbarism of the fight ring. She did, however, make the fleeting comparison that the activity she dwelled on was at least as primitive and certainly as devastating as Bertie's boxing.

"Lord Greville was right on the nose!" Bertie crowed, jerking Frankie momentarily from her reverie. "He said Burke would finish Frederick off in the sixth—you remember him saying that, don't you, Frankie?" Then, when she nodded, he continued. "Though I must say that Frederick was a game 'un." Bertie glowed with admiration. "He'd been gushing blood since the third round when the Bulldog had landed him a facer and one eye was already closed."

"Bertie!" Frankie protested, looking slightly sick.

"But Frederick wasn't a quitter. Game to the end, he was. But when the Bulldog hit him with a left hook to the temple and I saw his knees begin to buckle, well, I knew that it was curtains."

"Really, that's disgusting." He had her full attention now. "How you can sit there and gloat over some poor man's misery, I'll not pretend to understand."

"I'm not gloating over his misery, damn it, Frankie. Didn't I just congratulate Frederick on being such a game 'un? Pay attention. If I'm gloating—and I ain't—it's over what a famous mill it was. But you can't expect a female to understand a thing like that, and I was sapskulled even to try." He lapsed into a sulk to equal her dejection, and the rest of the journey was finished in heavy silence.

But it was impossible for Bertie to remain out of humor long once exposed to the spell of Astley's famous Royal Circus. He and Frankie joined the crush at the covered amphitheater and he elbowed their way to a choice vantage point in the first tier of balconies. "A fellow told me we can actually see better from up here than from one of those boxes down at ringside. I say now, ain't this famous?" He stared down at the spectacle below, oblivious to the glare of a fat lady and her diminutive escort whom they'd squeezed aside to gain their vantage point.

Frankie had to agree that indeed it was quite famous. She was soon diverted from her mopes by the antics of a trick rider on a dappled stallion that was speeding at a prodigious pace around the ring. The rider, standing upright upon the horse's back, was studying the label on a bottle he held there in his hand. Then all of a sudden, while the crowd let out a screech, he somersaulted high up into the air, a double rotation, landing successfully upon his feet to wild applause. "It says to pour into a tumbler," he announced, and put the bottle to his mouth while the horse continued its wild circle and the spectators laughed uproariously at the daring joke.

There were performing monkeys, songs, and pantomime. A bespangled lady, famous for cutting and slashing with the broadsword, displayed her skill and body to the admiration of the crowd. "You have to admit, Frankie, that she beats your Elgin Marbles by a mile" was Bertie's verdict. "I'd just about decided that sight-seeing in London was a complete waste of a fellow's time, but this is a lot more like it."

The Royal Circus was most famous for its equestrian show-manship and justifiably so. Frankie and Bertie leaned far over their balcony so as not to miss a single movement of a lovely gauze-draped dream who danced with the grace of Taglioni on the back of a snow-white steed. As the lovely dancer pirouet-ted almost beneath them, Frankie was momentarily distracted by a plume of orchid ostrich feathers towering above a head of lovely golden hair. There was something vaguely familiar about the lady's crowning glory, though from a bird's-eye view identification was difficult. Frankie tugged at Bertie's sleeve.

"Oh, I say, do watch the tailoring, will you, Frankie?" he complained. "It ain't like I've got a valet hovering in my rooms just hoping to iron the wrinkles out."

"Look down there, will you?"

"Where?"

"There. Right down below us. The woman with the purple plumes. Do you recognize her?"

"How could I possibly," he retorted, "from just the top of her head and her—and her bare"—he choked and turned a trifle pink—"well, you know." In addition to the golden hair they had a good view of the lady's décolletage.

"It's the Gilded Lily. I'm almost certain of it."

"Oh, I say." Bertie's interest was now completely diverted from the horseback dancer. "How could I recognize her? Told you I'd never set eyes on her, but I've been dying to. They say"—he lowered his voice—"there ain't a ladybird in the whole of London to match her for looks. Wish I could see her

136

face. Though what I do see of her's not all that bad." His leer cost him a dig in the ribs from his partner's elbow.

"Men!" Frankie's voice was lathered with disgust. "You're as bad as those other two, aren't you, Bertie?"

"What other two?" He clutched his side.

"Never mind that now. Oh, yes, it is the Lily." The vision below them had tilted her head upward in response to a remark from a tall gentleman beside her, and Frankie was able to confirm that it was indeed the woman who had accosted Evelyn in Hyde Park.

"Would you look at that." Bertie's eyes were popping from his head. "They didn't do her justice, not by half. She's a Nonpareil and no mistake."

"No doubt." But Frankie came nowhere near matching the other's enthusiasm. Then as the lady lowered her upturned face, both pairs of staring eyes refocused on her chest, although from two entirely different motives. Frankie, on her part, suddenly let out a gasp and grabbed her escort in a frenzied grasp.

"For heaven's sake, Frankie, I do wish you'd watch what you're doing. It ain't as though this coat's really up to snuff, and if you will keep mauling it this way—"

"Look down there at what she's wearing. I just noticed—on her neck!"

Bertie obligingly leaned precariously far over the balcony. "She's wearing a necklace," he reported as he straightened up to look into his companion's agitated face. "What's so odd about that? Most females do. You're wearing one yourself."

Frankie was staring at him in horror. "She's wearing Lady Venetia Sellars's necklace. That's what's so odd about it."

"Don't be daft. She couldn't be."

"I tell you she is. It's the same necklace Lady Venetia had on at the opera when I saw her there. It was made of diamonds and pearls and must have cost the earth. I commented on it most particularly. And she told me that her father had had it copied from one belonging to the Empress Josephine."

"Well, then, there you are." Bertie dismissed the subject. "If he could have had it copied, so could any other cove. There are probably dozens of 'em floating around England. Not even to mention the Continent. It's absurd to think—"

"You don't understand," Frankie interrupted, fighting to stay calm. "When we were discussing Lady Venetia's necklace that night, she adjusted it and the clasp broke. Evelyn took it from her and put it in his pocket. He was to take it to the jeweler's for her the next day."

"Oh, my God!" Bertie had gone quite pale. "What are we going to do?"

"I don't know," Frankie answered miserably. "We can't just go up to that woman down there and ask, 'By the by, where did you get the lovely necklace that you're wearing?'"

For possibly the first time in their lives it was Bertie who hit upon the course of action. "Come on." He grabbed Frankie by the hand and began to bull his way once more through the throng of spectators around them. They had collected a "good riddance" from the fat lady and a curse or two from the unfortunates whose toes they trod upon before they finally emerged from the amphitheater. Getting a hackney took a bit of time. The jarveys weren't expecting any passengers while the performance was going on. But finally they were once again ensconced inside a carriage pulled by a pair that Bertie diagnosed as "one step from the knackers" as they plodded at a snail's pace toward Grosvenor Square.

"What are you going to do?" Frankie asked.

"Take you home first and then go find Evelyn" was the grim-faced reply.

"I'm going with you. Tell the driver to go straight to Manchester Street."

"You'll do no such thing. Evelyn ain't likely to be home in the first place, and I can't have you following me to White's or Boodle's or God knows where. Besides, this is all bound to turn out to be a hum," he added stoutly. "There's bound to be more than one of those damned necklaces around. Probably Lord Wellington himself gave one to the Lily." His face contorted into what he meant to be a smile. "I know Evelyn's pretty ramshackled, Frankie," he continued, "but dammit, he ain't a thief."

"I know that," she replied with slightly less conviction. For the truth was, she realized, she did not know Evelyn Yarwood at all. "And you're right, of course, about the necklace having been copied countless times."

Just the same, as the hackney pulled up in front of her house she made Bertie promise to come right back and report to her. He put up some resistance but capitulated when she said if he did not, she'd show up at Evelyn's rooms and wait for him.

"Oh, very well. But it could be all hours."

"That's all right. I certainly won't be asleep. If everybody else is, just throw some pebbles at the window and I'll sneak out."

"That's a stupid thing to ask a man to do. Bound to break the glass. Oh, all right, then. I can't stand here and argue. Drive on there, will you?" Bertie called to the jarvey, and the hackney coach went creaking off.

As it turned out, Bertie did not have to resort to cracking her chamber window. He was back in a remarkably short time. "Got rid of that damned hackney and walked" was his explanation after Dearborn had shown him into the front parlor with marked disapproval for the lateness of the hour.

"Do hurry and tell me what happened before Aunt Maria gets home." Frankie had previously provided herself with a tea tray. Now she poured out a cup for him but withheld the seedcake so as not to impede his power of speech. "She and Lord Wainwright went to Drury Lane. They could be back any minute. Tell me, did you see Evelyn?"

"Yes," the other answered miserably. It was a mark of his dejection that he did not protest the withheld cake. "Caught him before he left for Brook's. And oh, my God, Frankie, you were right." He choked suddenly, to Frankie's horror. "That is Lady Venetia's necklace. And Evelyn did give it to the Lily."

"Oh, no," Frankie moaned softly, setting her cup down on the sofa table for its security. She had supposed so all along, of course. But suspicion at its worst was not the reality of knowing.

"The thing is, you see," Bertie continued, "Evelyn owes the Lily money. A lot of it. They'd been—uh—good friends, you know—"

"Oh, for heaven's sake, Bertie, I know what they've been. Do get on with it."

"Well, the thing is, she actually liked Evelyn a whole lot." A touch of pride crept into the younger brother's tone. "In spite of looking like an angel, the Lily's a real hard-headed business-woman, you see. In the ordinary way of things she doesn't have anything to do with anyone who's not a Nabob. And she certainly never lends money. That ain't her style at all. But the thing is, she had a real soft spot for Evelyn." Frankie had no difficulty at all believing that. "So she put up with a lot from him actually. And she kept making Evelyn these little 'loans,' she called 'em, to gamble with. Which, of course, he lost," his brother added in disgust. "Evelyn had considered them gifts, actually, not loans, he said. And he swore that that's the way she'd meant them too till things started to change between them—and he didn't want to be seen around with her anymore. For naturally he couldn't have you and Lady Venetia—or me when it comes to that—thinking he kept a ladybird."

"Or that a ladybird kept him." Frankie set the record straight and he turned red.

"All right, damn it. But don't keep interrupting if you want me to get this told before your aunt gets back."

"I'm sorry," she murmured contritely, and he hurried up his narrative. "Well, the upshot was that when Evelyn turned cool, the Lily started to press him for repayment of the loans she'd made him. And he said he was knocked for a loop when he found out it amounted to over five hundred pounds."

"Oh, dear heavens!"

"He kept trying to stave her off, promising to get the blunt somehow. But when she tracked him down to the park he knew his goose was cooked. What was it that poet cove said? 'Hell hath no fury—' "

" 'Like a woman scorned.' " Frankie finished the quotation.

"Well that's the Lily for you. She's out to ruin Evelyn and that's the long and short of it. That morning in the park she threatened to expose him to the rest of you. And if he didn't pay up, she planned to set that tame ex-boxer she keeps for pro-tection onto Evelyn. 'To make sure his face wasn't so pretty

140

from now on' was the way she put it." Bertie shuddered and Frankie looked a little sick. "Well, the upshot was that Evelyn gave her the necklace, to hold as collateral, he told her, till he could pay her back. He had it with him, you see, planning to go from the park to the jeweler's. And if all that ain't bad enough, now Lady Venetia's onto him about the thing. He kept putting her off, saying the jeweler hadn't gotten around to it, but then she started getting suspicious and wanted to know which jeweler had it so she could get it back, ready or not, and that kind of thing. And now she'd told him that if she doesn't get it back immediately, she'll go to her father. And that old behemoth is bound to go straight to Bow Street. Oh, Lord, Frankie, my brother's as good as in Newgate," he wailed, "and what will Papa say?"

"Stop it, Bertie." Frankie spoke sharply. "If you break down now, I shall start to howl and we'll never find a way out of this coil—besides having to explain to Aunt Maria why we're sniveling."

Bertie glared indignantly. "I ain't 'sniveled,' as you call it, since I was five, and I'm not about to start up now."

"There. That's more like it. How long do you think Evelyn has?"

"Before the Runners pick him up? Oh, God, I don't know. He told Lady Venetia that the jeweler has promised it day after tomorrow without fail. So she won't start her hue and cry till then. And I suppose the Lily is satisfied as long as she's got the necklace. But then there's always the chance that somebody else will recognize the thing, the same as you did, and tell old Lord Sellars about it. Oh, God," he groaned again.

"Not likely. Or even if they did, it wouldn't put the fat in the fire much faster. What it all boils down to is that Evelyn has about thirty-six hours to come up with the blunt for the Lily and get the necklace back to Lady Venetia."

"Which is the same as saying he's Newgate meat already."

"Oh, Bertie, don't be such a defeatist. We have to think of something."

"What do you suppose I've been trying to do? And Evelyn's been thinking of nothing else for days. First he went to Carter the moneylender, who laughed right in his face. Then the sap-skull pawned the gold fob and the set of enameled snuff boxes the Lily had given him, and—can you believe it, Frankie?—put the blunt on Ferocious Frederick to beat Bulldog Burke! Of all the thick-headed nincompoops! I swear I almost gave him a facer then myself. Anybody would have known that Ferocious Frederick couldn't—"

"Bertie! Don't start up again about that awful fight. Keep thinking. Let's see. I could get the money from Uncle Matthew, I expect. An advance on my inheritance. For as little as he'd approve of what Evelyn's done, he wouldn't want to see your father suffer for it."

"No!" Bertie almost thundered. "I won't hear of it. Neither would my father. Besides," he added practically, "there ain't time."

"No, that's the problem. Do you think Carter the money-lender might give you a loan? No, you'd be tarred with Evelyn's brush."

"The name Yarwood ain't exactly up there with the Rothchilds for solvency," Bertie said bitterly.

"He might let me have one, though," she mused. "After all, my prospects are quite good."

"Well, I won't hear of you doing that. Besides," he qualified, "there still wouldn't be time enough. You don't just walk into the place and say, 'I'd like five hundred pounds, please,' and the moneylender wraps up a parcel in brown paper. He'd first have to make sure you're good for it, and that would take more time."

"It's worth a try at least. We haven't exactly come up with anything else yet, have we? Besides, I'll wager that those cents-per-centers hand over cash like that all the time. Usury is their business, and they just raise the interest to match the risk."

"You may be right, but we ain't going to find out, Frankie. It's enough that Evelyn's dished his own family without starting in on yours. No, there's no help for it that I can see. I'll just have to try Evelyn's caper-witted scheme. Even if it does work, which ain't at all likely, it still won't be a permanent so-

lution. But it will at least buy Evelyn some more time. Yes"—
his jaw set stubbornly—"I'll just have to do it."

"Do what, Bertie?" she demanded, her blood chilling at his
expression."

"Steal the necklace from the Lily," her best friend replied.

*Chapter
Fifteen*

"**S**TEAL THE NECKLACE!" FORTUNATELY FRANKIE'S
vocal cords had suddenly constricted and a low croak
was all that she could manage, for footsteps were heard coming down the hall and there was barely time to work on composing their expressions before Lady Maria accompanied by
Lord Wainwright and his grandson joined them.

"Oh, tea. What a marvelous idea," her ladyship said lightly,
though giving her niece a rather searching glance. "Dearborn," she called, raising her voice to the butler hovering in
the hall, "do bring a fresh pot, please. How was the circus,
children?"

"The what?" Bertie looked at his hostess blankly. She might
have introduced the subject of electricity for all he seemed to
comprehend it.

"The circus, goose." Frankie substituted a warning frown
for the kick she longed to give him. "It was famous, wasn't it?"
Even to her own ears her enthusiasm sounded forced. "We
loved the dancer on horseback best of all, didn't we, Bertie?"

"Oh, yes," he agreed, rallying. "And the tumbler cove with
the wine bottle. Jolly good. It seems so long ago I almost forgot."

"Been a trying evening, has it?" Lord Greville inquired as Dearborn entered with the tea.

"Trying? Don't be absurd," Frankie intervened. "What could be trying about visiting Astley's Circus? It's one of the most memorable evenings I've ever spent, in fact."

"You're right on the nail there," Bertie agreed a shade too grimly, but fortunately Lord Wainwright launched forth on the circuses of his youth, and the attention turned politely his way for a while, except, that is, for his grandson, who still seemed more intent upon studying Frankie's face.

Lord Greville had no opportunity to speak with her, however, until the ladies accompanied the gentlemen to the hall, where they collected their respective cloaks and hats and gloves and canes. He managed then to take her to one side and murmur, "I need to talk to you. When may I call tomorrow?"

"Tomorrow?" The word had a doomed and hollow sound. "Oh, but I'm sorry, Lord Greville. Tomorrow's out of the question, I'm afraid. Besides," she hastened on as he seemed about to argue, "if you merely wish to apologize for that little incident this afternoon, well, there's no need for that. Indeed, I'd almost forgotten it." Surprisingly, she realized, that was so. Which went to show, she reflected, how desperate the situation was.

"Thank you." His lordship spoke dryly. Whatever else he might have said was cut short by his grandfather. "Come along, Greville. Don't keep Dearborn holding the door open. It's freezing cold out here."

As Lord Greville reluctantly complied, he was joined in the exit by Mr. Yarwood, who seemed, in fact, to be using him as a sort of blind in order to ease out of the door unobtrusively. It did not work. For the third time that evening Frankie clutched his coat sleeve in a grip of iron. "Just a minute, Bertie." Her spontaneity rang a trifle false. "Do let me run get the book I borrowed. I know you wanted it right back. And I'm finished with it."

"The what?" Bertie looked at her blankly.

"The book of poems," she said between clenched teeth. "You remember, surely."

"No, he doesn't," Greville remarked pleasantly, though his

144

eyes were hard with suspicion. "But I'm sure it will all come back to him. But poetry? Really, Miss Armstead. You should keep your excuses more in character." He did, however, cooperate by giving Bertie a push back inside the door, which Dearborn then closed behind him.

"If you have something to say to Bertie, do be quick about it, dear," her aunt said. "I realize I'm not in the best position to preach propriety, but it is late and servants do gossip." She kissed Frankie lightly on the forehead. "I'm off to bed."

"I'll just be a second. I promise," Frankie told her. "I only wish to—"

"I know. Give Bertie back his poems." The other smiled. "Good night, both of you."

Frankie waited till the coast was clear, then dragged her friend into the music room off the hall. She closed the door behind them, then motioned him to the center of the room away from listening ears. There she clutched his sleeve again, much to his annoyance. "What do you mean, steal the necklace?" she whispered.

"Just that. Couldn't put it any plainer, could I?"

"You most certainly can. Tell me how you propose to go about it."

"I ain't going to tell." He set his jaw stubbornly. "You'd be bound to set a rub in my way if I did."

"I'll set one if you don't. I'll go to Lord Wainwright and get him to send a message to your father."

"You wouldn't!" Compared to Bertie's, Caesar's look at Brutus was forgiving. "I swear it, Frankie. I never would have thought—"

"Oh, do hush, Bertie. The thing is, if the necklace has to be stolen, and I'm not conceding that point for a moment, why doesn't Evelyn do it himself? I'd think that was more in his line of country than in yours."

"He can't. The Lily's given orders to the Bruiser to keep him away from her unless he's got five hundred pounds tucked in his pocket."

"Oh, dear. Well, that's that, then. But the thing is, you'll never bring it off alone and you should know it. Somebody's got to help you. And it will have to be me," she finished resolutely.

"Well, you can't and that's that." His tone shut off the subject. "No, don't go into your high flights, Frankie. If I were going in for the ordinary kind of robbery," he continued, "like holding up a stagecoach or tackling the Bank of England, I'd let you in on it in a minute. But robbing a light-skirt, well, that's something else entirely. In the first place, it's got to be done at the Cyprian Ball."

"The Cyprian Ball!" Frankie echoed. She had heard whispered stories of an annual dance given by the Fashionable Impures, but she had always supposed the affair to be the figment of someone's imagination. "You mean there really is such a thing? And if there is, why on earth would you steal the necklace there?"

"Because that's where the Lily will be, of course," he answered patiently. "And since there's no question of your going there—"

"Of course I'm going," Frankie interrupted, shocking him to the soles of his evening pumps. "Don't argue, Bertie. You're going to need me. I have it on the best authority that pickpockets always work in pairs. One distracts the intended victim, don't you see, while the other one palms the goods."

"There's no point in your pretending to be the expert that you're not," he countered, "for it ain't her pocket I'm going to pick. She'll be wearing the cursed thing."

"Well, in principle it's still the same."

"No, it ain't. Not a bit of it. Besides, I've got a plan, and you don't come into it."

"Well, it won't work. I can tell you that much right now."

"How the devil can you say that without knowing—" he was stung into replying.

"Well, tell me, then. Wait, don't go off in a pucker, Bertie. Just think a minute. If there's any flaw in your plan, it's better that I'm the one to find it and not the Gilded Lily."

"Oh, all right, then. But I can tell you right now, you ain't going to approve."

"That's completely beside the point. I don't approve of stealing at all, as a general thing."

"Well," he began awkwardly, "I thought I'd—uh—ask her to go upstairs with me after we got through dancing."

"Go upstairs? Whatever for?" she asked, then watched him turn a fiery red. "Oh. My goodness, do they do *that* at the ball?"

"Of course. What do you think Cyprians do, drink lemonade and eat cake like at Almack's and go home at ten?"

"Well, I didn't know," she said humbly, "but anyhow it's a good thing you told me, for it won't work."

"Why won't it work?" he bristled.

"Because in the first place I don't think she'll go upstairs with you. You yourself told me that she only goes with Nabobs. And if you had that kind of money, we wouldn't need to steal the necklace. Oh, I know what you're hoping, but you are *not* Evelyn. Besides, even if you did succeed in luring her to bed with you," she finished practically, "she might take off many things, but I doubt the necklace would be one of them. No, that settles it, Bertie. I'm going with you. You go home now and get a good night's rest." She began to tug him across the room again. "But be back here by nine in the morning. We've got lots of planning to do. And do contrive to look less like a condemned man on the way to Tyburn Tree. Dearborn's out there waiting to let you out, and we mustn't make him suspicious. He'll tell Aunt Maria."

After seeing Bertie out the door under Dearborn's disapproving eye, Frankie bade the exhausted servant a good-night and went to bed. But not to sleep. The more she told herself that she needed to be rested and alert for tomorrow's activities—no, make that *today's* activities—the more wide awake she became. All the memories she'd kept staunchly at bay came crowding in—the sensation of being pulled roughly against a certain greatcoat and kissed beyond imagination. The shock of seeing the man she loved sprawled on top of the woman who stood in loco parentis to herself, a woman old enough to be his—aunt.

She tossed and turned and fought her pillow until finally she began to drift toward the longed-for oblivion. Then a final thought jerked her wide awake again. Why was it that the idea of Evelyn as lover to the notorious Gilded Lily had bothered her so little, while the thought of Bertie in the same role had seemed totally unacceptable? Quite shocking even. Were Lord Greville and her aunt both aware of something she was hiding from herself? And had she been both too quick and too puritanical when she'd talked Bertie out of his own scheme to steal the necklace? No, of course not. She firmly discarded that notion. Bertie was her friend, and it would have been wrong of her to consent to a plan, no matter how pleasurable for its perpetrator, that was doomed from its conception. It was folly to think that he'd ever be able to steal the Empress Josephine necklace without her aid. She owed that much to him for friendship's sake. With that ennobling thought, she finally drifted off to sleep.

When Bertie dutifully hammered the brass knocker at nine next morning it was a matter of speculation as to who looked the worse for wear, he or Dearborn. He was soon greeted by Miss Armstead, no less haggard, while the butler, grumbling to himself, went off for tea.

"I don't know what I'm doing here," Bertie observed a few minutes later while slathering a roll with butter. "Would have done better to stay in bed. Barely got to sleep before I had to pop back up again."

"What's Evelyn doing?" Frankie asked while noting that fatigue and anxiety had not affected Bertie's appetite. He swallowed the roll almost whole.

"What would he be doing?" Evelyn's brother answered thickly. "He's sleeping, of course. Like every other civilized person's doing."

"He would be." Frankie wrinkled her nose with deep disgust. "Here we are, trying to save him from ruination, while he sleeps like a baby. But then, why not? Someone always pulls Eveyln's chestnuts out of the fire for him. How often have you played cat's paw, Bertie?"

"I ain't doing this for him." He helped himself to another roll. "Thought I explained all that. It's my father I'm concerned

148

with." He paused a moment, however, to think over what he'd just said. "No, actually, that's wrong by half. I am mostly concerned about my father, but the fact of the matter is, no right-thinking chap wants to see his own brother in debtor's prison, never mind that he's a sapskull. And if it makes you feel better, Frankie, Evelyn's been running around like a rat in a rat pit with a terrier after him. He's put the touch on everybody he knows. But everybody so far has turned him down. He says he'll try again today, though. Waste of time, if you ask me. Everybody knows he's too far up the River Tick for them to ever get a farthing back. He might as well sleep while he can. Besides, I was deuced glad he didn't wake up. I didn't want to have to tell him where I was going. For he's as bad as you are, Frankie, when it comes to worming stuff out of a person who don't intend to tell. And I'll say this much for Eveyln: He's ramshackled all right, but he ain't ramshackled enough to let you go to the Cyprian Ball. So if he gets that out of me, you can be damn well sure he'll throw a rub in the way of that little expedition."

Frankie wasn't nearly as convinced as Bertie that if given the choice between his neck and her reputation, Evelyn would lift a finger in her behalf. But she refrained from saying so. Instead she lowered her voice in a conspiratorial tone. "Let's lay our plans; then you can go back to bed. Tell me everything you know about the ball."

That turned out to be next to nothing. It seemed that Evelyn had produced his card for the occasion a few days before and had made the "joking" suggestion that Bertie take it in his place and steal the necklace. But when Bertie indignantly refused, Evelyn had dropped the subject. And it never occurred to Bertie, he explained, to quiz his brother about any of the particulars concerning the Cyprian Ball, "because Evelyn was really only funning, you understand. He wouldn't let me go try to steal the necklace. And even if he should stand still for that, he ain't about to let you go." But Evelyn had left the invitation lying on the mantelpiece, and Bertie had later pocketed it.

If Frankie harbored doubts about Evelyn's motives in leaving the card lying around, she stifled them and set to work laying plans and counterplans based on their very sketchy knowledge of the mores of the Cyprian Ball. She and Bertie had their heads together in whispered argument when Dearborn reappeared. "Lord Greville Wainwright wishes to see you, miss."

"My God, doesn't anybody sleep anymore?" Bertie exclaimed.

"Apparently not, sir." Dearborn's voice was heavy with unspoken meaning.

"Well, I can't see him now," Miss Armstead answered. "Will you tell him I'm still in bed, please?"

"Very well, miss. And if he inquires about Mr. Yarwood, whose cane and hat are in the hall, what shall I say?"

"Tell him Bertie is back for another book of poems." Frankie giggled while both the butler and the guest looked pained.

"Now, where were we?" As Dearborn left upon his mission, the two heads bent together. The conspiracy was rejoined. It was completed, through necessity, though not satisfactorily, before Lady Paxton was astir. Bertie left then, and the day stretched out like eternity before his colleague.

When Lady Paxton proposed a series of morning calls, her niece pleaded a sudden headache, then was forced to lie down in her room to give the ailment verisimilitude. Frankie bounced up again, however, when she heard her aunt leave the house and, making sure first that Maud had joined cook in the kitchen and the coast was clear, spent several minutes rummaging in Lady Paxton's wardrobe. Then praying that the absence of the garments she had borrowed would not be noticed, she hurried back to conceal them underneath her bed. This flurry of activity over, there was nothing left to do but wait. Wait and refuse all callers, including two more visits from Lord Greville Wainwright, to whom she was determinedly "not at home."

Dressing for the Cyprian Ball turned out to be not nearly as problematic as Frankie had feared. She assured Maud that the services of a dresser would not be needed, since she and Bertie were invited to dine with an elderly (and imaginary) relative of his from Hampshire who was also a close friend of her uncle Matthew. And since the Old Dear was afflicted with failing eyesight, it hardly mattered how she looked. Her aunt Maria, on the other hand, was due at an assembly where it was hoped the Prince of Wales himself might make an appearance. Frankie magnanimously volunteered the services of her chambermaid to assist Maud in the task of making sure that Lady Paxton outshone every other female there.

It was only when Frankie had succeeded in dressing herself without detection that the thought occurred that the domino and loo mask necessary to keep her incognito at the ball hardly fit her story of dining with the Ancient. Her best hope, she concluded, was to slip outdoors unobserved and wait for Bertie in the shadows, trusting to luck that when it was discovered she had already gone, Dearborn would simply assume that one of the footmen had admitted Bertie to call for her.

And so she waited till the coast was clear, then raced on tiptoe down the stairs and across the black and white marbled hall, opened the front door noiselessly, and hurtled through it into the arms of Lord Greville Wainwright.

"Well, I've caught you at last," he remarked, holding her upright. "I thought I was supposed to be the one who came leaping out of doors."

Frankie was trying to extricate herself as a hackney clattered to a halt, but his grip on her shoulders only tightened. "Oh, here's Bertie now," she exclaimed. "Do excuse me, Lord Greville. I really must run."

"Why do I get the feeling you're avoiding me? I've been trying to see you all day. Good God!" he broke off suddenly. "What in hell do you have on your face?"

Frankie felt that face go redder still underneath the heavy rouge she'd applied in an effort to blend in, so she imagined, with the ambience of the Cyprian Ball. And before she could prevent it, Lord Greville pushed the concealing hood back from her face and pulled apart the edges of her cloak. The pale beams of the street lamp revealed her aunt's claret-colored satin gown, complete with sophisticated train and cut so low on Frankie's slighter bosom as to be almost indecent. "Good God!" his lordship repeated as Bertie, now at his elbow, gave a noisy gulp. "Where the devil do you think you're going dressed like that?" Greville Wainwright thundered.

There was a moment's awkward silence, then, "To do theatricals," Frankie offered while simultaneously her escort offered, "To a masquerade."

"To do theatricals at a masquerade," Frankie amended.

"Has Maria seen you got up like that?"

"Of course. My aunt is not a prude."

"She doesn't want for sense either. No young lady, barely out of the schoolroom, goes around looking like a—a—Cyprian."

"Oh," Frankie brightened, "is that what you think I look like?"

"It's no compliment, Miss Armstead."

"No, no, of course not," she said hastily. "But you must excuse us, Lord Greville. Bertie and I are running late. Rehearsal first, you see."

"Yes, and don't worry too much about the rackety way Frankie's dressed," Bertie offered, feeling the need evidently to meld all their various stories. "The theatricals are at the house of an old relative of mine who's blinder than a bat. She won't notice a thing. Good night now."

He was gradually edging Frankie away. Then the two of them wheeled suddenly and raced toward the waiting carriage. As they rattled their way down Grosvenor Square, Frankie turned to look back just once. Lord Greville Wainwright seemed turned to a salt pillar on her doorstep, staring after them.

Chapter
Sixteen

THEY ARRIVED EARLY, WHICH FRANKIE SAID WOULD never do. They had hired the vehicle for the evening, so when the coachman was informed that they intended to wait inside it for a bit, he merely shrugged. Whether he waited with a carriage occupied or empty was a matter of indifference to him. Frankie had already anticipated doubling his usual fare to ensure his silence. The evening was going to leave a terrible hole in her quarterly allowance, but if they accomplished what they'd come for, she'd consider the expenditure worth her while.

Bertie soon grew restive. "How much longer do we have to sit here?" he complained as they watched the press of carriages discharge their passengers before the Argyle Rooms. Frankie had been rather taken aback by the elegance of so many of the equipages. She had spotted more than one golden crest upon their doors. "What did you expect?" Bertie had replied in a world-wise tone when she commented on it. "Told you it was an exclusive affair, didn't I?" But now the suspense of waiting was wearing down his thin veneer of sophistication. "Come on, let's go. No sense sitting here all night. If you've lost your nerve, Frankie, I'll go in alone. Ought to, anyhow."

"I haven't lost my nerve," she said indignantly. "I just don't want us to have to be in there any longer than necessary, and I haven't seen the Lily arrive yet."

"That's not to say she ain't in there. We could have missed

her in the crush. Or she was probably already in before we came."

"Don't be a goose. She's the type to make an entrance. Mark my words. She'll not get here till everybody else has."

Then, as if on cue, a very smart chaise rolled past them as they cowered down once more out of sight. It came to a halt by the rich red carpet run from the doorway to the street, discharged its passengers, then moved away, allowing Frankie and Bertie a clear view of the magnificent Gilded Lily, her golden tresses topped with a tower of equally golden plumes, her figure swathed in a golden shawl of Norwich silk. "My word, she looks like King Midas just up and touched her," Bertie breathed.

Frankie made them wait several more minutes, "till she settles in, you know." Then, at last, they made their entrance.

For a very few seconds Frankie clung to the comfortable illusion that she had just entered an ordinary ballroom for an ordinary evening. The elegant decor, lavish with statuary and gilded carvings; the orchestra, ensconced on a raised platform, might have served as background for an evening spent in the company of the ton. And for just a fleeting moment, the guests assembled at the Argyle Rooms also seemed interchangeable. In point of fact, with many of the gentlemen it was no illusion, for they were equally at home in both societies.

For as Frankie gazed around her she soon realized that here were the very same gentlemen of quality who graced the drawing rooms of London's most fashionable houses, whose names were to be found on the exclusive membership rosters of White's and Brook's and Watier's. And, she also noted, they were dressed as impeccably as they would have been to spend an evening at those tony establishments.

But their behavior, she realized with a shock, was not the same at all. The gentlemen now dancing were holding their partners far too close for the dictates of propriety. Indeed, Frankie saw as she blushed behind her loo mask, male hands were inclined to wander most lasciviously over the anatomies of their partners. And those partners, who at first glance seemed so like the ladies whose style they tried to ape, on

154

closer inspection were painted and powdered and plumed and turbaned out of all reason above their décolleté gowns, while beneath those gowns, Frankie suddenly suspected, they wore little if anything at all. Then the awful fact struck her and Bertie at the exact same time. "They ain't masked," he whispered in her ear.

"I can see that," she whispered back. "Why on earth did you tell me that they would be?"

"Just stood to reason," he said simply.

"That's just how it doesn't stand" was her retort. "They've got nothing to hide. It's the men who should be masked, but just look at them."

"I am looking. But I don't think you should be. Come on, Frankie. I'm taking you home."

"You are not," she answered stoutly. "We've come this far, so let's get on with it. You go ask the Lily to dance. I'll stay nearby so when you get the necklace undone you can slip it to me."

"My God, what if she ain't got it on!" The thought obviously had not occurred before.

"She has to be wearing it." Frankie clutched his arm though, then relaxed her grip as the Lily moved into view, her beautiful bosom indeed adorned, like Napoleon's Josephine, in diamonds, pearls, and cameo.

As Miss Armstead and Mr. Yarwood edged their way round the room, squeezed in between the whirling dancers and others of the sisterhood and their admirers occupying chairs along the wall, they could not help but notice that several heads turned to stare in their direction. So when they found themselves beside two empty chairs, Bertie jerked Frankie down to sit beside him. "You've got to take that domino off," he whispered. "Stands out a mile. People are staring."

Obligingly she obeyed, dropping the black garment over a chair back. Bertie's eyes bugged out even farther than nature's slight flaw had placed them. "Well, I must say you blend in better, but I pray to God your uncle Matthew never gets wind of this. What about your mask? It's got to come off too, I guess."

"It can't," she groaned. "I've seen at least half a dozen men that could recognize me."

"Well," Bertie remarked philosophically, "if it leads folk to guess you really don't belong here, maybe they'll think you're Lady Caroline Lamb. Sounds like the kind of start she might get up to."

If Frankie thought privately that even the notorious Lady Caroline would stop short of attending a Cyprian Ball, she still appreciated Bertie's effort to put the best possible face on a situation that was likely to ruin her for life. Still, if they did not retrieve the necklace, there was no doubt at all that Evelyn was ruined. She set her mind determinedly on the task at hand.

"Let's dance over near the Lily," she said, "so you can be in line. Oh, my heavens!" she broke off short. "Bertie, I think they're waltzing!"

And sure enough, as far as she could judge by the tempo of the music and the whirling of the dancers, the revelers were throwing themselves wholeheartedly into the risqué dance craze that was all the rage upon the Continent but considered too shocking to be countenanced in proper English ballrooms.

"Oh, I say. I think you're right. That must be the waltz." Bertie was momentarily distracted by the gyrations on the dance floor. "Looks like fun, actually."

"Well, I think it's shocking. I certainly never expected that they'd waltz."

"Don't be such a widgeon, Frankie. Waltzing is the most respectable thing that's likely to be done in this place, so come on. Let's get at it."

"But I don't know how!"

"Neither do I. But who's to notice?" So saying, after one more concentrated stare at the revolving waltzers, he planted one gloved hand firmly on her waist, took her right hand in his other and whirled her with more determination than skill out onto the floor. "Ouch!" Frankie complained as he trod upon her toe.

"Sorry," he muttered grimly between his teeth. "This is harder than it looks, you know, especially when you're trying to catch up with someone in this crush." Indeed after a few more measures during which he attempted to keep the rhythm of three-quarter time, twirl his partner, and still work his way across the crowded floor toward the golden plumes that floated gracefully above the crowd, "The devil with this waltzing stuff," he whispered in his partner's ear. "Don't know about you, Frankie, but I've never been so dizzy. One more twirl and I hit the floor." With this pronouncement he modified his technique by setting a straight course for his target, omitting turns, but dipping one knee slightly on the first beat of every measure as a concession to the tune. If Frankie found this somewhat heavy going, propelled backward as she was, one glance at his grimly set jawline persuaded her not to say so.

But even as the waltz came to its merciful conclusion they actually wound up in the vicinity of the Gilded Lily. Bertie wasn't quick enough, however, to beat out the swarm of applicants for the beauty's hand. "Damnation," he muttered underneath his breath. And the maestro waved his orchestra into another waltz.

"Oh, Bertie, I can't go through that again," Miss Armstead wailed.

"I can't either," her companion answered. "Let's just track her from the sidelines and see if we can figure out where she'll stop when the cursed music ends so I can grab her. But I've got to tell you right now, Frankie, if they play another waltz then, well, I'm dished. How the devil I can be expected to go whirling around the floor without trampling her to death or falling in a dizzy fit is more than I can see, let alone get that cursed necklace off her neck all at the same time."

"Well, remember the catch is faulty. One good jiggle ought to do the trick."

"Don't you believe it" was his glum reply. "Any jewelry that's managed to stay on through two waltzes is on to stay."

But Lady Luck seemed to smile suddenly on Bertie. Not only did the Lily whirl to a stop right before them; she seemed quite genuinely pleased by the determination with which Mr. Yarwood elbowed a portly would-be partner out of the way and proclaimed in resounding tones with an aristocratic bow, "I believe this is our dance, Miss O'Malley." But there his good fortune failed. The orchestra, by popular demand, struck up another waltz.

It had not been part of the plan for Frankie to dance also. Her role was simply to be on hand to receive the stolen goods. So when a tall gentleman with ginger whiskers and a gleam in his eye approached, she politely declined his invitation. "I never waltz," she added primly.

The tall man roared with laughter. It occurred to Frankie that he was more than a trifle cast away. "Now, by God, I've seen it all—a missish light-skirt." So saying, he jerked her onto the dance floor.

"The fact is, I do not know how to waltz." Frankie tried vainly to extricate herself from the man's clutches. She was losing sight of Bertie and his partner in the crush. Then she briefly spied them just long enough to ascertain that the Gilded Lily had turned to dancing mistress and was trying to instruct her partner in the movements of the waltz. The man who now held her odiously tight had much the same idea. "Well, I'll teach you, little ladybird; then I dare say you can teach me a few tricks, eh?"

Frankie beat down her panic and concentrated on the task at hand. Since it was evident she could not rid herself of the inebriated gentleman, she determined to make use of him. After a few measures of "one-two-three, one-two-three" dinned into her ear with a breath that reeked unpleasantly of stale smoke and staler brandy, she said craftily, "Let's dance over near the orchestra. I'm rather hard of hearing, don't you know, and I'm sure I'll do much better there." She winced as her partner stepped down on the same tender toe Bertie had trod on. Satin slippers, she decided, were inappropriate for the waltz. One needed armor plating.

Ginger Whiskers obligingly set off in the general direction of the orchestra, the point targeted by Bertie for their rendezvous. But it was heavy going. For one thing, they kept colliding with other couples, due entirely to her partner's condition, Frankie thought, though he seemed to blame her own ineptitude, frowning reprovingly at her each time they crashed. For another, as she and Bertie had just discovered, the dance was not designed for reaching a certain goal. Each time they whirled, her partner seemed to tack in a new direction, making the orchestra appear as unattainable as the grail. Nor could Frankie decide whether her predicament was made worse or better by the fact that Bertie seemed to be having the same navigational difficulties. Throughout her own careening course Frankie had somehow managed to give the Lily's golden plumes the same zealous attention that the Children of Israel must have lavished upon the pillar of fire by night. And though at times the feathers did seem to whirl and twirl in the musicians' direction, at other times they seemed to fly entirely out of orbit, cut loose within the cosmos of the dance floor to travel God knows where. The only hope was chance. For the plan to meet on purpose at the orchestra together was obviously foredoomed. Frankie only prayed that they stop somewhere within range of each other. And to that end she tugged her partner once more in the direction of the plumes.

The maneuver did not work. In fact it had the opposite catastrophic effect to what she had intended. Her partner came to a complete halt in the middle of the whirling dancers and glared down at her.

"Whoever you are behind that mask, one thing's for sure. You ain't an opera dancer. In fact, if I may say so, you are possibly—no 'possibly' to it—you are absolutely the worst dancer I have ever had the misfortune to try and steer around a dance floor."

"I'm sorry," Frankie said humbly, watching the plumes fade in the distance. "I will try to do better this time. Let's go that way." She pointed toward the vanishing headdress.

"No, my little mystery ladybird, there's bound to be something you can do better than dancing or you wouldn't be here, now, would you?" He gave her bottom a sudden pinch.

"Sir!" Frankie gasped indignantly.

"That's the ticket," Ginger Whiskers bellowed as the couples around them turned their heads to grin encouragement. "Play it like a lady. Makes the game all the better, what? I tell you, little one, you'll go far. With that voice of yours, you make even the Lily herself sound downright common. Of course, she dresses better," he qualified. "And I ain't seen behind your mask yet, but by God you've got possibilities, and I ain't waiting another moment to explore 'em." He took Frankie by the hand and began to drag her off the floor.

Frankie was so intent upon spotting Bertie and the Lily that for a moment she did not comprehend what her partner had in mind. She had seen other couples depart the floor, clinging to one another, sometimes mouth to mouth in a passionate embrace, and exit through the same door toward which they headed. But she had closed her mind to the significance of those departures. Now it hit her with a sickening thud.

"Oh, you don't wish to see underneath my mask, sir," she improvised, trying to free herself from the viselike clasp of his hand upon her wrist. "Me face is 'orribly poxed, sir." She also tried to shed the cultured accent he so much admired.

"Is it now?" He sounded quite interested in that fact while he propelled her through the door. Frankie turned cold with fear as they approached a stairway. Another couple was halfway up it. The gentleman had already removed his cravat and was jerking feverishly at his waistcoat buttons, while his partner giggled at such unseemly haste.

"Well, now," Ginger Whiskers was saying as he dragged her up the first step, "no need to be concerned about me being disgusted by your face, love. We'll just leave the mask on, eh? Nothing like a touch of mystery to add spice to the romp, eh? And the rest of you's a bit of all right, I wager, judging from what I can see." His free hand moved toward her breasts as she shouted, "Bertie!" in a strangled cry.

Suddenly Ginger Whiskers was jerked off the step with a force and rapidity that gave him no time to let go of Frankie, who stumbled after him. But when a fist cracked against his jawbone, he went limp, both in hand and knee, sagging to the floor alone in a black and white, open-mouthed, ginger-whiskered heap.

"Is he dead?" Miss Armstead whispered.

"No such luck," Lord Greville answered grimly. "But he should be harmless for a while."

"Thank you." Her voice broke. "I can't tell you how grateful I am that you chanced along just this moment. Though I must say," she railed a bit, pushing the loo mask up to brush at some tears, "I am a trifle shocked to see you here. Though I shouldn't be, I suppose," she added, recalling a certain scene in a high perch phaeton that now seemed centuries ago.

"You're shocked to see *me* here! My God!" his lordship exclaimed, choking. He grabbed her by her now-smarting wrist. "Let's get out of here."

"Oh, but we can't!" Frankie was suddenly recalled to duty.

"Don't tempt me to throttle you, Miss Armstead." Her rescuer glared angrily. "I've just leveled that lecher there"—he pointed to the ginger-haired man, who was beginning to groan and open up his eyes—"and I'm planning to kill Bertie Yarwood when I get my hands on him. Don't make me add you to my list of victims."

"Oh, my goodness, Bertie!" Frankie was looking up at Lord Greville, and even a loo mask could not conceal all the horror on her face. "The music's stopped! Oh, please, I've got to hurry. There's no time to explain." She tugged him back toward the ballroom as he kept an iron grip upon her rapidly numbing wrist. But no sooner had they burst through the door than the party chatter was overset by a piercing shriek. "Thief! Thief! Stop that thieving toff!" the Lily screamed.

"Oh, dear heaven, we're too late," Frankie moaned.

The plumes, she saw, had indeed made it to the orchestra. And she herself was the one who had missed the rendezvous. The disaster was all on her own head. She had failed Bertie. Miserably.

As Frankie elbowed her way through the ring now gathered around her accomplice, the reproachful look he gave her cut to her heart like an assassin's knife. An immense bruiser with a flattened nose was holding Mr. Yarwood upward by the collar. The white folds of his cravat might well have been a hangman's noose. Yet despite acute discomfort and embarrassment he was still clutching Lady Venetia's necklace in his fist, managing somehow to keep it out of the Lily's grasping fingers while the Bruiser shook him like a puppy held by the neck scruff.

"Give it to 'er!" the Bruiser directed.

"Let go of him!" Lord Greville Wainwright, late of His Majesty's quarter deck, taught the Bruiser a thing or two about barking orders.

"You go to 'ell, sir," the Bruiser told this new annoyance just before the fist landed on his often-targeted nose which, in lieu of Achilles Heel, had served to finish him early in the fight game. He went down like timber, taking Bertie with him. The Lily, scrambling for the necklace, joined the heap.

While the Bruiser lay there hors de combat, the other two struggled to their feet with Bertie still miraculously in charge of the jewelry but with deep scratches lining his young face to prove that the victory had not been cheap.

"Are you just going to stand there and let him steal my property? Get him!" The Gilded Lily tried to exhort the crowd to action. But whereas the females of her own trade guild began to mutter threateningly, the gentlemen of the ton seemed to hesitate. Bertie in his turn played upon their obvious loyalty to one of their own kind. "The necklace ain't hers!" he informed them loudly. Lord Greville's eyes widened at that declaration. He too seemed to recognize the Empress Josephine design.

He turned to the Lily then and spoke with amazing courtesy, Frankie thought, given the recent combativeness of his temperament. "I'm Lord Greville Wainwright. I'm sure there's been some sort of misunderstanding here. Is there a less public place we could go to straighten this matter out?"

As she and Bertie followed the Lily and Lord Greville up the stairs, Frankie tried to close her ears to the squeals, giggles, and moans that drifted out into the hall from behind closed doors. At last the Lily found a room with its door ajar and led them into a small sitting area. There were chairs aplenty grouped around a cheery fire, but no one thought to sit. They all stood instead in a hostile huddle while the Lily and Bertie glared at each other and Frankie removed her mask.

"I should have realized earlier who you are," the Lily spit. "You're Evie's brother, ain't you? I can see the resemblance now, though you can't begin to touch him for good looks."

162

"I say," Bertie sputtered, and looked more pained than ever but evidently could not think of a suitable set-down.

The Lily kept the floor. "But you're every bit as sneaky as Evie, though; I'll say that much for you. Lifting the jewelry right off me neck! He put you up to it, though, now didn't he?"

"No. Well, yes, in a way, you could say that, but . . ." That protest, too, died suddenly on Bertie's lips.

It was Lord Greville's turn to glare. Only Frankie was his target. "You actually came to the Cyprian's Ball to steal a necklace for Evelyn Yarwood?" His voice was heavy with disgust. "My God, he really does have you besotted."

"No!" she answered heatedly. "I mean, yes, I came here to help Bertie get the necklace back. But I am not besotted over Evelyn. I just don't wish to see him go to prison, that's all. At least," she amended, "I don't wish to see his family see him go to prison. Actually, I think a few weeks spent in Newgate might do Evelyn a great deal of good."

"Well"—the Lily jerked her head toward Bertie—"it looks like it's this one who'll be Newgate bait, while as usual His Nibs goes scot-free. You're a bigger fool than I am, little brother."

"Let's not be hasty," Lord Greville drawled. "Will somebody please tell me what this is all about? Though I think I can guess the most of it, I'd as soon not try."

Bertie, with several corrections and additions from Miss Armstead, proceeded to unfold the story of the faulty necklace clasp, the debt owed the Cyprian, and the necklace held as surety on the debt, and the pressure the rightful owner was putting upon Mr. Evelyn Yarwood for the return of her property. "I intend to pay what Evelyn owes you," Bertie informed the Lily with stiff dignity. "But the thing is, I can't get my hands on that much blunt immediately, and I didn't reckon you'd take my note any quicker than you'd take Evelyn's."

"You're right there." The beauty gave him a chilly smile. "In fact, even if you had the cash in your fist right this minute I wouldn't let you have the necklace. It's mine now. And Evelyn can squirm out of Newgate the best he can."

"I think not." Lord Greville spoke matter-of-factly. "I

think you'll take my note for the amount Evelyn owes you—plus interest for your trouble and for forgetting tonight's little incident. Where's something I can write on? You'll have your money, I promise you, as soon as the bank opens in the morning."

The Lily called him a name that put Frankie to the blush but left the ex-sailor quite unruffled. "You don't hear so well, now, do you?" she continued. "I said I mean to keep the necklace. If you try to walk out of here with it, there's a roomful of people down there"—she gestured dramatically toward the ballroom—"prepared to swear that this one"—she glared at Bertie—"took it off my neck."

"There's a roomful of *prostitutes*"—Lord Greville gently stressed the word "—who may or may not testify to what you say. Your sisters aren't too fond of courts of law, you know. But on the other hand, my father, Lord Wainwright, and Mr. Yarwood here and I are prepared to say that you accosted Evelyn Yarwood in the park while he was carrying the jewels for Lady Venetia and likely picked his pocket." Frankie opened her mouth in the cause of justice, but Bertie poked her in the ribs and glared a warning. "Now, which of us do you think the judge will believe?" Lord Greville asked the Lily.

The courtesan stood with clenched fists, her lovely face contorted and Frankie could not help but feel a bit sorry for the impotence of her position. So, perhaps, did Lord Greville, for he said gently, "Come on, Lily, it's the way of the world, you know. And you aren't going to lose by keeping quiet, I promise you. Besides, making trouble for Yarwood would be bad for trade. Gentlemen might be a bit reluctant to become entangled with a ladybird, even one as lovely as you, who puts vengeance ahead of business. Come on, Lily. You've always been known for having a cool head. What shall it be?"

In answer, the Gilded Lily, plumes held high, strolled across the room to where pen and ink were waiting on a rosewood desk. She opened and slammed shut several drawers before finally unearthing a sheet of paper. "All right, then, you win." She gave Lord Greville a frosty smile. "Write me your note."

She watched him as he did so, her eyes widening just a bit at the increased figure that he jotted down. When he handed the paper to her, she waved it gently back and forth until the ink dried, then folded it over and over again until she'd decreased the size sufficiently to be concealed in the abbreviated bodice of her dress.

Frankie could only admire the courtesan's grace and poise as she walked with stately dignity toward the door. The Lily opened it and started out, then turned to scorch the three of them with a scornful glance. "And the 'ell with the lot o' you!" she screeched.

Chapter
Seventeen

A SILENCE HAD DESCENDED UPON THE HACKNEY FROM the moment the three passengers had clambered thankfully into it and left the Argyle Rooms behind. Frankie, swathed once more in her reclaimed domino, sat beside Bertie and faced Lord Greville, who had produced a cigar from the recesses of his coat and was now, without a by-your-leave, blowing a cloud that filled the confines of the coach with smoke. Frankie wondered if he could be feeling even half as cool as he managed now to look.

Bertie broke the silence. After clearing his throat a time or two, he finally produced a halting speech. "Don't really know how to set about thanking you, Lord Greville. It was a piece of luck, your happening to be there. We'd have been dished if you hadn't turned up when you did. I just want you to know you won't be out of pocket for anything. If you'll just tell me how much you gave the Lily above Evelyn's debts"—even in the dim light afforded by the street lamps it was evident that the thought sent Bertie rather pale—"I'll see that you get that too, of course."

"No." Greville looked at him through the smoke with narrowed eyes. "You only need pay me back the principal. The extra that I added was my own idea entirely. Let's just call it payment for the hiding I'm about to give you for taking Miss Armstead into such a place. My God, boy, what could you have been thinking of? And there's no need saying it was all her own idea; that does not excuse—"

"I wasn't going to say it," Bertie interrupted with a mulish expression on his face. "And if you think you can say anything to me I ain't already saying to myself, you much mistake the matter and might just as well save your breath to smoke with. Now that I know what a Cyprian Ball is like, I never would—well, there's no need in going into all that now. But at the time, getting the necklace back was all I could think of and it did seem as if we could pull it off—go in and pocket it, I mean, with no one wiser. And it almost worked, too. I'd palmed the cursed thing, ready to hand it over, but there was nobody there to take it. Got caught red-handed!" He shuddered at the memory. "Where the devil were you, Frankie?"

"She was being dragged upstairs by a very drunk but still very determined man; that's where she was." Lord Greville's eyes were steely.

"Oh, my God."

"You'd have admired the way Lord Greville here milled the fellow down, Bertie," Frankie said nervously, thinking it time to lighten the conversation up a bit. "I do believe it was even more expertly done than the way in which he milled down the Bruiser, who held you by the collar. You were certainly right when you said he was handy with his fives." She subsided as the two stared coldly at her. "Milled him down? Handy with his fives? Those are the right expressions, aren't they, Bertie?"

"Frankie, do be quiet." Mr. Yarwood turned his attention back to Lord Greville once again. "I realize I should have

166

known better, only I didn't really know by half. But I mean to make it as right as I'm able to. I plan to offer for her."

"You'll do no such thing!" Miss Armstead exclaimed.

"Certainly I will. Stands to reason I have to. Of course, I want to, too," he amended as Lord Greville choked suddenly on his cigar.

"Well, I don't want you to."

"For the Lord's sake, Frankie"—her suitor stared at her in complete disgust—"you surely ain't sapskulled enough to still want to marry Evelyn after all of this?"

"Of course not. In fact I have not wished to marry Evelyn for—goodness only knows how long. But I do not wish to marry you either, Bertie Yarwood."

"Well, dammit, Frankie, you have to marry somebody. And if the word of this ever leaks out"—he shuddered—"coves won't exactly be lining up for the honor, you must realize."

"You seem to forget, old boy," Lord Greville remarked idly, "that she's secretly engaged to me."

"That isn't funny." Frankie glared his way, then turned her fire back onto Bertie. "I do not 'have to marry somebody.' I'm an heiress and can live independently."

"Some life that would be," the other snorted.

"Children, children," Lord Greville chided, "here we are." The hackney had come to a stop at Grosvenor Square, where despite the lateness of the hour the houses of Lord Wainwright and Lady Paxton were both lit from top to bottom. "Let's continue this fascinating discussion inside. Oh, the devil. Just a minute, Frankie." He paused in the act of helping Miss Armstead from the coach to produce a snowy handkerchief and apply it vigorously to her face. "Ouch!" she complained loudly as he scrubbed. "Let's get some of this paint off before we go in," he said. "It's going to be hard enough to explain this evening satisfactorily. It would help if I could spit on this. No? Well, then, just elbow grease." After a moment he gazed intently at her face. "Yes, that's definitely better." He lifted her, quite unnecessarily, so she thought, down to the street, then turned to pay off the driver.

Inside they were confronted in the hall by Lady Paxton, who

looked worried, and Evelyn Yarwood, who looked incensed. "Where the devil have you been?" he demanded of his brother. "Papa and Mr. Armstead had the maggoty notion to drive up from Hampshire together and got here two hours ago. You can imagine how well it went down with our father—not to mention Mr. Armstead—when Lady Paxton here informed him that you'd gone visiting a relative of ours that doesn't exist."

"Uncle Matthew's here? Now?" Frankie exclaimed. That, she felt, was all the evening needed.

"Not at the moment." Her aunt was ushering them upstairs, where she ordered tea brought to the yellow saloon. "Lord Wainwright has taken them to his club. He was here when they arrived and has very graciously invited them to stay next door."

"Oh, Uncle Matthew will be pleased," Frankie said ingenuously, and Lord Greville smiled.

"Oh, yes, it's just one big Hampshire reunion," Evelyn declared while Dearborn placed the tea things. "One would think your grandfather was their bosom beau back home unless one knew better." He gave the younger Wainwright an unfriendly smile.

"My grandfather's London visit has done wonders for him," the other answered evenly. "He's completely forsaken his reclusive habits."

"Will there be anything else, madame?" Dearborn inquired, and then withdrew. No sooner had the door closed than Evelyn wheeled on Bertie. "Do you intend to explain yourself or not, little brother? Where have you been?"

It was the wrong tone entirely. Bertie, who had been seething since his brother's initial greeting, now exploded. "I'll tell you where I've been." He produced Lady Venetia's necklace with a flourish any conjurer could have been proud of. "I've been getting this back for you. That's where I've been."

"You went to the Cyprian Ball?" Evelyn's aplomb deserted him. "And took Frankie with you?"

"Oh, my God," Lady Paxton said weakly, her teacup frozen halfway to her mouth.

"Yes, we went to the Cyprian Ball." Bertie sounded dangerous. "That was what you wanted me to do, wasn't it?"

"No! Well—perhaps. But I certainly didn't want you to take a young lady there! My God, Bertie, I never dreamed that even you would do such a thing."

"There's a lot you never dreamed of, Evelyn."

The older Yarwood groaned. "Why didn't you tell me what you were up to, Bertie? If you had only seen fit to confide in me, I could have scotched this whole disgraceful scrape. You see, I raised the blunt myself this afternoon."

"You did what!" Frankie choked. Bertie's unblinking eyes never left his brother's face.

"I borrowed the money this afternoon," Evelyn repeated for Frankie's benefit. "And I intended to get the necklace from the—moneylender—in the morning and return it to Lady Venetia. So that would have been that, little brother, without all your rackety exertions."

"No, it wouldn't have been."

"I beg your pardon?"

"It would not have been that." The scales seemed to have fallen from Albert Yarwood's eyes. He was glaring at his brother with something bordering on contempt. "The thing is, the Lily was going to dish you. She wouldn't have given you back the necklace. She wanted you to stew in your own juice, Evelyn, and it would have been Newgate for sure, big brother, if Lord Greville here hadn't told her he'd swear she picked your pocket. What's more he paid her half the amount again. So you wouldn't have pulled this off without my 'rackety exertions,' Evelyn. And in case you forget it, I intend to draw your cork for you here and now." Bertie had risen and was taking a menacing step toward his older brother, who hastily put down his teacup and backed away. Lord Greville stood too, rather reluctantly, and laid a restraining hand on Bertie's sleeve. "Much as it pains me to say so, old man," he said gently, "I don't think you should right now. The ladies have been through a lot already. Besides, our respective relatives are due back any moment."

"Later then, brother," Bertie said between clenched teeth.

"Certainly, if you think you're man enough," Evelyn retorted, *sans* a good deal of his usual bravado.

"And I'll tell you something else right now." It was obvious to all present that the worm had really turned. Bertie was spoiling for a fight. If it could not be physical, verbal would have to do. "Frankie ain't about to run to Gretna Green with you. She don't want to in the first place, and in the second place I wouldn't let her even if she did. The fact is, you ain't nearly good enough for Frankie, Evelyn."

"I know that, Bertie." For once Evelyn managed to sound humble.

"Is it true, Frankie?" Lady Paxton asked gently, looking searchingly at her niece. "That you don't wish to marry Evelyn? You've had a tendre for him since you were in leading strings, I believe."

"Yes, I know. But I'm grown-up now, and no, I do not wish to. I'm sure you understand, Evelyn." She gave him a wan, apologetic smile. "For now I know, of course, that except for my fortune, you never really wished to marry me. I do hope that my crying off won't inconvenience you too much."

Evelyn, who actually looked abashed, said, "No, of course not. But believe it, Frankie; I'm very fond of you."

"That ain't good enough," his brother remarked darkly.

"Well, at any rate"—Lady Paxton, who alone had not risen from the tea table during the threatened fight, motioned the others to take their seats again—"this makes my—our—announcement a bit easier. I think you should all know, before the others get here, that Evelyn and I plan to be married."

"Aunt Maria!" and "My God!" Frankie and Bertie gasped simultaneously.

"Congratulations, old boy." Lord Greville saluted Evelyn with his teacup. "You are one for landing on your feet."

"Aunt Maria, how could you?" Frankie blurted, then turned beet red.

"How could I marry someone so much my junior?" her aunt countered. "Quite easily, in fact. Having married two charming gentlemen so much my senior, I'm quite curious to try the other way."

"I d-didn't mean," Frankie stammered. "That is to say, you don't actually look—"

170

"Of course you meant," her aunt answered pleasantly. "And so will everybody else. I'm quite prepared to be the *on dit* of all the drawing rooms, you know, my dear. In fact, I shall rather enjoy it."

"Evelyn ain't good enough for you, ma'am," Bertie suddenly declared.

"Why, thank you, Albert," Lady Paxton laughed. "But actually I think you're wrong. We are in fact quite well suited, I believe." She gave Evelyn a dazzling smile. "I dare say we understand each other very well and shall deal famously together. But do you know"—she turned back to Bertie—"the thing I most look forward to in marrying Evelyn is having you for a brother." She stopped abruptly then and chuckled. "Or are you to be my nephew? This really is confusing. But am I wrong in my impression that you're working up to a declaration? You do intend to offer for Frances, do you not?"

"Yes, I do," said Bertie with firm resolution. "In fact, I think I did already. Back there in the coach. I did make you an offer, didn't I, Frankie?"

"No, you did not!" Miss Armstead was having difficulty keeping her emotions under control. It had been a most trying evening. "I mean, you may have, but I have made it clear that I have no intention of letting you do such a cork-brained thing."

"And I," Lord Greville interposed blandly, "keep trying to point out a fact that everyone seems determined to ignore. Miss Armstead here is betrothed to me. Indeed, she has been ever since I fell helplessly in love with her at your house party, Lady Paxton."

"How dare you!" Frankie almost upset the tea table jumping to her feet. She turned to face his lordship with clenched fists and a threat of tears. "That remark on top of everything else that's happened is really the outside of enough. Your sense of humor, Lord Greville Wainwright, is most abominable. It's worse even than that. It's—it's—"

"Despicable?" Bertie offered helpfully as she then fled from the room.

Frankie raced up the stairs, into her bedchamber, and flung herself upon the bed. But then, before letting loose the storm of emotion that had been building throughout the long, hideous evening, she got to her knees and pulled the curtains closed around her. After that, just as she was about to refling herself and howl, she was hampered by the twisted folds of the concealing domino that she had not dared remove downstairs. She jerked off the offending garment and tossed it through the curtains.

"Oof!" a male voice protested. The draperies around the four-poster parted, and Lord Wainwright crawled in to sit beside her. "I thought of waiting to see what other garments you might hit me with," he offered, "but it didn't seem the sporting thing."

"What do you think you're doing?" Frankie gasped. "Get out of my bed, sir. Have you lost all sense of propriety?"

"I'm sure I must have," he answered soberly, pulling off his black long-tailed coat and consigning it to the same fate as Frankie's domino. He propped one of the pillows on the headboard and leaned back against it. "You tend to have that effect on a fellow, Frankie." He reached out and pulled her to him.

Suddenly there was nothing she wanted quite so much as to throw her arms around him, press her face into the shoulder of his frilly shirt, and get on with her plan of howling. But a sudden vision of her uncle Matthew served to remind her of the compromising position she was in. With even more strength of will than armpower she managed to brace her hands against his chest and shove them apart. She then sat on her knees facing him while he continued to lounge against the pillow. His face was far too shadowed for her to read his expression, but she did not need to.

"I realize I'm responsible for your conduct," she said bitterly. "Not only did I kiss you like a wanton—yesterday, was it?—but tonight I went to the Cyprian Ball. So it's little wonder that you feel free to take any sort of liberty. But short of ringing for the servants, I'd like to convince you that you much mistake the matter. So would you please remind yourself that you are a gentleman and get out of my bed and out of my room. Though when it comes to that"—she was momentarily diverted from the main issue—"for the life of me I cannot understand why I'm sunk below reproach for both those things, and

172

yet you can kiss me and go to that horrible place with perfect impunity and still be thought a gentleman."

"It's an unfair world," he murmured, reaching for her again. She continued holding him off, however. "But I will say in my defense that I'd not ordinarily take in the Cyprian Ball. That was on account of you, of course."

"Was it?" Her eyes widened. "My governess used to tell me that. But I never believed it for a minute."

"Your governess? Frankie, has anyone ever mentioned how hard your conversations are to follow?"

"My governess always said that a lady never encourages a gentleman in the matter of physical intimacy, because it, ah, stirs him up in that particular way and practically drives him to seek out women of ill repute. But I never believed her. She was a platter-faced old maid, you know. Now I suppose there must be some truth in it. Who would have thought that old Miss Killen would have been so worldly-wise."

"Frankie"—his lordship was having difficulty keeping his laughter muted enough not to pass the confines of the curtains—"do you honestly believe that you roused all my animal instincts there in St. James's Park and sent me on a Cyprian hunt?" Before she could reply, she was shocked to silence by the sound of the opening door.

It was no doubt in an effort to help maintain her noiseless state that his lordship drew her close and planted his mouth firmly upon her own. She was dimly aware of the sound of the coal scuttle being placed upon the hearth and the poker being wielded with some vigor. But after that she was aware of nothing more except that Greville Wainwright's lovemaking was even more devastating than she remembered it.

"She's gone now, I think," his lordship remarked after a bit. "What were we saying?"

Frankie's "How dare you, sir!" rang a little hollow even to her ears, perhaps only because her face was now buried in his shirt.

"You were accusing yourself of sending me to the Cyprian Ball, I believe. Well, that's true, but not in the way you meant it. I followed you there, of course."

She raised her head at that. "Followed me! Whatever for?"

"Well, when I saw you dressed the way you were, I knew that you and Bertie were up to no good, though in my wildest dreams I never imagined what you had in mind." He choked a bit again. "I can see that life with you, Frankie, is going to be filled with surprise. But as I was saying, at the time I thought you were about to elope with Evelyn and were trying to look older or some daft thing. And I meant to put a period to that nonsense, of course."

"Of course?" she echoed. "I thought you said Evelyn and I deserved each other."

"Did I say that? Well, disregard it. It was just the last futile thrashings of a man beginning to realize that he's been well and truly hooked."

She tried hard in the dim light to read his face. "You mean, I hooked you?"

"That's it, I'm afraid."

"Well, that's a revelation! You certainly managed to hide it well."

"Thank you. I tried. But I had a feeling I'd botched the job."

"So I expect you're about to make an offer of carte blanche."

"I most definitely am not."

"Good. For even though there's no use saying I'd not be tempted, I'd never consent to such a thing. I'm not really a wanton, you know. It's just that you keep catching me off guard."

"I know." He pulled her into his arms again. "It's most unfair," he murmured just before kissing her again.

This encounter took even longer than before. It was Lord Greville who at last called things to a halt with considerable reluctance. "I'm afraid we'd better climb out of this bed, little love, and go downstairs. The Hampshire gentlemen should be back by now. And they'll be waiting to toast our betrothal. They must be wondering what's taking us so long. No, cancel that. They can't be that old."

"Waiting to what?" Frankie gasped.

"Toast our betrothal. I told your aunt and the Yarwood brothers that I was going after you to go down on one knee, so to speak. But that was God knows how long ago." He was climbing out of the four-poster and pulling her after him. He grinned at her in the firelight and the gleam of a single candle. "I do think you'd better change that gown and do something about your hair, though, before your uncle Matthew sees you. He may send for a clergyman on the spot."

"You're certainly sure of yourself," she retorted. "What makes you think I'd marry you?"

"Because you're no wanton" was the prompt reply. "Besides, we love each other."

"Oh." The answer sounded reasonable enough.

The group collected in the yellow parlor gazed at them expectantly as they entered. Bertie was sprawled in a chair with his cravat loosened, looking completely exhausted and a trifle disgusted. Lady Paxton and Evelyn Yarwood were side by side on the sofa holding hands. The three gentlemen from Hampshire were seated at the tea table sipping contentedly, though tea had been replaced by champagne all around.

"Well, my lad"—Lord Wainwright beamed fondly at his grandson—"as you can see, we've anticipated the toasts a bit, but I gather we may finally wish you happy?"

"You may indeed," his heir said solemnly. "Miss Armstead has agreed to marry me and make me the most fortunate of men."

"Hear! Hear!" The glasses clinked and all imbibed again.

"But what I don't understand," Mr. George Yarwood remarked after the congratulations had subsided, "is why all the secrecy? As I understand it, you two have actually been betrothed for donkey's years."

"Oh, that was all a h—" his second son was beginning to explain when Lord Greville cut in smoothly. "You're right, of course. I fell head over heels in love with Frankie when I first saw her at her aunt's house party." He refused to glance at his beloved, who was choking on her champagne. "But because of her youth and limited exposure to members of the opposite sex—no offense, gentlemen"—he bowed to the Yarwood brothers—"I thought it only fair to allow her to make her come-out and enjoy a London Season. Then if she was still of the same mind—Well, as you can see, my gamble has paid off."

Mr. Matthew Armstead, rapidly approaching Bertie's degree of mellowness, beamed at the pair through misty eyes. "I should have known that Frankie there was hoodwinking me when she tried to pretend there was nothing between you two. Shame on you, miss." He wagged a finger roguishly.

But a thought had suddenly struck that newly affianced lady. She looked up at her betrothed accusingly. "Greville, I have just thought why it is you wish to marry me in particular."

"Oh?" He cocked an eyebrow. "I can hardly wait to hear. Why is that?"

"Because I said that any proper-thinking wife should be quite willing for you to continue in the navy."

"Well, you're wrong there, love." Oblivious to his audience, he drew her close again. "For to be perfectly honest," he said huskily, "once I'm wed to you I don't think I'll ever want to go to sea again."

A hoot of laughter coming from the direction of Bertie Yarwood shattered the tender scene. "That's easy enough to say, you know," he said, choking. "For any cove who marries Frankie is bound to be at sea already. And you may not know it yet, but going down on the HMS *Arrow* won't be a happenstance to what your future's got in store. After a few years with Frankie you'll probably look back on that as the tamest thing that ever happened. Well, you did survive being shot out of the water and you survived Trafalgar, so there's hope for you."

He struggled to his feet and raised his glass. "Here's to Lord Greville Wainwright, a true hero if I ever saw one. And here's to Frankie, the best friend a cove ever had. And to all the little Wainwrights who'll be sent to plague us." He drained his glass, then threw it in the Russian fashion. It missed the Adam fireplace by a mile.

Miss Romney
Flies Too High

Chapter One

LORD PETHERBRIDGE LAY DYING—ONCE AGAIN. BUT IF the angel of death was indeed hovering, as the two nephews who had dutifully obeyed the summons to attend his lordship's final hours were prone to doubt, that dread messenger could possibly have been put off by the invalid's scowling countenance. The old gentleman was propped up by a mountainous pile of pillows against the headboard of a mahogany four-poster bed. His nightcap was askew on his puckered forehead. His bushy gray eyebrows beetled over protuberant pale blue eyes that glared at the young men who had been attending him for the better part of an hour.

"What's keeping Gray?" his lordship snapped. "I said I wanted the three of you here at two o'clock. It's almost four."

As if to be perverse, the clock in the hallway whirred a bit and then struck hollowly. "It's just three, sir." The Honorable Randolph Milbanke had taken the trouble to count, in defense of his absent brother. His tabulation earned him an offended stare from his great-uncle and a wicked, if swift, smile from his older cousin.

"Sit down, will you, Randolph." His lordship waved impatiently toward the carved and gilt armchair that the lanky young man in riding coat and buckskins had recently vacated. "You're pacing like a caged beast in the tower menagerie. I'll say this much for Gerard, he ain't fidgety." He bestowed an almost benign look upon the exquisite sprawled in a wing chair

179

in front of the Adam fireplace—not for warmth, since the grate was empty and the month was June, but because the chair happened to be placed so and he had seen no need to expend the energy it would take to shift it.

Mr. Gerard Langford, elegantly clad in bottle-green long-tailed coat, champagne breeches, and shiny Hessians, yawned lazily and stared at his cousin through his quizzing glass. "Uncle's right, you know. One might suspect you're uneasy over Gray's defection. The sentiment shows commendable loyalty, I suppose, but a deplorable lack of self-interest, I must say." He smiled mockingly at Randolph.

No one, least of all his cousin, would have accused Mr. Langford of such a lack. The mistake that casual acquaintances often did make was to be led astray by some carefully cultivated mannerisms into writing him off as merely a fop. Fooled by the conjurer's trick of diversion, they noted the handsome face and the artfully curled fair hair and overlooked the muscular shoulders under the Weston coat and the calculating look that lurked behind the lazy azure eyes. His cousin Randolph was not so easily deceived. "Gray ain't defected, Gerry. He'll be here." He gave the other a challenging stare and obediently resumed his seat.

"Shows a want of feeling." There was injury in his lordship's tone. "When a man sends a message to town to say he's dying and wants his family at his side—well, he certainly expects punctuality. Could've already breathed me last as far as Graymarsh knows."

"Oh, I don't think that Gray expects . . ." Randolph's disclaimer sputtered and died under his uncle's glare. Gerard's muffled chuckle was its death knell. Randolph reddened to the roots of his Brutus-styled brown hair. But once again fraternal loyalty overcame self-interest. The usually amiable boyish face set stubbornly. "Since this ain't the first time we've been sent for, sir, I expect that Gray hopes for the best. Or"—Randolph Milbanke clutched at straws—"more likely, he never got your message."

"Oh, he got it all right." Mr. Langford casually picked an imaginary piece of lint from the sleeve his valet had brushed lovingly and unnecessarily a few hours before. "Saw him at

White's. Said so." He met his cousin's indignant gaze with an ingenuous smile.

"Well, then, he'll be here," Randolph said staunchly, just as the sound of metal wheels on gravel and heavy, plodding hoof-beats came drifting through the open windows. "What in the—" He broke off.

"I would hazard a guess that the laggard has arrived," his cousin replied lazily.

"Can't be." Randolph was on his feet, though, hurrying toward a window that overlooked the carriage drive. He leaned perilously far out of it. "It is him! My God!"

His shocked tone was enough to spur his languid cousin into action. Gerard followed Randolph to the window and peered through his quizzing glass past the other's shoulder. "My God," he echoed softly.

"What is it? What's going on?" His lordship's voice boomed with surprising vigor as he sat upright. "Somebody tell me what's going on!"

"Lord Graymarsh has finally arrived, sir," Mr. Langford drawled as he turned away from the window and strolled back to collapse once again into his chair, heaving a weary sigh. "In a horse cart. Perched on a load of straw. Driven by a rustic."

"Wha—wha—" His uncle's prominent eyes protruded even farther as he sputtered, "Don't bam me, boy, just because I'm dying. What would Graymarsh be doing on a load of hay?"

"Cursed if I know." The other yawned. "But like you, I await the explanation with bated breath."

The wait was not a long one. Lord Petherbridge continued to sit bolt upright; the Honorable Randolph Milbanke stood rooted in mid-chamber, staring at the door; and even Mr. Langford exerted himself so far as to shift his chair a fraction to provide a better view of the entryway. They remained in a tableau while the sound of hurrying footsteps taking the stairs two at a time echoed down the hall. The chamber door opened a second later and Winfield Milbanke, the sixth Baron of Graymarsh, strode in.

It was not immediately apparent that he and Randolph were brothers. He was half a head shorter than the nineteen-year-old, who had shot to an amazing height during the past year. And

181

while he possessed only a medium-size frame and trim figure, he was well-muscled and filled out in contrast to his brother. His hair was darker, almost black, and there was nothing boyish about his face. In fact, the high cheekbones, angular jaw, and slightly hawkish nose made his countenance appear forbidding at times. This effect was slightly softened by clear gray eyes and a charming smile, which was now directed at his uncle.

"Oh, good. You're looking quite the thing. I had hoped so. Though that doesn't wash as an excuse for being late. I must seem positively rag-mannered. I beg your pardon for it."

Lord Graymarsh's terminology could have been called into question. His uncle while obviously not expiring, did not, however, look "quite the thing." In point of fact, his mouth was gaping in a fishlike manner—the resemblance heightened by his popping eyes—as he took in the appearance of the late arrival.

At the best of times, the sixth Baron of Graymarsh could lay no claim to dandyism. But he was, as a rule, quietly up to snuff. And if not precisely fastidious, neither was he careless. At least that had been the case. At the moment, however, his lordship's gray riding coat was flecked with mud, and there was a large triangular tear in the left sleeve. His buckskins were even muddier than his coat, while his top boots, in spite of some efforts to clean them off, had obviously been wading in the muck. Here and there, wisps of straw clung to his apparel.

"Gray—What on earth!" Lord Graymarsh's brother gasped while at the same time Lord Petherbridge gave tongue. "They said you came here in a hay cart." Despite the tangible evidence clinging to his nephew's clothing, his voice was rich with disbelief.

"I'm afraid I did, sir." Petherbridge's favorite nephew walked over to the four-poster and looked ruefully at his uncle. "It wasn't my intention. I left from outside London by balloon, you see."

"You did what?" his uncle roared, while his brother gasped and exclaimed, "Oh, I say, did you?" and his cousin shook his head despairingly.

"Came in a balloon!" Lord Petherbridge's voice dropped a bit in volume but retained its disbelief.

"Didn't you know, Uncle?" Gerard drawled. "It's his latest start. My scientific cousin has forsaken the steam engine for balloons. Really, Gray," he said with a sigh, "why can't you be content being a bang-up-to-the-nines whip like anybody else? Balloons! Terribly bad form. Not at all the thing."

Lord Petherbridge seemed of the selfsame mind. "You came from London in a balloon?" From the heightened ferocity of his frown, this sin far outweighed tardiness. "After I'd sent word to you I was on me deathbed, you took a balloon to get here? Why, the public coach would have been more respectable. I must say, Winfield, I'm disappointed in you. Wouldn't have expected such rackety behavior on your part. From Randolph maybe, but not you. You'll soon be thirty. Besides, it ain't respectful at any age to come to somebody's deathbed by balloon. Shows a want of serious feeling."

Mr. Langford seemed to be enjoying his cousin's setdown, while Randolph looked offended by the reference to himself. Only the chief recipient of the old gentleman's displeasure appeared unaffected. "Well, actually," he explained amiably, "at daybreak it seemed quite a good idea. All the conditions were favorable for a flight. I should have been able to come down somewhere in the vicinity. But unfortunately the wind shifted and I was carried miles out of my way and wound up in a bog. By the time I'd rescued myself and the balloon—and walked for several miles before the farmer's cart came along . . . Well, instead of stealing a march on my brother and my cousin, I've kept you waiting. Again, I do beg your pardon for it." His smile took in the other two as well as the old gentleman.

"I could've been dead by the time you got here," the latter said petulantly.

"*He* could have been dead, coming by balloon!" Randolph protested.

"There was little chance of either." Because of his muddy clothes, Lord Graymarsh carefully avoided the upholstered furniture and pulled a spoon-backed chair with a cane bottom up close to the bed. "Ballooning's not as dangerous as it's popularly conceived to be"—this was said to his brother as he sat down—

"and, Uncle, I presume that there's something besides dying on your mind."

Randolph gasped at his brother's forthrightness and braced himself for the explosion that was sure to follow. But surprisingly, the old gentleman appeared less angry than embarrassed. "Cried wolf too often, have I?"

"Well . . ." His nephew crossed his muddy top boots at the ankles. "You do seem to find it necessary to take to your bed when you want us here on business," he offered mildly.

"There's a good reason for it," Petherbridge replied.

"I supposed there might be."

"It's your aunt."

"Oh. Our aunt. I see."

"No, you don't," his uncle corrected, and Lord Graymarsh's expression acknowledged the accuracy of the hit. "I think the world and all of your aunt." Lord Petherbridge fixed each nephew in turn with a belligerent gaze as if daring them to contradict his statement.

They had no intention of doing so. Not only politeness interfered. They all knew that this statement was true, even if they didn't pretend to understand it. A care-for-nothing and member of the Regent's raffish set, Petherbridge had, in his late middle age, begun a relentless pursuit of their do-gooder aunt Augusta. And when she had finally consented to abandon her advanced maiden state and marry him, it had been the *on dit* of the ton for an entire season. But no one, least of all the lady's nephews, had doubted for a moment that it was a love match. Miss Milbanke was of course, quite well-to-do. But Lord Petherbridge was a nabob. And during the ensuing years, unlike many grand but short-lived passions, their attachment had increased, underscoring the truth of the principle that opposites attract.

"I think the world of your aunt," his lordship repeated for extra emphasis, "and the last thing I want to do is cause her grief. That's why I had to send word to you that I was dying."

If the young men found some incongruity in that statement, they didn't say so. All three were, figuratively at least, on the edges of their chairs. "The thing is, you see," Lord Petherbridge said solemnly, "Augusta thinks I just want to say me last good-byes. But the truth is, I've important business that needs discussion. I brought you here to talk about my will."

If he had thought to drop a bombshell, his lordship was disappointed. Lord Graymarsh waited politely for him to continue. Randolph nodded as in confirmation of a fixed idea. Mr. Langford carefully inspected his manicured nails. When it became apparent that no one chose to comment, Lord Petherbridge forged ahead. "I think you've guessed that I'd always intended the three of you to share in what I leave behind me." He paused. No one replied. But what, in point of fact, they might have said was that no one had to guess. Once it had become established that his lordship's marriage was not to be blessed with progeny, the heirless nobleman had been quite vocal. He let it be widely known that his wife's great-nephews—the two sons of her brother, the fifth Baron of Graymarsh, and the only son of a sister improvident enough to have married a handsome ne'er-do-well to disoblige her family—stood to inherit the bulk of his estate. "Of course," his lordship continued, "I hadn't quite decided on the particulars, like who'd get the Hall." He looked around him fondly as if he could see through the bedchamber walls to the rest of his palatial residence. "That put me in a quandary. Gray has his own seat and might prefer to live there. Gerard ain't got much taste for country life."

"Oh, I say!" For once the dandy was jolted from his lethargy while his younger cousin broke into a grin. The grin faded as the old man continued. "And Randolph's too much of a green 'un. Can't say what sort of a landlord he may be. So that part's never been quite settled in my mind." He mused over the problem once more for old times' sake. "But never mind all that." He jerked himself back into the present. "It don't matter now how my mind was running when I led you to think you'd all inherit. Because the thing is, I've changed it. That's why I called the three of you down here."

He had already claimed their attention. Now the atmosphere fairly crackled with suspense. Even Mr. Langford had dropped his pose and was looking at his uncle warily. Randolph wore a worried frown. Lord Graymarsh was the only one whose interest seemed merely academic and detached.

"It's nothing personal," Lord Petherbridge assured them. "I couldn't think any more of you if you were me own flesh and blood and not Augusta's. But that's the point, you see."

All three young men looked equally bemused, but it was Graymarsh who asked politely, "What point exactly, sir?"

"That you ain't me own flesh and blood." His lordship frowned at the other's denseness. "You see, I've a mind to leave the hall and most of what I've got to me own offspring. Oh, there'll still be a bequest for each of you. But nothing like you've been led to expect. Which may be a bit hard for you to understand at your age. But it takes a man that way as he gets older. A man wants his own flesh and blood to follow in his footsteps. So that's what I've decided. Hope you'll come to understand in time."

The three were totally bewildered now, searching their uncle's face for other signs of dementia. It was young Randolph who blurted, "Surely you ain't thinking of setting up your nursery at this late date!"

He was squelched by a withering, "At Augusta's age? Don't be sapskulled." But then his lordship's scowl turned into an expression close to embarrassment. "The thing is—and, mind you, if you breathe a word of what I'm going to say outside these walls, you'll be cut out of me will entirely—that part's already been taken care of."

"You mean you already have a child?" Again, the indiscretion came from Randolph. He turned beet red.

"I mean I already have a daughter." There was pride now mixed in with the embarrassment. "She ain't a child, though. She's twenty-one. Or maybe twenty-two. Can't be sure now. But anyhow, she's what I've brought you down here to talk about. You see, it's been growing on me gradually for a long time now that she's the one I want to settle the bulk of my fortune on. A man likes to think of his own bloodline continuing on his land, don't you know," he explained apologetically once more. "But the thing is, I don't want to upset Augusta. It would go hard on most childless women, I collect, having their husband's by-blow sprung on 'em after he was dead and gone. But Augusta . . ." He shuddered. "Well, it just don't bear thinking on."

The stunned young men were quick to see his point. There were some women who were prepared to blink at the fact that their husbands had produced progeny on the wrong side of the blanket. Lady Petherbridge was not one of their number.

"So you see, even though I've always wanted to name me daughter Sarah as me heir, I didn't like to cause Augusta grief. But the other evening over port it came to me—like one of those revelations you always hear of—how I could work the thing with no one the wiser, least of all Augusta." He beamed at his nephews, awaiting congratulations for his brilliance. When none was forthcoming, he gave them the same kind of look they all remembered receiving from disappointed schoolmasters. "Don't you get the point, lads? I'm leaving the hall and the bulk of my fortune to whichever of you marries little Sarah."

"I beg your pardon?" Gerard Langford didn't bother with his quizzing glass. The stare he bent upon his uncle was intense enough. "I'm not at all sure I heard you right. Or if I did hear right, I'm not sure I understand."

"Well, you ought to have done. Didn't I just explain it? I can't name me bastard"—all three young men flinched at such forthrightness—"in the will. It would upset Augusta. Not to mention giving the gossipmongers a juicy bone to gnaw. So I'm leaving the lion's share of me fortune to one of you. After all, that's what everybody expects me to do. The thing is, the one that gets it has to marry Sarah. Then that will settle everything right and tight."

The old man leaned back against his pillows and surveyed his nephews. His look of self-congratulation was not reflected on their faces. There was a long, awkward silence. Mr. Langford recovered first. "And just how do you propose we, er, set about this, ah, project?" he drawled.

His uncle snorted. "Coming it a bit strong, ain't you? Happen to know there's nobody more in the petticoat line than you are, Gerry. Why, there was one particular little ladybird in Covent Garden, I recall, when you weren't even as old as Randolph here. And now, if I can believe even half the stories—"

"I think what my cousin means," Graymarsh interposed, "is that you haven't told us anything about your daughter

187

yet. Except that she's called Sarah and one of us is supposed to marry her."

"And that she's twenty-one. Or twenty-two," his brother offered for the record.

"For starters, where do we find the, uh, quarry?" Gerard inquired.

Randolph added, "What does she look like?"

"Most likely like her mother." Lord Petherbridge chose to deal with the second question first. "Girls generally do." Involuntarily, all three stared at their host's bulbous nose and bulging eyes as they mulled over this novel theory of heredity. "Oh, how I hope so," Mr. Langford opined, sotto voce, as Lord Petherbridge continued. "Best as I can recall, her mother was a prime 'un. Would have had to've been," he added reflectively.

"Don't you remember?" Randolph sounded shocked.

"Just told you. It was twenty-one—or twenty-two, I ain't quite sure which—years ago. Before I met your aunt Augusta, anyhow. Besides, a cove can't be expected to remember every bit of muslin from his salad days." He glared at Randolph.

"Except that this particular dalliance seems to have left a rather lasting impression." Mr. Langford helped himself to snuff from a silver box.

"Naturally, I've provided for the girl." Lord Petherbridge felt pushed onto the defensive. "Not handsomely, mind you. But well enough. Back then I didn't want to give her ideas above her station. Never expected not to have offspring in wedlock, don't you see. But I did see to it that she went to school. So she shouldn't disgrace the one of you who gets her. Besides, she's an actress. Should be able to carry off being a lady. Sort of thing they're trained to do."

"An actress!" Randolph gasped. "One of us is expected to marry an actress?"

"I'll admit it don't sound quite the thing at first," his lordship conceded. "But when you stop to think on it, it ain't all that unusual. It's always happening—actresses sweeping coves off their feet, I mean. I've known any number of men in the first circles to be completely besotted about actresses. Why the Regent himself—"

"Yes, but His Highness never actually married his Perdita," Lord Graymarsh offered.

"Well, he couldn't, could he? Stands to reason. The crown and all. And, well, I'll grant you, in our world it is more the usual thing to offer a carte blanche. But still, this won't be the first time a gentleman was knocked off his feet by an actress and lost his head enough to marry her. Oh, you'll set the tongues awagging for a while. But the gossipmongers will soon move on to something else. Always do. And then everything will be right and tight."

"I don't wish to be indelicate, sir," Mr. Langford drawled, "but since you don't seem to know what your daughter looks like, what makes you think the thing will wash? Take Gray there, for instance. You must be aware that he's the prime catch of the marriage mart. Every diamond of the first water who comes along casts out lines for him. Been doing it for years. Not to mention all the encroaching mamas who fling their daughters at his head. And young Randolph, while far more callow and a lot less moneyed, is personable enough— for a mere stripling—and certainly wellborn enough to snare himself, a, uh, respectable heiress. As for myself, well, modesty prevents my comment. The point is, your daughter would have to be something out of the ordinary to make such a flagrant misalliance believable."

"No, she wouldn't." This flat statement was loaded with conviction. "No accounting for tastes when it comes to falling in love. Just look around you. Very few love matches make sense. Take your aunt and me. Think we didn't know we were a nine-days' wonder?"

"I take your point," his nephew remarked dryly.

"Besides, ain't I been telling you to overlook the gossip? The thing to keep in mind is that I want me own daughter to inherit while me wife stays none the wiser. And having one of you marry the girl is the way to do it. I don't mind saying it's a dashed fine scheme."

"Yes, I can see that from your point of view it's a solution worthy of Solomon." Graymarsh settled back in his chair, moving from his recent position on its edge. "But it must

189

have occurred to you that the three of us might not be quite so enthusiastic."

"No, it didn't. I may not be one of your intellectual coves, but I do know human nature. There's a fortune at stake here. At least one of you will come up to scratch. And one's all I need. Now I've told you me terms. All I have to add is that me girl's appearing with a traveling company at Portsmouth Theatre. You can take it from there." Lord Petherbridge reached up and gave the bellpull a tug. "Oh, I almost forgot. There is one other thing. I ain't getting any younger. And one of these days when I take to me deathbed there'll be no getting back up again. So I'm giving you just six months to fix your interest with me Sarah. If one of you hasn't done the thing by that time, well, I'll put my Yorkshire cousins in the field. One way or another, I mean to have me flesh and blood at Pether Hall."

An ancient butler, who looked as if he, not his employer, should be recumbent, answered the bell's summons. "Me nephews are just leaving, Mason. Give 'em a glass of port in the library if they want it." Lord Petherbridge settled his nightcap and fluffed up his pillows. "It's past time for me nap," he remarked petulantly. "All your fault, Gray. Traveling by balloon. Of all the havey-cavey things. Wouldn't've been done in me day, I can tell you."

The three candidates for the hand of Lord Petherbridge's byblow did opt for port. They seemed to be in need of a restorative. When Mason had deposited a decanter and glasses on the mahogany pedestal library table and then departed, there was a few minutes' silence while each drained his glass more quickly than gentility decreed. Randolph was the first to find his voice. He gazed about him at the rich paneling of the room; at the floor-to-ceiling shelves filled with handsomely bound, if seldom touched, rows and rows of books; at the Turner painting hanging over the black marble chimney piece. Then he said, "I think I'm going to like living here."

His brother strangled on his port. His cousin raised an eyebrow. "Wouldn't you call such an observation a bit premature?"

"Why, no. Stands to reason I'll inherit. I'm the only serious candidate."

The other reemployed his quizzing glass. "The *only* candidate? Whatever gave you such a maggoty idea?"

"What's maggoty about it? Gray's already as rich as Croesus and doesn't have to dangle after any kind of heiress. And a high stickler like you ain't about to marry some chit actress. My God, a provincial player! Why, it ain't like she was at least from Covent Garden or Drury Lane. Portsmouth!" He wrinkled his nose. "And heaven knows what she'll look like, let alone how rag-mannered she's bound to be. And it ain't as though you're desperate. It's the latest *on dit* in town that old Scriven's widow's mad for you. Besides, Aunt Augusta's bound to leave you something. You're her favorite."

"True," his cousin answered softly. "But have you stopped to think that both those ladies' fortunes taken together don't even begin to touch our uncle's?"

"Maybe not. But his is a bird in the bush, don't you know. The widow's a sure thing."

"I don't think you'll make Gerard cry off with that kind of reasoning, little brother," Lord Graymarsh interposed. "When it comes to birds in bushes, don't overlook our cousin's most important trait. Gerry's a gambler, first and foremost. Can't resist a challenge. Don't take my word for it. Go have a look at White's betting book. Nobody's name appears with more regularity than his. Right, Coz?"

Mr. Langford raised his glass in acknowledgment. He studied the other thoughtfully. "And how about you, Coz? Is your little brother right in thinking that you've no use for another fortune and will stick with your balloons and engines and God knows what else to give him a better run at our uncle's heiress?"

Graymarsh examined his crystal wineglass thoughtfully, perhaps looking for sediment in the vintage. The beginning of a smile played in his eyes. "I'm not sure myself, actually. I haven't quite decided. But I do believe that, just as in your case, my brother has overlooked my most important trait."

"Greed?" Mr. Langford asked politely.

"No." His lordship grinned. "Curiosity. Our uncle Pether-bridge has made me very, very curious, Cousin."

Chapter Two

MISS SARAH ROMNEY STOOD AT THE BACK OF PORTS-mouth Theatre to count the house. The job was depressing but not difficult. A sweeping glance over the pit, boxes, and gallery sufficed to show that the place was only a quarter filled. Or three-fourths empty, she thought gloomily.

Not that Sarah was surprised. She'd shared none of her step-father's conviction that the public would flock in droves to see Master Tidswell Romney. She'd done her part, however, to make it a success: going to prominent homes in town to sell subscriptions, doing a large woodcut for posters of a small Master Tidswell dressed in armor.

But the public in 1816 was not as taken with infant prodigies as they had been some ten years before when Master Betty had taken the London stage by storm and, hailed as the wonder of the age, had been presented to the king and queen. But the manager of the Romney Company of Players for some five years now had hoped to re-create the craze with his own off-spring. His optimism was undeterred by the fact that Tidswell had none of the charm of a Master Betty or the talent of an Edmund Kean, once a "celebrated theatrical child" and now the star of Drury Lane. And to add to these other drawbacks, nature was about to deal Mr. Romney's hopes a cruel blow. Though still mercifully small for his age, at twelve Tidswell was rapidly phasing out of prodigy range. The thought caused Sarah to heave a heavy sigh.

"Oh, m'dear, did I not say so?" A voice spoke suddenly in her ear. "Our success is now assured."

Startled, Sarah turned to see if her late mother's husband had parted with his senses. The manager's appearance confirmed that dismal diagnosis. He was looking out over the near-empty auditorium, his ample face, forever amiable, now beaming; his hands gleefully washing each other, a gesture he'd often used to point up Shylock's greed. "I always knew my son would make our fortune. Did I not say so, Sarah?"

Sarah was looking at him anxiously. If rarely in accord with her stepfather's point of view, she was very fond of him. It distressed her now that, under the threat of losing his theatrical company, he might, in truth, be coming quite unhinged. "But Adolphus," she said gently, "there's hardly anybody here."

"Numbers! Pooh!" Mr. Romney dismissed the head count with the same airy wave he'd used as Claudius in *Hamlet*. "It isn't the quantity of the audience that ultimately matters, m'dear, when theatrical reputations are being made. It's the quality. Remember that," he added pontifically, rubbing his straining waistcoat, a Falstaff mannerism so overdone that a button had popped off. "Have you seen who's in the stage box?" he crowed.

Sarah had not. Indeed, from that vantage point it was all that she could do to see that the box was occupied. And the fact that it was hardly seemed to warrant Mr. Romney's degree of jubilation.

He explained, "There are three young gentlemen in it, m'dear. None of your yokels. Regular swells. Members of the ton. Types found at Covent Garden. Seen at Drury Lane. Used to the highest levels of performance. In evening dress. Came by private carriage. Sarah, m'dear, the veritable crème de la crème of the polite world is here now in our theater! Lured by the reputation of our Tidswell! Our fortunes are made! Mark my words, m'dear, after tonight's performance, word of your brother's genius will spread like wildfire."

Sarah Romney refrained from comment. She hadn't the

heart to prick his bubble. It would burst of its own accord far too soon. There was no aspect of the company's endeavor she was not involved with, including its finances. Like her stepfather, she knew that tonight's house would not pay their bills. Unlike him, she did not think that the presence of three temporarily displaced young men from the first ranks of society would in any way affect their dismal future.

"Heavens, child, you aren't in costume!" Mr. Romney pulled himself back from a rosy contemplation of that future to exclaim. "Mustn't hold up the curtain. Most unprofessional. Now, get along with you."

While under discussion, the three gentlemen of the ton sat side by side in the stage box—disdainful, keyed-up, detached, as befit their various personalities. Their senses were assailed by the sights and sounds and smells of a provincial theater. Especially the smells: tallow, sawdust, orange peel, and the patrons of the pit. Mr. Langford pulled a lacy handkerchief from his sleeve and applied its perfume delicately to his nose. "Do you realize we've still some five hours of this to endure?"

"Want to go now? I won't stop you." The Honorable Randolph Milbanke received a cool stare in reply.

For probably the first time in their aristocratic lives, the three cousins had arrived for a performance before curtain time. Back at the inn where they'd engaged rooms for the night, they had discussed the matter at some length. The problem was the playbill. After arriving in Portsmouth expecting an ensemble performance by the Romney Company, they had been taken aback to discover that they'd stumbled instead upon a solo benefit by Master Tidswell. They were, however, somewhat heartened to read in fine print at the bottom of the advertisement that this performance was to be "assisted by Miss Romney." The rub was that the gentlemen had no idea of the scope of this assistance. So when Lord Graymarsh had advocated waiting until seven—or possibly even eight—to arrive at the theater, his younger brother had pointed out, "Won't do. She could assist in the first half hour and never be seen onstage again." And when Mr. Langford had advocated that they "stay in the inn, have the landlord mix a bowl of punch, and deal the cards till the whole thing's over and we can go backstage with a bouquet apiece," it was again Randolph who had immediately seen the flaw in this course of action. "Too risky. If the girl's a fright, it's better to find it out from the audience beforehand. Bad form to drop our flowers and bolt the minute she's presented." For once, the counsel of youth had won out over older, wiser heads.

The company manager's views on a prompt curtain had proved to be a theory, not a fact. Miss Romney, however, was not the cause of the delay. Though not due onstage for ages, she was ready at curtain time, waiting in the wings to prompt. Master Tidswell was the problem. First, he had to race outside to the alley to throw up. Next, he flatly refused to go onstage. Finally his distraught father personally dragged him onto the boards, meanwhile hissing to a stagehand to raise the curtain before the Prodigy could bolt. Unfortunately, the manager had no talent for invisibility. He was caught beating a fast retreat and was awarded catcalls and loud guffaws from the pit "groundlings."

Master Tidswell looked around him for an escape. There was none. His sister blocked the stage-right exit. His father beamed encouragement from the left. He considered leaping over the orchestra pit, then abandoned the idea as impractical. There was no help for him. He closed his glass-green eyes, drew a deep breath, and launched into his song.

Except for his father's fond and tone-deaf ears, Master Tidswell's voice had never been more than mediocre. Now, the threat of puberty had given its soprano a growing tendency to crack. Fortunately, the worst of these occurrences were drowned out by the scraping of three fiddles that served as the orchestra. Still, it was hard to say which was more relieved, audience or performer, when the aria finally scraped and cracked its way to a conclusion. Thereupon the Prodigy opened his eyes, unclasped his hands, which had been held in piteous supplication, assumed a noble stance quite at variance with his strawlike hair and freckles, adjusted the flowing cape he wore, and, as evidence of his versatility, began a recitation. "*The Merchant of Venice*, by William Shakespeare," he announced.

"Good God!" After fifteen minutes of the bard, Mr. Langford's whisper from the stage box had a carrying power that the leading tragedian of the Romney Company had cause to envy. "Is he going to do the whole bedamned five acts?"

"Probably." His younger cousin joined in the titters that were coming from the pit. "It's the sort of thing these infant prodigies get up to."

Mr. Langford's ensuing groan distracted Sarah from the prompt book she was holding. She raised her eyes from the printed page, peered around the flat that concealed her in the wings and, for the first time, perused the occupants of the stage box.

For once her stepfather had not exaggerated. The three gentlemen were undoubtedly members of the quality. The fair-haired one, peering at her brother through his quizzing glass as if at some curious specimen of bug, was both the most handsome and the most disdainful-looking man she'd ever seen. The younger one beside him, his shirt points endangering his ears and his hand clapped hard against his mouth, was trying not to laugh aloud as the Prodigy's voice changed alarmingly halfway through the "quality of mercy" speech. Sarah appreciated the effort on his part. He looked quite nice. The third man, though not as handsome as the first and dressed more soberly than the second, somehow managed to appear of more consequence than either. Instead of looking amused or disgusted by the struggling performance, he seemed merely bored. No, Sarah amended her impression, *bored* was not the word. He looked detached. As though through an act of will he had removed himself from the tedium of his surroundings. Sarah found his attitude far more offensive than that of the other two.

So absorbed had she become in her observations that she had forgotten what was happening on stage. Only gradually did she become aware that something was amiss. And then she noticed the silence. Dread, ominous silence. Suddenly, it was punctuated by a snicker—then two, then several—from out front. Sarah jerked her attention away from the tonnish gentlemen and back onto the stage.

Master Tidswell had gone dry. He stood mutely, blinking up at the enormous chandelier suspended above the pit for inspiration. No help came from the crystal pendants. The dripping candles held no clue. Nor did his sister's frantic promptings from the wings ring a mental bell. Finally, after growing hoarse in the failed attempt to jog her brother's memory, Sarah accepted the fact that Shakespeare's jig was well and truly up. Fencing was to be the next display of the Prodigy's versatility. She threw down the prompt book, snatched up two swords, and rushed onstage to rescue Master Tidswell by launching him, a full half hour ahead of schedule, into phase three of his "bespeak" performance.

"Oh, my God!" This time Mr. Langford's exclamation was far more heartfelt, though, generally, not as audible. It did, however, carry down to the stage, where Miss Romney offered Master Tidswell a sword hilt with a snarling "En garde!" She heard, and had no doubt that it was meant for her.

As the duel began, the occupants of the stage box watched with horror. The Infant Prodigy was supposed to be the center of attention. The three men hardly saw him. Their eyes were riveted upon Miss Romney.

What they saw was a slight, graceful female form wearing a loosely flowing cambric shirt tucked into black satin knee smalls. A red sash was tied around her waist. It was obscure just what she was supposed to represent, a circumstance that bothered some members of the audience. "Is that the merchant of Venice?" a voice asked loudly. "No, it's a pirate," came the reply. But the men in the stage box were not concerned with pinning down the cast of characters. They had a far more pressing matter on their minds. Randolph at last voiced it. "She does look like Uncle Petherbridge," he croaked.

And indeed she did—at least in one overriding, appalling aspect. She was afflicted with his lordship's very prominent, very bulbous nose.

There was no need to call attention to that deformity. Randolph moved on to lesser things. "Don't think I've ever seen hair quite that carroty," he whispered hollowly. It *was* unlikely. For Miss Romney's crowning glory, while not quite the disaster of her proboscis, still left a great deal to be desired. "Don't think Petherbridge can take the blame for that."

"Her mother, then," Mr. Langford groaned. "And to think our uncle said she was a 'prime 'un.' Should have known better, though, than to trust his judgment. After all, he picked out our horror of an aunt."

Lord Graymarsh's mesmerized gaze followed the duelists. Sarah had attacked the Prodigy with snarling fury but was now being beaten back into a corner amid the frenzied clash of swords. For fencing was the only part of his repertoire that Master Tidswell relished. "Take that, you villain!" he shouted. Sarah barely managed to sidestep his lunge.

Suddenly Graymarsh's shoulders began to shake. He collapsed back into his chair, weak with silent laughter, while the other two glared at him. "At least she's got good legs," he choked out.

"It ain't funny," his brother spat out.

"I heartily concur," their cousin agreed. "It's all very well for you to laugh"—Gerard's voice was bitter—"but the future for one of us is now making a spectacle—no, forgive me; I should not shift the blame. God or our uncle made the poor girl a spectacle. She is merely making a complete cake of herself."

The onstage battle raged furiously. As the Prodigy threw himself wholeheartedly into the fray, the bored audience came alive. This was, indeed, more like it. They cheered the thrusts of the young hero in the flowing cloak and booed the villain's parries. Such unaccustomed accolades went straight to Master Tidswell's head. He began to milk his part. When the trapped pirate—or whatever—managed to slip underneath his sword blade and began to back cravenly toward center stage, the spot chosen for the skirmish that would do him in, the hero could not resist the urge to play his audience. "Varlet! Poltroon!" he shouted, holding his sword aloft. "You'll not escape the taste of my cold steel so easily!" To underscore this point, he flourished his weapon in a furious arc that sliced off one of the candles from a sconce above his head. Neither he nor the enthralled audience was aware of its slithering descent down through the back folds of his cloak. Nor did his adversary realize what had happened until a tongue of flame licked above the hero's shoulder as he lunged at her. Sarah's scream owed nothing to dramatic art. She

198

leaped forward to go to her brother's aid. He beat her back with a furious onslaught. The roar of the audience, now aware of the fire onstage, drowned out her voice as she shouted, "You're on fire, Tids!" His assailant's horrified expression and the audience's frenzy only served to heighten Tidswell's performance. His sword waved wildly as his sister dived once more to save him. It caught her broadside and knocked her flat. But even as she fell, she saw that help was on the way.

Like his cousin and his brother, the sixth Baron of Graymarsh had had his attention so fastened on the pirate—or whatever—that he was almost as slow as the onstage hero to realize that actor's plight. But in the instant he first saw the flames, he leaped from the box. He landed on the stage, dived underneath the flailing sword blade, and tackled Master Tidswell by the knees at the precise moment the Prodigy finally realized he was on fire. The boy's screams now outdid those from pit and gallery as the audience, far too aware of the hazards of fire to await the outcome, began to run and push and shove toward the various exits. Graymarsh rolled the panicked boy over and over while furiously slapping at the flames. At the same time, Sarah went racing toward the wing, where a water bucket was kept for such emergencies. Gray had just succeeded in getting the smoldering cloak off the hysterical Prodigy when Miss Romney charged back onstage with the dripping pail and dashed its contents at her brother. Her aim was off. The water missed its proper target. It caught his lordship full in the face. "Bloody hell!" he sputtered.

The stage was crowded now. Always the consummate professional, Mr. Romney had waved the curtain down as he and the rest of the company came rushing onstage, followed by the two remaining gentlemen from the box. The manager was now enfolding his sobbing son in his arms while assuring the young thespian that except for some singed hair he had escaped, miraculously, unscorched.

The same could not be said for Graymarsh. He felt the pain in his palms even as he wiped the streaming water from his face and gazed into the bluest pair of eyes he had ever seen. And the most expressive. They suffered with remorse for the drenching she had given him. As his lordship finished mopping himself with a snowy handkerchief and turned his attention to the damage done to his hands, he felt a twinge of sadness for nature's caprice. How ironic to put those lovely eyes and that hideous nose together in one face.

The pirate—or whatever—was now taking his hands tenderly in her own. The eyes in question filled with tears as she looked at his palms. "Oh, you are burned. I feared so. I don't know how I can ever begin to thank you—" She choked.

Sarah's quandary proved academic. She never even got the chance to try. She was now upstaged by an effusive rush of gratitude from her stepfather that left Lord Graymarsh embarrassed and impatient to be gone. He kept trying to rise from his kneeling position to his feet. The attempt was thwarted by a large presence looming over him, blubbering out gratitude for his son's miraculous salvation. "If it had not been for your heroic action, sir"—the tears streamed down Mr. Romney's face—"the world of the theater, I fear, would have lost its fastest-rising star."

"Indeed? Anyone we know?" Mr. Gerard Langford, who stood above the tableau, looked puzzled.

"I am, of course, referring to my son, Master Tidswell Romney"—the company manager was shocked that such a swell should prove to be slow-witted—"whose fame, thanks to the heroic action of this gentleman, will in time eclipse the reputations of the great Garrick and the mighty Kean."

Mr. Langford slowly turned and raised his quizzing glass toward the sobbing Prodigy, who was now being comforted by various female members of the company, as if to ascertain if there was perhaps something in the young actor's mien that he had missed. From his expression, it might have been concluded that there was not.

Lord Graymarsh, meanwhile, kept trying to extricate himself from Mr. Romney and out of a situation that was becoming more and more distasteful to him. But a new obstacle to this action appeared. As he tried once more to rise, a pair of hands grasped his shoulders and pushed him firmly down into a sitting position on the stage.

"What the devil—" He glared up into his brother's face.

"Here comes Miss Romney." Randolph spoke out of the corner of his mouth. "Don't forget why we're here."

"Don't be daft. Surely you can't still—" Gray began angrily.

"Of course he can," Gerard, his young cousin's unexpected ally, murmured in his lordship's ear. "Silly, don't you think, to have put up with that ghastly performance and then leave just as we're smoking out the quarry." He dabbed his handkerchief to his nose as the acrid smell of charred wool heightened the aptness of his phraseology.

Miss Romney was indeed returning from some mysterious errand that had taken her offstage. She quickly extracted Graymarsh from Mr. Romney's groveling gratitude by the simple expedient of pointing out that the Prodigy stood in need of his father's company.

But again Lord Graymarsh was foiled in an attempt to rise. Miss Romney knelt before him and took one hand gently in her own. The luminous eyes looked with pity at his palms, now completely blistered. "Oh, dear," she said, moaning.

"It looks worse than it is." For some reason, Gray felt a need to relieve her distress. "The burns are superficial, I believe."

"I feel so responsible," she murmured. "I should have got to Tidswell right away myself."

"You certainly tried." His lordship unexpectedly broke into a grin at the memory of her efforts. Sarah, who had thought him more distinguished than good-looking, suddenly revised her opinion. "I don't think Wellington's army could have broken through your brother's guard. Has Master Romney ever considered a military career?"

"Instead of acting?" The young woman was quick, Gray noted. "Unfortunately, I think not." She had released his hand and was opening a small, round box. "This salve should take most of the sting away." She dipped her fingers into the ointment and began to spread it tenderly on the burns. The mixture did seem to have healing properties. Or perhaps there was something in her gentle manner that his lordship hadn't experienced since his nursery days. At any rate, the stinging palms

201

were soothed as the baron looked into the lovely eyes while tactfully managing to keep his gaze from straying to her nose.

His brother, towering above them, stagily cleared his throat. "Oh, I say. I do think we should introduce ourselves, Miss Romney. The gentleman whose hand you're holding is my brother, Lord Graymarsh. This is our cousin, Mr. Langford, and I'm Randolph Milbanke. Let me just say—though I must admit it seems dashed out of place now, what with all that's happened—how much I was admiring the, er, performance . . ." The prevarication died on his lips as the clear blue gaze seemed to look right through him. "I daresay," he stammered on, "I've never seen anything quite like it in my life. Have you, Gerry?" He turned in desperation to his cousin.

"Never," the other offered dryly, and earned himself an equally searching look. He half bowed in her direction. "Charmed to make your acquaintance, Miss Romney." He might have been in some fashionable drawing room.

"Thank you, sir," she answered coolly, wiping a wisp of hair off her forehead with her wrist. The awkward gesture, made in deference to the ointment on her fingers, had an unsettling effect on Mr. Langford. He reemployed his quizzing glass. "I say, Miss Romney, forgive my mentioning it, but your hair seems somehow to have slipped its moorings. A wig, perhaps?" he added hopefully.

"Oh, my goodness!" For the first time, Sarah became aware of her appearance. With a complete disregard now for the effect of burn salve upon false hair, she snatched off the wild red wig that the company manager had decided would make her appearance more villainous. The three relatives stared with fascination at the tightly coiled, cloth-banded locks that were now exposed. Under the stage lighting, her own hair glowed a rich, dark brown. A soft sigh of relief escaped from the Honorable Randolph Milbanke.

Mr. Langford, on the other hand, was still studiously employing his quizzing glass—in the direction of Miss Romney's nose. His eye was as out-of-proportion magnified as that enlarged feature when he asked, "Er, do I dare hope, Miss Romney—frightful gaffe, of course, if I'm proved wrong—that your hair is not your only affectation?"

"Oh, my heavens!" Miss Romney clapped her hands in horror on her forgotten nose. It, too, had been the manager's idea. "Can't have the audience preferring you to the Prodigy," he'd chided when she'd objected. She was now pulling at the false proboscis. And if the residue of putty left clinging to her own quite small and classic feature might have seemed untidy at another time, to the fascinated gentlemen who were staring at her, it mattered not a whit. What had emerged from underneath the stage disguise was a young woman who, though red of face and flustered from being ogled by the three most distinguished gentlemen she had ever met, could most decidedly be termed personable and, most probably, when proper attention to her appearance had been paid, could even be classified as pretty.

An hour later, back at the Royal Hart and settled in their bespoken parlor around a steaming bowl of punch, the gentlemen in question pursued that very point. "I say, she's a beauty," Randolph opined.

"Nonsense," Mr. Langford drawled. "She's merely presentable, that's all. You've let yourself be carried away by the transformation. I collect that any time a frog suddenly turns into a prince, he's automatically pronounced handsome by contrast. Don't you agree, Gray?"

The object of the query was gazing absentmindedly into the depths of his punch cup but looked up when he heard his name. "I beg your pardon. I'm afraid I wasn't listening."

"My God, you can't be smitten!" His brother looked appalled. "Don't tell me you got more than your hands burned back there onstage, that your heart was singed as well!"

"What a perfectly ghastly play on words." The aesthetic Mr. Langford looked more pained than his cousin did with his blistered hands.

"Well, even if it ain't quite the way Lord Byron might put it, you do see what I mean. When a cove meets an heiress and then stops attending to conversations, well, what's another cove to think?"

"He could think," his brother said, "that the other fellow found the conversation boring and was trying to think how best to repair his damaged balloon."

"Fustian, though speaking of your balloon—" Randolph began, but Gerard refused to allow the talk to be diverted.

"We were discussing Miss Romney's physical attributes, Gray," he interrupted. "Randolph thinks her a nonpareil. I find her merely passable. What do you say?"

"Oh, I think you're right, Gerry. Ordinary. Except"—he paused thoughtfully for a moment—"except for her eyes. They are extraordinary."

"Didn't I tell you!" Randolph pronounced. "I knew he wasn't indifferent. Balloons, indeed! And," he added glumly, "I guess you know, Cousin, he's already stolen a march on us. As though it ain't bad enough that he's the one with the fortune that Miss Romney's bound to favor, anyhow. Well, now the poor, deluded female thinks he's a hero. Gerry, did you see how she looked at him with those 'extraordinary' eyes? Damme, why couldn't I have noticed that that Shakespeare spouter had caught on fire? Or for that matter, I'd sooner it had been you, Gerry, who went leaping out of the stage box to the rescue."

"What an odd idea." His cousin's eyebrows rose. "As a matter of fact, I did see that the aging prodigy was on fire. But such an exertion on my part would never have occurred."

"You mean you saw—and just sat there? You're bamming me." While Randolph did not hold his cousin's character in high esteem, he was finding this revelation a bit much. "You ain't serious. Couldn't be."

"Why couldn't I?" The other paused to sip his punch. "Oh, I suppose if I had been the only person for miles around when the brat decided to turn himself into a torch, I'd have attempted to extinguish him. Though only after extracting a solemn oath that he'd never inflict a recitation of *The Merchant of Venice* on any hapless audience again. But with a whole company of theater types there in the wings having, I presume, little better to do than to snuff out one of their own—Well, really, old boy"—he turned with disapproval toward Lord Graymarsh—"I found your conduct in rather questionable taste."

"That's as may be"—Randolph kept the floor while his lordship merely smiled enigmatically—"but a pair of blistered palms may be a small price to pay for Uncle Petherbridge's fortune. And I tell you again, Gerry, he's stolen a march on us. It ain't easy to compete for a girl against a man who's just saved her little brother's life. And who has twelve thousand pounds a year to boot."

"Ah, yes, discouraging on the surface." Mr. Langford yawned. "But think of Aesop and take heart."

"Why on earth should I do a rum thing like that? Who's Aesop?"

"I collect your cousin's referring to the tale of the hare and the tortoise," Gray said. "The race isn't always to the swift, eh, Coz?" Gerard saluted Gray's erudition with his punch cup, and his lordship turned back to his little brother. "Well, he's right, you know. At least he is if I'm the hare. For I must confess that now that I've satisfied my curiosity and seen Uncle Petherbridge's by-blow, the contest fails to rouse my sporting blood. Bores me, in fact. So I'm here and now withdrawing from the pack. Abdicating. Leaving the field. You may rest assured, gentlemen, that I no longer have the slightest interest in winning the hand of the fair or the commonplace—Miss Sarah Romney."

Chapter Three

ABOUT HALF OF THE PREVIOUS NIGHT'S PATRONS WERE gathered in front of the Portsmouth Theatre when a curricle drawn by a handsome pair of grays drew to a stop.

Randolph Milbanke turned the reins over to his tiger and climbed down to join the group gathered around the box office. A crudely printed notice announced: Theater closed indefinitely due to fire.

Randolph had stolen a march on his rivals, who were still sleeping in the inn, and had set off in pursuit of the unaware heiress. Now it would seem that he might just as well have stayed in bed himself.

"Fire, me eye!" A stoutish crone who, from her aroma, must have been an occupant of the pit, snorted with indignation. "The only thing what got burned in there was us. If you ask me, they've just used the fire as an excuse to split with our sixpences in their pockets." The rest of the rabble seemed to agree with her. Delegations of them were pounding on the various doors, shouting for the manager, and demanding their money back.

Finally, a small, rat-faced man opened the pit entrance just wide enough to be more inside than out and shouted, "Go away! Nobody here but me, and I'm naught but the caretaker! The Romney Company's left town!" After this announcement, he quickly oozed out of the crack and slammed the door, being steeped enough in dramatic lore to know that far too often it was the messenger with bad news who innocently suffered.

The crowd hung around a bit longer to grumble about actors, thieves, and swindlers and to vent their spleen by tossing a few souvenirs left by passing horses at the theater doorways. Randolph waited patiently until they'd all dispersed and then strolled around the building. He rapped sharply on the stage door with his walking cane and called out in his most authoritative, aristocratic tone, "Oh, I say, you in there! Caretaker! Open up!" After a few more poundings and, essentially, repetitions of the same command, he was rewarded by the stage door cracking open a tiny bit. "Nobody here but me," Rat Face said grudgingly.

"I already know that. What I now need to find out is how I can locate the Romneys." Randolph clinked some coins together in his hand.

The door opened a bit wider. "All I know is they closed down on account of the fire. Maybe they've gone on to

Brighton," Rat Face added in a flash of inspiration. His eyes widened, though, as Randolph opened his hand. As the caretaker weighed the sixpence he'd been given to keep the whereabouts of the Romneys a secret against the young swell's silver, he found the former sadly wanting. "There's more blunt there in your fist," he blurted, "than you ever laid out for the ticket price."

"I'm not wanting my money back," Randolph explained patiently. "I just need to find Miss Romney."

"Oh, well now, that's something else again, I'd say." Rat Face broke into a lascivious grin that displayed his blackened teeth. "Well now, it wouldn't be splittin' to help a gentry cove like you track down a bit o' muslin, now would it?"

Though inclined to deliver a facer along with the six shillings he paid for the Romneys' direction, Randolph contented himself with wiping his fingers clear from their contact with filthy, grasping hands. After all, the evil-minded caretaker wasn't as far off the mark in his assumptions as the gentleman might have wished.

The boardinghouse was quiet when a slatternly-looking landlady admitted him. Hers was a theatrical residence, she informed Randolph, where the paying guests normally slept late, but he'd find Mr. Romney already at his breakfast. She thereupon ushered him into a small back room where the company manager sat at a table, clad in a well-worn but scarlet-brave dressing gown, consuming toast and sweetbreads. There was more dismay than pleasure on his face when he looked up and spied his caller.

"I've come to inquire about Master Tidswell's health," the young man was inspired to reply to his reluctant host's choked greeting, and as a reward he saw the broad countenance first awash with relief, then wreathed in smiles.

"How kind! How uncommonly thoughtful!" Mr. Romney kept repeating as he insisted that the other man join him at the table. Randolph was more than happy to comply. He had left the inn too hurriedly to partake of breakfast and now realized that he was ravenous. He gratefully accepted the cup of tea his host provided and helped himself liberally from a mound of light wigs, while nodding sympathetically as Mr. Romney poured out a sad tale of the havoc that had been wrought upon the Prodigy's nervous system by his ordeal the night before. "The artistic temperament is a delicate thing." The manager sighed. "Though my son emerged practically unscathed, thanks to the heroic actions of your brother, sir"—the large man's eyes misted with gratitude—"I fear that the fire has seared his soul and it will take some healing time before his muse returns. In short, sir," he finished more prosaically, "the Prodigy refuses to go back onstage."

"Tsk! Tsk!" Randolph hoped that his clucking noises disguised his lack of true sympathy for a state of affairs he considered to be a blessing.

"It is a tragedy." The other man seemed to find no hollow ring in his guest's condolences. "But my consolation is that it can only be a temporary aberration. A talent like my Tidswell's cannot remain the victim of vile circumstance for long. Er, by the by"—he abruptly changed the subject—"you did say you came from the theater, did you not? Was there, er, anyone else there?"

Randolph reluctantly relayed the information that a large proportion of the previous night's patrons had turned up hoping to get their money back.

"Dear me. Dear me. I was afraid of that. And you, sir?" the manager forced himself to ask.

"No, no, of course not," Randolph assured him. "I felt more than recompensed by the first part of the performance. Wouldn't dream of profiting from your near tragedy."

It was not stage technique, Randolph concluded, that caused the manager's eyes to brim with tears at the slightest pretext. Mr. Romney was a very sentimental man. "Thank you, sir, for articulating so well my very own feelings," he choked out. "I, too, felt that the audience had, for the merest pittance, been allowed a cultural feast. And even though the feast had to be shortened, alas, by several courses, I cannot believe that so many were so crass as to ask for refunds. Well, well—in time, when our Prodigy attains the dramatic stature that fate has in store for him, those oafs will thank me for not allowing them the humiliation of being reimbursed for a foreshortened Tidswell Romney performance. In the meantime, I can only thank you for displaying in these trying times the sensitivity of a gentleman."

While Randolph basked in so much approval, the time seemed ripe to inquire after Miss Romney's health. And after being assured that the young actress had survived the previous night's ordeal like a veteran trouper, it seemed an even better notion to ask if he might see her.

But no sooner had the request left Randolph's lips than a subtle change came over the company manager. Though Mr. Romney continued to smile affably, Randolph did not miss the hint of suspicion lurking in his eyes. "Alas, my daughter's frayed nerves require rest and solitude. I'm sure you understand." And there was something in Mr. Romney's tone that made Mr. Milbanke think twice about pointing out the discrepancy between the trouper image of Miss Romney and this latest version of her mental state.

Randolph Milbanke's instincts did not play him false. Though overprone to toadeat the quality, Mr. Romney drew the line where his daughter's well-being was concerned. And though inclined to give reality a wide berth in the main, he allowed himself no such latitude regarding the motives of gentlemen in pursuit of actresses. Even this fresh-faced stripling was not likely to be exempt from temptations of the flesh. So without putting his position crassly into words, Mr. Romney made it quite clear to the slightly red-faced young gentleman that Miss Romney never socialized with her audience. "It destroys illusion," he explained. "Aesthetic distance must be maintained, you see." He smiled apologetically.

Foiled in his pursuit of the Petherbridge fortune for the day, Randolph was anxious to know where the Romney Company would go from there. This wasn't easy to pin down. There was quite a lot said about "pausing at artistic crossroads" and "weighing the various possibilities." An "almost certain booking" seemed anticipated, but only "if this or that takes place." A lot more bluster followed in a similarly optimistic vein. But when the young gentleman finally took his cordial leave of the actor-manager, he was left with the distinct impression that the Romney Company was well up the River Tick and hadn't the slightest notion what it would do next.

It was a very thoughtful Randolph Milbanke who drove the ten miles to Pether Hall. How he was to be expected to pursue a young female who was guarded at home by a suspicious father and taken out of the public domain by the collapse of her career was more than he could fathom. Even keeping track of Miss Romney's whereabouts could prove impossible. Adolphus Romney's rambling references to Bath and Bournemouth had been duly noted and filed in memory. But then, when the sanguine manager had begun to talk of London, Randolph realized that all of his plans were just so much moonshine. The Romney Company had been delivered a knockout blow and would likely remain down for the full count.

Randolph's only comfort was that if he was stymied in his pursuit of his uncle's heiress, his rival—or rivals, for he was not fully convinced of his brother's withdrawal from the chase—was completely in the dark. The coins he'd given the theater caretaker had persuaded that worthy to lock up his doors and visit the nearest tavern. Randolph didn't doubt that he'd be there for the day, and anyone else looking for the Romneys would find only an empty theater.

As for himself, he'd no intention of being questioned about his morning's activities, hence his decision to head for his great-uncle's house. At least he'd be in the vicinity of Portsmouth and could check on the Romneys' movements while, he hoped, his two rivals headed back to London. Besides, it might be helpful to report the current state of affairs to Lord Petherbridge. After all, it occurred to the nephew, the old rake had had experience in pursuing actresses and might be persuaded to part with some helpful advice.

But Randolph was doomed to disappointment on that score. When he arrived at the hall, Lord Petherbridge was sequestered with his bailiff and likely to remain so for some time. Lady Petherbridge, however, the butler informed him, was in her chamber. Randolph suppressed a sigh and went in search of his prosy relative.

"Oh, it's you." Lady Petherbridge looked up from her cluttered writing table with a preoccupied gaze. "Good. You can help me."

Randolph stared back at his elderly relative with some astonishment. He was not accustomed to her ladyship being pleased to see him. Well, not *pleased* precisely, he amended. Her expression was more of the "any old port in a storm" variety.

Indecision did not become Lady Petherbridge. The frilled cap that almost obscured the iron-gray hair, and whose ruffled fasteners shored up several chins, outlined a face accustomed to command. The snapping eyes below a beetled brow and above a nose fit to grace a Caesar could, under normal circumstances, pale a butler and reduce a housemaid to tears with a single stare. But now the face appeared as close to bemusement as such an august assortment of features could permit. "Sit down, Randolph." Her ladyship waved imperiously at a chair. "I need your advice."

It took all her nephew's self-control to keep his chin from dropping. Indeed, a summons from His Majesty to discuss affairs of state would have been no more astounding. Randolph obediently pulled the chair closer to the table, collapsed in it, and looked at his aunt warily.

"It's your uncle," she said abruptly. "I'm worried about him. Do you realize he's been on his deathbed three times in the last six months?"

"That often? Well, no, er, yes. But I, uh, don't think, actually—"

His aunt waved him to silence. "Oh, I know Petherbridge ain't really dying. That's just the point. He's turned morbid. And it ain't like him to be blue-deviled. So it's up to us to cheer him up."

"Us? Well, I, er—"

Lady Petherbridge rolled once more over the interruption. "I hold myself responsible." To her nephew's astonishment—and horror—he saw tears begin to form in her ladyship's eyes. "I fear that my more serious-minded nature has put your uncle under a great strain. He was used, you know, before he met and married me, to live a frivolous, pleasure-filled existence. And

211

while I cannot but condemn a life given over totally to the pursuit of pleasure when there are so many worthy causes crying for attention, still I can see that for a person of your uncle's temperament such a radical change from the frivolous to the significant could in time exact a toll. And in your uncle's case I believe this excess of morbidity is the direct result of this change in his mode of living. And since I value your uncle's well-being even more than the demands of principle, I have decided to take drastic measures." She paused dramatically while Randolph gazed at her, wide-eyed. "I shall give a house party!"

Her voice rang out with martyred resolution. Her face glowed like Joan of Arc's. "That's why I'm glad to see you, Randolph," she added in more normal tones. "I need your suggestions on how to entertain my guests."

If thereupon Randolph stared at her, transfixed, it was not, as Lady Petherbridge suspected, that his faculties had stalled. In point of fact, his mind was racing at an accelerated speed that he found frightening. It struck him that in just such a sudden burst of frenzied inspiration might the "Hallelujah Chorus" have occurred to Handel. None of this, however, conveyed itself upon his vacant countenance. Indeed, Lady Petherbridge was moved to snap her fingers in his face.

"Don't gawk, boy. I'm making a perfectly reasonable request of you. You go to parties, don't you? Of course you do. And while you ain't an arbiter of fashion as Gerard is, you must surely know how the frivolous amuse themselves. I certainly do not. The only houses I ever went to were the ones where the talk was serious."

Randolph repressed a shudder. There was a time, he recalled, when his aunt had been affiliated with the Society for the Suppression of Vice, whose members warred on Sabbath breakers, licentious books, dram shops, county fairs, and all other distractions of the devil. Her marriage had modified her zeal, however. Her causes now took a more positive turn.

"Speak up, Randolph." She was looking at him impatiently. "You must surely have some suggestion for entertaining our houseguests."

Randolph beamed. His hour had come. "As a matter of fact, I have. Theatricals."

"Theatricals!" Her ladyship thundered like a major prophet as her black eyes snapped their disapproval. And only then did her great-nephew recall that private theatricals were among the vices that the Society for the Suppression of Vice had targeted. Even so, Randolph held his ground.

"Just the ticket for Uncle," he said firmly, although he dropped his eyes before the gimlet gaze. "Nothing like a play to take a chap right out of himself. I refer, of course, to the highest type of uplifting drama that points up a moral principle," he threw in with a cunning Machiavelli could have admired. "I mean the sort of thing those old Greek coves seemed to think could purge the soul." He risked a look at his aunt. Her expression had transposed from outraged to thoughtful. "Hmmm," she said.

Rightly interpreting the syllable for indecision, Randolph pressed on. "It's done, you know, in the very best houses. Uncle would like it above all things. And there's a bang-up theater in the hall."

"That's true, but—"

Under normal circumstances, Randolph would never have dared to interrupt his august aunt. But there was nothing normal about this situation. Handel's misplaced muse still whispered in his ear. "And you wouldn't have to concern yourself at all. The custom is to invite some professional actress to take—"

"Randolph!" Lady Petherbridge trumpeted. "Have you gone mad?"

"W-why, no, ma'am." He gulped.

"Then I can only assume that you're indulging in some tasteless joke. But I assure you, I am not amused."

"It ain't a joke, ma'am." The thought of the fortune at stake gave the young man courage. "It's quite the thing. To bring in somebody who knows what's what to pull everything together. And maybe to play the lead while the houseguests do the other parts. But mainly to direct the thing."

Any charity Lady Petherbridge had momentarily felt for her

nephew was fading fast. The frosty look she bent upon him raised gooseflesh despite the sun-drenched room. "I cannot believe, sir, that you are seriously suggesting that I extend the hospitality of Pether Hall to a creature of that ilk! An actress! As my houseguest! Never!"

"But I ain't suggesting *that* sort of actress. Wouldn't dream of it. Had in mind someone more like the Kembles—a terribly respectable theatrical family, you know. Received in the best houses. Friends of Lord and Lady Egerton. Spotless reputations."

Her ladyship wavered. "Well, yes, the Kembles. But you must admit, Randolph, they are the exception and not the rule in what is generally a degenerate profession."

"All the more reason, don't you think, to lend a helping hand to actors trying to lead decent lives. There's this one theatrical family in particular—not well known like the Kembles, but they've managed to uphold high moral standards in their profession, too. But now they're down on their luck, due to an accident to their child prodigy."

"To their what?"

"Child prodigy. That's an odd sort of youngster who recites Shakespeare by the bucketful and gets up to all sorts of other queer starts that children ain't usually up to doing."

"I know what a prodigy is, Randolph," his aunt said witheringly. "And I must say I abhor the very idea of a mere child being exploited."

"Well, I'm with you there, ma'am." Randolph shuddered at the memory of *The Merchant of Venice*.

"It should be stopped."

"Well, in this particular case it has been," Randolph began, but the light of zeal was beginning to glow in his aunt's eyes, and she did not hear him.

"This is a *respectable* theatrical family, you say?"

"Oh, yes, indeed." Randolph began to describe the Romneys in glowing and fictitious terms that included Sunday school for the Prodigy and baskets of theatrical oranges distributed to the needy by Miss Romney. "But now they've been forced to close their engagement early—and, well, they're des-

214

titute. So I thought it would be an act of charity to engage Miss Romney for the theatricals, don't you see, and save a deserving family from sinking to the level of those types you disapprove of. And at the same time, a play could give Uncle a real lift."

Lady Petherbridge was almost convinced. "You are quite certain, Randolph, of the young woman's character?"

"The very soul of respectability, I assure you." There was a sincerity in his tone that nipped the seeds of suspicion in his aunt's mind as to his motives before they could begin to sprout. "And she looks and talks like a lady." He pressed his advantage. "Wouldn't put off your other guests. Uncle would—"

"Very well, then." Lady Petherbridge had made her snap decision and was ready to move on to other things. "I shall write to Miss Romney and engage her and her little brother."

"Her b-brother? Oh, I say, I don't really think that the Prodigy'd fit in at a house party." Randolph was appalled. "Besides, he wouldn't be up to performing just yet. Had an accident, you see."

"That, Randolph, is the point." His aunt stood dismissively, glaring down her impressive nose at her great-nephew. "He shall not perform. I intend to give the child the benefit of the country air, good food, and a moral environment. I want to expose him to life away from the evil theater and plant his feet on the path of righteousness. I'm beginning to regard this house party as heaven-sent. What I had considered selfish indulgence and crass frivolity can now serve a higher purpose. I shall reclaim this child from his sordid calling."

"B-but—"

"Don't try to dissuade me from my duty, young man." His aunt thrust a sheet of paper into his hands and gestured toward the pen and inkwell on the table. "Just write down the Romneys' direction and I will do the rest. My conscience would not be easy if I ignored the plight of that hapless child. Indeed, Randolph, I see the infant prodigy as a brand that must be plucked immediately from the burning."

"Oh, no, Aunt Augusta. That ain't necessary. You see—"

"A brand to be plucked from the burning," she stated once more, emphatically.

"But I don't think you understand, ma'am." Confused by the biblical terminology, Randolph felt a need to set the record straight. "Don't know how you could have learned about the burning part, but the thing is, Gray's already done the plucking. No need to concern yourself at all."

"The Romneys' direction, Randolph." Lady Petherbridge snapped her fingers.

"Yes, Aunt Augusta." With a sigh for a brilliant scheme gone half awry, the Honorable Randolph Milbanke seated himself, dipped the pen in ink, and began to write.

*Chapter
Four*

THE LONDON STAGE WAS DUE TO DEPART IN FIVE MINUTES, and the Royal Hart bustled with activity. So much so that the landlord hadn't time to assess properly the young woman inquiring after Lord Graymarsh. His first inclination as he glanced at her respectable-looking, if unfashionable, dark walking dress and listened to her modulated, cultured voice was to have the boot escort her to a private parlor, then go fetch his lordship. No sooner had the thought occurred than the boy himself staggered down the stairs lumbered by a pile of luggage bound for the metropolis. "Who'll I say's calling?" the host inquired as he settled the reckoning with the owner of the baggage.

"Miss Romney from the Portsmouth Theatre," the young woman replied, and earned a startled stare. That settled that. An actress. Didn't look the type, but facts were facts. At ten in the morning. By herself. Bold as brass. The landlord, a family man, tried to stifle a look of disapproval. Business was business, and he couldn't afford to antagonize the gentry. Having the likes of Lord Graymarsh in his inn was bound to do wonders for the reputation of the Royal Hart. That is, if he didn't set the Quality's backs up by not blinking at their rakeshame ways. Funny thing, though. He'd have thought that his lordship was the least likely to . . . Well, it was none of his concern. "Upstairs, left corridor, third door on the left," he said dismissively as he counted out the traveler's change.

Sarah hadn't missed the landlord's disapproval and for the first time paused to consider that her mercy mission might be open to misinterpretation. Certainly Miss Marshall at the Marshall Academy for Young Ladies, a second-rate boarding school with pretensions of gentility, had drummed it into her pupils' heads that no proper young lady went abroad unaccompanied. As for visiting a gentleman in his rooms—well, that was so unthinkable as to have never been discussed. Miss Romney was, however, of the theater, which had a different code. And if, in her case at least, that code did not include the type of behavior that Lady Petherbridge so heartily disapproved of, still it did embrace a degree of independence. Even so, Miss Romney was prey to second thoughts as she rapped rather timidly upon the designated chamber door.

Inside, Lord Graymarsh had, for once, regretted traveling without his valet. His hands, while not seriously burned, had smarted enough during the night to make sleeping difficult. He had counteracted this by drinking a great deal more brandy than he was used to. As a result, he had a throbbing head as well as smarting palms. Shaving had been an ordeal, since the razor had been difficult to hold. The nicks on his face testified to the difficulty. The soft tapping on the door hit his head like drumbeats, causing him to flinch and to add a new notch to his chin. "Damnation!" he swore as he dipped the corner of a towel into the washbowl and growled, "Come in."

Sarah stepped inside and then felt her face flame red. His lordship, stripped to the waist, was standing in front of the washstand holding a towel to his chin, his full attention focused on the looking glass as he tried to staunch the flow of blood. Later she was to remember, in a rush of embarrassment, that if she hadn't been so stunned by the sight of broad shoulders, rippling muscles, and a thatch of dark chest hair, she could have simply backed out of the doorway and disappeared. But for some reason Lord Graymarsh in dishabille affected her wits adversely. Her widened eyes traveled down skintight pantaloons, registered muscular thighs, and came to rest with a shock on his lordship's bare feet. This homey sight jarred her back to reality once again, and she was just about to do her disappearing act when Gray glanced her way and the opportunity was lost forever.

Lord Graymarsh, who had expected to see a servant, was almost as jolted as Miss Romney. But in his case surprise was quickly displaced by disappointment, a reaction that, if he'd stopped to analyze it before it quickly faded, would have surprised him.

Lord Graymarsh was well accustomed to pursuit. In fact, he had become bored by it in all its forms, whether exhibited in the coquettish glances over French silk fans at Almack's or by the more blatant sexual advances of the Fashionable Impures. Even so, his moment of disappointment had come from one more illusion shattered. Miss Romney of the clear blue eyes and tender concern had not struck him as a lady of easy virtue. Still, as her presence here in his room reminded him, she was, after all, a common actress. And her mother's daughter. As well as Lord Petherbridge's.

If Sarah had been quick to notice the landlord's attitude, Graymarsh's was even clearer as he looked at her with a cynical, and bloodshot, stare. "I—I came to inquire about your hands," she stammered in a rush of embarrassment that might have given Gray second thoughts if he hadn't concluded that she was acting.

"Thank you," he said dryly, hanging up the towel but not bothering to put on the dressing gown flung carelessly on a bedpost. The sight of the unmade bed, which seemed to be expanding before her eyes until it filled the entire room, made Sarah even more uncomfortable. With an effort, she wrenched her attention away from it. Lord Graymarsh looked down at his palms indifferently. "The burns are beginning to heal." He held his hands out toward her. "Would you like to take a look?" This time she did not care for his smile—or leer—at all.

Again it took an effort to remind herself that she had come on a mercy mission. "Did the salve help?" She might have been a doctor inquiring clinically about a patient's treatment.

He laughed softly. "Come see for yourself." She hadn't moved from her station by the door.

"You forgot to take the ointment with you," she continued, "and I thought you might be needing it. We've found it to be very efficacious."

" 'Efficacious'?" His gray eyes mocked her use of the high-toned word. "Oh, I'm sure it's all of that and more."

"Well, at any rate, here it is if you need it again," she said primly, preparing to set the ointment on the chest of drawers next to the door and then take her leave. She was inwardly up-braiding her foolish conduct. And wondering why this odious man had appealed to her so much the night before. It hadn't been just his physical attraction, which he seemed so well aware of, that she'd found compelling then. There'd been something else that she'd fancied she had seen in him. Sarah felt a sudden rush of disappointment that put Gray's similar re-action to shame. For after all, her experience with the opposite sex had been far more limited than his. Her disillusionment came harder.

"That ointment can't be 'efficacious' unless applied, now can it?" he said mockingly as she set it down. "Last night, you put it on for me." He found her missishness a bit absurd under the circumstances and was baiting her. Sarah realized this, re-sented it, and decided to settle the matter once and for all.

It was certainly out of character for her to be so unnerved by a shirtless, bootless gentleman. There was no time in the the-ater for such niceties as the insistence on privacy for costume changes. She'd seen many an actor in worse states of undress than this, she told herself as she snatched the box of ointment off the chest and took a determined, if unwary, step in his di-rection. It was her misfortune then to trip over his carelessly discarded Hessians and go sprawling into his arms.

Lord Graymarsh may have been disgusted by Miss Romney's blatant pursuit, but he was also human. When he found himself supporting a young woman who was clinging to his naked chest and whose "extraordinary" blue eyes widened with feigned shock as they met his narrowed gray ones, he did what any other red-blooded gentleman would have done. He kissed her.

And it came as no surprise that Miss Romney cooperated. The only surprise was the heady pleasure the encounter brought him, a feeling almost, but not quite, new. Indeed, the softness of the lips that met his own with unexpected sweetness and then parted in response to his awakened passion was enough to make him forget his stinging hands and throbbing head.

Sarah, on the other hand, had no basis for comparison. She was caught off guard by this new development. Indeed, so bombarded was she by a variety of strange emotions that being lifted off her feet at first appeared to be just natural cause and effect, a normal state of levitation. The contact of their kiss was, however, fortuitously broken as he deposited her upon that disconcerting bed and climbed in beside her. The momentary release brought Sarah to her senses. "What do you think you're doing, sir?" she yelped.

Gray, who had momentarily upstaged his headache with desire, felt it return full force, and all his ill humor with it. "Look, Miss Romney—Sarah, or whatever it is you're called—don't you think it's time you dropped the missish role? I'm in no mood for plays. What I'm doing is precisely what you came up here for, so let's get on with it. Now, where were we?" He reached for her again. Sarah boxed his ear and leaped off the bed.

"Oh, I say, Miss Romney, is my cousin annoying you?"

Gray groaned. Whether it was the ringing slap or the sight of his dapper cousin lounging in the doorway with his infernal quizzing glass in place that had increased the pain in his throbbing head was merely academic. "Go straight to hell, Gerry," he muttered.

"On the contrary, dear boy. I should say that it's you who are on the path to perdition. Assaulting young ladies? In

Portsmouth? In midmorning? Not at all the thing, you know."
The blistering look his cousin flashed his way did nothing to
disturb the expression of shocked rectitude on Gerard's face.

Sarah, in the meantime, was looking around for her bonnet,
which had gone missing somewhere along the line. It did nothing for her agitation to discover the demure dark blue headgear
underneath the bed. The final indignity was to go down on her
knees to retrieve it under the jaundiced eye of Lord Graymarsh
and the interested gaze of the Corinthian by the door.

Well aware of her flaming cheeks, she clapped on the bonnet and fastened its ribbons with a jerk that nearly choked her.
The salve, too, had landed on the floor. Sarah scooped it up de-
fiantly. Let his lordship's roaming hands heal themselves! As
far as she was concerned, they deserved to smart.

It took all her actor's training to hold her head high. She
made her exit without a backward glance at the half-dressed
gentleman still seated on the bed watching her. But she could
not avoid looking at Mr. Langford. He blocked the doorway.
Sympathy was written largely upon his face. He was enjoying
the scene immensely, though, Sarah was sure.

"Allow me to see you safely home, Miss Romney."

"That won't be necessary."

"Beg pardon, but I have to differ. You need a protector, obviously. This world is filled with villains just waiting to take
advantage of unescorted ladies, I'm afraid." He smiled wickedly over her shoulder at his cousin. Gray's bloodshot glare of
bottled-up outrage made his grin grow broader.

Sarah was too anxious to leave Graymarsh's odious presence to stand and argue. She feared she might succumb to impulse and hurl the salve at his lordship's aristocratic head. But
after she'd stalked down the stairs in embarrassed, indignant
silence, run the gauntlet of the landlord and his servants' curious eyes, and emerged finally into the inn yard, she turned to
her companion. "Really, sir, I thank you for your consideration, but I should prefer to go on alone."

"It isn't done, you know," the other replied pleasantly, taking her arm. "You must break this habit of going unescorted. It
gives the wrong impression."

She opened her mouth to protest, but the innkeeper had brought his curiosity to the door. Defeated, she turned toward home with the Corinthian in tow.

"Really, Miss Romney, I must protest the pace!" After they'd walked rapidly for several minutes, Gerard broke the silence. "My weak heart may not stand the strain."

She gave him a withering glance that took in his muscular physique. "It's my guess that in addition to being an accomplished horseman—as your kind always seems to be—you spar in Cribb's Parlour. Am I not right?" He nodded. "Then I do not think that this little bit of exercise will harm you. But if you're concerned, you may stop and rest. I did not desire your company, you recall."

"Really, Miss Romney." He regained her arm, which she'd removed from his, and slowed her down. "It's most unfair of you to heap my cousin's sins upon my innocent head." His smile was intended to disarm.

Sarah, though, had no reason to revise her first impression, that he cared not a fig for anyone but himself. She still considered him the handsomest man she'd ever seen. He looked almost as elegant in his tall beaver hat, dark spencer jacket, and biscuit-colored pantaloons as he had in black and white evening clothes. And he was obviously exerting himself to charm her. What she couldn't understand was why.

Mr. Langford, aware of her suspicion, heaved a heavy, stagey sigh. "I really can't blame you for being out of charity with my 'kind.' I believe that was your term. My cousin's caddish behavior is enough to prejudice any sensitive young lady. Let me see if I can reconstruct what happened."

"That won't be necessary," she said between stiff lips. "What happened was quite evident."

"Yes, but actions divorced from motives are most unsatisfactory witnesses of character. Don't you agree?" He gave her a moment to comment, then, when she failed to do so, went on. "You, for instance, felt compelled, out of gratitude for Lord Graymarsh's rescue of your brother and a genuine concern for the hurt he suffered, to seek out my cousin this morning with

222

your cure-all. Your motives were pure and altruistic. Am I not right?"

Sarah refused to look at him or to acknowledge that she was listening. For in truth she had no desire to explore her motives. But Mr. Langford was forcing her to admit—only to herself, of course—that she really had wished to see Lord Graymarsh once again. But she certainly had not wished to be kissed by him or to be . . .

Gerard continued his one-sided conversation. "But looked at from my cousin's point of view, your visit took on an entirely different connotation. You see, my dear Miss Romney, Gray's been terribly spoiled from the cradle on. You are aware that he is most sinfully wealthy, are you not?" Sarah wasn't and said as much but didn't think the Corinthian believed it for a moment. "He's never been denied anything, don't you see. And that includes the, er, favors of the fairer sex. I'm afraid, Miss Romney, that females have the regrettable habit of flinging themselves at my cousin's head."

Sarah's cheeks, which had finally cooled down, heated up again. "Fling themselves." That's exactly what she'd appeared to do, thanks to his lordship's ill-placed boots.

"And if you'll forgive me," the gentleman was saying, "your habit of going about without a maid or footman in attendance only served to reinforce my cousin's, er, regrettable misconception."

"Mr. Langford." For the first time, Miss Romney looked him full in the face. "I am well aware that Lord Graymarsh took me for a trollop." The Corinthian's eyebrows rose at such plain speaking. "And you are right. I did bring the slander upon myself. I'm afraid I tend to forget that actresses have that sort of reputation, whether deserved or not. Another characteristic of actresses is that, except for a highly successful few, they do not have maids or footmen at their beck and call. However, my mistake was not in going unaccompanied to see your cousin. It was in going to see your cousin at all." They had reached the gate that barred the path to her rooming house. She forestalled Gerard's gallantry by opening it herself. "Good day, Mr. Langford," she said firmly. "Thank you for your escort."

He cocked an eyebrow and smiled winningly. "May I not come in and recover from our canter?"

"I think you will survive it. If there's doubt, you'll find a coffeehouse one street over."

"Heartless! When may I see you again?"

"Watch for the playbills. I'm sure the Romney Company will be back in production soon."

"That was not what I meant, vixen, and you know it."

"It was what I meant, Mr. Langford," she answered coolly. "The only communication I intend to have with any member of the quality again will be from stage to audience. Good day, sir." Sarah walked swiftly up the gravel pathway and disappeared into the house without a backward glance. Mr. Langford stared at the closed door speculatively.

Chapter Five

THE HONORABLE RANDOLPH MILBANKE HAD NEVER BEEN impressed by his own intellect. But now he was seriously contemplating a life in government, guiding the ship of state through troubled waters. For getting his aunt Augusta to invite Miss Romney to Pether Hall had been a diplomatic coup.

True, having the prodigy included in the invitation was a bit depressing, and finding his brother's and his cousin's names on the proposed guest list was downright dampening. But as his uncle's valet withdrew after putting the final touch to the young visitor's cravat, Randolph preened in the cheval glass at the memory of the inspired way he'd scotched his rivals. He'd subtly persuaded his unsuspecting aunt to extend invitations to Lady Scriven, the wealthy widow who was determined that Gerard Langford fill her late lord's shoes, and Miss Evelina Crome, the newest candidate for his brother's hand.

He could count on Lady Scriven to keep Gerard occupied. But Miss Crome, he realized, though a beauty without peer, would not, on her own, pose much of a threat to Gray's bachelorhood. She was fresh from the schoolroom, and shy to boot, with none of Lady Scriven's determination. But that lack caused him no concern. Randolph was well aware that the beauty's mama possessed the required resolution by the bucketful. And since there was no question of Miss Crome's being invited without Lady Emma as a chaperon, Randolph was assured of having the unwitting heiress, Miss Romney, to himself. He was humming a cheerful little tune as he left his bedchamber to go in search of whatever diversion might be found that morning at Pether Hall.

He was not alarmed when Mason announced lugubriously, "Lord Petherbridge would like a word with you in the library, sir." There was nothing unusual in the butler's mournful attitude. A simple announcement such as "Dinner is served" had a way of sounding like the trump of doom from Mason's mouth. So Randolph was still humming as he opened the library door.

The sight of his uncle's livid countenance froze the melody on his lips. "Close the door, Randolph," Lord Petherbridge commanded with hard-won control. No sooner was the heavy portal in place, however, than he exploded. He took a threatening step toward his nephew. "What the devil are you up to, you—you bedlamite!"

"I—I don't think I understand, sir." Randolph placed a shaky hand upon the doorknob, considering flight.

"*You* don't understand!" his uncle thundered. "*I* don't understand! What possessed you, lad?" Lord Petherbridge's wrath suddenly gave way before his sense of injury. To his nephew's increased horror, his chin quivered and his eyes brimmed with tears. "How could ye betray me?"

"B-betray you, sir? Oh, I say! There's bound to be some sort of mixup. I haven't betrayed you, sir. Wouldn't dream of such a thing."

Anyone else might have been struck by the young man's obvious sincerity. Not so Lord Petherbridge. The only effect it had was to swing his emotional pendulum back to wrath. "Do ye deny, sir, that you've hoaxed your aunt into inviting me by-blow to this house?"

"Oh, that." The mystery was apparently cleared up, but for some reason Randolph did not feel enlightened.

"Yes, that! Of all the shabby, underhanded, scurvy, knavish—"

Just as the uncle ran out of adjectives, the nephew's sense of injustice shored up his manhood. "Oh, I say, sir. That's coming it a bit strong!"

"Not a bit of it. It don't begin to describe what I think of your treachery."

"Treachery!" Randolph gasped. "What does treachery have to say to anything? I think that having Aunt Augusta invite Miss Romney to direct her theatricals was a capital idea, if I do say so myself. And for the life of me I can't see why you're in such a pucker over it."

Randolph regretted the words immediately. The resulting near-apoplexy was indeed alarming. He was contemplating ringing the bell for Mason when his lordship recovered enough to gasp, "You actually think it's 'capital' to have Augusta find out she's playing hostess to me bastard?"

Randolph did wish his uncle would be less basic in his terminology and almost said so, but on further reflection decided to save such chiding for another day. "Of course I didn't think it would be capital for Aunt Augusta to find out that Miss Romney's your daughter. What an extraordinary notion. There's no way she'll find out. Who's going to tell her?" His eyes were filled with injured rectitude. "You should know that Gray won't. And even Gerry, who's rackety in some ways, wouldn't dream of doing such a shabby thing. So you must mean me. And I have to say it—in spite of all your years, and even if it means the inheritance—I resent your implications!"

Randolph's wounded attitude gave his uncle pause. The old

gentleman took a deep breath before he answered. His tone was almost normal. "It's bound to come out, though, once the girl gets here. Augusta will know at once. Never could keep anything from her."

"That's not exactly so, sir," Randolph ventured, and then hurried on as his lordship bristled again. "You've kept your secret for twenty-one or twenty-two years, and there's nothing in Miss Romney's appearance or manner to give you away."

"You're saying the girl ain't like me at all?"

Randolph couldn't tell whether there was relief or disappointment in his uncle's attitude. But he hastened to describe Miss Romney in glowing terms and to assure his lordship that the young actress, as predicted, evidently looked like her mother. "So nobody, not even Aunt Augusta, could possibly guess at the relationship."

"The girl could tell 'em."

Randolph's mouth flew open. That thought hadn't occurred to him. "You mean she knows?"

"I've no idea. Her mother died when she was still a child. So I doubt the two of them ever sat down to chat about the thing. But mark me words, her mother's bound to have told somebody who's bound to have told the girl. Oh, you've put the cat among the pigeons for sure, lad, by asking that young woman to come and stay here."

"But sir, you did go on and on about wanting to see your own flesh and blood under your roof."

"That's when I'm dead and gone, you ninny. I certainly didn't intend to stir up a hornets' nest while I'm still alive."

"There won't be a hornets' nest," his nephew replied with firm conviction. "I'll bet a monkey Miss Romney don't know a thing about the relationship, and even if she does know, it don't signify. Actress or no actress, Miss Romney's a lady. She ain't at all the type to tie her garters in public; you can rest assured of that, sir. Besides," he pointed out, "if you're serious about wanting one of us to marry her, it's a risk you'll have to take. For frankly, if she don't come here, I don't know how the deuce we'll get the chance to court her." He then went on to inform his uncle of how the stage manager kept Sarah cloistered when not performing. "And the company's folded, sir. She ain't likely to be acting anytime soon. So we can't go backstage to dangle after her."

Randolph continued to press his points and finally convinced his uncle that the visit of his illegitimate daughter, while not the most comfortable of arrangements, was necessary for the continuation of the Petherbridge line. After a dismissal that, though grumpy, was still a thousandfold more cordial than his reception, Randolph closed the library door behind him and mopped his brow. "For a cove so deuced anxious to have his own flesh and blood here at the Hall, the old boy certainly kicked up a dust when I tried to help it happen," he muttered to himself. "You'd have thought he'd want to thank me. Fall on my neck in gratitude and all that sort of thing. Just goes to show. Virtue has to be its own reward." On that self-righteous note, he headed for the solace of the billiard table.

Miss Romney was only slightly less disturbed than Lord Petherbridge over the fact that she was being invited to Pether Hall. When her crested invitation arrived, she had to read the crossed message several times and then recheck the outside of the missive to see if she was really the intended recipient. For the invitation made no sense. Sarah had never heard of Lady Petherbridge and could not imagine what had possessed the noblewoman to engage her to entertain the guests asked to Pether Hall. She took the note and her puzzlement to Adolphus Romney.

" 'O my prophetic soul!' " The company manager struck an attitude. "Did I not predict that something like this would happen? Our fortunes are made!"

"I wouldn't go quite that far," Sarah said dryly. She had found the manager sitting morosely in the front parlor, gazing with glassed-over eyes through the window at the bustling street. But now he leaped from the slough of despair and became his old ebullient self again. "I'd hardly call a pound apiece for Tids and me a fortune. For a fortnight's work, it's hardly handsome."

Mr. Romney's gesture waved away such monetary consideration. No one but Sarah would have suspected he hadn't a feather left to fly with. "What payment you receive for your contribution to the success of her ladyship's house party is totally beside the point, my dear. What is important is that you and Tidswell will find yourselves at last in your proper milieu. And to think I was concerned over our closing! The Portsmouth Theatre—bah!" His sneer recalled Richard III's contempt. "We'll be able to bid farewell to the provinces after this and take our rightful place on the London stage."

Sarah was too accustomed to her stepfather's high flights to refine much on them. Instead, she kept frowning at her letter as if by staring long enough she'd unravel the mystery of it. "I still don't understand why they're asking us," she muttered.

Her stepfather looked slightly offended. "That should be self-evident, my dear. Where else would her ladyship find a juvenile of Tidswell's genius and an actress with your birth and breeding?"

"Almost anywhere," Sarah was on the verge of saying, but held her tongue.

"After all, my dear, breeding tells. You must recall that I did explain when you were but a child, though the subject was almost too painful for me to broach, that you yourself are of the aristocracy. I do not condone your poor, dear mother's folly"—he wiped an eye rather ostentatiously—"nor do I condemn it. But I have found comfort in the fact that her earlier love was of the highest rank. There could be no question of marriage, needless to say. They were as star-crossed as Romeo and Juliet. Their tragedy was, of course, my own good fortune. Otherwise I might never have won your mother's hand." He wiped the other eye.

It was a story Sarah had heard several times before. The main difference in this telling was that Mr. Romney's recital was without benefit of port. And she had noticed through the years that her natural father's rank tended to increase with repetition. She would not be surprised, she was used to think, if one day her begetting was credited to the crown prince himself.

Sarah had never refined much upon the story. Illegitimacy was not uncommon in her world, and many actresses were fond of assigning noble antecedents to their nameless off-spring. The great Edmund Kean was a case in point. He claimed to be the son of the Duke of Norfolk, a relationship that the nobleman had declared was news to him.

Sarah had always preferred not to think too much about the matter. When she did allow herself to do so, her best guess was that she was in actuality the manager's true daughter. Since her birth had anticipated his marriage by several months, it would have been quite in Adolphus Romney's character to weave some fanciful, romantic tale to account for this discrepancy, which he would in time come to believe himself.

"So I'm sure," the manager was saying, "that when Lady Petherbridge was casting about for a suitable person to provide theatrical professionalism, while mingling comfortably with her highborn guests, she naturally thought of you."

Refraining from pointing out the absurdity of his state-ment, Sarah merely asked, "But however did she learn of my existence?"

"That part should be self-evident. Did I not say when I first set eyes on the three young gentlemen in the stage box that Tidswell's fame would spread? 'Oh my prophetic soul!' " he declaimed once more.

Sarah, of course, had thought of that same possibility. Still, she knew of no connection between Lady Petherbridge and the threesome. But even the possibility was enough to bring a rush of embarrassment to her cheeks at the memory of her latest en-counter with two of the three young swells. "I really don't think I care to go," she said diffidently, and braced for the storm of protest that was sure to break upon her head.

"Not go?" Mr. Romney surely did not hear aright. "Not go!" Mr. Romney was appalled. *"Not go!"* Mr. Romney was wounded to the soul. He talked at length about the Prodigy's career. How could that dear child's own sister stand in the way of certain patronage for Tidswell? This was the lad's big chance. With friends among the aristocracy, his meteoric rise would be the marvel of the theatrical world. Surely his sister would not be so mean-spirited as to . . . And on and on.

In the end Sarah capitulated—not for any of the reasons the

manager put forward but because they were nearly destitute and the wages plus her and Tidswell's meals and lodging for a fortnight would take some of the strain off their rapidly dwindling funds.

Tidswell, though, proved even more recalcitrant than his sister. The combination of his terrifying lapse of memory in front of the Portsmouth audience followed by being set on fire had caused him to have serious second thoughts about the brilliant career his father envisioned for him. And the glowing descriptions of the grandeur of Pether Hall, gathered by Mr. Romney in various alehouses in the neighborhood, did nothing to alleviate his fears. "I ain't going," he pronounced flatly, sending his father into a fit of histrionics that made the manager's remonstrances to Sarah seem but a pale rehearsal. It was only after Tids's sister had taken the boy aside and promised he'd not have to perform unless he wished to—a promise he must not, under any circumstances, divulge to his doting father—that he finally agreed to go.

Mr. Gerard Langford considered his invitation a decided bore. His first inclination was to scrawl a reply saying that urgent business required his continued presence in the city. But upon reflection he realized the folly of offending his aunt. Besides, he thought as he frowned over the almost unintelligible communication, there might be more to it than met the eye. For his unsocial aunt to plan a house party . . . Damn it all, he'd have to go!

But despite his resolution, when he tooled his team of perfectly matched grays through the park during the fashionable hour the next day and was flagged down by Lady Scriven, who informed him that she, too, had received an invitation to Pether Hall, the instincts that had stood him in good stead in many an all-night card game made him look pityingly at the lady. "How tedious for you," he drawled. "You'll cry off, of course. I did." He smiled his slow, handsome smile, lifted his curly-brimmed beaver to the lady, nodded at her entourage of strollers, flicked his reins, and drove on, thinking furiously.

* * *

Miss Evelina Crome was as fully alarmed as Tidswell by her invitation. A shy young lady, she found the social rounds more frightening than pleasurable. And in spite of her mother's constant harping on the subject, she remained quite unconvinced of her extraordinary beauty. She saw nothing remarkable in diminutive, fragile fairness and envied the statuesque, dark goddesses of her acquaintance. And her confidence in her appearance was not increased by her mother's constant reminders that it was her duty to trade in on it and restore the family fortunes by capturing a rich husband. Lady Emma Crome was the daughter of an impoverished nobleman and had married, as she was fond of telling her only child, quite beneath her. All of her considerable ambitions now focused on Evelina.

So when Lady Emma sailed into her daughter's bedchamber holding the Petherbridge invitation like a talisman, the young lady, who was sipping chocolate in her bed, gazed at the note with apprehension. Like Mr. Romney, she would have uttered "O my prophetic soul!" had she been acquainted with Lord Hamlet's line. "Do we have to go?" she asked timidly after she'd deciphered the scrawled message.

"What a question!" Lady Emma, who had all of the imposing stature Miss Crome envied but no claim to beauty, frowned down at her young daughter. "Do you realize who Lady Petherbridge is, my dear?" Evelina pleaded ignorance. When her mama informed her that their hostess-to-be was none other than Lord Graymarsh's aunt, her spirits plummeted even lower.

For Lord Graymarsh was the matrimonial victim her mother had targeted for her. It was useless for Evelina to point out that his lordship was the most sought-after catch on the marriage mart or to mention that he had failed to show the slightest interest in her. Her mother merely snorted with more emphasis than refinement. "Nonsense! Lord Graymarsh has never failed to stand up with you."

Though Miss Crome was certain that any number of beauties could make that claim, it would have been a waste of breath to say so. For in her own way, Lady Emma was fully as optimistic as Adolphus Romney. That she had as little basis for her sanguineness, her next utterance revealed. "Indifferent, indeed!" She scoffed at her daughter, who had allowed her chocolate to grow cold during this social crisis. "I'm convinced that Lord Graymarsh is behind the invitation. Why else would Augusta Petherbridge be asking us? Our acquaintanceship is slight." Since her daughter had no answer to this poser, Lady Emma considered the point well made. She nodded several times to underscore it and then sailed off to pen her acceptance of such a "gracious invitation."

Except for Lady Emma and possibly Randolph, the only other person who looked forward to Lady Petherbridge's house party with any degree of pleasure was the hostess. The primary purpose of the social gathering was, of course, to divert Lord Petherbridge from his doldrums. And it was already having the desired effect. If the mere anticipation of the party had so captured his attention and blotted out all thoughts of dying, just imagine the salubrious effect the event itself would have!

Lady Petherbridge had been greatly pleased when her husband had taken an interest in the guest list. When he exerted himself to the extent of wishing to know which chambers would be assigned to the various members of the party, Augusta Petherbridge's cup of happiness overflowed. To have raised her husband's spirits to this degree exceeded her fondest hopes. He made a few suggestions that she was happy to comply with, such as isolating one gentleman whose snoring could be "heard above cannon fire." So when he asked with elaborate casualness, "Where are you putting the actress and her brother?" she found nothing at all odd about the query. Her plan, she explained, had been to house them in the rooms next to the housekeeper, "between stairs," as it were.

"Won't do," his lordship said emphatically.

His wife looked up from the list with mild surprise. "Whyever not?"

"Have to treat 'em like the other guests."

"But Petherbridge, they are actors." The term might have been gypsies from the way she rolled it off her tongue.

"I know that. But you expect 'em to mingle with the guests. Ain't like they were hired to perform here on their own. They'll be acting with the others you invite. Like the Kembles do at Oatlands. Can't send out invitations, then treat the ones who get 'em like servants. Ain't done."

"But I'm paying them," his wife objected.

"The others won't know that. Ain't the thing, Gussie, not to put 'em with the guests."

Her ladyship sighed and capitulated. While she bear-led her more pliant husband in most of life's decisions, she bowed to his superior wisdom where social niceties were concerned. It all seemed rather eccentric to her mind—putting a provincial actress on the same footing with the cream of polite society, but Petherbridge undoubtedly knew best.

As for his lordship, he'd surprised himself by such uncharacteristic assertiveness. But when he mulled it over later, he was well satisfied. "Can't have me own flesh and blood treated like a servant here at Pether Hall," he muttered to himself, "no matter which side of the blanket she was born on. Wouldn't be the thing at all."

Chapter Six

LORD AND LADY PETHERBRIDGE KEPT COUNTRY HOURS and saw no reason to change their habits just because they were entertaining. So when the house party convened, dinner was served promptly at five, and it gave the ill-assorted guests their first opportunity to size one another up.

Lady Emma Crome had, of course, taken precedence in the march to the dining room. Miss Romney, equally of course, brought up the rear. Now, though seated figuratively below the salt, Sarah was not far enough away from that formidable dowager to escape her ladyship's inquisitive stare. The actress amused herself by attempting to read Lady Emma's mind.

The first stare had been used, Sarah felt sure, to ascertain whether the only other young lady present might prove to be a rival to her daughter. Sarah was well aware that she passed that muster—or failed, depending on the point of view. For in no way did her appearance pose any threat to the reigning beauty. It would be a rare gathering indeed, in which Miss Crome could be overshadowed. Sarah had never seen such a lovely female. But after apparently satisfying herself upon that score, Lady Emma still continued to stare down the table. It was evident that her ladyship didn't know quite what to make of Miss Sarah Romney.

Sarah was dressed in the best that the Romney costume wardrobe offered. But while her British net over blue satin frock might have given an illusion of elegance from the stage, its inferiority was immediately apparent when compared with Miss Crome's deceptively simple white muslin round dress, the work of a fashionable modiste. Lady Emma first categorized Miss Romney as a governess. But she quickly dismissed that notion as absurd. To her almost certain knowledge, the Honorable Randolph Milbanke was the youngest member of the Petherbridge connection. She mentally reran the list of possibilities and stopped on "poor relation." Yes, of course. That had to be it. Miss Romney must be one of Those.

The table conversation had ground to a halt during the first remove. Lady Emma took advantage of the lull to fasten her barrister's eye on Sarah and inquire across and down the table. "Are you perhaps related to Lord and Lady Petherbridge, Miss Romney?"

His lordship thereupon strangled on his wine and had to be pounded on the back by the nearest footman. When quiet was restored, Sarah answered clearly and politely, "No, Lady Emma. I am an actress, come to direct the theatricals."

"Indeed?" the other replied frostily, and Randolph quickly changed the subject.

The party was not as large as Sarah had expected. She looked around the table with an eye toward casting. She dismissed Lord and Lady Petherbridge as unlikely participants in the entertainment. Sir Peter Sherburne, now attacking the roasted pheasant with greedy single-mindedness, seemed equally in doubt. A gouty bachelor crony of Lord Petherbridge, Sir Peter would surprise her if he showed an inclination for performance. Nor did she have more hope for Lord and Lady Stanhope, also antiquated. No, she'd have to depend on the younger members of the group.

Sarah had been unnerved but not too surprised to find the Honorable Randolph Milbanke and Mr. Gerard Langford among the company. She had prepared herself for the possibility that her stepfather might be right for once and there could be a connection between the tonnish gentlemen of the stage box and the Petherbridge invitation. At least, she consoled herself, Lord Graymarsh wasn't present. It was embarrassing enough, meeting Mr. Langford. An encounter with the other man didn't bear thinking on.

Well, either of those two young gentlemen could play the hero's part. And despite his handsomeness, there was something decidedly villainous about Mr. Langford that assured his versatility. Nature had certainly formed Miss Crome for the perfect heroine. If only the young lady weren't so shy. Sarah sighed inwardly. She herself would be forced to take a role— or roles. She'd hoped to concentrate fully on direction. She began to regret her rash promise to Tids that he'd be exempted from performing. Still, sheer boredom might cause him to change his mind. What on earth had possessed Lady Petherbridge to ask him here? He was now dealing with a tray in his room and pretending to be a prisoner, too intimidated by the grandeur of his surroundings to venture out of the sanctuary of his bedchamber and explore the grounds as she'd suggested.

Sarah continued to study the dinner guests covertly. Her eyes darted quickly away when they reached Lord Petherbridge. Her host had been staring at her throughout the entire

236

meal in a manner she found disconcerting. Her gaze lighted once more on Lady Emma, engrossed in conversation with Sir Peter. Her ladyship had definite dramatic possibilities. She would make, for instance, a marvelous witch for the opening of *Macbeth*. If only there were a few more people here to choose from . . .

Sarah proved not to be the only one whose mind was on the guest list. "I'm sorry your friend Lady Scriven could not join us," Lady Petherbridge said abruptly to Mr. Langford.

"Oh, was Lucy asked here?" Gerard inquired innocently. "Pity she couldn't come."

"Wrote she had a putrid throat," his aunt informed him.

"Glad she didn't come, then." Sir Peter spoke through a mouthful of prawns. "Very catching, putrid throats."

Lady Stanhope shuddered and launched into a recital of the various times she'd succumbed to the same illness.

"I didn't know Lady Scriven was ailing. Did you, Gerry?" Randolph seemed suspicious.

"That I did not." The guileless blue eyes met his cousin's stare. "I must have a posy sent around."

"And speaking of persons who ain't here"—Lord Petherbridge entered the conversation suddenly—"what's keeping Gray?"

The query shattered the calm of the two young ladies present. They had both breathed private sighs of relief at the baron's absence.

"Oh, is Lord Graymarsh expected?" Lady Emma could not conceal her delight at this bit of news. "Such a charming young man. So attentive to my Evelina at her come-out. Put the dear child quite at ease."

Sarah doubted that. She stole a look at the beauty and felt a pang of sympathy as the girl's face flamed red.

"Oh, yes. My cousin is noted for his attention to young ladies." Gerard smiled his enigmatic smile at Sarah, who willed herself not to engage Miss Crome in a blushing contest.

"Don't know what's gotten into the boy." Petherbridge clung to his train of thought. "Used to be the soul of punctuality. Now it seems as if he's late for everything." A terrible notion struck him. "You don't suppose he's coming by balloon," he said to the world at large.

"Don't be ridiculous, Petherbridge." His wife disposed of that subject and turned back with martyred resignation to her duty as hostess as Lady Stanhope exhausted putrid throats and moved on to the history of her frequent megrims, sparing no detail.

At the end of the interminable meal, it was decided that the guests would take a garden stroll, then afterward enjoy their tea in a lakeside pagoda. Sarah took advantage of the interval required for the gentlemen to enjoy their port to go and rescue her little brother. She neither knew nor cared whether it was proper to include Tids in the outing. She only knew that he could not remain cowering in his room for an entire fortnight. They joined the group as the party was leaving the house by way of the conservatory.

It was obvious that Tidswell's presence did little to enhance Sarah's social status. That fact perturbed her not at all. What did disturb her was the way he quaked under the censorious stare of Lady Emma. To offset his fear, she took him firmly by the hand, a state of affairs he would have fiercely resisted under less intimidating circumstances.

As the group began its promenade around an artificial lake, the younger members of the party soon outstripped their elders, who were inclined to take advantage of the various seats and rotundas that they passed. Away from at least that much intimidation, Tids shook off Sarah's hand. He looked back over his shoulder at the imposing stone exterior of Pether Hall reflected in all its formal symmetry in the lake. He gazed around him at the seemingly endless expanse of garden whose "natural" vistas belied the army of gardeners and the hours of work needed to create them. Tidswell began to feel that he was fortunate to be there after all. He paused a moment on an arched bridge that crossed a narrow finger of the lake to gaze at some fishes swimming there, marking them for a return engagement with a fishing pole. As he caught up with the other strollers, he fell into step with Miss Evelina Crome, much to his sister's astonishment.

Instinctively, Tids had recognized someone at least as intimidated by their circumstances as he was. Under Evelina's shy and lovely gaze, he began to lose his inhibitions and to revert to his natural ebullient state. She too seemed to forget her self-consciousness and giggled like a schoolgirl, when an enraged goose he'd paused to tease came hissing out of the water after him. Even Mr. Langford dropped his world-weary pose and smiled at the beauty's infectious laughter.

Now that she'd ceased to worry about Tidswell, Sarah was puzzling over the behavior of the two gentlemen. To her way of thinking, their conduct defied all logic. Ignoring the beauty, they had attached themselves to her. She could better understand Randolph's actions. He seemed a kind young gentleman who would go out of his way to make a social inferior feel at ease. But she was unable to think the same of Mr. Langford. Self-interest seemed to be his guiding principle. So why he, who could barely suppress a shudder at the dowdiness of her gown, should be vying with his cousin to entertain her was certainly perplexing. Especially when Miss Crome was in the party.

True, Miss Crome's mother was enough to put off any number of potential suitors, Sarah thought, but still . . . She stiffened suddenly as she recalled that compromising situation Mr. Langford had recently interrupted. If he, like his odious cousin, thought for one minute that she was the kind of young woman he could count on to take the tedium away from a boring party—well, he was in for a bit of disillusionment. She gave the elegant gentleman, who was walking unnecessarily close to her, a telling look. Gerard was astute enough to take her meaning and turned to enter Tids and Miss Crome's discussion of the delights of country fairs.

Sarah was glad to see Tidswell enjoying himself, but she almost wished he'd not come out of his shell quite so far. He now held center stage. And Sarah was suddenly aware of the Yorkshire overtones in her brother's voice. Mr. Romney came from the north, and the company had spent a great deal of time there. Sarah's stint in Miss Marshall's Academy for Young Ladies, plus the natural ear invaluable to an actress, had left her speech free of the regional dialect that now seemed so out of place. If

Tids did fulfill his father's dream of Drury Lane, he was destined to play the rustic, Sarah thought as her little brother considered aloud the possibility of mastering the sword-swallower's technique he'd witnessed at a fair and including it in his own performance.

Mr. Langford thought it an excellent notion. "Your *Merchant of Venice* recitation seems an ideal time to swallow something," he offered. "During the first scene, don't you think?"

Just as Tids had worked out that he was being insulted and was wracking his brain for a setdown that would take some starch out of the puffed-up swell, Miss Crome made her first contribution to the general conversation. "Oh, my goodness, what is that?" She craned her pretty neck and squinted skyward.

Outlined against a vivid blue background and floating among powder puffs of clouds was a small, spherical object that had absolutely no business being there. It came from the northeast and moved toward them slowly, catching the reflected rays of the low-lying sun like a mirror flashing signals, causing the gaping observers to shade their eyes with their hands in an effort to identify the heavenly body.

"Lord save us!" There was terror in the Prodigy's voice. "It's a meteor from outer space, and it's headed straight for us!"

"At a celestial snail's-pace? Don't be sapskulled," Mr. Langford drawled.

The phenomenon shifted slightly in the breeze then, and whatever there was about it that was picking up sunbeams with such blinding intensity went out of focus, and the object, though still small and distant, lost its mystery and became easily discernible.

"It's a balloon!" Master Tidswell whooped.

"Oh, my God, Gray!" His lordship's brother groaned.

"What a bore." His cousin brought his quizzing glass into play and gazed skyward with distaste.

"Do you mean that's actually Lord Graymarsh?" Sarah stared with horrified fascination as the balloon drifted inexorably their way. It was now possible to see its metallic silver coloring and the band of crimson-bordered blue that encircled its circumference like a broad equator. "Surely it can't be!"

240

"Bound to be him." Randolph sighed. "Can't think of anybody else around here queer enough in the attic to be flying one of the things. For the past six months, it's been all he thinks of. Bound to break his neck one of these days. Oh, it's Gray all right."

"How awful!" Miss Crome's murmur was so heartfelt as to cause the others to switch their attention from the balloon to her. It was hard to tell whether the exclamation was for Lord Graymarsh's peril or his imminent arrival.

The balloon, still headed in their direction, seemed to be sinking rapidly. It was now possible to make out the rope netting that covered the silk cylinder and to at least identify the lone figure in the boat dangling beneath it as a dark-haired male. The Prodigy was suddenly overcome by excitement and began to jump up and down, waving both arms ecstatically. "Oh, I say, this is famous!" he crowed repeatedly. The figure in the boat obligingly waved back.

"My God, would you look at that." Even Mr. Langford was forced to mutter a grudging tribute to his cousin's navigational skills. Gray was obviously controlling his descent rate versus his projected distance with a mind toward landing on the grassy, level expanse just beyond them. It was possible now to get a good view of the aeronaut as he intently worked his valves, letting the air escape in properly controlled amounts to guarantee a safe and accurate meeting with terra firma. But just as Randolph and Tidswell broke into spontaneous huzzahs, a sudden, capricious breeze sprang up and focused like a bellows upon the deflating silk. The gust changed the balloon's direction and aimed it straight at the watchers.

"Get down!" Mr. Langford yelled, then saw to it that his command was at least in part obeyed by the simple expedient of snatching Miss Crome off her feet and flattening her beside him on the turf. The others dived in similar fashion just as the blue and crimson boat sailed over the space where moments before their heads had been.

"Bloody hell!" Lord Graymarsh was heard to say as he floated gracefully over five prone bodies and headed toward the lake.

Chapter Seven

THE WALKING PARTY SCRAMBLED TO THEIR FEET, THEN stood like the monoliths at Stonehenge as the balloon continued its capricious descent and came to rest, like a huge swan settling, near the center of the lake. The gossamer silk balloon, almost deflated, stayed aloft, breeze-held, for a second, then with a soft, rustling sigh, floated downward to meet the rippling water.

"Come on, Gerry!" Randolph had shrugged out of his form-fitting evening coat and was hopping on one foot when his cousin laid a restraining hand upon his shoulder.

"Don't be such a gudgeon." Mr. Langford spoke reprovingly. "Gray's a better swimmer than either one of us."

"Yes, but he's underneath that damned balloon and he could have hurt himself."

Randolph had succeeded in ridding himself of his black slippers and would have leaped into the lake except for the firm grip that held him. "No need for both of you to take a ducking, you know."

"Dammit, let me go!" Randolph was growing frantic. He leveled a punch in the direction of his cousin's jaw that the star pupil of Cribb's Parlour had no difficulty dodging.

"Look there, you hothead." Gerard nodded toward the water. "If you want to spoil your clothing, go ahead. God knows it's no great loss to the world of fashion. Who does make your shirts? But as I predicted, your heroics will be ridiculously misplaced."

Just as the silk descended to obscure him, Gray had dived out of the boat. He'd shrugged out of his jacket and kicked off his boots, glumly wondering what his valet would have to say over the second outfit ruined in a fortnight's time. Though tempted to turn toward the bank opposite his watchers, he decided that that would be too craven. He regretted not having taken the coward's way, however, when he pulled himself, dripping, out of the water and confirmed the fleeting impression he'd registered from his bird's-eye view of the figures throwing themselves upon the ground. Miss Sarah Romney was indeed among them. She was now staring at him with a face free of all expression but with disapproval written largely in her luminous blue eyes.

Sarah might have been the only person present. "I had not expected to find you at Pether Hall, Miss Romney," Lord Graymarsh said formally, while at the same time he peeled a water lily petal, which clung like a mustard plaster, off his thigh.

"Nor I, you," she replied haughtily. "But in your case, Pether Hall is the mildest of the unexpected possibilities. I had not expected to see you flying overhead. Or playing Triton the sea god rising from the water, when it comes to that."

"Sea god, Miss Romney?" Gerard gazed at his dripping cousin. "Wouldn't beached mackerel be more accurately descriptive? Really, Gray, this habit of yours of coming to light in awkward places is the outside of enough. First a bog. Now a lake. Is there some balloonist's rule against landing on solid ground?"

His lordship grinned sheepishly, accepted the handkerchief his brother offered, and began to wipe the streaming water from his face and eyes.

What had happened to the cool, elegant fashionplate she had first seen at the Portsmouth Theatre and found so disconcertingly attractive? Miss Romney asked herself. That sophisticated image was fading rapidly; superimposed, perhaps forever, was this second view of Lord Graymarsh in dishabille. So tightly was his linen plastered to his torso that he might have been shirtless once again. His pantaloons, close-fitting due to his tailor's art, now served as a second skin. Sarah glanced at Miss Crome just then and found that she was blushing. Her eyes were demurely averted from what might as well have been his lordship in the raw. Sarah was caught off guard by an almost uncontrollable desire to giggle. Fortunately for her dignity, the Prodigy suddenly redirected the group's attention. "How long do you think it will stay afloat?" he asked anxiously, his troubled gaze intent on the mass of silk floating in the water.

"That's a good question," Gray answered grimly. "I think the boat's fairly watertight. But a soaking won't do the balloon much good. At any rate, I'd better round up some help and get it out while there's still light enough to see by."

"Don't look at me, old boy." Mr. Langford yawned. "Pulling balloons out of lakes holds little appeal for me. Besides, we're due at the pagoda for tea."

"I'm sure he wasn't expecting any exertion on your part." Randolph's voice dripped acid. "My God, Gray, it was Portsmouth Theatre all over again. Anybody who wants to can burn up or drown before our cousin will risk rumpling the cravat it took him forty minutes before a looking glass to tie." By lashing out at his relative, the young man was finding release from the scare he'd just been given.

"Forty minutes? You malign me. I assure you that I can, on my better days, achieve the perfection of the Langford fall in less than twenty. Only a clutch-fist would require forty."

"Oh, the devil with your deuced neckcloth. That ain't the point, and you know it. The point is, you weren't about to put yourself out to rescue Gray."

From Randolph's point of view that might have been the main thrust of his tirade. But from the manner in which the two Romneys were staring at Mr. Langford, it was evident that they had not missed the oblique reference to the Portsmouth Theatre. As far as they were both concerned, Mr. Langford's action—or lack of it—there was the only point.

That astute gentleman took note of their reaction. "I never

believe in unnecessary exertion, dear Coz." Gerard's tone was careless, but the look he bent on Randolph was filled with venom. Whether or not his cousin had intended to alienate Miss Romney was a moot point. The fact remained that he'd dealt Mr. Langford's pursuit of the heiress a severe blow. "At Portsmouth, Gray here had the young thespian's cloak off before, alas, I'd become aware anything was amiss. Did the same not apply to you? As I recall, you arrived onstage as tardily as I." He noted that some of the Romneys' hostility was fading. "And just why," he continued, "you thought I should immerse myself in that filthy lake to keep Gray company is more than I can fathom. Surely he can make a private cake of himself without turning it into a family affair. My only regret in this sordid episode is that I prevented you from joining him. Your hot head could use some cooling."

"Stop it, you two." Dripping wet or not, the baron sounded every inch a lord. "Randolph, I take it that you wish to help. Would you round up some gardeners? Tell them to fetch a boat. In the meantime, Gerry, you might escort the ladies and, er, Master Tidswell on to tea."

Randolph loped off on his mission, but the Prodigy's face fell. "Oh, can't I stay and watch? I don't want any old tea, and I've never seen a balloon pulled out of a lake before. I'd like to above all things. Is it all right if I stay, Sarah?"

"Certainly." His sister enjoyed overruling their imperious dismissal and annoying Lord Graymarsh. "I think I should like to see the rescue myself. Miss Crome, will you not join us? I'm sure Mr. Langford will make our excuses to the others." Seating herself upon the grass as though settling in for a Vauxhall Gardens spectacle, Sarah didn't bother to suppress a smile at the disgusted look on his lordship's face. She didn't mind at all that he knew she was enjoying his discomfort.

Torn between embarrassment at his lordship's revealing dampness and the prospect of strolling along with Mr. Langford, who made her even more uncomfortable, Miss Crome elected to remain. For she was quite certain that Lady Emma would wish her to hold her position near Lord Graymarsh, despite his shocking state, rather than to walk unaccompanied with his slightly scandalous cousin. So after placing a dainty handkerchief on the grass, she sat down beside Miss Romney. "Yes, I think I should like to see the balloon rescued, too," she said, though without much conviction in her voice.

"I'm aware that Pether Hall is hardly the Royal Pavilion," Graymarsh remarked dryly, "but I didn't expect my uncle's guests to be this hard up for entertainment."

"Didn't you?" Gerard answered. "Can't have thought much about it, then; that's obvious. Well, if beauty has elected to stay here," he said with a sigh, "I hesitate to join the crones. I except your mother from that general description, of course, Miss Crome. Still, one hates to forgo one's tea for the dubious excitement of seeing several soaking yards of silk pulled from brackish water. By George, I have it! We'll have tea brought here. Young Tidswell!" The Prodigy turned from trying to ascertain whether more of the balloon had become submerged than when he'd looked a second earlier and eyed the starchy cove warily. "I don't suppose you could be bribed to go tell the servants to—Never mind." He abandoned the notion before the lad's look of horror. "They'd never do anything on your say-so, anyhow. What a bore. I'll have to go myself. Don't do anything till I get back, Gray. The rescue of your balloon, I'm sure, will quite eclipse Miss Romney's theatricals for excitement and suspense." He bowed to the ladies and set off at a leisurely pace to retrace their footsteps along the gravel path.

The Prodigy joined the two ladies on the grass and continued his anxious balloon surveillance. Lord Graymarsh stood awkwardly, pulling covertly at his clinging shirt and breeches. He felt more uncomfortable than at almost any point in his memory. Certainly more than at any point in his entire adult life. And he had no problem accounting for his loss of poise.

Its cause was not the young beauty whose cheeks flamed with embarrassment and who could not bring herself to look at him directly. As always, he felt only sympathy for Miss Crome. He was well aware that her dragon of a mother was determined that the beauty bring him to heel and lead him to the altar. He also realized that Evelina was more terrified of succeeding in that Herculean task than she was of failure. When

246

Lady Emma had maneuvered him into standing up with her daughter for the second time at the girl's come-out, he'd thought, Why doesn't the old witch find some nice young squire at home for her? He was usually adept at sidestepping such manipulation. But the desire to save Miss Crome from a scold about her shyness overrode his judgment. Now, as he looked at the girl's flushed cheeks, he wished that he'd squelched that kindly impulse. He'd only managed to stoke the fires of her mother's high ambition. Hence their presence at Pether Hall. Gray wondered if his cousin's fine Italian hand was behind their invitation. It never occurred to him that his little brother would set such a trap for him.

No, it was not Miss Crome's presence that was discomforting to his lordship. He could live with her averted eyes. It was the mockery in the beautiful blue eyes of the other female and the suppressed laughter that caused her tightly pursed mouth to betray itself ever so slightly now and then in the beginnings of a grin that made him long to snatch her up and toss her headlong into the lake. To prevent himself from possibly doing the unthinkable and also to break the weighty silence, he remarked, "I believe my cousin mentioned something about theatricals, Miss Romney."

"Yes, I believe he did," she replied gravely, then loosed the threatened grin as his lordship, upon shifting his position slightly, gave a sudden hop. The suppressed giggle broke free of all restraint as Gray stood on one leg like a stork and pulled a burr off the sole of his wet and muddy stocking.

"You will, I take it, be performing, then?" he asked between clenched teeth.

"Directing, at any rate." She choked back the laughter under the full force of his glare. "Lady Petherbridge has *hired* me"— Miss Crome gave her a startled glance as Sarah emphasized the word—"to help entertain her houseguests. I do hope that explains my presence here sufficiently. I can see it puzzles you. Did you think, perhaps, I was here on your account?"

"No. You quite mistake the matter. Believe me, I have not concerned myself about the whys and wherefores of your being here."

"Fustian!" Sarah replied pleasantly. "You might have seen a ghost when you floundered out of the lake."

"Floundered?" He looked dangerous.

"Whatever. I do not expect you to believe this, sir. I offer it merely for the record. I had no idea that you were connected in any way with Lady Petherbridge. Not that such knowledge would have kept me away," she added in a burst of candor. "No matter how I may have wished it otherwise, I fear that the proffered wage would have outweighed even my desire to avoid your lordship. The Romney Company is down on its luck, you see."

Miss Crome looked ready to faint at such plain speaking. And his lordship was regretting not having stayed on board his doomed balloon in the noble tradition of sea captains, when the Prodigy, who had paid no attention to his elders' conversation, exclaimed with distressed single-mindedness, "Oh, I do wish they'd hurry. I'm scared it's going to sink."

In spite of a growing desire to strangle the boy's sister, Graymarsh was moved by the Prodigy's concern. "No, I think it will be all right. The boat should float forever."

"It will soon be dark, though." It occurred to Gray to wonder if the loss of the balloon wouldn't pain the lad at least as much as it would bother him. The Prodigy's next speech erased all doubt. "I never saw anything to touch it," the boy confided in an embarrassed rush. "Just floating through the sky like a bird. A big silver bird. It was famous, sir. The prettiest sight I've ever seen. There you were, floating up there in the heavens just like you belonged. I can just picture what it must be like. Why, looking down on all the poor creatures stuck tight to the ground must make you feel like a god or something. It must be the grandest feeling in the world."

"It is all of that." Gray was looking at Tidswell with new respect and thinking how much more appealing the eager face and shining eyes seemed now in the grip of real emotion than in all the posturing and swaggering upon the stage. He smiled at the boy. "When we get the balloon out of the lake and have it sufficiently dried out, would you like to see for yourself? Go up in it, I mean?"

"Oh, sir, could I really?" Tidswell could hardly contain himself. "You ain't bamming me, are you, sir? Of course I'd like it. I'd like it above all things. I'd like it more than—"

"No!" The word rolled off Miss Romney's tongue with dramatic force and echoed across the water. She had leaped to her feet and was staring at the two enthusiasts with horror. "Tidswell, you are not even to consider such a possibility. The idea is unthinkable. I forbid it! Absolutely!"

"You wouldn't do that. You couldn't!" Her brother turned toward her, aghast. His voice was choked. "You don't even know what you're saying."

"I certainly do know." In the face of his obvious distress, Sarah tried to soften her strident tone. "I'm well aware of the dangers of ballooning. And I'm also aware that our father would never consent to your doing such a foolhardy thing and would completely disown me if I allowed it."

"But Sarah!" The Prodigy's wail was stricken. It came from his very soul.

"I hope your lordship is satisfied." She directed her bitterness to where it belonged. "Break your own neck if you've a mind to, but pray, sir, leave my brother out of your harebrained schemes."

"Thank you for your kind permission, but I've no intention of breaking my neck or anybody else's. I assure you there's very little danger in balloon flight."

"Oh, yes. I'm sure it's perfectly safe." Her tone was withering. "You made that abundantly clear when you chose to bring your craft down in the middle of the lake. Why, you might just as well have landed in a treetop—or on a church steeple, or in the channel, or—or—" She sputtered to a close, more from a threatening fit of apoplexy than from the fact that she'd exhausted the list of dire possibilities.

"Trust an actress to make a Cheltenham tragedy out of a simple balloon ride," Gray remarked to the world at large, then, to the Prodigy, "I'm sorry for your sister's prejudice. Though I'm not surprised at such a reaction from a female."

"A female!" Miss Romney choked. "Some of the world's

foremost balloonists have been females, I'll have you know. And died for their pioneering. Sex has nothing to say to anything."

His lordship ignored that and addressed the boy. "As I was about to say, since you are not of age, I'm afraid I can't take you up in opposition to your sister's wishes."

Tidswell glared at Sarah, then burst into tears.

"Oh, thank you very much." The actress looked daggers at the nobleman.

"But if, on the other hand," Gray continued, "your father were to grant that permission—well, that would be another matter, would it not?"

"Divide and conquer?" Sarah inquired.

"Certainly not. I just hate to see a fellow enthusiast suffer from a stupid, baseless prejudice, that's all."

"All? Is that all, indeed?" she began but, fortunately perhaps, was prevented from elaborating by the simultaneous arrival of the tea and the rescue team.

Rescue came by water in the form of two flatboats. One headed directly toward the center of the lake while the other made for shore, where his lordship stood impatiently waiting for it. Since he'd not begun the drying process enough to matter, he waded in to help the burly punter nose his boat onto land so that Randolph could climb out.

"You're sure you don't need my help?" Randolph eyed the baskets that two footmen were placing on the grass.

"No, have your tea."

His brother's testy voice gave Randolph second thoughts. "Wouldn't dream of deserting you in your hour of need," he pronounced stoutly. "Let's shove off."

"Don't be such a gudgeon." Gray managed a weak smile in lieu of saying that Randolph was in no way responsible for his irritation. "I'm grateful to you for fetching help. I'd have hated to trudge the distance stocking-footed. Go on now." He held the boat steady so that his brother could climb out, then jumped in himself. The gardener pushed off.

"Oh, I say, sir." Tidswell was too embarrassed by his recent tears to manage more than a mumble. But fortunately his lordship heard and told the punter to hold up. "Would you like to come along, Tids?" he called back over his shoulder.

"Oh, could I, sir?"

"Certainly. I should have thought to ask you." Without even glancing Miss Romney's way for her permission, Gray jumped into the water, which was waist-high, and waded to the shore. "Climb on my back," he commanded, kneeling down. "And for God's sake, keep your feet up. I don't want to be held responsible if you soak your boots."

Tidswell followed his instructions to the letter and was deposited into the flatboat high and dry. The craft rocked dangerously as Gray pulled himself up over the side, but a shift of balance by the gardener soon steadied it. They moved rapidly toward the other boat as the shadows lengthened across the lake.

In the meantime, the footmen had spread a linen tablecloth upon the grass and had distributed china, silver, napkins, and mounds of cakes. After a second's indecision, the silver teapot had been placed before Miss Romney, the senior of the ladies. The footmen then retired to a respectful distance to allow the alfresco party to have the semblance of privacy even as they watched discreetly in case something was required.

"Well," Mr. Langford remarked indifferently as he accepted a Dresden cup from Miss Romney's hand, "I see that the fleet has arrived in time. The imperiled vessel will be towed to dock."

"I wish it would sink like a stone."

"Surely, Miss Romney, you don't really mean that." Randolph spoke through a mouthful of cake.

"Oh, do I not! Lord Graymarsh has offered Tidswell a ride in the horrid thing. And I've forbidden my brother to set one foot inside that hanging coffin. Nothing but a watery grave for that cursed balloon will save Tids and me from the worst—indeed, I think the only—row of our entire lives."

Mr. Langford gazed toward the center of the lake. "It pains me, then, to inform you that it appears they've worked out a salvage plan. The modus operandi seems to involve placing the collapsed balloon in one flatboat and allowing its carrier to trail behind, while pulling the two in tandem with the other. Oh, I say, your little brother seems to have decided to climb into the balloon boat."

"Oh, bother!" Sarah scrambled to her feet to confirm this, wondering what had become of Graymarsh's concern for Tidswell's best boots. "It's bound to leak."

"Well, at least now he can say he's had a balloon ride," Randolph remarked.

"Think that will satisfy him?" Mr. Langford asked the question without much interest.

"Of course it won't," Tidswell's sister retorted. "It will only serve to whet his appetite. Oh, blast his lordship for a villain! A 'bloody, bawdy villain! Remorseless, treacherous, lecherous, kindless villain!' " The Shakespearean oaths came tripping off her tongue. She might have been the Romney Company manager at his most fulsome.

"Miss Romney!" Miss Crome gasped. At first she looked shocked at Sarah's tirade, then she suddenly broke into a spontaneous peal of laughter that caused the other three to turn and stare. Stripped of her shyness, the beauty had never looked more appealing. Randolph's eyes widened, as if really seeing her for the first time. Gerard, in the act of taking snuff, paused halfway to his nose. "Miss Romney, you are a caution." Evelina chortled. "I've never met anyone so divertingly original. Just imagine calling Lord Graymarsh a 'bawdy villain'! And all the rest of it! I vow, my m-mother would expire to hear you. However do you manage to think up these things?"

"I really couldn't say," Miss Romney answered levelly, while Mr. Langford's snuff, inhaled too quickly, sent him into a sneezing, coughing fit. "The words just seem to come to me."

Later that evening, when the members of the house party had retired, Randolph made his way to his cousin's chamber carrying a candle that trailed a smoke line in the drafty hall. He found Gerard, clad in a magnificent gold brocade dressing gown, propped up in bed with Byron's latest volume discarded at his side while he slowly sipped from a crystal wineglass. Uninvited, Randolph helped himself to the decanter and pulled up a chair. The other man frowned. "Prepared for a coze, are you?" he asked pointedly.

"Yes. Wanted to get your opinion on our progress."

"Progress? In what respect? I wasn't aware that we'd made any. Unless you call surviving one full day of our aunt's tedious hospitality progress. Which is a point, I suppose." He took another appreciative sip. "Uncle's cider is the only bright spot in a dull prospect, Randolph, so please do not toss your wine off in that oafish manner. Savor it like a gentleman."

"Dammit, Gerry, don't try your poses on me. I know you too well by half. You know perfectly well what kind of progress I'm talking about. Progress with Miss Romney. But you did speak the truth without meaning to: you and I ain't made any. At least not so far as I can tell. There's one good thing, though. Gray's definitely been eliminated. That's something positive to drink to, anyhow." He misread the other man's speaking look as he stretched his long legs in a forty-five-degree angle and rested his slippers on the white coverlet. He had left his coat back in his room. To add to his comfort, he unwound his elaborate cravat.

"Staying long?" his cousin murmured.

"Oh, I know what you're thinking." Randolph ignored the interruption and kept a single-minded grip on his train of thought. "Gray was already out of the competition. That's what he gave us to believe, at any rate."

"And you doubted it?" Gerard asked sarcastically.

"Oh, I didn't doubt that he believed it at the time. Pursuing a female without her having the slightest notion why goes against the grain with Gray. I know him well enough to be sure of that. Don't like it above half myself. But I rather thought that in spite of what he had said he was attracted to Miss Romney. She's surprisingly likable, ain't she?" He spoke with obvious relief, and his cousin nodded. "And I was sure that she was taken with him. Females generally are. And that rescue thing at the theater made him the odds-on favorite. But she's really turned against him since he offered the Prodigy a ride in his balloon. He couldn't have done us a bigger favor if he'd planned for days just how to go about it."

"You think so?" His cousin's look was enigmatic.

"I know so. Miss Romney really has it in for my brother now." He chuckled as he took a gulp of wine. "For God's sake, Gerry, weren't you listening? Didn't you hear all those different kinds of villains that she called him? By the by, whichever of us wins Miss Romney in the end should have a private word with her on that sort of thing. All right for the stage, perhaps, but won't do in the polite world. But that's neither here nor there just now. The point I'm making is, no matter how smitten Miss Romney may have been at first, Gray's really managed to get himself in her black book. She actually detests him now!" crowed his lordship's brother.

Randolph paused for a response from his other rival. When none came, he gave vent to his exasperation. "There's no use looking so Friday-faced, Gerard. Come on, admit it. You're as relieved as I am that Miss Romney's taken a violent dislike to Gray."

"Oh, no, you're wrong there, Coz. I am not relieved at all. And if you are, as you claim, it only goes to show that you have a lot yet to learn about the other sex. Now if Miss Romney were indifferent to your brother, *then* I'd be relieved. But that she despises him? Frankly, I find that sufficient reason for alarm." He yawned elaborately.

"Oh." The wind was obviously leaving Randolph's sails. He did not for a moment question his cousin's superior knowledge of the female nature. Gerard had been on the town too long for Randolph to doubt his insights. But after a moment's silence, the resilient young man brightened. "Well, there's still Miss Crome."

"Ah, yes. The fair Evelina."

"Her mama wants Gray for her."

"You noticed that."

Randolph ignored the sarcasm. "He could do worse, you know," he continued thoughtfully. "Oh, I didn't think so at first. For in spite of Miss Crome's being the prettiest female I've ever seen, bar none, I thought her insipid, didn't you?"

"Shy is the term I might have used."

"But I think that if you could get her away from her odious

mother long enough she'd be a different person. Don't you agree?"

"The possibility has occurred to me."

"I mean, did you see her when she was laughing at Miss Romney? I found her quite a taking little thing. Didn't you think so, Gerry?"

"I suppose my reaction could be so described."

"So even if what you say is true, about Miss Romney's not being indifferent to Gray, I mean, I think Miss Crome—and her mother—can be counted on to cut him from the competition. And you can thank me for that, Gerry. It was my idea to have Aunt Augusta ask 'em."

"So I surmised. And I also gather it was your idea to invite Lady Scriven to join our happy gathering." Gerard's eyes narrowed.

Randolph grinned sheepishly. "Well, yes, as a matter of fact, it was. You can't actually blame me, now can you? I ain't a complete ninnyhammer, you know. I realize any female's bound to prefer you or Gray to me. So I thought it a rather good notion to keep you both occupied. Too bad Lady Scriven had to go and develop a putrid throat."

"Checkmate, Coz."

"You mean you put her off? Damnation. Well, one out of two ain't all that bad. At least I've flung Miss Crome at Gray's head. A pity the girl ain't rich."

"Why? That should make no difference where Gray's concerned."

"I know. But I wouldn't mind dangling after the beauty myself now." Randolph heaved a heavy sigh. "Lord, I'd give a monkey not to be required to find an heiress. It's dashed inconvenient not having a fortune of one's own."

"You don't say so." The bitterness in Gerard's voice caused his cousin to look up sharply. But he was met by the usual lazy smile. "Do go to bed, Randolph," Mr. Langford said with a dismissive gesture. "One needs one's rest. How else to face the tedium of the morrow?"

Chapter Eight

MISS ROMNEY WOKE UP EARLY AND TAPPED SOFTLY ON Tidswell's door. It was opened almost immediately by the Prodigy, who was dressed in oversized buckskins and riding boots. Sarah had fared slightly better from the same costume source. Her slate-colored, braid-trimmed riding dress, while of inferior cut and cloth, had at least been sized for her. "I don't think anyone's up yet," she whispered. But to safeguard the secrecy of their departure, they stole down the servants' stairs.

As Sarah had hoped, in his mounting excitement Tidswell seemed to forget his balloon grievances as they approached the stables. "Are you sure the nobs won't care?" he asked anxiously.

"Don't say nobs, Tids. Lord Petherbridge made it quite clear that his guests should use his horses."

"Yes, but I'll bet a monkey he took it for granted that everybody knew how to ride."

"Undoubtedly. That's why I wanted us to practice before we're asked to join in some excursion. There was talk last night about exploring the scenic areas in the neighborhood."

"And do you think they'll have a hunt?"

"I've no idea. But I certainly hope not."

"I think it would be famous," her brother crowed. "Riding to hounds! Jumping fences!"

256

"Don't get above yourself. We'll do well to manage a sedate pace."

"Well, it can't be all that hard. Seems to me the horse does all the real work."

In actuality it proved far more difficult than Tids had predicted. Sarah ordered the horses saddled with a careless assurance that caused the stable boy to overestimate greatly her ability. The mount he brought her, though schooled to carry ladies, was by no means a plodder. And when the Prodigy requested a "prime goer," the groom, barely Tidswell's senior, was willing to comply.

He stood by to watch them mount, an act that Sarah, with her stage training, had observed closely and now tried to imitate. But the horse she had watched hadn't persisted in going around and around in circles. Finally aboard, and noting that Tids had also reached the saddle after several abortive tries, she then declined the groom's rather anxious offer to accompany them. Under the stable boy's doubtful gaze, Sarah clucked to her mount, a technique gleaned from observing Lord Petherbridge the day before. Nothing happened. She tried again, this time with more success. The mare turned her head and looked at the groom in protest.

Observing his sister's problems, Tidswell varied her technique. Along with the prescribed cluck, he dug his heels into his horse's flanks. Results were instantaneous. His mount shot off. And Sarah's mare, at last realizing what was expected of it, immediately followed suit.

The Prodigy's instinct for self-preservation wiped out his sister's lectures on equestrian skill. He flung himself forward, his stomach rattling on his horse's back, and somehow managed to fling his arms around the creature's neck. Screeching bloody murder all the while, Tids hung on for all that he was worth.

Sarah was not so fortunate. As her horse, panicked by Tids's screams, broke into a gallop, her instincts were to wrap herself, Tids-style, as close to the animal's hide as possible. But her lady's saddle prevented this procedure. As it was, her knee, crooked around the pommel, acted as an axis. This focal point remained a constant as she bounced around, teeth rattling, spine jarring upward through her skull, never alighting in the same spot twice. How she and the horse remained tenuously united defied all natural laws. On one bound, she dipped so far over to the side that her head paralleled the ground they were flying over. With a mighty effort, she saved herself from falling and struggled upright, only to be immediately flung backward where her head rattled on the horse's croup. If I survive this ride, she thought, my future is assured. Astley's Royal Circus is bound to find a spot for me. Just then an especially hearty jolt helped Sarah gain a more or less upright position once again. They were speeding across a meadow now. And while she bounced erratically, like a backward toddler's first rubber ball, Sarah observed three things: that her horse and Tids's mount still maintained the same distance ratio they'd started with; that they were running pell-mell toward a patch of woods; and that they had been joined in their headlong gallop by another rider.

Even as her rattling teeth connected with her tongue, even in her shocking state of terror, even as she dipped perilously close to the horse's side once more, Sarah still managed to feel a rush of indignation that it was Tidswell whom Lord Graymarsh was intent on saving and not her.

It was a near thing altogether. When Gray, out for an early-morning ride, had seen two horses flying across the meadow, his first reaction had been annoyance for the end of his solitude. Then, as the mounts drew nearer with unnerving speed, he mentally cursed the two fools for their neck-or-nothing race. But when they drew close enough for him to see one rider plastered like a poultice on his charger's back and the other rattling around like errant hail, he woke up to the fact that he was witnessing two runaways. He knew that once the horses reached the woods, both riders were going to be scraped off the horses' backs like barnacles from a ship's hull. He dug his heels into his mount and rode like the very devil.

Gray approached Tidswell at a ninety-degree angle that forced the Prodigy's horse to swerve just before it reached disaster. He managed to chase the maddened animal down and

258

then clutch its bridle, meanwhile yelling to the boy, "Stop your caterwauling. This poor beast's panicked!"

"H-he's panicked!" Tids wailed, his terror overridden now by bitterness as his horse decreased its pace. "How the deuce does he think I feel?" The Prodigy didn't wait for a complete cessation of all movement. A normal canter was good enough. He rolled off the creature's back and hit the ground with a grateful thud.

Sarah's horse, she had discovered, had no character of its own. A natural follower, it had swerved after Tidswell's mount. It now came thundering toward its stable companion with Sarah shouting "Whoa! Whoa! Whoa!" in a voice fit more for lament than for equestrian direction.

But in its first independent action of the day, the mare declined to rendezvous and dashed on by the others. Cursing like the cavalryman he wasn't, Lord Graymarsh set off in hot pursuit. Once again he was able to catch hold of a bridle and slow a terrified animal down. "There, there, old girl, everything's all right." He clucked soothingly. "No need to panic. You're fine now."

"That's easy for you to say. I know I've bitten my tongue in two, and I think my neck's most likely broken."

"I was talking to the horse, Miss Romney."

"I should have known," she answered bitterly.

"If you think you can manage to hang on for a few more seconds, I'll lead this poor beast back and see about your brother."

"Of course I can hang on." Sarah spoke with more bravado than she felt. She then chose to ignore his lordship's derisive snort.

Tids's bay was peacefully cropping grass when the other two riders joined them. The boy had progressed to a sitting position. But he was reluctant to distance himself from terra firma any more than that.

Lord Graymarsh dismounted. He looked at Tids with more disapproval than sympathy. "Are you all right?" he barked.

"I g-guess so."

Thus reassured, Gray turned to help Sarah dismount. She had anticipated him, however, and was determined to prove herself a horsewoman by getting off alone. He was just in time to be in the way when a tangle of boots and skirt and stirrup sent her sprawling. She clutched at him to break her fall, caught him off balance, knocked him off his feet, and landed on top of him. "Ooff!" his lordship commented as the wind escaped his lungs.

It was the bedchamber in the Portsmouth inn all over again. Why she found being enfolded in this odious man's arms such a homey sort of feeling was more than Sarah Romney could understand. Nor could she ever hope to anticipate the Graymarsh reaction to such proximity. In one instance, it had turned him lecherous. In this case, furious.

"I don't appreciate your language, sir." Despite the fact that her body was plastered on top of his with an intimacy that even her heavy riding clothes could not obscure, her tone was prim. "I am well aware that I'm an actress, therefore not a lady. But since you are supposed to be a gentleman, I find your conduct inexcusable."

Lord Graymarsh looked into the beautiful, censorious eyes just above him, stared at the disapproving mouth, and came within an ace of kissing it. Just in time he recalled the folly of succumbing to his baser instincts. He swore again instead. "Get off me, woman," he commanded.

"You needn't take that tone. I intend to." She struggled upright, leaving Gray feeling far more bereft than he was prepared for or would admit, even to himself.

A natural reaction to this undefined emotion, which had followed hard upon the fear that he'd be too late to prevent the Romneys from breaking their fool necks, was an increase of fury. "What the devil did you two think you were up to?" he demanded as he rose and dusted himself off.

Sarah, who was feeling the Prodigy for broken bones, grew at least as haughty. "We were out for a morning ride. What else would we be 'up to'?"

Tidswell chimed in defensively. "Lord Petherbridge did say we could use his horses anytime we'd a mind to."

"Did his lordship realize that neither one of you had ever been on a horse before?"

"What an absurd notion." Sarah was glad her back was turned. "Whatever gave you the idea we'd never ridden?"

"Perhaps," he replied dryly, "it was Tidswell clinging to his horse like a monkey on a bolting tiger. Or it could have been you flapping along like the wash caught in a high wind." Graymarsh choked suddenly at the recollection.

Sarah spun to face him. "I'm glad you find it so amusing that we were almost killed. And we can hardly be held responsible for the fact that our horses ran away."

"Oh, can you not? I beg to differ. You are right about one thing, though. The whole thing's not funny. If I hadn't come along—"

"I assume you're waiting for us to thank you. Well, consider it done."

"I don't want your thanks," he said explosively. "What I would like is an explanation of why two complete novices chose to take out two of the most spirited horses in Petherbridge's stables without letting the groom know you'd never ridden before in your lives. And don't bother denying that fact again. It won't wash with me."

"I did not expect riding to be so difficult," Sarah answered defensively.

"And I didn't expect you to be so calf-witted."

"Well, it looks easy enough." She bristled. "And we're actors. Imitators by trade. I observed the riders closely yesterday and didn't foresee any problem in simply doing as they did."

"Of all the daft—Why didn't you just admit you didn't know how to ride? One of the grooms could have instructed you."

"Because," she blazed, "people of your sort simply assume that everyone knows how. In the same way it's simply assumed that people own their own carriages, and have a house in town, and—and attend Almack's assemblies. When those people"—she gestured in the direction of the hall—"were planning their horseback excursions, it didn't occur to anyone that we mightn't know how to ride. And I—I just didn't want to admit it, that's all." She glared at him. "Do you think you aristocrats are the only ones entitled to their pride?"

"I think I've no intention of getting into a class war with you."

"You'd better not." Tidswell surprised himself by horning in. Graymarsh might be the owner of the marvelous, if water-logged, means of flight, but blood was thicker than balloon air. "The fact is, Sarah's at least as well born as you are."

"Tidswell!" Sarah gasped in horror while Gray looked rather worse than startled.

"I don't care. It's true. Papa says so. Sarah's only my half sister, you see." The Prodigy's voice filled with pride. "And her father was a lord. So for all we know, he could have been a higher-up kind of lord than you are."

"Tidswell!" Sarah repeated. She was ready to sink with mortification. Graymarsh watched her curiously. "That's nothing but a Banbury tale and you should not repeat it. Besides, my parentage has nothing to say to anything."

"Yes, it does." Her brother stuck to his guns stubbornly. "It must be the reason you wouldn't admit you'd never ridden. At least I know I would have," he added virtuously.

"Well, never mind all that." Graymarsh thought it was time to change the subject. He felt a protective rush of sympathy for Sarah's embarrassment. "You both are about to get your first lesson now."

"Really, my lord, that won't be necessary." Miss Romney was all icy dignity.

"I ain't about to get back up on that vicious monster," her brother declared.

"Oh, yes, you are. It's the first rule to riding. When a horse dumps you, you climb right back on. And, yes, Miss Romney, it is necessary. For one thing, I don't want my uncle's cattle or your lives imperiled."

"Thank you for the order of your concern."

"And for another," he continued as though she'd never spoken, "it's a long way back. All right now. Please bring your famous actor's training into focus and observe. This, Miss and Master Romney, is the proper technique for mounting. Understand? Now then. Try to imitate me exactly."

Chapter
Nine

*L*ORD AND LADY PETHERBRIDGE'S HOUSE PARTY WAS PRO-
ceeding, for the most part, along traditional lines. Breakfast was served at ten, dinner around five, supper at ten-thirty.
Between breakfast and changing for dinner the gentlemen
went shooting or fishing. They joined the ladies for a walk, on
an outing, or in their dressing rooms. They played billiards in
the hall. The ladies spent part of the morning in their own
dressing rooms or their hostess's, then walked around the lake
or garden, watched the gentlemen fishing, or went for a drive
to the neighboring village. Occasionally, visitors called. Wet
days were largely spent in the library, rummaging among the
books, doing needlework, playing anagrams and backgam-
mon, or simply chatting, as their fancy was struck.

There were some variations, however, in the time-honored
routine. Before breakfast, Lord Graymarsh and his reluctant
pupils met for riding lessons. Then when he had eaten,
Tidswell joined, with even greater reluctance, his hostess's
class in moral instruction for the children of her tenants.

Tids considered it quite the most tedious hour imaginable
and found his ladyship too prosy again by half. He was filled
with wonder at the compliance of the other children until he
discovered that they welcomed these classes as a respite from
their labors.

At first, Tids had been flattered by Lady Petherbridge's attention. He could imagine his father's delight when he learned

of it. But gradually the boy began to wonder about her motives and found it more than coincidental that her ladyship chose the works of Hannah More for their spiritual edification. Lady Petherbridge prefaced each selection from *Practical Piety and Christian Morals* by telling them once again how a misguided Miss More had been associated with the wicked stage, had, in fact, had a flourishing career as a writer of tragedies, but had seen the error of her ways and turned her pen away from the theater toward higher things. The inference was plain. If Miss More could redirect her life, well, so could Master Romney.

"What would Miss More say about your theatricals?" Tids was bold enough to point out some discrepancy in Lady Petherbridge's preaching and her practice.

"There is a world of difference between ladies and gentlemen reading uplifting material for private amusement in their own houses and actors giving sordid performances for hire," was the haughty, less-than-satisfactory reply.

Tids was not the only one puzzled by Lady Petherbridge's choice of entertainment for her guests. Sara confided her confusion privately to Randolph when the two of them arrived onstage early for the first rehearsal.

She had not yet recovered from the shock of seeing the hall theater. It far eclipsed in grandeur, if not size, any of the provincial playhouses she'd appeared in. The decor was a riot of gilt paint. Golden cupids were in large supply. Ornate plasterwork was rampant. Sconces and chandeliers gleamed with gold and crystal. Miss Romney ran an expert eye around the house. From pit to balcony, she estimated that the theater could seat almost two hundred. She voiced her concern obliquely. "When Lady Petherbridge engaged me to organize her theatricals, I really expected a much larger house party than this one."

"Did you?" Randolph said uneasily.

"Well, yes. It is a bit unusual for the cast to outnumber the audience, don't you think?" (Actually, in the Romney Company experience, it was not really all that rare.)

"Oh, well." Randolph dismissed such trifles carelessly. "As for that, if we come up to snuff in our performance, I expect my

264

aunt will provide us with an audience. Be a good chance for her to have the county in. Noblesse oblige and all that, don't you know."

Sarah did not know. But if Lady Petherbridge's own nephew was not concerned about the oddness of the engagement, well, then, she needn't be. "Oh, there's no question that our performance will come up to snuff," she remarked with a bravado worthy of Adolphus Romney.

The young director had many occasions to eat those words. The first came about half an hour later when the rest of the young people were assembled upon the stage and she attempted to assign the parts.

Sarah had devoted much time and effort in choosing the right vehicle for these amateurs. She had decided upon *The Gamester*. The play had several qualities to recommend it. For one thing, it was written in prose, not verse, and would be less difficult for nonprofessionals to tackle. But more important, the cast of characters exactly fit, in numbers, anyhow, her little group of players.

Before assigning the parts, Sarah outlined the plot. This proved no small task, for the play was complicated, not to mention convoluted. "The male lead, Beverley," she explained, "is a gamester who squanders his own fortune then sells his wife's jewels. He's led astray by a false friend named Stukeley, who is scheming to win Mrs. Beverley for himself. Mr. Lewison, who is in love with the gamester's sister, discovers Stukeley's villainy. Stukeley tries to murder him. In the meantime, Beverley, who has been languishing in debtors' prison, takes poison in despair, then discovers too late that he's inherited another fortune. Mrs. Beverley dies soon afterward of a broken heart."

"My God," Gray was heard to groan underneath his breath.

Given the limitations of her group, Sarah was satisfied that she'd done an excellent job of casting. Mr. Langford's exceptional good looks made him a natural choice for Beverley, the male lead. For the same reason, but with less conviction, she'd given the part of Mrs. Beverley to Miss Crome. She had not hesitated a moment over the villain's role. Lord Graymarsh would do the part of Stukeley. That left the virtuous Lewison to be played by Mr. Milbanke. She herself, in addition to directing, would be obliged to take the minor role of the gamester's sister.

Sarah had not anticipated the amateurs' reactions. Her cast assignments met with instant opposition. Miss Crome, apprehensive of participating in the theatricals at all, had grown quite pale when given the lead role. She asked in a trembling voice to be excused. After Sarah's attempts to persuade her to at least read through the part had failed and Randolph's entreaties hadn't moved her, the Prodigy offered his opinion, with more truth than tact, that anybody who looked like Miss Crome could make a complete cake out of herself onstage and nobody would even notice. But on this issue the pliant Miss Crome proved intractable. Sarah finally offered to exchange parts with her if she would not abandon the project altogether.

That crisis settled, the director hit another snag. Lord Graymarsh declared that he'd no intention of being involved in such a piece of flummery. He'd work backstage if necessary, but he was damned if he'd play that sapskulled part.

"What's the matter, Gray?" his cousin twitted. "Nose out of joint? Want to be the hero?"

"Not at all. Getting to do you the dirty is the only appealing aspect of the whole silly plot." It was his lordship's considered opinion that the villain Stukeley was *The Gamester's* choicest role. "Which is about like saying you'd prefer the pox to leprosy." And all his brother's wheedling could not induce Graymarsh to change his mind. As for Sarah, she refused even to try, but turned in desperation instead to her brother. "Tids?" she pleaded.

His face was set stubbornly. "You promised I wouldn't have to take a part. I'm stage manager."

"I know I promised. But I did not think to be short one male." The speaking look she shot Graymarsh failed to disconcert him. Nor did her pleading budge her little brother.

"Perhaps if Mr. Milbanke would play Stukeley, you could have the smaller part."

"No! You promised!" But then a look of cunning crept into

the Prodigy's eyes. "Of course if you was to do me a favor, I might do you one."

"And what would that favor be?"

"Let me go up in his lordship's balloon."

"No!" There was a long pause while the two Romneys glared at each other. Then Sarah closed her script dramatically. "We'll just have to choose another play, that's all."

"Oh, what the devil. I'll do it." Lord Graymarsh suddenly capitulated with great martyrdom and little grace. "Only how about trading parts with me, Randolph? You did say the part of—who was it, Lewison?—was smaller, didn't you, Miss Romney?"

Sarah nodded, relieved but at the same time feeling things slipping out of her control.

"So, little brother, wouldn't you like a juicier role?"

"But Gray," Gerard protested with a mocking smile, "that's no good. No one will take Randolph seriously as a villain."

"Whereas they would me? Thank you, Coz. What do you say, Miss Romney? The part of Lewison would give me more time to help the Prodigy backstage."

"Very well, then," Sarah grudgingly agreed. She suspected that all this maneuvering was designed to avoid playing romantic scenes with her. Or perhaps he merely wished to place himself opposite Miss Crome. Well, if he had but noticed, her original casting had served both those ends. She pulled herself together and attempted to regain the reins of this runaway rehearsal. But the initial read-through left her even more discouraged and depressed.

Nor did subsequent evening practice sessions serve to lift her spirits. She blamed herself for the lack of progress they were making. As a theater professional, she should, she felt, be able to surmount enough of their difficulties to bring about a creditable performance of *The Gamester*.

The problem was, she could find no similarity between the production of social theatricals and the serious pursuit of earning one's bread and butter. It wasn't that she aimed so high. Heaven knows, the Romney Company had dealt with its own share of miscasting. But never had she had to cope with a character who quailed and quaked as Miss Crome did. And Randolph, though more courageous, was just as hopeless in his role. As for his recalcitrant lordship, any hopes she'd had that he might pick up a bit of zeal for acting faded after one or two rehearsals. Boredom was Lord Graymarsh's overriding emotion. It set the key for his so-called performance.

If there was any bright spot where Graymarsh was concerned, and Sarah tried her best to view it so, it was that his boredom evaporated when Tids introduced him to life behind the scenes. Here Gray's bent for invention ran such riot that the director felt compelled to launch a protest, "All these scenic effects will upstage the drama."

"Good. So much the better for the audience," the nobleman–stage apprentice replied as he and the Prodigy went onto plot a regular orgy of thunder, lightning, hail, fog, wind, and rain.

Mr. Gerard Langford, however, proved the outstanding exception to the general ineptitude. He had, in fact, turned out to be a genuine dramatic find. Well aware of the Corinthian's striking good looks and supreme self-confidence, Sarah had expected a certain aptitude for acting on his part. She had not expected such extraordinary talent. Had Mr. Langford been less well born, Sarah soon decided, the Garricks, Kembles, and Keans of the professional theater might well have had a strong contender for their laurels.

But what was undoubtedly the production's biggest asset also had its down side, the director soon discovered. It was bad enough that Gerard completely overshadowed his fellow amateurs' performances; what was worse was that Sarah was obliged to push her own talents to the limit to reach his level. And she blamed Lord Graymarsh for the fact that she found this so difficult to do. It was humiliating when she, a consummate professional, was reduced to a self-conscious parroter of lines merely because his lordship, hammer in hand, was watching from the wings. And at no point was her craft put more to the test than when the script called for a passionate embrace between the gamester and his wife.

Wearing her director's hat, Sarah had explained how the

love scene should be played. Mr. Langford should take her into his arms, then bend her body away from the audience so that the back of his head obscured her face. Thus they would give the illusion of a long and ardent kiss, whereas in reality their lips would never meet.

"Nonsense," said Mr. Langford as he enfolded her in his arms. "Here's how I envision this particular scene." His lips met hers just in time to shut off her protest. Not only did the leading man actually kiss the leading lady, but he continued the intimacy well beyond the scene's requirements, not to mention the bounds of all propriety. Nor did it help matters at all that when Sarah emerged, red of face and gasping, from this expert, unsettling, unprofessional embrace, the first thing she saw was Graymarsh's level, censorious stare.

An unexpected side effect of Mr. Langford's excellence was that it spurred his cousin Randolph on to greater effort. Mr. Milbanke seemed to grow painfully aware of his own inadequacies and pressed his director for private coaching sessions. Sarah soon found this rather wearing, especially since he, like his cousin, seemed to place far too much emphasis on his love scenes at the expense of the rest of his appearances. So she was guiltily grateful—for Randolph's acting needed all the help that she could give it—when at the end of a particularly trying group rehearsal, Mr. Langford took his cousin firmly by the arm. "No private session tonight, cub. Miss Romney needs a rest. And I need you for billiards."

Sarah took full advantage of her reprieve and went immediately to bed. But after a full hour spent tossing and turning in the unsuccessful endeavor to find a comfortable position, she finally abandoned the notion of sleep and lit her bedside candle. Reading would rid her mind of its disconcerting tendency to dwell upon a particular, odious member of the aristocracy. She picked up the three leather-bound volumes stacked on the bedside table and examined each in turn. They proved to be a weighty collection of sermons, the inevitable copy of Hannah More, and *The Mysteries of Udolpho*. The last, Sarah surmised, must have been left by some former guest. It hardly seemed to reflect the literary taste of Lady

Petherbridge. She decided to read it. Though possibly less soporific than the other two, at least the Gothic novel would keep her mind from dwelling upon a certain incident in a Portsmouth inn and the feel of a bare chest, strong arms, demanding mouth . . . Resolutely, she opened the work of Mrs. Radcliffe.

The cure proved worse than the disease. Sarah did forget all about Lord Graymarsh, but she became so obsessed with the possibility of clanking chains and fearsome cries and moaning specters that she raised her eyes from the printed page every few seconds to peer around her, trying to penetrate the deep shadows that lay beyond the small pool of candlelight. The room that by daylight seemed so welcoming had suddenly turned sinister. The dark mass that once had been a wardrobe appeared ominous, undefined. Surely it had moved! Was creeping toward her! And was that a bulge behind the damask drapery? Could something inhuman, unthinkable, be lurking there, choosing its time to pounce?

Don't be ridiculous. You're letting your imagination get out of hand. Sarah gave herself a mental dressing-down. What you need is rest. Blow out your candle and go to sleep! So screwing her courage to the sticking point, she inhaled a deep breath, then watched the yellow candle flame bend and elongate, sputter, and go out. And at the precise moment of total darkness, she realized three things: she had heard an ominous, prolonged creaking; she was not alone; and she had not exhaled her breath. She took care of the omission immediately in a long, bloodcurdling scream.

The Honorable Randolph Milbanke had not wished to advertise his presence to anyone else who might be abroad in Pether Hall. So he had made his way down the corridor without benefit of candle, relying on the faint moonlight drifting through the open window at its end. Not being a disciple of Mrs. Radcliffe, he took no notice of the slight breeze that fanned his carefully styled hair. What he did observe was a trickle of light beneath Miss Romney's door. The actress, he deduced, was still awake. The gentlemanly thing would be, of course, to knock. But prudence and the proximity of other houseguests demanded a different course. Randolph turned the doorknob very slowly, trying to reduce its tendency to squeak. He eased the door ajar, thereby creating the fatal draft that snuffed Miss Romney's candle.

Her piercing shriek caused him to drop the tray he bore. The ensuing clang and clatter, combined with a sharp, crashing, splintering sound, compounded Miss Romney's terror and increased the volume of her screams.

Instinctively, Randolph sprang toward the bed. His one thought was to persuade its occupant to cut the caterwauling before she waked the dead. The maneuver was to prove a grave mistake. Unlike the Gothic heroines she admired, Miss Romney was not prone to swoon in a crisis. Instead, as the dark form lunged her way, she snatched the heavy brass candlestick from its stand and swung it with all her might. The blow was glancing, but if suffced. It sideswiped Randolph's nose, which immediately gushed blood. His howl of pain now merged with Miss Romney's shrieks of fear.

"Sarah! My God, Sarah! What's happening!"

Lord Graymarsh had been awakened from a deep sleep to dash groggily toward the outcry. It was plain good luck and not acuity that caused his bare feet to spring safely over two shattered crystal goblets as he honed in on the dim figure attacking the damsel on the bed. In actuality, Randolph had just succeeded in clapping his hand over Miss Romney's mouth and was trying to explain his presence the best he could when a pair of rough hands jerked him backward off the bed. A source of light miraculously materialized and shone on a familiar gold brocade dressing gown. "Damn you, Gerry," his lordship croaked, "this time you've gone too far!" Gray swung the midnight marauder around and delivered a right cross to the jaw before he realized his mistake. Randolph groaned, his legs buckled, and he sank limply to the floor.

"I do think you owe me an apology, Gray, old fellow." Mr. Langford held his candle aloft and looked down at the stricken Randolph. "And did you have to bloody the poor idiot's nose? He's bled all over my best dressing gown."

"He didn't bloody my dose." Randolph thickly set the

record straight. "Miss Romney took care of dat. Gray merely broke my jaw."

Lord Graymarsh glared at his brother with less pity than distaste. "It's more than you deserve. What the devil were you up to?"

"Don't be obtuse." Mr. Langford's eyes wandered from his pilfered dressing gown to the broken goblets; to the wine bottle, mercifully still intact, that had rolled in the direction of the wardrobe; and finally came to rest on Miss Romney, who was sitting upright amid the tumbled bedclothes and trying to adjust her ruffled nightcap and regain her poise. The latter endeavor was not aided by the fact that her two gallant rescuers were clad only in their nightshirts. "I'm afraid, Graymarsh, it's all too obvious what your brother was up to." Mr. Langford clucked his disapproval.

"I just wanted Miss Romney to help me with my lines, that's all," the guilty party muttered. And three pairs of eyes took due note of the well-worn copy of *The Gamester* resting not far from the dented tray.

"There's a theater for that sort of thing." Lord Graymarsh sounded dangerous. "Are you all right, Miss Romney? Did he hurt you?"

"Did *I* hurt *her*?" Randolph's sense of injury was mounting. What he'd envisioned as a romantic interlude had become a classic nightmare. "She damned near killed me. I never laid a hand on her except to try to stop her screeching before she roused the household. Which I obviously did not succeed in." He eyed his kin with loathing.

"Oh, my goodness!" Sarah suddenly awoke to the fact that, horrifying as this imbroglio was, it had the potential to become far worse. "Do you think the others heard?"

"I doubt it," Gerard reassured her. "If they had, they'd be here by now. The Stanhopes across the hall are as deaf as posts. The Prodigy's next door? Well, then, I assume he's dead."

"Oh, Tidswell can sleep through anything."

"Evidently. So, except for us, everyone else is in the east wing. Let's trust that even your professional projection can't carry quite that far."

272

"You know, Miss Romney, it really wasn't necessary to go screeching like a banshee and then nearly kill me with your candlestick." Randolph felt his nose gingerly and eyed her with reproach. "If you didn't want me here, all you had to do was say so. I'd have left. A gentleman, don't you know."

"That, dear brother, is open to question." Graymarsh pulled him to his feet. "Apologize to Miss Romney, and let's leave her in peace."

"I won't apologize for what I'd no intention of ever doing." Randolph set his swelling jaw stubbornly, then winced. "You and Gerry ought to know I'd never attack Miss Romney, even if she does seem to think I would."

Sarah suddenly felt sorry for young Randolph. At best, he was quite unsuited for the Don Juan role he'd tried to play. And to be so humiliated before his more sophisticated relatives must be far worse punishment than his bloodied nose and battered jaw. Now that she'd recovered from her fright, Sarah felt more than a bit embarrassed herself that she'd not handled the incident with more aplomb. Under ordinary circumstances, she might have sent the callow youth off with a flea in his ear but with his dignity more or less intact. She tried now to smooth things over for him a bit.

"Though it was inexcusable for you to invade my privacy, Mr. Milbanke, I am sorry that I screamed and hit you. I would not have done so had I realized just what, er, who you were. But the fact is . . ." She was bogged down in a fresh rush of embarrassment as the truth of what she'd actually supposed came home to her.

"Yes, Miss Romney, you were saying?" Lord Graymarsh prodded politely as her silence lengthened.

"I lost my train of thought," she mumbled, while Mr. Langford, who'd been looking puzzled, drew near and held his candle over the open volume beside her. He gave a wicked chuckle. His cousins looked offended by such misplaced mirth. Miss Romney's mortification mounted. "*The Mysteries of Udolpho!* You were reading this, Miss Romney, when my cousin came creeping in?" She nodded, and he laughed again. "Well, that does explain a lot. Poor Randolph. What abysmal timing! May I suggest, Miss Romney, that you place a chair underneath the doorknob after we are gone and confine your future reading to Hannah More? Come, gentlemen."

He moved to the door and opened it the merest crack to assure that the coast was clear. The three young men eased out into the hall, two of them ghostly specters in their bedclothes, the other a fallen angel in bloodstained gold. Gerard lighted the threesome down the hall. "You owe me a dressing gown, Randolph." He spoke in an undertone. "And if you'd bothered to ask my permission before you took it, I could have saved you some pain with a bit of free advice. Never pay clandestine, nocturnal visits to Gothic novel readers. Scaring a lady out of her wits is no fit prelude to seduction." Graymarsh shook suddenly with laughter, and his brother gave him a dirty look.

"Still," Gerard continued thoughtfully, "I should be grateful you didn't ask. My conscience would have been sorely tried. As it is, I didn't have to feel obligated to try to stop you from ruining your chances with Miss Romney. On further consideration, you needn't bother to replace my robe. A dressing gown is a small price to pay for a rival's elimination. Uncle's fortune should buy no end of gold brocade. Sleep tight, Cousin Randolph. Sweet dreams."

"Go to hell, Gerry." As he stepped inside his threshold, Randolph blew his cousin's candle out. "You go there, too, Gray." He directed this remark toward more smothered laughter in the darkness just before he slammed his chamber door.

Chapter
Ten

"H URRY UP, WILL YOU, SARAH!"

Miss Romney gave her brother a jaundiced look. He had no right to appear well rested. Or so eager. She settled the tall riding hat on her chestnut curls and pinched her cheeks to restore a little color. Satisfied that they now harmonized with her bloodshot eyes, she sighed and turned from the cheval glass. "I thought you hated riding." It had been true. Tids was used to approach his horse like a Montague eyeing a Capulet.

"Where'd you ever get such a maggoty notion? I like it above all things."

"That's not what you used to say." She reluctantly followed him out of her chamber door. "You used to say that you wanted no part of anything that has a leg fastened on each of its four corners."

"That was before I became such a bang-up rider."

It was true. Tids had made amazing progress. He was, of course, an athlete whose natural abilities had been increased by all the tumbling, swordplay, and dancing he'd mastered for the stage. Still, Sarah conceded mentally as they made their way down the azalea-lined walkway toward the stables, much of the credit had to be given to his instructor. Not only was Lord Graymarsh an accomplished horseman—a nonpareil, in fact— he had approached his tutorial task with amazing tact and patience. Insofar as the Prodigy was concerned, at least.

Tids paused at a turn in the path to allow Sarah to catch up.

"What's wrong with you this morning, anyhow? You're slower than treacle and crosser than anything." He peered up at her puffy eyes and haggard face. "What's more you look like the very deuce," he added clinically.

"Thank you. I did not get a whole lot of sleep last night."

"Didn't you?" He seemed interested. "Come to think on it, I didn't rest too well myself. Kept dreaming there was a regular rumpus going on. People up and down the hall. Doors slamming. Somebody screeching. Maybe it wasn't just a dream. Did you hear anything?"

"No. That is, well, I'm not really sure. Perhaps I did hear something. Do you have to walk so fast?"

"Don't be such a grouch. Don't you want to ride?"

Sara did not. At least she did not want to ride with Graymarsh. Or even to see him, when it came to that. She'd been tempted to flee Pether Hall altogether rather than face any of the trio who'd come barging into her room the night before. Only the thought of facing Adolphus Romney had kept her there.

As they passed through the stable-yard gate, Sarah's faint hope flickered and went out. She'd clung to the notion that Graymarsh wouldn't appear. He'd naturally oversleep. Or he'd feel too awkward after last night's fiasco to want to confront her. But there he was, dressed in an impeccable dark-blue riding coat, rested and unflustered, leading a small, spirited chestnut around and around in the yard. From the cool, impersonal glance he gave her as they approached, no one would ever have suspected he'd come rushing into her bedchamber, barefoot and in his nightshirt, in the dead of night.

"Oh, I say! Is that for me?" Tids's eyes glowed as he ran toward the baron and the chestnut.

"Whoa there. Steady now." Gray spoke as much to the boy as to the horse. He relinquished the bridle to the Prodigy. "Walk him a bit. Get acquainted. I suppose you brought some sugar along? Yes, of course."

"Ooooh, he's beautiful," Tids breathed. "I can't believe I'm actually going to ride him. He really is a prime bit of blood." The Prodigy was so taken with the phrase that he repeated it. "A prime bit of blood if I ever saw it."

276

"Well, I do think you're ready to graduate from the hack that you've been using."

From Gray's disparaging tone, no one would have suspected that he himself had personally chosen the hack for Tids. After the Romneys' first disastrous ride, he had given the poor stable boy a solid dressing-down for not recognizing "complete flats" when he saw them and had ordered him to saddle the two most plodding, docile animals in his uncle's stables. Now the same mare, the actress noted, was once more saddled and stood waiting for her. She felt her resentment surge. Her progress had been every bit as good as Tids's. But trust his nibs to ignore that fact.

As Tidswell eagerly scrambled onto the chestnut's back, Gray strolled over to help Sarah mount. "Don't bother," she said waspishly. "The poor thing needs to lie down, anyhow. Then I can merely step on."

"Nose out of joint?" He grinned suddenly and then helped her into the saddle. "I could order you another horse, of course, but I thought you might be a bit fatigued this morning."

"Lord Graymarsh, if you dare to refer to last night's odious affair, I shall endeavor to have this ancient nag collapse on top of you."

"Last night? Now why would I mention last night? Actually, I had planned to discuss literature. Have you read any interesting books lately that you'd care to recommend?" His face was tightly controlled, but he couldn't subdue, nor could she miss, the laughter in his eyes. Sarah dug her heels into her horse's flanks. The ill-favored equine gave the world an injured look and plodded off in the direction the galloping chestnut had taken.

Lord Graymarsh maintained a sedate pace by Sarah's side, though it was obvious that his mount was chafing at the bit. They rode in silence for a while. "Lovely morning," he finally observed.

"I think it looks like rain."

"Well, yes. Bright sunshine. Cloudless sky. Bad signs, those."

"I was referring to the breeze. It has a decided dampness. And the sky's not cloudless."

He rose in the stirrups to squint with intense exaggeration

277

down the meadow they were crossing and up above a tree-crowned hill where one tiny puff-of-cotton cloud was seen to float. "You're right. I stand corrected. It does look ominous."

She giggled then, and he sighed with relief. "Thank God. I was beginning to think you'd lost your sense of humor."

Sarah reverted to her scowl. "I assure you, sir, my sense of humor is quite intact. It has simply found no cause for amusement in any of the happenings of late."

"None at all?"

"None." She firmly closed that subject. Then after a lengthy silence, she broached another. "What I do not understand at all is why I was asked here."

The question had an odd effect. For a moment, Graymarsh actually looked startled. But he reined in his horse just then to allow her to precede him through a narrow opening in the hedgerow they'd been following, and by the time he drew abreast again, his face was quite composed. "Surely there's no secret about why my aunt asked you. She wished to amuse her guests. Theatricals are quite the thing at country houses. They help break the tedium."

"Not here they don't. In the first place, there aren't enough people to justify the endeavor."

"I beg to differ. A larger group might not so soon grow sick of one another."

"And in the second place," she continued, ignoring the implication, "there's little interest in dramatics. Poor Miss Crome is absolutely terrified at the thought of performing. And you would prefer being stretched out on the rack."

He laughed. "Oh, that's coming it a bit strong. I'll admit I haven't any desire to disport myself for public amusement, but you have to admit my scenic effects are rather good."

"Rather good? Oh, you are far too modest, my lord. Your fog is spectacular. It will no doubt obscure the entire second act, and"—she held up a restraining hand—"before you tell me that could be a merciful occurrence, let me just say that I'm well aware of it."

"You wrong me." He grinned, reminding her suddenly of why she'd initially found him so attractive. "I wasn't about to

278

make such an ungentlemanly remark. Besides"—he grew serious once again—"it would have been untrue. You and Gerry are very good together."

"Mr. Langford does show an amazing ability as an actor."

"I find nothing amazing about it. Gerry has been acting all his life." He paused deliberately. "He is especially skilled when it comes to love scenes."

"I beg to differ. I think Mr. Langford and I do deal well together onstage for the most part. Where our performance breaks down, though, is in the love scenes." She was attempting to sound professional and detached but was actually feeling quite uncomfortable. "Mr. Langford, as I've tried to point out to him, quite fails to maintain the proper esthetic distance."

"That's one way to put it. Another is that he acts like a whoremonger."

Sarah's embarrassment was replaced by anger. "Your lordship certainly has a way with words. But never mind. I'll accept your delicate turn of phrase—which you would never dream of employing in Miss Crome's presence, by the by. But I am, after all, an actress. Yes, Mr. Langford does use the excuse of the play's stage directions to take certain liberties. Your brother, it seems, needs no excuse to treat me like a Cyprian. And we both know that I have you to thank for their attitude."

"Me to thank?" He looked astonished. "I assure you, Miss Romney, I've no notion of what you're talking about."

"Oh, have you not? Well, perhaps I do overstate the case a bit when I blame you entirely for the liberties the others take. Like you, they simply make certain assumptions about actresses. We are all women of easy virtue and"—her tone was bitter—"fair game. Especially for the gentry. But I do think Mr. Langford's attitude is rather more understandable than yours was. He did, after all, find the two of us in a most compromising situation."

"That has nothing to say to Gerry's behavior. I'm sure he—"

"Of course it has," she interrupted. "And I've no doubt that he told your brother of it. The fact that Mr. Langford caught us—well, you know how," she said, coloring, "simply reinforced the general belief that *actress* and *light-skirt* are interchangeable

279

designations. But since I do not require the good opinion of any of you *gentlemen*"—she placed undue stress upon the term—"I will not waste my breath in trying to convince you that you're wrong."

"You are bitter, aren't you?"

"Bitter? That three gentlemen of the ton should try to give me a slip on the shoulder? La, sir," she mocked him, "I'm that honored I'm fair beside myself."

"You're wrong, you know." He held a tight rein on both his horse and temper. "Never mind Gerry and me for the moment. Let's talk about last night. No, I insist." He waved away her protest. "That's what's put you up on your high ropes, isn't it? My brother was stupid, gauche. He behaved abominably. But he was not trying to give you a slip on the shoulder, I assure you."

"Fustian. Why else would he pursue me? Or why would Mr. Langford? But to set the record straight, I no longer count you as a potential seducer."

"Thank you. I'm glad to see your estimate of my character rise."

"On the contrary, it hasn't. I merely think that there's nothing like being made to feel ridiculous—as when Mr. Langford interrupted our little bedroom farce in Portsmouth—to cool the passions. For the same reason, I don't expect to be pursued by Mr. Milbanke any longer. But to be quite honest," she admitted with sudden candor, "I don't think you were ever all that eager. I believe you merely thought you were obliging me. And I must admit, if one ignores the fact that I stumbled over your boots, as you seemed determined to overlook, it must have appeared that I was flinging myself at you. Especially since, according to your cousin, you take pursuit for granted."

"Gerry said that, did he?"

"Oh, yes. He insisted on walking me home from the inn that day and made all sorts of excuses for your behavior. It seems you are rich as Croesus and, consequently, the constant prey of fortune hunters of all descriptions. Some with matrimony in mind. Others—and I'm sure you placed me in this category— more than willing to settle for a carte blanche."

From the grim set of Gray's mouth, Sarah had the satisfaction of concluding that she'd touched him on the raw.

"As I noted," he shot back, "you do sound bitter. And, if I may say so, quick to misinterpret the attentions of gentlemen. Perhaps your own . . . obscure parentage has made you too suspicious. No, before you fly off into the boughs again, I'm not referring now to my ill-advised attempts at lovemaking in Portsmouth. To set the record straight, I do regret that. And beg pardon for it. If I have an excuse, it's that I'm not nearly so widely pursued as my cousin intimated. In fact, he painted a rather distorted picture. You see, it was an entirely new experience for me to find an unaccompanied young lady in my room. That—pray forgive me, Miss Romney—is more the behavior of women of another stamp."

"Oh, I'm quite aware of that now. And it's useless to say that I intended to see you in the public parlor. And that I was merely concerned for the burns you had suffered. You will not believe it, and I do not need your good opinion. But I would like to clear up one point you tried to make. I am not bitter about my parentage."

"Oh, no?"

"No. I have never had any reason to be other than proud of it. My stepfather is kind and affectionate. He saw to it that I received an education he could ill afford. Most important, he has schooled me in a profession that I take great pride in—in spite of its occupational hazards, such as loss of reputation."

"But Tidswell said your father—"

"Was a nobleman? That's moonshine."

"Very well, then. That wrecks my explanation for your bitterness. And explodes my theory that would account for your prejudice against gentlemen. Oh, yes, don't deny it. You've made heavy weather about how all actresses are tarred with the same brush because a few are no better than the Cyprian sisterhood. But aren't you just as hard on gentlemen who dangle after actresses? Do their motives always have to be suspect? All right, then, I've already pleaded guilty to misconduct in the Royal Hart. As for Gerard, you'd do well to be warned against him. He's at least the libertine he'd have you believe that I am.

But I do take exception to your views on Randolph—in spite of last night's escapade. Undoubtedly he's pursuing you. But there's no reason for you to conclude that his motives are dishonorable."

"That, begging your lordship's pardon, is the biggest pack of nonsense I've ever heard. Of course his motives are dishonorable. Honorable would imply intent to wed. And for a gentleman of your class to pursue me with a view toward marriage—well, I'd either have to be another Helen of Troy, which my looking glass denies, or be possessed of a fortune to rival yours. So I don't think your younger brother is quite the innocent you take him for. What do you say to that?"

"Perhaps you'd better get another looking glass."

Unfortunately, the Prodigy came galloping back just then to ride beside them and expound at length on the remarkable merits of his horse before Sarah could collect herself enough to ask just what on earth his lordship had meant by such an odd reply.

Chapter
Eleven

"AUGUSTA PETHERBRIDGE'S ECCENTRICITY IS WELL known and accepted. But I do think that in this case she has gone far beyond the bounds of what is proper." Lady Emma Crome did not have to rearrange her facial muscles much to show disapproval. That was their natural set. Even so, there was a subtle alteration of expression that caused her daughter to brace herself for what was to follow.

It was midmorning, and her ladyship had seized the chance

to get her daughter alone on the pretext that they should jointly pen a letter to Mr. Crome. Evelina had dutifully seated herself at the rosewood writing table in her mother's bedchamber, only to find that correspondence was not uppermost on Lady Emma's mind.

Her parent found it helpful to pace about the room as she unleashed her feelings. The chamber assigned to her, which had been recently and cheerfully redecorated in the Chinese fashion, seemed an inappropriate setting both for Lady Emma and her lecture. "As much as it pains me to say so," she continued, "as much as it goes against the grain with me to criticize a personage of Lady Petherbridge's social standing—for think what you will of her, Evelina, her antecedents are above reproach. The Milbankes are one of England's oldest, most distinguished families, a fact I cannot stress too often in your hearing, daughter. But while it is true that rank carries with it privilege, and we can, therefore, forgive some degree of eccentricity in those well born—the Regent's conduct, for example, would never be tolerated in a personage of lesser degree—I do believe that in the case of this house party Augusta Petherbridge has gone well beyond eccentricity." Lady Emma paused dramatically. "She has reached impropriety."

"I don't quite understand," her daughter ventured.

"I know that you do not understand, Evelina: You are far too young, too unworldly to understand. You must simply take my word that it is not at all the thing—and an insult, however unwitting, to you, my dear—to have that actress person as the only other young lady—no, I will not use that term—the only other young *female* present. And to treat a person of her station as a guest! It really is too much to countenance! Lady Petherbridge, in my opinion, has a great deal to answer for."

"But I like Miss Romney." Indeed, no greater proof of that regard could have been offered than that Miss Crome dared to voice an opinion counter to her parent's. "And her manners are quite proper. Really, if it were not for the theatricals"—the very term made Evelina shudder—"one would never suspect she was on the stage. And she truly is amusing. She says the most diverting things." Evelina giggled at the memory. "S-she called Lord Graymarsh a villain! Not an ordinary one, mind you. She had all sorts of descriptions to go with it. I never was quite so diverted, I declare."

"Well, I must say!" Lady Emma stopped her pacing to glare at her daughter. "I am shocked that you, Evelina, should be amused by such rag-mannered outbursts. I need no better illustration of the point that I strove to make. You should not be required to associate with that type of person. Lord Graymarsh a villain, indeed! I am shocked. The young woman is coarser than I imagined."

"Actually, I think she was merely quoting something or other. At least that is what Mr. Langford says." Miss Crome tried valiantly to champion Sarah, but her defense was weakening. "The others seem to like her quite well," she finished lamely.

"Humph! You are speaking now of young gentlemen, who will always like females of a certain stamp."

"Oh, I don't believe Miss Romney—"

"Of course she is." There was no arguing with Lady Emma in full spate. "She is an actress, a member of a notorious profession. Why, the stories that circulate about Edmund Kean alone are enough to— But I will not sully your tender ears, Evelina. The point I intend to make is that I wish you to have as little as possible to do with that Romney person."

"But—" her daughter began, and was once more interrupted.

"I know. I know. You have been placed in an intolerable situation where she is the only other young woman in the party. It will be impossible to shun her altogether. If only Lady Scriven had come." Lady Emma sighed.

"But Mama," Evelina protested, "Lady Scriven's behavior is most improper. She is known to actually do all those things that you only suspect Miss Romney of."

"Lady Scriven is one of the nobility. She has been married. Two facts that set her above the harsher judgments of society. And while I do not approve of her mode of living and would not under other circumstances consider her a fit companion for a young lady of your tender years and strict upbringing, when I consider her influence in contrast to Miss Romney's, well, I can only repine that she is not among us. Lady Scriven's place in society is unquestioned. She is received everywhere. Whereas only Augusta Petherbridge would permit a third-rate actress to mingle with her guests. Avoid Miss Romney, Evelina," her mother ordered.

"That is the first thing I wished to speak of," she continued. "The second is even more vital to your future happiness. And here I must confess that I am not pleased with you, my dear. You have been given a heaven-sent opportunity to fix Lord Graymarsh's interest, and instead of profiting from the intimacy a house party offers, you actually appear to go out of your way to avoid his lordship."

Evelina picked up the quill pen from the desk and began to run its feather nervously between her fingers. "But Mama," she protested, "Lord Graymarsh does not appear to have an interest in me to fix."

"Nonsense." Her mother seated herself on the other side of the desk and removed the pen from her daughter's fingers. "You must learn to value yourself more highly, Evelina dear. Lady Petherbridge and I have only recently discussed this very subject. And I will say that Augusta, for all her oddities, is very sensible in these matters. She agrees it's time Graymarsh married. His dear father has been gone for some three years now." Lady Emma dabbed her eyes affectingly with a handkerchief despite the fact that her acquaintanceship with the late baron was slight. "And she thinks that you and he should deal very well together. 'Graymarsh does not care overly much for society and would probably like someone who is quiet' was the way she phrased it. But the thing is, my dear, you must make a greater push to captivate his lordship."

"But I do not know how to set my cap for a gentleman." Evelina was looking more and more distressed.

Her mother spoke in soothing tones. "I know you do not, my dear. That is why I must contrive to help you."

And not being one to let the grass grow underneath her feet, that very afternoon Lady Emma forged an opportunity to bring her daughter and Lord Graymarsh together.

The day being particularly fine, the entire party had moved

outdoors, with the exception of Lady Stanhope who, complaining of the staggers, had dosed herself with calomel and gone to bed. The gentlemen, joined by Lady Petherbridge and Master Tidswell, planned to fish. Miss Crome and Miss Romney elected to sketch.

Miss Romney had gone ahead and was on a grassy rise that afforded a good view of the lake when Miss Crome, under her parent's disapproving eye, actually had the temerity to ask, "May I sit beside you?" Lady Emma was just about to open her pursed mouth and point out that sketching, like fishing, was best done in solitude and suggest that Evelina find another location, when Lord Graymarsh, after rejecting several other spots, decided to wet his line in Miss Romney's vicinity. Mr. Langford, who had had the same idea, gave him a speaking look and moved on past. Randolph, coloring at the sight of Sarah, seemed relieved when Lady Petherbridge commandeered him to bait her hook. They and the other anglers spaced themselves around the lake.

The good tactician must be flexible. Lady Emma revised her plans. Rather than remove her daughter from a strategic location so near Lord Graymarsh, her ladyship decided to shift Sarah instead. "My dear Miss Romney," she remarked as she spread her handkerchief, inadequate for her designs, upon the grass and lowered her ample posterior onto it, "I do believe your brother requires your assistance."

Sarah glanced down the lakeshore where Tidswell did have his line tangled and was struggling with it. "Oh, I'm sure he will manage," she said carelessly.

"He seems rather young to be left unattended. Do you not agree?"

"Tidswell? He's twelve." Sarah was not slow to comprehend the motive behind her ladyship's maneuvering and was amused. She was determined to hold her ground.

"I myself would never dream of leaving a small child alone so near the water." After delivering this setdown, Lady Emma lapsed into icy silence that lasted only until Lord Graymarsh, moments later, hooked a fish.

"Oh, Evelina!" She was in transports. "His lordship has caught a fish! Isn't it thrilling? Do go see!"

"Mama, please!" Miss Crome whispered in an agony of embarrassment.

"Come, Evelina. You are longing, I know, to see it. We must observe how he removes it from the hook." She lumbered to her feet, then thrust out a commanding hand to help her daughter up. "I'm sure Lord Graymarsh deserves our admiration for his sporting feat."

"Will you not come, too, Miss Romney?" Misery cried out for company.

"No, thank you," Sarah replied politely. "The excitement might prove more than I could stand." Then aware that none of their conversation had escaped his lordship, she added mischievously, "But I do agree wholeheartedly with your mother. That fish should be seen at close range. Its size prohibits any more distant admiration."

Gray had just enough time to stare at Sarah in a manner meant to be repressive, but which, in spite of himself, evolved into a broad grin before he was beset by Lady Emma and a mortified Evelina.

After the fish had been exclaimed over, nothing would do but that Lord Graymarsh should share his singular skill. "My daughter has been yearning to learn to fish for the longest time. Have you not, Evelina dear?"

Sarah did manage to choke off a giggle as the red-faced Miss Crome stammered, "Oh, yes. For ages." But when Lord Graymarsh, proffering a worm, asked solemnly, "Would you like to bait the hook?" and Evelina shrieked and backed away, a fit of coughing was the only outlet she could find to offset a burst of laughter.

Ashamed of his mischievous impulse and amazed that he was at the same time longing to laugh with Sarah over it, Gray obligingly baited the hook and handed the fishing pole to Miss Crome with a few instructions on what to do if she felt a nibble. The poor girl looked so mortified that Graymarsh took pity on her. He did his best to set her at ease, chatting easily and at length about the choice fishing sites in the county, as though believing that Miss Crome really had developed a consuming passion for the sport.

Graymarsh actually had a double motive for prosing on about the art of angling. Beside wishing to spare Miss Crome the agonies of upholding her part in a conversation, he hoped to bore her behemoth of a mother into going about her business and leaving them alone. In the first instance he was quite successful. Miss Crome seemed to realize he wished to make her feel at ease and was touchingly grateful for it. But in the latter he was doomed to failure. A powder blast would not have sufficed to remove Lady Emma from Evelina's side. The scheming mama had too little faith in her daughter's powers of entrapment to risk leaving her on her own.

Feeling that the fishing maneuver had been singularly successful, Lady Emma launched a new offensive. "Evelina will give me a scold for saying so, your lordship," she gushed, "for you know how young ladies hate to admit they even think of—let alone discuss—young gentlemen, but my daughter was saying just the other day how much she envies you."

"Indeed? And why do you envy me, Miss Crome?" Gray was immediately sorry for the question when it became evident that the young lady addressed had not the slightest notion of an answer.

"No need to be missish, dear." Lady Emma tried to cover her daughter's bewilderment. "You may just as well admit it. You were envying his lordship's freedom to soar in the air in his magnificent balloon. You were saying that if you were a man you would like ballooning above all things."

Hearing another choking fit from the grassy slope behind them, Gray raised his voice a bit. "How refreshing, Miss Crome, to find a young lady so enthusiastic. It will amaze you to learn, I'm sure, that some females are actually prejudiced against ballooning. Some have the hypocrisy to term it hazardous while at the same time approving of far more dangerous sport. Take fencing as an example. I once knew a female who was knocked flat by a sword—almost decapitated, in fact—but who still thought ballooning suicidal. I find such an attitude incomprehensible."

"Quite absurd." Lady Emma shook her head disdainfully. "But then what could one expect from a female who would actually engage in swordplay?" She seemed to have a strong suspicion of that female's identity. "I can assure you that my daughter would never do anything so vulgar. But I certainly see nothing at all either unladylike or dangerous in a balloon ascension. That is if you, dear Lord Graymarsh, were at the helm, to borrow a nautical figure of speech. I am convinced that Evelina would be perfectly safe with you. Will you not grant her fondest wish and take her up with you?"

There was a gasp. Evelina turned white. Her fishing pole dropped from nerveless fingers. Just as Lord Graymarsh plunged an arm elbow-deep in after it, Miss Crome, uttering a soft moan, crumpled in a heap of blue-sprigged muslin in the green grass at his feet.

The collapse precipitated a rush of activities. Gray consigned his fishing rod to its watery fate and wheeled to help Miss Crome. Miss Romney dropped her sketchbook and came running down the slope. Equidistant but in opposite directions from the fallen beauty, Tidswell Romney and Gerard Langford abandoned their fishing rods and sprinted toward the scene. The only person who stayed calm was Lady Emma. Annoyance seemed her overriding humor. She pulled a vial of sal volatile from her reticule and held it to her daughter's nose.

Gerard and Tidswell arrived in a dead heat. "Is she d-dead?" the latter said, gasping.

"Don't be ridiculous," Lady Emma snapped. "My daughter has merely swooned."

If the race along the lakeshore had been uncharacteristic of the languid Mr. Langford, the look of concern on his handsome face seemed even more misplaced. As the young lady began to cough and stir, it was relief as much as anger that caused him to turn to his cousin. "What the devil did you say to her to bring this on? Surely you must realize how sensitive Miss Crome is?"

"What did I say? Don't be daft, Gerry. The girl just collapsed. I don't know why."

"Oh, no, you are unjust, Mr. Langford. You must not blame

his lordship." Lady Emma seemed much more perturbed over this possibility than over her daughter's condition. "It's the heat, I'm sure. Poor Evelina is so delicate."

"Nonsense!" Sarah was having her own reaction, brought on by fright when Miss Crome fainted, now fueled by guilt. How could she have been amused by a scene that had caused her new friend acute distress! "The heat has nothing to do with any of this. The poor girl's terrified at the prospect of going up in that—that odious balloon. That's why she fainted."

"You're actually proposing to take Miss Crome up in that flying coffin! Damn you, Gray!" Mr. Langford's eyes glittered dangerously. He spoke through tightly clenched, perfect teeth.

Lord Graymarsh looked sufficiently annoyed to welcome a battle. But before he could pick up the challenge, the Prodigy, whose concern for the beauty had evaporated with this new development, chimed in. "You're taking the balloon up again, sir? Oh, when? Please, sir, may I go? Please say yes. I'd be no bother. You'd hardly know I was there."

"Oh, Tids, do be quiet!" his sister commanded.

"I will not! If a mere female like Miss Crome, who's scared of her own shadow, can take a balloon ride, I don't see why you won't let me go. I'm sure Miss Crome would like to have my company. Or, better yet, would let me take her place, for I can't believe she actually wishes to take a balloon ride."

That young lady's lids had fluttered open under her mother's ministrations. She was gazing uncomprehendingly at the many faces staring down at her. But at the sound of the word *balloon*, memory came flooding back. She gave a piteous little moan and swooned again.

"I swear it, Gray," Mr. Langford blazed, "you'll answer to me for this." He then knelt down with a complete disregard for the effects of grass upon biscuit-colored pantaloons. Ignoring the formidable Lady Emma, he picked up the beauty's limp fair hands and began to rub her wrists briskly with strong, slim fingers. "Miss Crome," he murmured softly. "Miss Crome." The eyelids fluttered open once again and fastened on the face behind the soothing voice. "It's all right, Evelina," Mr. Langford continued in the same calming tone. "There's no need to

290

be alarmed. Lord Graymarsh has no intention of taking you up in his balloon. Have you, Gray?" He shot a lethal look up at his cousin.

"No, of course not," the sorely tried aeronaut answered. "And I never have had, as anyone but a gudgeon would realize." The words were intended for his lordship's cousin. And no one but Sarah saw the offended look they brought to Lady Emma's face. Once again the unfortunate actress had to bring all her theatrical training into play to keep from giggling.

"I don't see why everyone is so dead set against balloon rides," the Prodigy muttered. "I'd do it in a minute."

"Miss Crome, do you think you can sit up now?" Mr. Langford tenderly helped the beauty to do just that. Lady Emma opened her mouth. Her intention was to protest the fact that Mr. Langford's arms were around her daughter. But with a sudden burst of inspiration, she put its position to better use. "Lord Graymarsh, perhaps you could help dear Evelina home. I really do think the sun is too much for—"

"I will see to Miss Crome." Mr. Langford spoke with a firmness that stopped Lady Emma cold and caused his cousin to look at him curiously. Before the dowager could recover, Gerard had scooped Evelina up into his arms and had gone striding off toward Pether Hall with the beauty clinging pathetically, her head nestled against his shoulder.

"Well, really! I must say!" Lady Emma gasped. She stood for a moment, stunned into uncharacteristic indecision. Then she announced, "Upon my word! This will not do!" to no one in particular as she hurried off after her imperiled daughter.

"I'm going fishing," the Prodigy remarked sullenly, still aggrieved over his sister's unreasonableness where balloon ascensions were concerned. With a black look in her direction, he went striding off toward his abandoned fishing pole.

Lord Graymarsh and Miss Romney stood looking at each other. "She's really very nice," Sarah said.

"Who?"

"Miss Crome, of course. If it weren't for her odious mother flinging the poor girl at your head, mortifying her and disgusting you, I expect you two would deal quite well together. She is without doubt the loveliest female I've ever seen. Don't you agree?"

"Yes," he said, a reply that, though given in acquiescence, did not completely satisfy the questioner. His lordship frowned at her. "Miss Romney, are you matchmaking?"

"No, of course not."

"Good. I find Miss Crome's mother more than sufficient in that area."

"I know. Oh, my heavens, th-that fish!" Sarah choked suddenly, and his lordship grinned. "But," she said, sobering, "that's just my point. I do feel terribly sorry for the girl. She needs to marry well, and with that ogre of a mother making such a cake of her, no one gets to really know her. She is a sweet, shy girl who's basically very kind and would, I expect, make some gentleman a perfect wife."

"And just why are you telling me all this?"

"In the interest of fair play, I suppose. I simply hate to see that old—Lady Emma, that is—ruin Evelina's chances of making a good match."

"You refer to me? How surprising. But then, of course, you're thinking of my fortune."

"Of course. She has to have a good income. But she also needs someone who would treat her kindly."

"Thank you for that much. But are you sure I wouldn't beat her? She looked as though she thought I would."

"Oh, it's not you she's afraid of. It's your balloon. And the fear her mother will force her into it. And Lady Emma would! That woman would stop at nothing to see her daughter marry well!" Sarah pulled herself up short and looked a bit embarrassed by her vehemence. "Well, now, Lord Graymarsh, before you give me the setdown you're longing to and tell me all this is none of my affair, I'll say so myself. I merely wanted you to have some idea of the daughter's true character and not be totally prejudiced by her horrid mother. You could do a lot worse than marry Miss Crome." Her voice trailed off. Sarah was confused by the way his lordship was looking at her.

"Thank you," he said dryly. "I'll add you to the long list of people nudging me toward matrimony. And I promise to look at Miss Crome through new eyes now. But your advocacy may come a little late. Improbable as it seems, I think my cousin may be smitten."

"Mr. Langford? But he's out of the question for Miss Crome."

"Oh, I don't know. I'll admit Gerry is a bit of a rake. But underneath it all his heart's in the right place."

"The location of his heart is to no purpose. Mr. Langford hasn't a feather to fly with, has he?"

"Well, no. Not now at least."

"Then that cooks his goose. For people of your class never marry except for personal advancement of some kind."

Gray stooped, picked up a stone, and skipped it across the water. "Miss Romney," he said, sighing, "as I pointed out before, your view of my class is cynical, to say the least."

"But the point I make is accurate?"

"In as far as generalizations can ever be, I suppose so. At least I will not argue the point with you." Indeed, he could not. For the memory of Lord Petherbridge's scheme for the disposal of his fortune had come rushing back to him.

Miss Romney found herself regretting her want of tact. The shuttered look on his lordship's face signaled the end of a conversation she'd enjoyed. Well, it was not surprising that he found her constant attacks upon his upper-class values distasteful. What was harder to account for was the distinct impression on her part that Lord Graymarsh was feeling guilty. She dismissed the notion as absurd.

Chapter
Twelve

*T*HAT EVENING WHEN THE GENTLEMEN JOINED THE LADIES in the drawing room, the Petherbridge house party, never rated high by any of the guests, seemed to sink to its lowest point. Perhaps because the solicitous inquiries into Miss Crome's health had set Lady Stanhope off into a detailed account of her own sufferings, the assembly seemed plunged into gloom. It might have been supposed that a natural reaction to the general mood would be to seek diversion. But the drama group did not excuse itself for rehearsal, the whist players did not deal the cards, and the gentlemen did not seize the opportunity to withdraw for billiards. Instead, the entire party was bunched together in one corner of the elegant, spacious room with a grand pianoforte, which no one deigned to play, as their focal point. Expressions ranged from martyred to vacant to resigned as Lady Stanhope droned on and on.

When her ladyship finally paused for breath between her rheumatism and her biliousness, Lord Petherbridge, who had been nodding, awoke to his duties as host. "And how are the riding lessons coming along, m'dear?" he inquired of his most-neglected guest.

The question took Sarah by surprise. She had been watching Lord Graymarsh, who was watching Mr. Langford, who was watching Miss Crome, and did not realize it was she whom Petherbridge addressed. "I beg your pardon, sir?"

"The riding lessons. The coachman tells me that Gray here

has been teaching you and your little brother to ride. How are you getting on?"

Lord Petherbridge had snatched the gathering from its stupor. Randolph and Gerard glowered at Gray. Lady Emma's frown of disapproval was directed at Miss Romney. Lady Stanhope looked peeved at having lost the floor. Lady Petherbridge, Lord Stanhope, Sir Peter, and Miss Crome seemed confused by the currents whirling all around them.

"Giving lessons, are you, Gray?" His lordship's younger brother was studiously polite. Only his eyes accused. "Never knew that sort of thing was your line of country."

"Yes, Gray." Mr. Langford's smile was devoid of warmth. "Do enlighten us. When did this come about?"

Petherbridge answered for him. "Oh, Webster says they've been going out every morning since they got here. How are your pupils doing, Gray?"

"Yes, don't keep us in suspense, Gray. We're on the very edges of our seats. How are you as a riding master?"

"As to that, I couldn't say. Miss Romney and her brother have made excellent progress, but the success lies in their aptitude, not in my teaching."

"I'm sure you are far too modest," his cousin contradicted. "Your dedication must have inspired your pupils. Just think of it, Randolph. Your brother, who professes to have no interest at all in"—he paused for a moment and then continued—"*others*, rises early every morning to ride forth with Miss Romney."

"We were not alone," Sarah protested after Lady Emma had sniffed a telling sniff. "Tidswell has also been a pupil."

"Ah, yes. The Prodigy. You are all heart, Gray," Langford drawled while his lordship glared daggers back at him. "It occurs to me that if you had not been born to your present position, you could have been quite successful as a tutor. There's no end to your talents, is there, Coz? Fishing instructor. Riding master. What will it be next? Sketching? Languages?"

"Dancing!" Lady Emma declared with such resonance that all heads turned her way. "Lord Graymarsh must put his instructive talents to work right here and now." The smile directed toward Graymarsh, while meant to dazzle, was dimmed by yellowed teeth. "I am assured, your lordship, that you are quite accomplished in the new dance craze. I refer to the waltz, of course."

"Indeed? And who would have told you that?"

"Why, it's common knowledge. And I myself have observed that your lordship is particularly skilled in all other modes of dancing, though of course we did not deem the waltz proper at Evelina's come-out. But since Czar Alexander has waltzed at Almack's, it is no longer thought a shocking fad. And one must always keep abreast of fashion. Therefore I am determined that Evelina should learn the waltz. And with a skilled instructor, as I've no doubt your lordship will prove to be, I'm certain my little girl will master it in no time. So, with Lady Augusta's kind permission, I am prepared to play while you lead Evelina through the steps."

"I don't think—" Gray had begun when his brother interrupted. "What a capital idea! Let's all join in. Do you waltz, Miss Romney?"

"Well, yes, but—"

"I am sure Miss Romney wishes to pursue her dramatic duties." Lady Emma dared anyone to differ.

"Ah, yes, but you really should take advantage of Randolph's enthusiasm." Gerard was unperturbed by a frosty look. "Actually he is a much more accomplished dancer than his older brother. I hope you take no offense, Gray."

"I try not to, Cousin."

"Oh, but I am sure that Miss Romney requires Mr. Milbanke's presence at the rehearsal, whereas Evelina's and Lord Graymarsh's parts are so insignificant that their presence would scarce be missed. Is that not so, Miss Romney?"

"Well, actually, if no one really wishes to rehearse, I suppose we might forgo it this one evening," Sarah said doubtfully.

"Not wish it?" With an effort, Gerard forced his thoughts away from the lovely Miss Crome and the memory of her arms clasped around his neck. He thought instead of her nonexistent fortune and of his uncle's wealth. Thus fortified, he contrived to seize the moment and turn it to his advantage. "I personally cannot face losing even one evening's practice without being beset by an onslaught of the quakes." His drawling tone gave no evidence of his inward state. "As you well know, Miss Romney, the success or failure of *The Gamester* is largely in our hands. That fact may not cause you trepidation—you are, after all, a professional—but I can assure you that the prospect fills me with terror. And Lady Emma is right, as usual. Miss Crome and Gray do not need as much rehearsal as we do. Nor does Randolph. So why don't we leave the brothers here to teach Miss Crome the waltz while we go to the theater and run through our scenes."

Sarah did not like the suggestion. Nor did Randolph and Gray look very pleased. Evelina was obviously upset. "Perhaps we should all go practice." The beauty showed rare spunk.

"Nonsense." Her mother overrode her easily. "As Mr. Langford has pointed out, minor characters do not need as much rehearsal as leading ones."

Sarah was still trying to find an acceptable alternative to Gerard's proposal when Lord Petherbridge spoke up dismissively. "That's settled, then. Gerard, you and Miss Romney go rehearse."

Reminded of her status, Sarah felt her face go red. She rose slowly to her feet, reluctant to be alone with Mr. Langford and made even more uneasy by the suspicious look in Graymarsh's eyes as he studied his handsome cousin. But Lord Petherbridge had made her position abundantly clear. She was not a guest. She was a hired performer.

In truth, such a setdown had been the furthest thing from Lord Petherbridge's mind. He'd been uncharacteristically quick to realize that Gerard was maneuvering a chance to be alone with Sarah. And though Mr. Langford was not his lordship's first choice as a secret son-in-law, he had to admire the skill with which Gerard disposed of his two rivals. Lord Petherbridge's single-minded concern was that a nephew win Miss Romney. And so far as he could tell, not one of the slowtops was making any progress. He did wish that somebody would get on with the job and bring an end to this infernal house party and leave him in peace. Hence his willingness to aid and abet Gerard. He rose to his feet to organize a table of cards, "as far away from that blasted waltz music as possible."

Sarah was on the point of excusing herself to go get Tidswell to hold the prompt book when she remembered that Tids was spending the evening conning a selection from *Practical Piety*. Lady Petherbridge had decreed that the Prodigy recite Miss More's work at the end of their performance as a sort of antidote to *The Gamester* and a salve to her conscience for allowing such questionable entertainment to take place. Poor Tidswell had been too frightened of her ladyship to offer any objection. In spite of Sarah's promise, it seemed that he was to perform after all.

"I hope you don't mind giving me this extra time." As they entered the theater, Mr. Langford appeared to read Sarah's thoughts. His blue eyes held a glint of amusement at her obvious discomfort at being alone with him. He looked even more handsome than usual in his black evening coat and white knee smalls.

"No, of course not. Indeed, I am quite impressed with your dedication."

He didn't miss the irony. "Oh, I really am quite dedicated. But whether the dedication is to the play or to the leading lady is a question I have not allowed myself to explore."

Sarah took refuge in professionalism and bustled about the stage arranging rehearsal props. "Is there some particular spot you're having problems with, Mr. Langford?" she asked in a firm, directorial voice, then could have cut her tongue out.

But much to her relief, he did not choose the love scene. True, the part he claimed to find difficult did lead up to their embrace. Sarah planned to bring the rehearsal to a halt at least a page and a half before that intimacy.

She did not plan for her artistic nature to get the upper hand of her good sense. But she soon immersed herself in the role of Mrs. Beverley, forgetting all else in the pleasure of playing opposite an actor of Mr. Langford's skill. Sarah dimly recognized that she had never performed better and began to wonder if, unhampered by the third-rate Romney players, she might not aspire to the stature of a Mrs. Siddons. It was in this euphoric state that she allowed herself to be swept on past the stopping place and ended up involved once more in an out-of-control love scene.

"Beverly! How dare you!" It said something for Sarah's state of mind that when she finally struggled free from an embrace that left her red of face and angry, she was still in character. The look of amusement on Mr. Langford's face brought her back to reality. She made an effort to retrieve the director's authority he'd usurped along with her dignity. "I think we've rehearsed quite long enough."

"Oh, but I disagree." They had moved, appropriately front and center. He reached for her again. She sidestepped quickly. Sarah's next impulse was to leap over the footlights and go sprinting for the door. Instead, she elected to face him down. The ambivalence seemed to amuse him even more. "No need to look so Friday-faced, Sarah love. Why not admit it? You enjoyed our rehearsal as much as I did."

"Oh, I admit it. Up to a point."

"And just what point was that?"

"When you dropped out of character and developed an extra set of hands, that's when. Mr. Langford, you are well aware that the scene, as you've just played it, wouldn't be allowed in Covent Garden, let alone in Lady Petherbridge's private theatricals."

"Oh, I intend to tone my performance down. Don't distress yourself on that score, love. But while we're alone, I see no reason to hide my true feelings." He moved toward her and she backed away. "Come now, Sarah." His voice was seductive. "Don't be such a tease. You must know how I feel by now."

"I most certainly do know," she retorted. "I not only know how you feel: I know where you feel, and I'm warning you that if you ever try those tricks again when we're rehearsing, I'll— I'll—" She sputtered to an impotent stop, unable to think of a threat with any substance to it.

He laughed huskily and pulled her into his arms again. At first she struggled, then, being no match for him in strength, sighed faintly and succumbed, melting against him, holding her slightly parted lips tilted upward to be kissed. There was a sparkle of triumph in his eyes as he bent his head to meet them. His lips teased, then grew insistent. Just before she wound up being caught in her own trap, Miss Romney stamped with all her might upon her lover's arch.

"Ow! Dammit! Ow!" Mr. Langford howled and pirouetted, clasping both hands around his injured foot while his thumbs explored the throbbing spot beneath his silken hose. "You vixen! You've broken it!"

"With these soft slippers? I think not, more's the pity. But if you're sufficiently cooled off now, Mr. Langford, I do believe you owe me an explanation for your conduct. Please notice that I did not say apology. For since I am not a lady, I don't suppose that you'd agree I'm due one. But neither am I a light-skirt. Pray in future bear that in mind. Now I await your explanation."

Gerard had sunk down upon one of the chairs that did temporary duty as windows, doors, and furniture upon the stage. He was massaging his damaged foot gingerly. It was hard to tell whether the grimace on his handsome face was for the pain he was suffering or the smudge upon his stocking. Sarah briefly considered making a dignified exit. Instead, she pulled up a chair to face him. "Would you care to explain just what all that groping was in aid of, Mr. Langford?"

"I should think that was obvious, Miss Romney," he growled.

"Not to me it wasn't." She paused then and looked thoughtful. "I suppose the logical explanation is that when a man finds himself in an intimate situation with a woman—any woman—it's his second nature to take liberties. Take your cousin's reaction in the Plymouth inn, for instance. It was exactly the same sort of thing. And I expect this kind of conduct is especially true of gentlemen of your class."

Gerard gave her a cool stare. No love light could be seen glowing in his eyes. "I feel I'm going to hate myself for asking, but why my class in particular?"

"Well, for one thing, you are accustomed to taking whatever you want as your unquestioned right. For another, I expect your type is rather unsure of your own manhood."

Mr. Langford's blue eyes narrowed. "What a novel notion. Not many of my acquaintance would dare subscribe to it."

"No need to take offense. I am speaking in general terms. It merely struck me that men of your class are for the most part useless, which undoubtedly is why they're obsessed with boxing in Cribb's Parlour, riding neck-or-nothing, hunting, wenching—all the rest. How else would they prove their manhood?"

"Since the activities you describe aren't limited to the ton, except perhaps in scope of opportunity, I find your thesis a little lacking, Miss Romney. Not to say bird-witted."

"Well, perhaps you're right, Mr. Langford. If so, we are back where this conversation started. I've no earthly notion then why you chose to behave as you just did."

Perhaps only a stage-trained observer would have noticed him ease back into character, so subtle was the transformation. Even Sarah came close to being dazzled by his slow, seductive smile. She had to remind herself that mere seconds before Mr. Langford had longed to throttle her. "Sarah, Sarah," he said, still using her first name with no by-your-leave, "why are you so determined to come up with all these daft explanations for my actions and ignore the obvious? Surely it's crossed your mind that I'm falling in love with you."

"Fustian!"

The flat retort took some of the wind out of his sails, but he quickly rallied. "Oh, come now, Sarah. You are not as indifferent toward me as you'd like to pretend. Can you deny you felt some response to my lovemaking—cold, heartless Sarah?"

"Of course I don't deny it." Her face grew warm at the recollection. "But I know as well as you do that it had nothing to do with love."

"Perhaps not on your part," he answered huskily. "But you have no right to weigh my feelings on the scale of your own indifference. Why can you not simply believe that I love you?"

"Well . . ." She took his question seriously and turned it over in her mind. "I could give you any number of good reasons, but I'll boil them down to two. First, I am an actress. And I recognize a performance when I see it. Oh, a good performance, I give you that much credit. I think you could have a glorious stage career, Mr. Langford, if you chose to. But your lovemaking was a performance all the same.

"And my second reason may also have to do with my stage training. At least I like to pride myself that I'm more observant than most. You see, I've seen the way you look at Miss Crome when you think you're unobserved. I think you're in love with her."

"And I think you, Miss Romney, have the most freakish notions of any person I've ever met. Even your preposterous attack on my manhood is not as absurd as that. My being in love with Miss Crome is not merely ridiculous: it's unthinkable."

"Well, as to that," Sarah answered slowly, "I'm sure you're right. Speaking practically, that is. But when did 'ridiculous' and 'unthinkable' ever have anything to say in the matter of falling in love? Now, marriage is another thing entirely."

"That's a very astute observation." From the back of the theater, a voice interrupted—brittle, sophisticated, and amused. "I await your comments with bated breath, Gerry, darling."

The onstage characters were startled into getting to their feet. Neither had heard the newcomer's entrance and had no idea how long she'd stood there listening.

Lady Scriven, as conscious as any actress of the effect that she was having, walked slowly down the aisle. She was not a beauty of the first rank. She was certainly beyond the blush of youth. Few would ever notice either fact.

She was elegantly dressed in black crepe over a sarsnet slip. Her hair, black as her adornments, was lightly covered by a long veil draped over a jeweled aigrette. In contrast to all the dramatic inkiness, her milk-white complexion appeared luminous, her lavender eyes intense. All in all, Sarah thought, she'd never seen a more striking woman. She disliked her immediately.

The interloper seated herself front-row center and looked up at the stage expectantly. "Pray do not let me interrupt your little scene. You were *rehearsing*, were you not?" The lips curved mockingly.

"Lucy, what the devil are you doing here?" Mr. Langford was jolted from his usual savoir faire.

The lady's eyebrows rose. Her amusement increased. "Why, Gerard, what an uncivil question. One could almost suppose, my dear, that you are not pleased to see me. But to give an answer that your rudeness does not deserve, I'm here because Lady Petherbridge invited me. Did I fail to mention that fact in London?" she asked innocently.

"As a matter of fact, you did say you were asked." In an effort to regain composure, Mr. Langford helped himself to snuff. "But I thought you had not planned to come."

"Did you, indeed? What a strange coincidence. I had the same impression about you." The voice purred, but the lavender eyes narrowed just a bit. "You were not by chance, Gerry darling, trying to put me off?"

"Of course I was." He had full command of himself once more. "Tried to do you a favor. Knew you'd find the place tedious beyond redemption. I hadn't intended to come myself. Sent my regrets, in fact. But the old gentleman wouldn't hear of my crying off. And I can hardly afford to cross him, so . . ." He shrugged elegantly.

Her smile was as false as his explanation. "You are the most accomplished liar I know, Gerry dear. Perhaps that's why I find you so amusing. But pray get on with . . . whatever you were doing." Her gaze shifted to Miss Romney. It made Lady Emma's similar appraisal seem almost approving.

Sarah turned to Mr. Langford. "I think that will be sufficient rehearsal for the evening, Gerry," she said coolly, using his first name just to be annoying. "Now, if you will excuse me." Without waiting for an introduction to the newcomer, she swept off the stage and up the auditorium aisle. She thought she did it very well, but her "Mrs. Siddons, famous actress" bubble was burst by the look of contemptuous amusement she glimpsed on the widow's face as she breezed on by her. All in all, Lady Scriven was the last straw in a thoroughly trying day.

Her solace was, Sarah concluded, as she decided to forgo the society in the withdrawing room and headed for her bedchamber instead, that those two sophisticates back in the theater deserved each other. But then she thought of Miss Crome with a sigh. She was almost certain that the beauty was falling in love with Mr. Langford. Why did females insist upon forming *tendres* for the most unsuitable members of the other sex? And with that poser, the vision of Lord Graymarsh took over center stage in her imaginings. "Oh, fiddle!" Miss Romney said explosively as she slammed her chamber door. "A pox on all of them!"

Chapter Thirteen

SARAH WAS NOT SURPRISED WHEN LORD GRAYMARSH failed to put in an appearance the next morning at the stables. Although she'd been puzzled by the reactions when the rest of the party discovered he'd been teaching Tids and her to ride, she did realize that the disclosure was going to put a period to the lessons. What she had not expected was that Randolph would take his brother's place.

The grooms were leading their horses up and down while Randolph stood by a marble watering trough, flicking his boot with his riding whip. It had taken a bit of courage to face Sarah. Since the embarrassing bedchamber scene, he'd done his best to avoid her. But now he was determined to put himself back into contention for his uncle's fortune. The time was ripe. Gray, whose clandestine meetings with the heiress were most suspicious, had seemed grateful nonetheless when he'd offered to substitute as riding master. And Lady Scriven's unexpected arrival had effectively disposed of Gerry. Randolph had a clear field and intended to make the most of it. He forced a smile as the Romneys approached. "Here you are, finally. You had me worried. I was afraid you weren't going to ride this morning."

"Oh, Sarah dropped her stupid glove along the path and didn't notice for ever so long and we had to go back and hunt for it." Tidswell sounded quite disgusted. "I told her we could just as well look when we came back. Ain't as if it's likely to rain or anything." Indeed, the weather remained amazingly fine. The morning air was cool and pleasant. "Can't see why she couldn't just as well ride with one glove as two. Oh, I say, where's Lord Graymarsh?"

"He won't be coming this morning. I'm taking over his pleasant duty."

Tidswell's look of disappointment was hardly flattering. Nor was the "Oh, blast!" the boy muttered under his breath.

"Tidswell!" his shocked sister exclaimed. "Do beg Mr. Milbanke's pardon."

"Oh, it ain't that I mind him being here," Tidswell said sulkily. "It's just that I particularly wished to ask Gray something."

Sarah, even more embarrassed, was about to lecture her brother upon the shocking familiarity of calling Lord Graymarsh by his shortened name when Randolph forestalled her by saying, "Well, if your question has anything to do with that infernal balloon, Tids, I think Gray means to work on it this morning."

"He does? This morning? Oh, I say, how marvelous! Do you suppose he'd let me go with him, sir? I'm sure I could be useful." Tidswell's eyes were filled with longing.

"Well, of course it ain't up to me to say, but I should think Gray would welcome your company. For it ain't often that he finds anyone to share his enthusiasm. His family's more inclined to pour cold water on his scheme."

That was all the permission the Prodigy needed. Pausing only to pop a sugar lump into his horse's mouth and to give the animal a pat on the nose and a promise to see it tomorrow, the boy was off, responding to his sister's shouted "Tidswell! I really don't think you should!" by running all the harder.

Sarah turned to Randolph in despair. "Oh, dear. I'm afraid his lordship won't be pleased."

"Nonsense. I meant what I said. Gray'll be glad of his company." His forced smile turned suddenly mischievous. "He'll be almost as pleased to have him there as I am."

"Am I to understand that you were trying to get rid of poor Tidswell?"

They were moving out of the stableyard. Randolph, who took his duties seriously, observed her closely. Only when assured of her competence as a horsewoman did he resume their conversation. "You mustn't say 'poor Tidswell.' It's nothing against the boy if I wish to be alone with his lovely, charming, talented sister."

Randolph, Sarah noted, was quite pleased with that fulsome speech. She chose to overlook it. But after several more callow attempts at gallantry, his flowery periods began to pall. For some unfathomable reason, Randolph seemed determined, once again, to turn himself into a poor imitation of his Don Juan cousin. It only needed the gold dressing gown! Sarah did wish he'd revert to his own personality, which really was quite likable. She was just about to say so when she recalled his youth. Coming on the heels of his midnight misadventure, such a comment might prove crushing. As an alternative to plain speaking, she urged her horse into a brisk canter that broke up their tête-à-tête.

Sarah slowed her horse to a walk as they climbed a grassy mound. Randolph reined in beside her. When he addressed her this time, she was relieved to note, it was as himself. "I say, Sarah—oh, may I call you that?"

"Of course."

"Good. You call me Randolph. It will make things easier."

What things? she wondered, and was about to ask when he forestalled her.

"I say, Sarah, could we get off and talk a bit? Seriously, I mean."

She was totally mystified now and a bit alarmed by his expression. His young face had grown quite intense; one could say it almost looked harried. Although the morning was still on the cool side, tiny beads of perspiration glistened on his forehead. What on earth can be wrong? she wondered as she dismounted.

306

Oh, my goodness, I'll bet a monkey he has stage fright and is trying to find the courage to tell me he won't do the play.

So when Randolph took her by the hand, led her over to a fallen log underneath a spreading oak, and bade her to sit down a moment while he spoke to her, her mind was busily sorting out proper phrases of reassurance. "Everyone gets butterflies at the thought of performance. It's only natural and soon passes." Or "But Randolph, you have made such splendid progress in your role. You must not—" Her thoughts were interrupted. Mr. Milbanke had suddenly gone down on one knee in front of her and was clasping his hands in supplication.

"What on earth!" she exclaimed. Then she thought, Well, really, there was no need to make a Cheltenham tragedy of the thing. If he felt that strongly about dropping the part . . .

"Miss Romney—Sarah." The sweat on Randolph's brow was increasing. "I know my declaration may come as a shock to you. But I can no longer hold my tongue."

"Well, after all, Randolph, if you feel you positively cannot appear, then I suppose—"

Randolph rolled over the interruption lest it divert him from the set speech he'd been practicing in his head throughout a long and sleepless night. "Forgive my abruptness in declaring myself. But I fear I may not soon find another opportunity to be alone with you. And the depth of my passion demands utterance, dear, dear Sarah."

"The depth of your what?" Her look of astonishment rather threw him off his stride.

"My passion," he said awkwardly.

"For me?" Her tone was rife with disbelief.

"Of course, you." Randolph was nettled by all these interruptions. They interfered with his train of thought. "Do you see anyone else around?"

"Randolph, is this some sort of joke?"

"No, dammit, I'm making you an offer. That is, I would be if you'd let me get on with it. I had the thing all worked out and now it's gone clear out of my head."

"An offer! Randolph, how old are you?" Sarah might have looked the same way at Tidswell caught in some transgression.

"How old am I?" Exasperation was getting the upper hand. "Nineteen. But what has that to say to anything?"

"Isn't nineteen a trifle young to be thinking of offering a carte blanche? Not to say that such a thing would be proper at any age."

"A carte blanche! Who mentioned a carte blanche? Such a thought never entered my head. My God, how could you be thinking I'd be offering a carte blanche? Why, I could never afford—that is, what I mean to say is, I would never . . . Dammit, Sarah, you've caused me to make a complete mull of my marriage proposal."

"Marriage? You're asking me to marry you? *Marry* you? I don't believe it!"

"I know it's sudden and all. But I may never get a better chance to be alone with you." He reached for her hand and gave it a tender squeeze. "Sarah, do say you'll be mine."

"Randolph, do please get up off your knees and stop talking nonsense." She tried to take some of the sting out of her words by smiling, though in truth she longed to box the young man's ears. "I don't know what sort of maggot you've got in your head, but I do wish you'd get rid of it to let us get on with our ride."

"Sarah." The pressure of his handclasp was intended to be ardent. She would have called it painful. "I love you, Sarah."

Miss Romney sighed. Really, this sort of thing was getting to be outside of enough. "You do no such thing."

She sounded much like a governess even to her own ears, and more so to Randolph's. It was appallingly clear to the young man that things were not going at all as planned. Well, then. If words would not convince her, he'd just have to take a page from his cousin Gerard's book and arouse her carnal passions. No sooner had the thought occurred than he was beside her on the log, crushing her in his arms and kissing her clumsily. Unfortunately, the very suddenness of his assault, coupled with her desire to elude the embrace, sent Miss Romney reeling backward. Equally off balance, striving—unsuccessfully—not to terminate the kiss, Randolph tumbled on top of her. His cousin Gerard would not have been deterred by such a circumstance. That beau would have simply reembraced and

308

started over. But Randolph found the fact that Miss Romney was suffering a giggling fit entirely offputting. The devil with Gerry, anyhow!

"I don't think that's a very proper way to act when a lover has just offered you his heart," he said sullenly, wiping the dirt off his buckskins and riding coat.

"I'm so s-sorry," she gurgled. "But you must admit, we did look ridiculous."

"Thank you very much."

"Oh, come now, Randolph," she chided, settling her cork hat straight and shaking out her skirt to rid it of debris. "Please don't put yourself into a taking. Things could be a lot worse, you know. Why, I might even have taken your proposal seriously."

"Dammit, I was serious!"

"Were you?" She looked at him speculatively. "If so, I wonder why." He reddened a bit, and she continued. "For you've not the slightest wish to be married to me. I'd stake my life on it."

"That's not true. I do wish it. The thing is, I happen to like you a lot."

"And I like you, too. But that's no reason to get married. So may I suggest that we simply drop the subject and continue with our ride?"

Randolph opened his mouth to protest, mumbled, "Oh, blast!" instead, and shut it again. It was obvious he'd made a shambles of the thing. Still, he thought with youthful optimism as they remounted and set off at a sedate pace, at least the ice was broken. She now knew he wished to marry and not seduce her. That should erase the bad impression he'd made by sneaking into her chamber and scaring her half to death. And once she got over the shock of his unexpected proposal and thought it over, she was bound to reconsider. After all, as far as she knew, he was a damn fine catch for her. Or any actress. Well above her touch in the ordinary way of things. But he would have to fix the matter right and tight before Gerry made his move. Better not put it off too long. Couldn't depend on Lady Scriven keeping his cousin occupied forever. Nor could he entirely trust Gray to keep his oar out of the matrimonial waters. By George, he'd propose again tomorrow. Bound to have the hang of it the second time around. Randolph began to whistle under his breath.

Sarah, who'd been stealing worried glances at him as they rode along, was glad to see his spirits so restored. Her conscience was troubling her for laughing at him. Well, laughing at herself, actually. "I don't think I've ever seen a lovelier countryside," she offered as a conversational gambit to ease his mind from the embarrassing incident. "This must be the most beautiful estate in Hampshire."

"I think so." He spoke with great conviction as he surveyed the lush, sloping green hills. "Can you imagine what it would be like to own it?" he asked slyly.

"Indeed I cannot." She laughed. "As an actress, I do live in a world of make-believe, but my imagination doesn't stretch that far. But how about you? It's certainly less far-fetched to ask what you would do if you owned such an estate."

"I'd modernize it," he answered promptly. "Bring in the latest methods of agriculture. Change the fusty notions Uncle clings to. My God, I could double the yield in no time." The young face was alight with enthusiasm.

"Why, Randolph, I'd no idea you were such a farmer."

"I'm not. Got nothing to farm, you see, the way things stand. The land all belongs to Gray."

"And does he share your enthusiasm?"

"Well, yes and no. That is to say, he keeps up with the times. His bailiff's top-rate and gets the best out of the land. So Gray leaves all that sort of thing up to him. He looks after the tenants himself, though: I'll give him that. There's nobody better. But Gray's interests are scientific. Like ballooning. He could drive you insane with all his talk of air currents and temperatures at certain altitudes and hot air as opposed to hydrogen. Before that, he was daft over steam engines."

"Well, could you not run his farm for him?"

"You mean take his bailiff's place? Of course not." From his tone she might as well have suggested he become a highwayman.

Sarah thought it time to change the subject. "Have you noticed that your cousin seems to be falling in love?" she asked.

310

"Gerry?" He tried to sound nonchalant, but the query jolted him. "Oh, Gerry's always falling in and out of love. Does it as often as he changes cravat styles. You mustn't take him too seriously. Fickle. That's Cousin Gerard."

"Really? Well, you certainly know him better than I. But I would have said he's formed a sincere *tendre* for Miss Crome."

"Miss Crome!" He reined his horse to a standstill, amazed and relieved at the same time. "Gerry and Miss Crome? But that's absurd."

"I don't see why." She turned back to let her mount graze a moment beside his. "Goodness, can you imagine the difficulty those two must have in finding others as dazzling as they? You must admit that as a couple they take the breath away."

"Yes, but Gerry's pockets are to let and Miss Crome hasn't a feather to fly with. It ain't like him to . . . Well," he mused aloud, "if he is dangling after her, it's just because she's meant for Gray."

"I don't think I understand."

"Simple enough. Gerry's green with jealousy over Gray. Always has been. They're the same age, you see. Been thrown together since they were in leading strings. Been rivals ever since Gerry began to understand how much Gray had and how poor his own prospects were. He tries to best Gray in every possible way. So I guess that could include Miss Crome."

"But that's terrible."

"Well, it's stupid, anyhow. For what Gerry don't realize is that Gray couldn't care less. At least I don't think he's interested in the fair Evelina," he amended. "But it could cook Gerry's goose if what you say is true and he gets carried away by the thing. Of course, Lady Scriven ain't likely to let that happen. She's got her claws hooked into Gerry. Good thing, too. Gerry has to marry an heiress. He's got no choice."

Sarah sighed and patted her impatient horse's neck. "The quality are certainly mercenary. I'll wager that Miss Crome and Mr. Langford could rub along quite well by most people's standards. They might not afford to keep a stable or—"

"Well, you'd lose," he interrupted. "They couldn't rub along well by any standard. Not in debtors' prison. Economies won't

311

help. Gerry's too far up the River Tick for that. If word got out that he'd married just for love, his creditors would flock like vultures. Gerry's a gambler, you see. Bets on anything and everything. Which raindrop will beat the others down the glass. Whether a certain cove will wear a buttonhole that day. Who'll manage to seduce a certain female first—Oh, I do beg pardon."

"Not at all." Sarah's eyes were wide. "You mean gentlemen would actually place bets upon a thing like that?"

He looked embarrassed. "Well, yes. Happens all the time, in fact. But I should not have said so. Didn't intend to shock you."

"Oh, you haven't shocked me. In point of fact, I think you've just enlightened me. I'm very glad to have this insight. I think it may explain—Well, never mind." The suspicion that was forming her mind could be explored alone and at her leisure.

As they resume their ride, Randolph's troubled conscience began nagging him a bit. "Don't want to give you the wrong idea about Gerry," he said abruptly. "Shouldn't make him out a scoundrel, for he ain't. Oh, what I said is the truth—about him being a gambler and jealous of Gray. He's all of that. But he's got another side. Like my brother says, Gerry might knife you in the back himself, but he'd stop any other cove from doing it."

"How chivalrous," Miss Romney murmured.

Randolph missed the sarcastic overtones. He was too busy mulling over what she'd said. "By George, I guess it is at that. Gerry would have made a real go of that sort of thing. Clanking around in armor. Jousting in tournaments." He went on pursuing that train of thought while Sarah's mind was on another tangent.

The manor house was back in view before she broke their silence. "Randolph, forgive my impertinence, but I've been thinking. Do you have any money of your own at all?"

Randolph's eyes sparkled at the question. By Jove, she was having second thoughts about his proposal! "A little," he answered. "And, of course, I do have some prospects."

"But I'm not talking about when this or that person should die. I mean, do you have enough brass, er, money, that is to say, to purchase a small farm right now?"

"Well, yes, I collect so."

"Then why don't you simply buy one and farm it yourself? Why, with your expert knowledge, I should think you'd make a success of it in no time."

His jaw dropped. She might have made an indecent proposal of some kind. "You mean you want me to be a *farmer*?"

"It's not what *I* want. It's you I'm thinking of. Doing something positive with your life. Isn't that what you'd like to do? Farm, I mean?"

"You must be bamming me." He looked shocked. "It simply ain't done, you know."

"No." She sighed. "I suppose it isn't. But somehow it does seem a pity."

They finished the ride in silence, both deep in depressing thoughts.

Chapter Fourteen

SARAH WAS MORE THAN WILLING THE NEXT MORNING TO join in the excursion to watch Graymarsh attempt to put his balloon back in the air. She needed the distraction. Yesterday's conversation with Randolph had cleared up a mystery but left her decidedly blue-deviled.

There was no further doubt in her mind that she was the object of a wager. Mr. Langford and Randolph were in competition to see who could seduce her first. What, she wondered, was the stake? No, on second thought, she'd rather not know her value. Was it recorded in White's notorious betting book?

Anger might follow, but at the moment she was simply

disillusioned. She was especially disappointed in Randolph Milbanke. That he should engage in such a business at all was unthinkable. But to dangle marriage like a carrot . . . that was reprehensible! Well, the ways of the ton were incomprehensible. Not to mention downright immoral. The sooner she could leave Pether Hall the better. She wished she'd never come. She almost wished that three young gentlemen of the ton had never entered the stage box of the Portsmouth Theatre.

Sarah was not the only one to welcome a diversion. The entire Petherbridge house party seemed to be sunk in despondency. Lady Scriven's arrival could have contributed to Miss Crome's dejection. And if, underneath his usual nonchalance, Mr. Langford was indeed furious, again Lady Scriven must bear the blame. But why Lady Emma should be out of sorts, Lady Stanhope suffering all her complaints at once, Lord Stanhope fidgety, and Sir Peter cross, was past understanding. Even the ebullient Randolph Milbanke appeared sunk in the general gloom. So when the Prodigy had come rushing in at breakfast to announce, "Have you heard? Gray—I mean to say, his lordship—plans to try his balloon today!" the whole party had come to life.

The day was bright and sunny with a gentle breeze, propitious for ballooning. The ascension site was within easy walking distance of the manor house. Servants were immediately dispatched with the provisions deemed necessary for the party's comfort and refreshment, and the guests set forth on foot soon after breakfast.

Sarah looked around in vain for the Prodigy. She had started back to find him when Randolph stopped her. "Don't be silly. He won't be there. You surely can't think Gray's been able to take a step all day without the boy right on his heels. Come on. It would be just like my brother to start without us and spoil the only bit of excitement we've any hope of."

The two of them fell into step with Miss Crome and her mother. Sarah was well aware that Lady Emma did not want her daughter associating with an actress, but the poor girl looked unhappy and in need of a friend. There was little doubt that the sight of Lady Scriven and Mr. Langford walking on ahead, with the lady's hand placed possessively on the gentleman's arm, was the main source of the beauty's misery. That and her mother's satisfaction at the sight.

"Mr. Milbanke, you must be very proud of your adventurous brother." Lady Emma beamed at Randolph. At the same time, she managed not to see Sarah at all. "Evelina and I were just remarking about how greatly we admire these intrepid aeronauts."

"Do you, ma'am?" Randolph's eyebrows ascended in surprise. "I've always held the opinion they're bedlamites myself."

"It does seem terribly dangerous." Miss Crome shivered. "Is Tidswell going up, Miss Romney?"

"Oh, no. And he'll never forgive me for not allowing it. He went over my head and wrote to our father. But, thank goodness, Papa was even more horrified at the notion than I was and flatly refused to give permission."

Randolph barely kept his face straight. "I'll bet a monkey he told Tids that a talent like his must be guarded for posterity or some such thing."

"You are exactly on target." Sarah chuckled, and Randolph felt free to release his grin.

When they arrived, the meadow looked like a scientific laboratory gone slightly mad. Even the cows appeared fascinated by what was going on. While they had prudently retreated to a safe distance, they'd ceased to graze and stood staring at the center of activity, chewing their cuds with that bovine passivity that is as close as cows can come to curiosity.

A huge mass of crumpled silk lay in the center of the field. Gray, Tids, and three burly gardeners were busily unloading casks of hydrogen and yards of hose pipe from a cart and placing them near the silver silk. This accomplished, a rubber umbilical cord was stretched between the cask and the collapsed balloon. The inflation process began.

Sarah shared none of Lady Emma's admiration for the "intrepid" aeronauts. She was, in fact, terrified for Lord Graymarsh's safety. It was her secret hope that there would be some defect in the balloon, left over from its unauthorized descent into the lake. A small tear, perhaps, that had gone undetected but that would suffice to prevent inflation. It had been a frail hope, and it soon expired. The mass of silk writhed sensuously on the ground, puffed a bit like yeasty dough, and then began to fill in earnest.

"Ooooh!" Even the timid Evelina Crome was moved to gasp in admiration as the balloon slowly took shape and began to rise above its boat, like an outsized bird venturing out of the nest to try the air. Up and up it rose, its crimson-bordered, bright blue band unfolding in all its bravery as the silken orb filled out, became tightly packed, and tugged against the ropes that kept it earthbound.

"Huzzah!" Tids shouted as he danced up and down like some North American tribesman in a ritual celebration.

"Huzzah!" the house-party spectators echoed back, with Sarah cheering and clapping as loudly as anyone, elated at the triumph against all instinct and better judgment.

The house party pressed nearer to inspect the colorful curiosity. Their ranks had been swelled by workers from the fields. Servants streamed toward the meadow from the manor house. Lord and Lady Petherbridge benignly turned blind eyes toward their flagrant truancy.

"Tidswell! You get right out of there!"

The Prodigy had climbed into the blue and crimson boat and was staring upward at the glory. He was the very picture of a fledgling aeronaut with his eye upon the future.

"It's all right." Lord Graymarsh, in consultation with his helpers about recovering the balloon, turned to reassure the Prodigy's sister. "I told him he might get in to get the feel of the thing. Never fear. I'll toss him out before I go." He smiled away her concern. She found herself smiling back at him.

The sudden warmth and total unexpectedness of her response was almost Gray's undoing. He stifled the impulse to sweep Miss Romney off her feet, toss her into the boat, and go soaring off into the sky with her. Instead, he reluctantly broke off contact with those lovely, extraordinary eyes and turned to continue his instructions.

Sarah, too, had trouble dealing with the moment. She also

316

turned away, back toward the balloon, where her little brother was stooped over, fascinated, it would appear, with the craft's moorings. So absorbed was she in sorting out her confused emotions that it took a while for the significance of her brother's actions to register. "Tids! What are you doing? Stop this instant!" Lunging for the boat, Sarah grasped hold of what in a proper seagoing vessel would have been the bow with some insane idea of preventing its ascent.

"Jump, Sarah, jump!" Tidswell yelled as the balloon began to rise and the crowd around—below—them let out a concerted gasp. "No! Don't jump! Dear heaven, no!" The Prodigy amended in a shriek. "It's too late now. Hang on, Sarah! Don't panic! I'll haul you in."

The horrified spectators stood frozen in tableau as Miss Romney's boots dangled, kicking, in the air. They watched them inch slowly upward while the balloon, as if to mock the snail's pace of the footwear, rose at an alarming rate. Then with a final kick the boots disappeared over the boat's side. There was just time for the crowd to expel their collective breath before Miss Romney's head was sighted, the merest dot, peering down at them.

"Oh, my God!" Lord Graymarsh croaked as pandemonium broke out. Some of the female servants began to scream. Lady Stanhope suffered palpitations. Miss Crome emitted a soft little moan and crumpled at her mother's feet. Lady Emma bent to succor her only child and was rudely pushed aside by Mr. Langford. He knelt beside the beauty, all anxious concern, and began to chafe her wrists, a technique he was fast perfecting. Lady Scriven, ignoring the runaway balloonists, observed this tender scene with narrowed eyes.

"Dear God, Gray, what can we do?" Randolph shouted as his brother began to race toward the cart that had hauled the casks of hydrogen. "Help me unharness this horse," Gray shouted back as he began uncoupling the animal from the wagon, all the while keeping an eye on the heavens. "I think the little fiend knows what he's about," he muttered as the balloon seemed to taper off its ascent gradually.

"Dear God, I hope so," Randolph breathed prayerfully from the other side.

"He's certainly asked enough questions to be an expert. Lord, what a fool I've been." Gray groaned as he pulled the reluctant dray animal away from its nuncheon of grass and climbed onto its bare back.

"What do you think you're doing?"

"Going after them, of course. Thank God there's no wind. He shouldn't go too far. That is if he can do what I'd planned to do, which was no more than get it up for a test and then right back down again. I'd hoped to bring it down at Pope Farm. There's more level ground there than anywhere else around here. Randolph, you get the landau and head there. Bring bandages, laudanum, smelling salts—whatever. Take Meadow Lane. That should bring you somewhere near my landing site—if the lad can find it and manage to bring the thing down. Oh, God! Don't just stand there—run!"

Randolph sprinted in the direction of Pether Hall as Gray gave the nag a swift kick with his boot heel. It lumbered off while his lordship's eyes fixed themselves on the balloon, an ill-mounted wise man following the natal star.

The aeronauts, after their shaky start, were having the best of it. When first hoisted on board, Sarah's initial shock had been rapidly followed by hysteria. "Oh, my goodness, Tidswell, Papa will kill you! And then he'll kill me for allowing you to get us into this scrape!"

"Now, Sarah, just stay calm. It won't help matters at all for you to go into one of your high flights." Tidswell choked suddenly and giggled. " 'One of your high flights'! Did you hear what I just said?" He whooped.

"I heard," his sister said, groaning at the ill-timed pun, then giggled, too. Tids's absurdity had snatched her back from panic. She was filled with a soothing calm. If these were to be their final moments, well, she'd make the most of them, treasure each fleeting second. She'd take her cue from an intrepid Tids, who was going about the business of ballooning with enthusiastic gusto.

"Would you look at that," she commented as she peered

318

over the side of their swaying craft. "The people are all staring up at us and they're shrinking to nothing as they do so."

"That's because we're going upward, stoopid."

"Funny. It doesn't seem that way at all. It appears as if they are going away from us."

"By George, it does!" Tids paused in his valve inspection to join her view. "Gray said it would be this way," he crowed.

The crowd in the meadow shrank away to tiny ants, then were no more as the balloon drifted and the two Romneys gawked at the awesome prospect far below them. Fields, hedgerows, canals, forest, blended into a mosaic—a winsome pattern put together by some craftsman with an eye for green in all its variations. "Oh, it's beautiful," Sarah breathed just before they were enveloped by a dense, damp fog that totally obliterated the view and caused her to exclaim, "Oh, my goodness, Tids, what's happening?"

"We're in a cloud, that's all." Her brother spoke soothingly. "Nothing to worry about." She was just about to observe that that was as calf-witted a statement as she'd ever heard when suddenly they drifted free and were back in the sunshine once again.

"See, what did I tell you?"

Sarah had only a moment's thankfulness for their deliverance before they shot suddenly upward, tossed by some mischievous airborne giant playing with a ball. Sarah let out a shriek as Tidswell yelled, "We've hit an air current," and jumped to operate the valve that controlled the hydrogen.

Far down below them, fear clutched at Lord Graymarsh as he watched the balloon rapidly gain altitude. "Oh, my God," he said, groaning aloud, "they'll freeze." He kicked his plodding nag viciously, urging it on, as if by sheer force of will he could turn it into Pegasus and go flying after the wayward balloon.

There was a sudden pain in Sarah's ears and she began to shiver. "I sh-should have worn something w-w-warmer than my riding habit had I known," she remarked through chattering teeth, hugging and slapping herself.

"Hang on," said Tids. "I'm going to try to bring her down a bit." As he worked the valve, they plummeted. Sarah felt her

319

stomach drop out from under her and her ears gave a horrendous pop.

"Oh, my God! Oh, please!" Lord Graymarsh, riding with his neck craned upward, combined prayer with expletive.

"Oh, my heavens!" Sarah gasped, then giggled hysterically. "Tids, there goes another pun!"

Her brother's mind was on other things. "It's all right now. I think I've got the hang of it." He began to breathe normally again as they stabilized.

Down on terra firma, Graymarsh shouted his relief. "Good lad!" The nag, thinking the annoyance on its back referred to it, stepped up its snail's pace.

The aeronauts floated leisurely for a while enjoying the view until Sarah forced herself to put into words the fear niggling at her. "Tids, do you have the slightest notion of how to get us down?"

"Of course I have." Sarah would have been more reassured if the bravado in his voice had not reminded her of his most successful stage role. "Keep your eye out for a meadow near a crossroads. That's where Gray planned to come down. He said it was the biggest, levelest spot around."

"I'm certainly in favor of that," his sister commented, squinting over the side. "Oh, Tids, there's no cleared place down there that looks any larger than a counterpane. I never realized that England possessed so many trees."

"Those counterpanes are acres wide, dummy. It'll be all right. You'll see."

But seconds after this reassurance, atmospheric conditions conspired to belie his words. A stiff breeze sprang up, gathered force, and propelled them at an alarming rate back in the direction they'd just come from. Tids frantically opened the valve again, and they began to descend out of the current's force. He heaved a sigh of relief as the balloon slowed down a bit.

But the sudden alteration in the flight plan had taken its toll of his confidence. "We'd better get this thing down in the best place we can find," he muttered. "Sarah, keep a lookout, will you?"

320

She sensed his anxiety and gulped. "All right," she managed to say as they descended even lower.

Gray watched with horror as the balloon was blown back toward him. He urged his reluctant beast to optimum effort and veered off toward a field that, though not as large or nearly as level as the one he'd chosen, was obviously Tids's best hope. "Bring it down, lad, bring it down," he pleaded aloud, then amended his command to a choked "Up, Tids! Up! Up!" when it looked as if the rapidly descending balloon was headed straight for a row of trees.

Sarah's scream warned Tidswell of the danger. He threw out some of the sand on board for ballast, and the balloon rose a hairsbreadth above the branches as Graymarsh croaked, "Thank God!"

The silver orb descended rapidly once again and came skimming low across the meadow as Gray and his reluctant steed approached from the other side. "Throw out the grappling iron, Tidswell!" he shouted, with little hope that the lad could hear him. But whether on command or by his own volition, the Prodigy did weigh anchor, seconds before he ran out of field.

For a bit, it seemed that the wind would defeat them. The anchor dragged, making a furrow through the meadow, slowing their progress but not stopping it. Then, just before they seemed doomed to hit the trees on the other side, the grappling iron caught on a bush and held.

Gray leaped off the nag and ran with a speed that put the plodding beast to shame. He grabbed the anchor rope and hung on with all his might, while the slowly deflating silk tugged at it. "Quick! Slide down the rope as close together as you can manage!" he shouted upward.

"You first, Tids. I'm right behind you." With a prayer of thanksgiving for their acrobatic training, Sarah came down on top of Tids, who'd struck Graymarsh with a thud. All three landed in a heap as the balloon, lightened of its load, pulled up the bush and went sailing off to clear the treetops and join the clouds again.

Tidswell leaped to his feet to scream, "Oh, no!" and then chased after the airborne orb.

Graymarsh also rose and pulled Sarah into his arms. His face was pale. His voice shook. "I thought I'd lost you." And being unable to express adequately the horror and the bleakness of that prospect, he abandoned the attempt and held her closer, then met her upturned lips with his.

No sooner was that contact made than Sarah soared again. She shot upward into flight, and all the variegated colors that had reflected and refracted from the vapors congregated around the balloon danced once again before her eyes with renewed intensity. She was light-headed—she was spinning—she was flying—it was glorious—beyond belief. Ballooning was indeed an experience she would not have missed for all the world.

Graymarsh, at last, reluctantly removed his lips from hers. He gazed into her luminous eyes and said huskily, "I love you."

I love you. The very familiarity of the phrase was Sarah's downfall. It forced her consciousness open like a valve and allowed euphoria to escape. She'd heard the words too often. She knew their false and hollow ring. Her high flight was finished. She experienced once again the terrible sinking sensation that came from falling too far, too fast. She hit earth with a thud, all her illusions left behind her in the clouds, her feet planted firmly on reality. She gazed up into the nobleman's bemused face as he observed this transformation. "I love you, Sarah," Gray repeated in case she'd failed to comprehend.

"I heard you," she replied as she sadly freed herself from his embrace. " 'Et tu, Brute?' " She sighed.

322

Chapter Fifteen

"Oh, sir, it's gone!" Tids wailed, his eyes full of tears.

He'd gone chasing off after the balloon, which had lofted over the woods, with some half-crazed idea that a miracle would send it floating back to where he could snatch the anchor and drag it down. Now, his tail between his legs, he rejoined his sister and Lord Graymarsh. He'd missed all that had passed between them and misinterpreted the bleak look on his lordship's face. "I never meant for this to happen," he said, blubbering. "It's awful. I've gone and l-lost your balloon."

"Good," Gray said tersely. "I never want to see the damned thing again."

"Oh, but you can't really mean that." Sarah had decided that her best course of action was to pretend their kiss had never happened. "I never thought I'd live to hear myself say so—indeed, for a few moments, I never thought I'd live to hear myself say anything—but I can quite see now why you're so enthusiastic about ballooning. It really is quite marvelous. Though not without its hazards." She paled a bit at the memory of the line of trees.

"No, it certainly is not." Lord Graymarsh's usually even-keeled nervous system had suffered too much recent strain. First he'd had to cope with terror. Then with the realization that he was in love. This was rapidly followed by rejection. Now anger was flooding in to add to the devastation of his psyche.

"Tidswell, for your sister's sake, I will not give you the hiding you deserve. But when I think that you could have killed Sarah, not to mention broken your own worthless neck . . ." Words failed him, and he shuddered involuntarily.

"Well, you can't blame me for Sarah," the Prodigy said sulkily. "I certainly didn't ask her to come with me."

Graymarsh closed his eyes and the vision of Miss Romney dangling over the side of the rising balloon boat came rushing back. He turned a sickly green. "I take it all back, Tidswell. I may kill you after all. To save me from the gallows, how about you taking that animal back to Pether Hall?" He jerked his head toward the dray horse that was placidly munching grass a few yards away.

Tids looked at it blankly. "How did it get here?"

"I rode it." Gray's voice was grim.

"That bag of bones? It don't look your style at all," the boy said disapprovingly. "Why, it ain't even saddled."

"I noticed that. I may never walk properly again for the chafing that I took, but I managed. And so can you. Ride or lead. I don't care which. Just go before I throttle you."

The Prodigy gave him an uneasy look, decided that he meant it, and, placing his palms on the animal's rump, leaped agilely on its back. The horse looked around to ascertain the source of this new disturbance, then plodded off.

"There's supposed to be a rescue party headed our way," Gray said to Sarah. "We can wait for it or start walking, just as you please."

"Oh, let's walk. You've no idea how much I'm enjoying direct contact with solid ground."

They trudged in silence for a few minutes, Gray more miserable than all the stinging from his barebacked ride could account for, Sarah trying unsuccessfully to recall the more glorious sensations of balloon flight. She needed that recollection to stave off a threatening bout of the blue devils. Her instincts warned that it would be the most dampening she'd ever known.

Graymarsh spoke first. "What did you mean back there, after I'd kissed you, by 'Et tu, Brute'?"

324

"Did I say that? Oh, well, it's a quotation. Actresses are full of them, you know. It's from *Julius Caesar*."

"I'm not a complete ignoramus," he said impatiently. "I know my Shakespeare—and my Latin—reasonably well. It means 'And you, Brutus?' or 'You, too, Brutus?'—something of the sort. Anyhow, Caesar said it just after the other had stuck the knife in."

"Yes. He was dismayed to find Brutus among the group," Sarah said sadly.

"So what exactly did *you* mean?"

"You know perfectly well."

"Perhaps. I'm not quite sure, though. Suppose you tell me."

She sighed. "You had just told me you loved me, you recall. You, the seventh Baron of Graymarsh, said that."

"Sixth," he corrected.

"You, the *sixth* Baron of Graymarsh, then. Titled—well, that's redundant—privileged, born with a silver spoon in your mouth, kowtowed to. That you should love Sarah Romney, out-of-work actress, of doubtful parentage, no beauty, questionable charm ... Well, it doesn't make much sense, now does it?"

"It doesn't have to. Besides, you can scratch the part about no beauty and questionable charm. You've got that wrong."

"Thank you. To be candid, I threw it in hoping you'd disagree. It was chivalrous of you. The thing is, though"—she concentrated on the narrow path that led them out of the meadow to the carriage lane—"in spite of the absurdity of it all, when you said 'I love you' back there, I probably would have believed you—we do tend to believe what we wish to, do we not?—if the words hadn't had such a familiar ring. You see, you are the third gentleman of quality to have spoken them to me since I came to Pether Hall. And even if I had not finally discovered the plot concerning me, I don't think I'm sufficiently convinced of my own worth to have swallowed so much coincidence. Even you must admit it puts a bit of strain upon credulity. I'm only sorry to have discovered you are part of the conspiracy. You see"—she raised her head for the first time to look at him and her clear, sad gaze seemed to pierce him to the soul—"I had hoped that you were not."

The shame and misery in Gray's face was all the confirmation of his guilt that Sarah needed. Not that she could any longer doubt that he was a party to the infamous wager. Still, she longed to take his word for it when he said, "I don't suppose you'd believe it if I told you I'm not involved, wanted no part of the thing, in fact?"

Instead, she shook her head. "It doesn't stand to reason, does it? Especially after the Portsmouth inn episode. You were almost the winner, were you not, before the competition even started?"

"Who told you about the 'competition,' as you call it?" he asked bitterly. "You weren't supposed to find out. Ever. Then you couldn't have been hurt by it."

"That's a notion only a man could come up with."

"Well, some women might consider themselves fortunate in a similar situation."

She whirled on him, eyes blazing. "Sir! How dare you! I find that disgusting. *Droit du seigneur,* I suppose. Nothing is to be denied a gentleman of rank."

"I don't find that antiquated term at all appropriate," he countered, angered at an attack he felt was unjust. They trudged in silence for a little longer. Then when he was forced to jump a hedgerow—very gingerly—and reached back to lift her over, she could not free herself from his touch quickly enough.

"What are you going to do about it?" he asked abruptly as they walked on.

"Do? Why, leave Pether Hall as soon as possible. I've never walked out on a performance before in my life. It's a source of pride—actresses do have pride, you know—with me. But since the theatricals were merely a pretext to get me here— well, I no longer feel that professional standards need apply. I don't think Lady Petherbridge will mind our leaving."

Gray looked alarmed. "My aunt knows nothing of this, you understand. And is not supposed to know."

"You need not think I'd tell her such a shameful thing," Sarah retorted hotly.

326

"You could be tempted. I wouldn't blame you overmuch. I just wanted you to know that it would wound her deeply."

"You're a fine one to lecture me! I'm aware of her ladyship's sensibilities. Indeed, believe it or not, they are not really so different from that of any right-thinking person, regardless of class."

Even if Gray could have dredged up a reply to quell so much righteous indignation, he had no chance to deliver it. A landau appeared over a furrowed rise, bouncing precariously cross-country. Randolph, holding the reins, stood upright to his peril and hallooed at them.

The trip back to the hall was made in a strained silence that Randolph incorrectly attributed to the ordeal of flight Sarah had just been through and Gray's guilt over being the cause of it. They soon overtook Tidswell, who had directed Randolph on his rescue mission. The Prodigy had climbed off the nag's back none too soon and was leading it, walking slightly spraddle-legged.

They reached the stableyard to find the group that had watched the unauthorized ascension collected in an anxious knot. The crowd had spied the balloon a bit before, the merest speck, heading toward the channel, and so had feared the worst. A wild cheer, in which even the ailing Lady Stanhope participated, went up when its former passengers arrived safe and sound. Miss Crome burst into tears and ran to throw her arms around Miss Romney as she alighted from the carriage. And Lord Petherbridge was moved to pat the actress on the shoulder and in a choked voice keep repeating, "Oh, I say! Oh, I say!" Indeed, the only person who appeared unmoved by the miraculous deliverance was Lady Scriven. All her attention was focused on the fact that Mr. Langford was at least as touched by Miss Crome's unseemly outburst as the beauty's mama was displeased.

The group moved together toward the hall. Lady Petherbridge decreed that Miss Romney and the Prodigy should be dosed with bark mixture and put to bed, a remedy sure to combat any resulting ill effects of balloon flight. Miss Romney did

327

not demur, but did ask for a private word with her hostess, at her ladyship's convenience.

Gray overheard the request and pulled Randolph aside. "We need to talk to Uncle right away. Pry Gerry loose from La Scriven's clutches and go to Petherbridge's bedchamber. I'll bring the old gentleman."

While Randolph attempted to carry out this mission, Lady Petherbridge visited Sarah's room and found her packing. The actress had badly misjudged her ladyship's reaction to their leaving. She was quite upset. Nor did her attitude improve when Sarah made it clear that she'd no intention of accepting payment for the time already devoted to the play. Instead, Lady Petherbridge drew herself up to a considerable height and looked down her nose. "The money was never at issue," she said haughtily.

"I beg your ladyship's pardon. I realize it's shabby of me to abandon the play that was to have entertained your guests. But perhaps now that Lady Scriven is here, she could read my part. The rest of the cast is sufficiently prepared to carry on, I'm sure."

"Oh, bother the play!" Lady Petherbridge dismissed *The Gamester* with a wave of the hand. "It's your little brother's recitation I'm concerned with. Do you realize, young woman, that Tidswell has committed to memory the most meaningful passages from Hannah More's great work?" Her eyes glowed with a fanatic light. "What a genius that young man is!"

"T-Tidswell?"

"Tidswell!" Lady Petherbridge sat down suddenly upon a japanned couch and motioned Sarah to join her. "I will have to make a confession, Miss Romney. When I asked your brother to accompany you here, it was with the intention of opening new horizons for him. I felt it wrong that one so young should be embroiled in such a dissolute profession." If Sarah bridled just a bit, her ladyship took no notice. "And so I meant to open up new avenues to him. Show him the value of honest work—tanning, blacksmithing, farming, whatever. But then when I had your brother recite *The Merchant of Venice* for me, I saw the error of my ways."

"You did?"

"Indeed. The lad's talent is truly prodigious." Her expression was reminiscent of Mr. Adolphus Romney. "So instead of putting this light underneath a bushel, my plan was to beam it in another direction entirely." She paused, perhaps awaiting congratulations, but Sarah was struck dumb. "Now you tell me that my guests are to miss the opportunity of hearing the words of that great moralist spoken by the innocent lips of a true child prodigy. For shame, Miss Romney. For shame!"

Sarah wilted underneath her ladyship's censorious eye. "Perhaps Tids *could* stay," she offered feebly, then quickly added as her ladyship's expression brightened, "Of course, that would be entirely up to him. And really I am not at all sure that he will do it."

But whether Tidswell was too overawed by her ladyship to cross her, or too flattered that for the first time in memory someone shared his father's assessment of his talents, or too covetous of the fee that Sarah was prepared to forgo—for whatever reason, the Prodigy agreed to stay behind to perform while his sister returned alone to Portsmouth. He went to her bedchamber and told her so.

"That's really noble of you, Tids." Sarah's eyes misted. "Papa will be so proud of you and so pleased that it was you they wanted all along. But are you sure you'll be all right alone?"

"Oh, I won't be alone. I can go to Gray if I need advice." His face clouded. "At least I could have done till I lost his balloon. But anyhow," he rallied, "it's only a few more days. Beats me why you can't stick it. I've rather learned to like this life."

Much to her surprise, Sarah laughed. A few moments before, she had thought never to laugh again. "Oh, Tids," she choked, "don't get too comfortable among the nobs. You're letting yourself in for a terrible come-down."

"That's as may be." Her little brother looked resolute. "How much does that Kean fellow make in a year at Drury Lane?"

"Barely enough to keep Lord Petherbridge in horses. Loath as I am to burst your bubble, dear Tidswell, I fear you have to be born into a life like this."

Master Romney heaved a regretful sigh.

Chapter
Sixteen

THE MEETING IN PROGRESS IN ANOTHER PART OF PETHER Hall was not proceeding half as smoothly as the tête-à-tête between Lady Petherbridge and Miss Romney. Lord Petherbridge had taken a wide-legged stance in front of his bedchamber fireplace and was glaring at his three nephews, who were seated like errant schoolboys in front of him. "What a bunch of nincompoops you three turned out to be. I never would have proposed this scheme if I'd thought you'd make such a shocking mull of it. It seemed simple enough. Practically any cove I know could have brought the thing about. And one of you ought to have been able to get the girl to marry you. Why, a penniless actress should jump at the chance to wed a man-about-town. But no—somebody here had to go spill out the whole story and get the girl's hackles up. And next thing you know, she'll be telling tales to Augusta. Dammit, most likely she already has!"

"No, she won't do that," Gray said.

"Fustian. Never knew a female to hold her tongue."

"Miss Romney said she was not going to tell our aunt and we can depend upon her to keep her word. Which is more than can be said for one gentleman present."

"What's that supposed to mean?" Randolph bristled.

"Yes, Cousin, before you begin your accusations, you might stop to consider that you're the one who's discussed the matter with Miss Romney. You can hardly be considered free of suspicion yourself, you know."

"Stop your wrangling!" Lord Petherbridge commanded in a terrible voice. "We ain't got time to discover who the tattler is. The thing is, what's to be done? The girl's leaving."

"Well, if you wish my opinion . . ." Gerard paused, apparently not considering the present dilemma as important as his snuff-taking ritual.

"Of course I wish it. I just asked for it, didn't I?" Lord Petherbridge glared while his nephew inhaled.

"Well, then, I think you should simply call Miss Romney in and make a clean breast of the whole thing. Evidently, the girl thinks she's been made a fool of. Here she thought we were pursuing her for herself alone, then she finds out there's a fortune involved. From one point of view, I suppose it is rather humiliating. But when she calms down a bit, I think she'll come to realize that feeling a trifle foolish is a small price to pay for going from rags to riches. She's a sensible girl. She'll respect your wish to keep your relationship a secret. She'll not want to upset Aunt Augusta—be a blot on the family escutcheon or whatever. Explain to her that part about wanting your own flesh and blood—a rather grisly term for offspring, don't you think?—here at Pether Hall. She'll come about. And then . . ." He paused again while they all waited.

"Well!" Lord Petherbridge barked. "Then *what*?"

"Why, then, let *her* choose one of us."

"But, you sapskull," Randolph said, giving him a disgusted look, "she's already turned us down."

"In the heat of the moment. A feminine reaction to discovering that her fortune weighed more heavily in our eyes than she did. Actually, it's a pity that the whole thing wasn't lined out for her in the beginning. I'm sure she would have been ecstatic. It's only this duplicity that's sent her up into the boughs."

"By George, you may be right." His uncle looked at the Corinthian with new respect.

"Of course I am. Call her in and let her choose."

"She could even draw straws." The suggestion came from Randolph, who did not think too highly of his prospects.

"What do you say, Gray?" Lord Petherbridge turned his protuberant gaze on Lord Graymarsh, who merely shrugged.

"That ain't exactly helpful," his uncle retorted. "But if no one's got a better plan, we'll talk to the girl. No use having her go off in a pucker. Might turn her even more stubborn." His mind made up, he gave the bell a pull and dispatched Mason to summon Miss Romney to the library. The three young men seemed to take that as a signal for departure and rose hastily to their feet.

"Sit!" his lordship barked in a tone usually reserved for his pet spaniel. "You ain't leaving me in the lurch. One of you is responsible for mucking up a perfectly good scheme for the continuation of the Petherbridge line, and by gad you'll stay here and help me put things to rights."

As a result of Petherbridge's exhortation to the troops, Sarah found all four gentlemen seated around the library table with the lord of the manor at its head and, for fortification, a port decanter at his elbow. Pausing on the threshold, her first inclination at the sight of her three dishonorable suitors was to turn on her heel and leave. But as the gentlemen all stood, Lord Petherbridge looked so perturbed that out of civility to her host, who certainly had intended her no harm, she made herself walk toward them.

"Do come sit down, Miss Romney." His lordship gestured to the chair at the foot of the table, which Mr. Langford was holding for her. "Didn't want you to leave in a pucker. Wouldn't be right. You're owed some kind of explanation."

Sarah struggled for composure. "Really, your lordship, I'd rather not discuss the matter, if you don't mind."

"Oh, but I say, m'dear, you have to let me try to set things right, you know. Wouldn't be the thing not to explain."

Sarah relented. Although her greatest wish was to forget all about the demeaning wager and get on with her life, she was touched by the fact that Lord Petherbridge was so upset over his nephews' odious behavior. If he wished to try and smooth things over, well, for his sake, she'd be civil. She accepted the chair that Gerard pulled out without looking at him or at either of his cousins.

The gaze that Lord Petherbridge then bent upon her was awash with emotion. Annoyance, embarrassment, befuddlement—all warred within him. Annoyance won.

"I have to tell you," he began abruptly. "I ain't at all pleased with these three nephews of mine."

"I did not think you would be, my lord," she replied with quiet dignity.

"Bungled the thing. Made a complete mull of it. I should have thought that any one of 'em could have brought the thing about. Nothing to it, really."

Sarah stared at the old gentlemen, stunned and appalled. Surely she had misunderstood what he'd just said. "You cannot mean, Lord Petherbridge, that you actually knew what these 'gentlemen' were up to."

"Of course I knew. Had to, didn't I?" he said impatiently. "It was me own idea, naturally."

Again Sarah almost rejected the testimony of her own ears. They must have played her false. She was actually more shocked by this elderly gentleman's disclosure than by the knavish behavior of the younger men. And she hardly trusted herself not to throw the inkpot before her at any one of the family group. Instead, she rose from the table, bent on stalking from the room. Her voice shook with righteous indignation. "You, sir, should be thoroughly ashamed of yourself."

"Ashamed of myself? Well, I say now, that's cutting it a bit rough." His lordship had the hurt look of a spanked puppy.

"Rough? I beg to differ. In view of your shocking disclosure, I consider my reaction quite restrained."

"For the life of me, can't see why you call it shocking. I'll not say what I did was quite the thing, but it ain't all that unusual. And not to put too fine a point on it, it ain't as if I forced your mother. Or didn't pay for your upkeep when it comes to that."

There really was something terribly wrong with her hearing. Or perhaps her wits were the real culprit. Since she'd walked through the library door, nothing seemed to be making any sense. Now she felt her knees grow weak, a prelude to comprehension. Sarah sat back down, her face drained of color.

Gray, who had been watching her intently, spoke up. His

voice was gentle. "Sarah, what did you think this was all about? All of us dangling after you, I mean."

"I thought it was a wager," she managed to say. "Randolph—somebody—said that it was common practice. For gentlemen to bet on which of them could seduce a certain female first. That was the idea, wasn't it?"

"Oh, dear God." Gray groaned.

"You muttonheads!" Petherbridge thundered. "You had the lass here thinking that all you wanted was a tumble in the hay! Of all the pea-brains I ever heard of . . ." he sputtered, and words failed.

"I did no such thing," Randolph protested. "I made her an honorable offer. Even said I loved her."

"I think we both—all?—said that," Gerard commented. "But I collect that Miss Romney here merely took our declarations for moonshine to cloak our less honorable intentions. Did you not, Miss Romney?"

Sarah, who could no longer persuade her vocal chords to work, merely nodded.

"Well, of all the bungling idiots! Of all the sapskulled clothheads!" Lord Petherbridge began his diatribe again, then just as suddenly calmed down. "Can't be helped, though. See now I was a fool. Should have made a clean breast of the whole thing to you from the start, Miss Romney—Sarah, I mean to say. But I didn't know you then, you see. Now that I've been in your company awhile, well"—he choked suddenly with emotion— "I'd just like to say that I couldn't be prouder if you'd been, well, uh, born on the right side of the blanket." He had a bit of trouble interpreting her look. "You do understand now that I'm your natural father?" She nodded, and he continued. "Well, now that I've seen for myself the kind of girl you are, I realize I could have trusted you not to let the cat out of the bag. Wouldn't do, you understand. Augusta's a very straitlaced woman. She wouldn't take kindly to me early, uh, indiscretions. But I should have told you right off that I want you to have me fortune. My only child, don't you see. But since I can't just will it to you in the ordinary way of things, I told these three I'd leave it to whichever one of them succeeded in marrying you. With you none the wiser as to why."

At this point, Miss Romney shifted her gaze from his lordship's face to look at each of his nephews in turn. The beautiful eyes remained fixed especially long on Graymarsh, who turned a deep, dark red.

"That's still the only way to handle things. Except now you'll know what's what. Well, then. I think we can just forget the courtship, which they don't have the slightest notion of how to go about, anyhow, and let you choose. Tell me, girl, which one of me nephews will you have?"

With great difficulty, Sarah pulled herself together. "Do I understand you right, sir? I will inherit your fortune if I marry one of these 'gentlemen'?"

"That's it." By now, Petherbridge was enjoying his fairy-godfather role. The girl was obviously overcome by the miracle of it all. "At least that's the gist of the business. Like I told you, you can't be named in me will. Wouldn't do, you understand. So it's your husband who'll do the inheriting. Comes to the same thing in the end. All you need to do is decide which of 'em it's to be."

"That's all?" she asked softly.

"I'll grant you it's a bit of a poser. Gray's me choice, I don't mind saying. Think he'd make you the best husband. But then, of course, Gerard's better-looking. Females set store by that sort of thing. And he needs me money more. As does Randolph," Lord Petherbridge added in the interest of fair play. "He's a good-enough lad, too. So which one will it be, girl?"

Again Miss Romney gave each gentleman an appraising glance. "As you say, your lordship," she then replied with a coolness that surprised her, "the problem is a poser. There is not, after all, a great deal to choose among them. I agree that Mr. Langford's need is greatest. His debts, I understand, are enormous. He's prepared, it seems, to go to any lengths to settle them. Any, that is, except to earn an honest living. He is, however, quite prepared to see the woman he loves sold to the highest bidder. And, as a last resort, to sell himself to Lady Scriven, whom he positively dislikes. It must have seemed very attractive, Mr. Langford, to have the opportunity to marry me, to whom you are merely indifferent. Especially since you would be able to control the purse strings, a thing impossible in Lady Scriven's case, I collect. Besides, I'm given to understand that Lord Petherbridge's fortune puts the widow's to shame. Is that not so?" Mr. Langford, whose composure was wearing thin, merely nodded. "So that puts me in the running well ahead of Lady Scriven. And leaves Miss Crome, the sentimental favorite, a distant third.

"As for Randolph, did you realize, your lordship, that he has a passion for the land? Not to teach you your own business, sir, but you really should be backing him to win me. He'd be the one who'd increase your holdings and turn your estate into an agricultural showplace. No wonder he was so eager to press his suit. His motives, at any rate, are not to be despised."

She paused a bit before continuing. "As for your choice, Lord Graymarsh—well, I understand he's at least as wealthy as you. But as King Midas demonstrated, one never seems to feel quite rich enough. So I expect greed was the emotion behind his lordship's pursuit."

"Oh, I say!" Randolph protested, observing the look on his brother's face. "It ain't fair to call Gray greedy. He never wanted any part of this business from the first."

"Never mind, Randolph. You're wasting your breath," Graymarsh said quietly.

"I think you wrong your nephews, Lord Petherbridge," Miss Romney said, ignoring the interruption, "by thinking they made a mull of things. Indeed, their courtships were all that one might reasonably have hoped for. They each had a great deal to gain and each gave the chase his best. Perhaps if I've failed to point out the lengths to which they were prepared to go to achieve their ends, it's because the language itself is lacking. If only there were some good term to describe the male of the species who prostitutes himself for money, you'd get the picture instantly. What an odd oversight, come to think of it, when our vocabulary is so rich with descriptions for the grasping female: Venus mendicant, light-skirt, bit o' muslin, Fashionable

Impure . . . Oh, I do like that one especially! Fashionable Impure. Now that label could do for either sex, don't you agree?"

"Oh, I say . . . Come now! Really, Miss Romney," Lord Petherbridge sputtered, "you go too far! There's no comparison between the, er, activities of the sort of female you refer to and this situation. I think you owe me nephews an apology. Except for the fact you didn't happen to know you were me heir, there's nothing unusual in this sort of arrangement. It's done all the time."

"I realize that. But I still maintain that the practice of selling one's self for money is a custom shared by the upper classes and the ladies of the evening. The rest of us, thank goodness, are able to choose our mates for love. That makes me the only free person in this room." She got to her feet. "Now, if you gentlemen will excuse me."

"B-but," his lordship expostulated, "you can't go yet. You ain't said which one of 'em you'll have."

"Oh, have I still not made it clear? I beg pardon, my lord. I thought you understood that I would not marry one of your nephews at gunpoint."

"But you have to!" Lord Petherbridge also stood. "I thought *you* understood. You can't inherit unless you do."

"Oh, I understand that right enough. But what your lordship fails to grasp is that I wish nothing from you. I know you mean well by me, sir, but your concern is quite misplaced. You see, I'm already an heiress. My *father*"—she stressed the word—"plans to leave the thing he values most, the Romney Company of Players, in my charge. So if you'll excuse me, I'm going home to help him get my inheritance back on its feet."

"Young woman, have you gone daft?" his lordship roared. "Do you understand what it is you're being offered? You can't know that you're whistling a fortune down the wind for the chance to work with a bunch of broken-down, third-rate, talentless actors!" Words failed him as Sarah started toward the door.

"I resent your name-calling, but never mind," she answered over her shoulder. "In reply to your question, I know exactly what I'm doing."

"My God!" His lordship stared at his nephews. "The girl's queer in the attic. I don't know what to say."

The actress broke her exit with one hand resting on the doorknob. She turned to gaze with pity at his lordship. "That, sir, underscores the difference between you and my real father—the one who loved and reared me. He is never at a loss for words. May I suggest that were he in your place—though, given our relationship, such a similar situation would not arise—but, hypothetically, if it did, he'd borrow this phrase from *Lear*: 'How sharper than a serpent's tooth it is to have a thankless child.' "

Adolphus Romney himself could not have topped her reading. Well satisfied with the dramatic climax, Miss Romney closed the door behind her.

The four men stood in silence, looking at one another. "I tell you the girl's queer in the attic," his lordship repeated. "Madder than old King George. Throwing me fortune back in me face that way. I tell you, there's bad blood there. Goes to show, lads. Don't pay to get yourself involved with cits. Stark, raving mad! And just what she thinks a bunch of toothless serpents have to say in the matter defies all understanding. Queer in the attic. Got to be. It's the only explanation."

Chapter
Seventeen

LORDS PETHERBRIDGE AND GRAYMARSH, THE HONORABLE Randolph Milbanke, and Mr. Gerard Langford had drained the port decanter when Mr. Langford pushed back his chair from the library table and rose rather unsteadily to his feet.

"Well, I for one am going to dress for dinner. Or should I say make myself 'fashionable.' Coming, fellow 'impures'?"

"That ain't funny," Randolph retorted. "I can't think what got into Sarah to say such a maggoty thing about us. 'Fashionable Impures,' indeed! I didn't like it above half."

"Yes, but you must admit it was 'a hit, a very palpable hit.' You see, Miss Romney isn't the only one who can spout Shakespeare. Coming, Gray?"

"In a moment. I'd like a word with his lordship first."

As the library door closed behind his brother and cousin, Gray turned to Lord Petherbridge, who was slumped down in his chair, staring morosely at the empty decanter. "I know my timing is poor," he said gently, "but since I plan to leave right away, I think we should discuss your will."

"Trying to steal a march on the other two, are you? My God, the chit was right. You are greedy."

"Perhaps. But not in this instance. I'm not about to suggest that you make me your heir."

"You ain't? Well, then, I hope you ain't planning to try to talk me into leaving something for that—that *actress*, for I won't do it. Most ungrateful female I—"

"No, I'm not going to suggest that either," Gray broke in. "Given her prejudice against being pursued for her fortune, I'm not eager for her to be an heiress. You see, I intend to marry Sarah."

"You what! Have you taken leave of your senses? The girl's a shrew! A termagant! Besides," Petherbridge added more practically, "she just said she wouldn't have you."

"That is a leveler," Gray admitted. "But once she realizes my motives aren't mercenary, I think I can bring her about."

"Don't see why you'd want to. She's queer in the attic, I tell you."

"Oh, I don't think so. A bit overly dramatic, perhaps. That's to be expected. And her background makes her look at things from a different perspective than we're used to—not such a bad thing, really," he mused. "Then, too, I suspect she's inherited an overdose of Petherbridge pride."

"Petherbridge pride? Oh, I say." His lordship perked up a bit. "By jove, do you think so?"

"Of course. Blood will tell, you know."

"Hmmm. Hadn't thought of that. Well, now, I collect there may be something in what you say. The chit does look a bit like me sister Fanny, come to think on it. And, God knows, Fanny was a great one for flying up into the boughs over the least little thing. Humph! Can't say I'm as keen on the notion as I once was, but, well, if you do persuade the girl to marry you, I expect I might reconsider and leave you me blunt as agreed on."

"No! No!" Gray almost shouted. "That's just what you are not to do! My God, my life will be intolerable if you name me in your will. The girl will never believe she was all I ever wanted. Which brings us to the matter I wished to discuss with you. Would you consider dividing your inheritance between Gerard and Randolph?"

Lord Graymarsh went on to outline his plan. "Leave Gerry the townhouse and all your assets outside of the estate. And if you could see your way clear to settling his debts right away, sir, then he could go ahead and marry Miss Crome on his prospects."

"Marry Miss Crome! Ridiculous! You've let yourself be gulled by that actress's ravings. An out-and-outer like Gerry shackled to a schoolroom miss? To a female who has the vapors every time you look at her at that? Preposterous! Makes no sense at all."

"Oh, I couldn't agree more, sir. But he does seem to love her."

"Why, he'd never be able to stomach Lady Emma Crome for a stepmama. Know I couldn't."

"Again I agree. But then Gerry should have to pay something for his sins. Will you think about it?"

"I'll consider naming the lad in me will, but I don't believe for a minute he'll be sapskulled enough to wed a penniless chit with a harpy for a mama. He can't be such a green 'un after all these years."

"Well, you could be right sir. Now about Randolph—"

"You're taking a lot on yourself, ain't you nevvy?"

340

"Well, yes, but I trust in no way you'll object to. My next suggestion is that you leave the estate to Randolph. And let him know it. But, most important, give him the running of it now. It will keep him occupied for the many years your lordship should still enjoy. And I don't think you'll regret it. The lad really does know what's what when it comes to farming."

"I'll think on it." Lord Petherbridge sounded grudging, but had, in fact, already begun mulling things over in his mind. "Can't expect me to come up with an answer now. There's been too much hubble-bubble already for one day. First that curst balloon of yours taking off with those actors aboard. Then me own little Sarah turning into a—what did she call it? A toothless child? Well, really, Gray, I think it's a bit much for you to be settling the terms of me will right now."

"I know, sir," the young man said smoothly. "Rotten timing, and I do beg pardon for it. Just let me point out, though, that when the dust settles, things should work out fairly close to the way you've always planned. Only instead of the three of us nephews inheriting—I'm speaking now of your original scheme—it will be a two-way thing. And even though your own flesh and blood won't be actually living at Pether Hall, well, they'll be in and out of here all the time if I've anything to say in the matter. So all's well that ends well. My God! Is that the bard, too? The curst habit's catching."

He pushed back his chair. "I shouldn't keep you. You'll need to dress. I'll say my good-byes now, sir. I won't be staying."

"Oh? Going after the girl now, are you?"

"Oh, Lord no. In her present temper, I wouldn't dare. No, I think Miss Romney will need a nice, long cooling-off period."

"So why not eat your mutton? No need to go rushing off."

"Oh, I'm afraid I have rather urgent business in town, my lord." Gray grinned. "You see, I have to see some men about a new balloon."

The Romney Company of Players was experiencing a turn-about in fortune. Adolphus Romney had found a backer for them—due entirely, so he said, to Tidswell's connections with the aristocracy. "Once it was learned, m'dear," he explained to

Sarah, "that the Prodigy had been engaged for a solo performance at Pether Hall, well, there was simply no scarcity of gentlemen eager to finance us. Our success is assured."

As usual, Sarah made allowances for exaggeration. But she didn't look the gift horse of a change of luck too closely in the mouth. She gratefully accepted the opportunity to immerse herself in work.

The company planned to reopen with *The Gamester*, with Sarah in the female lead. If the associations of that drama were somewhat painful, this drawback was outweighed by the fact that its small cast fit their dwindled company. And since Sarah had already learned her part, she could give more attention to other aspects of production, such as the playbills.

Mr. Romney had bespoken a ridiculous number of these broadsides. Sarah tried to remonstrate over the expense, then sighed and capitulated as he chided, "Think big, m'dear, think big."

Just how big the manager's thoughts on publicity had grown became abundantly clear when Sarah and Tids were on the way to the theater for dress rehearsal. They hurried across the cobbled street, with Tidswell talking a mile a minute about an improvement he had made in their wind machine, when suddenly he froze and clutched Sarah's arm while an outraged voice behind them roared, "Look out!"

Adjusting their position slightly so that a covered cart could go around them while its driver muttered curses, Tids pointed skyward. "Look up there, Sarah, would you?"

Her chip-straw bonnet being inadequate to the task, Sarah shaded her eyes with her hand against the sun. But even while squinting into the glare, she had no trouble indentifying the blurred object that bobbed their way. "It's a balloon," she remarked brilliantly.

"By George, you don't suppose!"

"Don't be ridiculous. His is in France by now, in case you've forgotten."

"Well, the wind could have changed," Tids muttered.

"Get out of the street, you numbskulls!" a gentleman in a phaeton yelled. The two obliged him. "Come on, Tids. We'll be late."

"I don't care. I want to see it." Tids planted himself in front of a draper's shop. Sarah glared, then sighed and took up a position next to him.

The balloon was close enough now for easy identification. The silk was a bright, bold yellow, banded with zigzag stripes of blue, the colors borrowed from sun and sky to appear at home in the alien heavens. "Oh, it's lovely," Sarah breathed, while her brother muttered, "Rats! I'd hoped—"

The craft was descending rapidly now, heading down over the High Street. "Oh, goodness, it's going to crash!" Sarah exclaimed.

"No such thing!" Tids yipped. "Look at that, would you!" A shower of leaflets came drifting down from the dangling basket as the balloon floated above their heads close enough for the lone aeronaut to be identified. "It is Gray!" Tidswell whooped, while Sarah's knees grew weak. A piece of paper drifted past her face and she automatically reached out and clutched it. "Portsmouth Theatre!!!" the broadside proclaimed in big, bold print, "This present Monday, July 15, 1816, the Romney Players will present—"

There was more, a whole sheet's worth, in fact, but Sarah never got to read it. "Come on!" Tidswell dragged her along in the wake of the balloon and amid the rushing company of every pedestrian and horse-drawn vehicle in sight. "By Jove, Gray plans to land in the park!" he shouted to her.

"Does he, indeed?" She panted. "Well, then, we'd best look for it anywhere. The church spire seems a likely spot."

But this time Sarah had unjustly maligned Lord Graymarsh's navigational skills. After hovering for some minutes over the grassy open space while he rained leaflets upon the gathering crowd, Gray descended among thunderous applause for a perfect landing. "Tids, help me!" he shouted as the Prodigy came bounding up.

Sarah stood on the fringes of the crowd, willing herself to leave but quite unable to do so as the two, with some volunteer help from several spectators, scrambled to make the balloon secure.

Once this thing had been accomplished, Lord Graymarsh declaimed with all the assurance and authority of centuries of breeding, "Ladies and gentlemen, may I present one of the stars of the internationally famous Romney Company? Here he is, Master Tidswell Romney—better known to his adoring public as *The Prodigy*!"

The crowd broke into noisy, if somewhat mystified, cheers and clapping. "Just tell 'em about the play, Tids," Gray whispered soothingly as the boy looked around him for an avenue of escape. The Prodigy gulped twice, took a monstrous breath, then launched into a spiel touting the merits of *The Gamester*. Gray waited till the lad was caught up in his own oratory, then pushed through the crowd toward Miss Romney.

" '*Deus ex machina.*' " She looked up at him wonderingly.

"You do have a quotation for every occasion, don't you, love?" His smile was tender. " 'The God from the machine'? Well, I've been called worse things. Even by you."

Sarah managed to wrench her attention away from the warmth of his eyes to ask, "But what are you doing here?"

"Besides the obvious? Well, in addition to publicizing *The Gamester*, I plan to operate the fog machine. It's all in aid of protecting my investment. I'm your new backer. Didn't Adolphus tell you?"

"No, he did not!" She found the revelation humiliating. "But then I should have known," she added grimly.

"Indeed, you should have. As you pointed out when you rang a peal over us all at Pether Hall, no one of my class ever weds except for profit. And since you are heir to the Romney Company, and since it's the *only* thing you'll ever be heir to . . . Oh, by the by, I should perhaps mention that Lord Petherbridge is leaving his fortune to Randolph and Gerry. Unconditionally. They can marry whom they please, uh, as long as it's not you, that is. Our Gerry has already taken advantage of this new freedom by eloping with Miss Crome."

"Oh, has he? I'm so glad."

"I thought you might be, since it was all your doing. You've sorted us out rather well, in fact. Or you will have done, as soon as you consent to marry me."

"As soon as I what? You aren't serious, surely?"

"Never more so, I assure you."

"But you can't possibly be offering for me, can you?" She looked about her at the park, the people, the balloon, and Tidswell, who was dominating the scene in a manner that would have made his father proud. "No, that's perfectly ridiculous. Of course you can't be."

"Whyever not? It may not be a very romantic proposal: I'll grant you that. But when else will I get the chance? I'm sure you won't miss a rehearsal merely to settle your future happiness. That's too unprofessional for Miss Romney. Damn!" He snapped his fingers. "I forgot to say that I have your father's permission to address you. Making an offer's more complicated than one realizes."

"My father's permission?"

"Yes. I am, of course, referring to Mr. Adolphus Romney. Oh, everything's all quite proper in spite of my bad choice of time and place. I asked, and he approves."

She gurgled suddenly. "Y-yes. I expect he would."

"Let's see now, that should about cover everything. Oh, blast! Have I said I love you? Granted, it's a touchy phrase where you're concerned and may simply put you into another taking. But I do feel that such a declaration is essential when proposing marriage. So it's a risk I'm prepared to take."

"It's good of you to be so conscientious."

"It's true, actually. I do love you." The light in his eyes intensified as he closed the gap between them. "I'm really quite humiliatingly in love, in fact. Find myself doing the damnedest things." He looked ruefully around at the strewn leaflets all about them. "Things completely out of character. Do you know, I think I loved you from the first," he continued huskily, drawing her into his arms. "I think I even loved you right through that awful fright wig and that appalling nose."

"You couldn't possibly have done so." Her voice remained unconvinced even as her arms found their way around his neck and her face turned upward.

"Oh, yes, I could have." Just before his lips met hers, he managed to murmur, "You see, you do have the most extraordinary eyes."

Time stood still. The world retreated. They were alone.

There was nothing but their love, their joy, their completeness. Nothing, that is, except a persistent, high-pitched voice in the background haranguing with an insistence that finally penetrated even love's defenses.

"Stop it, Sarah! Really, I must say! Tying your garters this way in public! It ain't at all the thing! And your lordship should be ashamed! What will Papa say?"

"Nothing, you odious brat, if you don't tell him." Graymarsh released his lady with reluctance. "Or better still," he added as the crowd, now collected around them, whistled and clapped, "just explain to your father that the two of us were doing a love scene from *The Gamester*, giving the public a brief preview."

"Was that really what you were doing?" The Prodigy looked skeptical.

"Of course. Oh, by the by, Sarah love, can I take it that your scandalous behavior means you've accepted me?"

She nodded, not yet trusting herself to speak.

"You mean you've actually asked Sarah to marry you?"

"Yes. I trust that meets with your approval."

"Meets with my approval!" The Prodigy whooped. "I should say! Well, yes, by George, it does! I say, this really is the most famous thing imaginable!"

"Well, thank you, Tidswell. I'm quite touched," the sixth Baron of Graymarsh said.

"By Jove, it's like some unbelievable play. An out-and-out fairy tale. Why, I couldn't have arranged things better if I'd had a lamp to rub, or three wishes, or a magic potion—any of that farfetched sort of thing."

"Why, thank you, Tidswell. And I'm proud, too, to have *you* for a brother."

"Brother?" The Prodigy looked blank. And then, suddenly, enlightened. "Oh, yes, I see now what you mean. The brother thing's nice, too, of course. But what I was really thinking of was how famous it's going to be to have a genuine, top-of-the-trees balloon right in the bosom of my family. How soon can we go up, sir?"